What I Say Instead of Nothing

Stories and Essays

By
James Brega

Published by James R Brega

jrbrega@gmail.com

First edition February, 2021

Author's Note: the stories and essays included herein are works of fiction, criticism, and humor. As such, they do at times make reference by name to real people who've chosen, with various degrees of commitment, to lead public lives. Excepting these, any resemblance of names, characters, locations, and events to real people, living or dead, or to actual events, is purely coincidental.

Author photograph by John Castell

Cover Illustration and book design Copyright © 2021 by John Castell

I owe my eternal gratitude to Alice Lowe, my writing chum of nearly a decade, who has been my guide, muse, editor, and taskmaster (when needed) and without whom, I have no doubt, this project would have never been completed.

Acknowledgements

"There Are Still Empty Places" was first published in *Red Savina Review*; "Realpolitik" received a public reading as a programmed event for the 2017 San Diego Pride Festival; "Panic at Twenty-Four Frames Per Second" was first published by *Lunch Ticket*; "I H8 David Sedaris" was first published in *The Ink and Code*; "Parking Signs" was first published in *Lime Hawk Review*; "Sandman" was first published in *Shadowgraf Quarterly*; "Spring Fever" was first published as "The Twisting Path" in *r.cv.r.y;* "Twenty Questions" was first published in *Hippocampus*; "The Wright Stuff" was first published in the anthology *Songs of Ourselves*; "A Letter to Anna Bell" was first published in *Haunted Magazine*; "Things Could Be Worse" was first published in the anthology *A Year In Ink 5*; "Little Red Bird" was first published in *Foliate Oak;* "Twenty-One" was first published in the *Hamilton Stone Review*; "What I Say Instead of Nothing" was first published in *Plenitude* as "Five Years and Four Months."

ISBN 978-1-7364853-1-6

For Ralph, who helped me understand what is important and what is not, and for John who, beyond all reason, has put up with me for twenty years.

Contents

What I Say
Instead of Nothing
Stories and Essays

There Are Still Empty Places in California

Drive east out of San Diego on Interstate 8, the main route over the Cuyamacas, toward the vast, vacant desert. The sun-bleached signs beside the road warn "12% grade ahead" and "next services 51 miles." You pay no attention to these cautions, cocky, air-conditioned traveler that you are, confident in your fuel-efficient engine, sealed radiator, smart phone.

It used to take either brains or dumb luck to make it safely across the desert. Even after they built the Interstate, you had to pay attention, check your fuel gauges, test your overheated brakes if you didn't want to end up on the road's shoulder among the other victims of heat and poor timing. Slow lizards, lingering too long on the cooler white highway stripe; crazy rabbits, running straight down the road instead of turning aside; rarely, an aged coyote, too old and tired and desiccated to make it safely across a twelve-foot-wide interstate lane—all tracked by the beady eyes of the ever-vigilant buzzards and carrion crows circling overhead, for whom they provide a steady if grisly diet.

The desert has a terrible, barren beauty, but it's a hard place to love. Still, if you slow down to search for it, you'll find life even in the driest, hottest fix: underground, in shadows, thriving against all odds on the blade-sharp edge of survival. Once you're on the 8, as San Diegans call it, the details blur. You don't notice you've crossed the Tecate Divide until the fringe of pines and live oaks that mark the drip line for water-bearing coastal clouds is fading in your rear-view mirror. In another moment you'll plunge over Horsethief Ridge—at 2,800 feet, not even a mountain by some folks' reckoning. Now there's nothing to distract you until, blowing like a hot wind past Plaster City, doing ninety in a seventy-five-mile zone on a road so straight that it must have been surveyed with a pencil and ruler, the desert floor drops fifty feet below sea level, and you start to catch whiffs of the stock yards in El Centro, still twenty miles or more away.

A hundred years ago, the last six and a half miles into Yuma would have been on the one-lane plank road built across the Algodones

Dunes—if you could find the wooden road beneath the drifting sand. Some of the dunes topped three hundred feet; it was said your horse would sink in up to its knees if you were to strike off across the open desert on horseback. The terrain seemed so peculiar they used an Arabic word to describe it: erg, which translates as "dune sea." Meeting a car coming the other way could spell disaster. It meant one driver would have to back off and allow the other to pass; whether or not the Samaritan could regain the road was a matter of luck.

Damaged by the sun's heat, splintered by the very scrapers designed to keep it free of drifts, its braces and supports hacked apart by travelers for use in campfires, only fifteen hundred feet of the ruined plank road still exist. But you won't see that fragment this day; today you glide by overhead on an interstate raised on concrete pilings, following the instructions of the navigator in your phone. They begin: *In eighty-five miles...* and you realize you're in for it: the 8 was not built to enjoy. It was built to take you somewhere.

Maybe, like me, you prefer more orthodox scenery. You'll head north instead of east, cling to the coast on Interstate 5, pass a strip of beach communities—La Jolla, Del Mar, Solana Beach, Encinitas—until, speeding out of Oceanside into the barren expanse of Camp Pendleton, the GPS screen goes white save for the tiny, pale blue avatar of your car on an endless purple ribbon beside the ragged cobalt profile of the Pacific coast.

Freedom! Gone are the dense rectangles of cities and towns with their stoplights and double-wide strollers in crosswalks. Now it's just the occasional on- or off-ramp, you and your car, and you're yearning for wasteland, for emptiness, falling in love again with the open road, mainlining RPMs like there's no tomorrow, pressing the accelerator toward the floor but hoping you'll never get "there," never get to the end of it!

Through rolled-down windows, gulping sea-fresh air, tasting the salt, you see the same limitless possibilities the conquistadores pondered two hundred years ago as they trekked north from Mexico on foot and horseback, taking days to cover what you can in an hour. The next seventeen miles cross the only remaining piece of undeveloped southern California coastline, but the pristine view is an illusion. Pendleton is not really empty any more than it was when the Spaniards arrived to displace the native Kumeyaay. Now the low summer-brown hills to the east conceal five thousand Marines and their tanks, artillery, amphibious vehicles, and movie-set Afghan villages, perpetually practicing war on the shores of an ocean named "peaceful."

All too soon you make out the edges of San Clemente ahead, just past the defeated dragons at its gate: the twin domes of the San Onofre Nuclear Generating Station, whose songs of death and disaster no longer hum through the miles of electrical wires that surround it. Nor does it exhale clouds of vaporized seawater from the hellfire in its belly as it once did. It simply sits and waits, as it will for a thousand years, for something to happen.

It's here that your lark becomes a slog; your foot spends more time on the brake than the accelerator as you shuffle through town after town. You leave San Clemente behind, pointing your grille toward Los Angeles, the very antithesis of the open road. You're only two and a half hours into it, and already your adventure seems destined to founder in the traffic jams born in the foothills of Anaheim's papier-mâché Matterhorn.

You're smarter than that. You don't stay on I-5 as it lumbers dutifully in the direction of the city's indeterminate center. You switch to the 405, which isn't pretty either but at least skirts the areas with the heaviest traffic and follows the coastline you can no longer see from the road. Then on to highway 101, and you're headed for the open road again; if you can only make it past Ventura, another fifty miles, it's a straight shot to Santa Barbara along an asphalt strip that embraces the shore with such abandon that you seem to skim along an inch above the high tide mark.

Leaving LA's smoke-choked spread of endless-seeming urban metamorphosis for other, smaller burgs, your spirits rise again. Indeed, if you ignore the beatification part, the names of the towns and cities you mouth as you pass seem like a guest list for a birthday party: Barbara, Luis, Simon, Joe, Francis. Viewed from your speeding car, the pastoral villages nestle among hills turned mustard-green by the waving fields of wheatgrass atop their domes; hills whose silhouettes rise up out of the coastal plain like those of sleeping buffalo.

This is the quintessential California geography I fell in love with as a child, an affair nourished during long vacations with my father at the wheel and my mother dozing in the car's front passenger seat, while my brothers and sister and I, in the back, played a game of our own invention (or so we thought) that required us to spot a license plate from every state in the union. One thing had changed, however. Back then, only small stands of dark green live oak trees interrupted the landscape's bovine beauty. Now, long, sinuous rows of grape vines are everywhere, flowing up, down, and around the hillsides like wind patterns on a meteorologist's map, turning the virgin soil's chemistry into grape juice for the wineries that have found a foothold a few miles inland.

At San Luis Obispo you'll have to make a choice: you can stay near the water and then, forty minutes ahead, launch yourself onto the fifty-mile rollercoaster of uninterrupted, gut-clenching twists and turns of Highway 1 (always seeming worse than you remember it), holding your breath as you swing around a curve to find yet another panorama—each more spectacular than the last—of cliffs, coast, spray, and sky. Smarter, perhaps, to match the footsteps of the more practical Spanish padres. They turned inland at this point, following a trail established by indigenous hunters and gatherers over thousands of years and kept open by constant use—essentially the same route highway 101 follows today. You pick the inland option, and soon are rocketing along two-lane roads past endless tidy rows of lettuce in every hue except orange.

This is what it was all about, you think, that famous exhortation to "go West" when "West" meant Illinois or Missouri: the inexorable (some would say inevitable) migration from the crowded eastern cities toward the territory beyond the setting sun, the search for "land, lots of land under starry skies above." But you'd be wrong; Cole Porter didn't write that "cowboy song" until 1934, when the western frontier of our imagination was already long gone and Americans were dealing with the psychic angst of having bumped up against the continent's limits.

You, too, feel it keenly: the pinch of limitations, the cramp of having nowhere new to go any more, the itch of fences that encircle, like choke chains, those few open stretches where you can really get a sense of what it used to be like. What is a twenty-first century boy, raised on the romance of the road and the uniquely American idea of "no limits," to do?

There are still empty places in California, even if none are undiscovered. You gas up and turn the car for home, nursing a love for the land that, like a mother in her dotage, no longer remembers you. Maybe you'll take the route down the central valley this time, dueling it out with the long-haul trucks that clog the straight, dusty interstate, taking you places you don't want to go. Maybe you'll find another way.

You press the accelerator to the floor, gathering speed, searching... searching.

Realpolitik

"What you've told me won't change our relationship."

Those eight words, written many years ago in my father's looping scrawl, were the closest he and I ever came to a discussion of the fact that I'm gay. I came across his letter today, among other papers long thought lost; reading it has re-awakened the disappointment I'd felt at the time. I'd hoped my revelation *would* change our relationship. I'd hoped it would make it better.

Now I realize how unreasonable my expectation was. I can't remember a single instance in which an issue affecting my family was resolved through reasonable conversation, loving concern or respectful debate. When we needed to communicate, we resorted instead to angry accusations, insults, and tears. Even my choice of college was dictated by my father in a way that seemed crafted to wreak maximum damage to my self-esteem: "The state college was good enough for your brother, it's good enough for your sister, and it's certainly good enough for you."

It's that "certainly" that really bites, as if we weren't real children, weren't individuals but generic entities to whom he'd given different names to avoid confusion.

My father issued this dictum in response to what was at the time a major political issue for men who had successfully negotiated puberty: the length of their hair and sideburns. My sideburns barely came to mid-ear, but in my parents' buzz-cut world any sideburn at all labeled me a "hippie" and caused them such acute embarrassment that they stopped going to their swim club for a time, afraid they wouldn't be able to look their friends who had "normal" children in the eye. My mother sniffed back tears, wondered out loud where she had gone wrong. She refused to buy any of my high school senior pictures, for which I'd donned a suit and tie, because, she told me, "Your hair makes your face look dirty."

"Really?" I wanted to reply. "Do you think Lincoln's face looks dirty? Do you think Jesus's face looks dirty?" But what would be the point?

I turned eighteen in 1969, the year a human first walked on the moon, the year of Woodstock, the year I registered for the draft. I didn't worry about which school I'd go to. Truth be told, my father was right: the state school *was* good enough. What worried me was the possibility that the fourteen-year-old war in Vietnam would outlast my student deferment; that I'd be drafted and sent to southeast Asia where, I was certain, I would be killed. I prayed every day to a god I didn't believe in that Secretary of State Henry Kissinger would employ his famed shuttle diplomacy to negotiate a cease-fire with the North Vietnamese Communists, thus ending the draft in the US and saving me from certain death. That's more or less the way it turned out. Then, as the world paused for a breath before plunging into the next crisis, I imagined Henry could shuttle over to our house and solve our family problems in five minutes. Now, *that* would be *realpolitik*!

My father wasn't the first person in my family I came out to. That honor fell to my sister, Rebecca, thirteen months older than I, my closest friend and confidante. When I was thirty-five, newly emancipated via therapy from decades of trying to "fit in" as straight, I traveled from New York to Orlando to visit her and the first of her two husbands, with my inaugural boyfriend, Louis, in tow. She caught on the minute she laid eyes on us, probably amused by our pitiful attempts at secret handholding and our stammering confusion over sleeping arrangements.

Rebecca never raised my sexual orientation as a topic of conversation; she simply moved smoothly from addressing me as you, singular, to you, plural. I broke up with Louis two years later in the finale of an argument over Ronald Reagan and the Iran/Contra affair. My exit speech— "I'd rather be a knee-jerk Democrat than an asshole Republican like you!"— was shouted over my shoulder as his office door slammed behind me. I stalked toward the World Trade Center's fourteenth-floor elevators through a thicket of averted eyes, Louis's coworkers scrambling to answer phones that hadn't rung. There were no fantasies of Dr. Kissinger and *détente* this time. Rebecca reverted to the singular "you" without comment, but in her eyes I saw the same look of resignation we'd shared as teenagers after one of my father's outbursts.

When he retired from the Federal Aviation Administration, my father landed a consulting job that gave him the opportunity to travel all over the world at his employer's expense. I had moved to New York City by then and had a good job as a software developer. He began to visit me during stopovers. To save his *per diem*, he'd sleep on an air mattress on the floor of my 350-square-foot walk-up on west 49th Street—seventeen blocks from the United Nations Headquarters. Against the background of the UN building and plaza, the very air seemed infused with the spirit of understanding and compromise. We were together in this intimate setting for many more hours than we had ever been when we lived in the same house, but my secret kept our conversations formal, halting, and completely lacking in substance. It was during one of those visits that he asked me if I ever went out on dates. I knew he meant with women, of course, but he'd caught me by surprise and, for a moment, I didn't know what to say. I was between boyfriends and had resorted to looking for sex partners via personal ads in one of the city's gay newspapers. I was pretty sure that was something he did *not* want to hear about.

"Well," I finally replied, "I don't go on many dates *per se*, but I do have dinner with friends occasionally."

After he left, I felt guilty. He'd asked a straightforward question, and my parsing of it felt like I was constructing a lie. I sat down and wrote him the coming-out letter to which, a week later, I received his eight-word response.

When I talked to my gay friends about my father's note, I was surprised that some saw it as hopeful. "See here?" Ray said. He stabbed at the small notecard with an index finger. "He promises the relationship won't change. The question is, does he think it's good or bad at present? If he thinks it's good now, he's saying it won't turn bad because of your confession."

"Look, little Mary sunshine," I said. "We're talking about a man who forced me to turn down a half scholarship to Reed as punishment for having hair that he thought was too long. A man who responded to my plea for a small loan for living expenses so I could finish out my last year of grad school by saying 'Why should I throw good money after bad?' Of course he's writing me off! He's telling me our relationship is never going to improve."

One thing did change though, after he received my letter. From then on, whenever he stayed in my apartment during a New York layover, he would ask me at some point whether I'd had any "dinners with friends" lately. Neither of us used the word "gay" or "boyfriend," but we both knew what he was asking. I was weary of secrets and dissembling, but never came up with an answer that told the whole truth. Why should I bother? After all, he had promised that nothing would change, that our relationship would never get better.

My father quit his job when he was diagnosed with congestive heart failure. There would be no more New York layovers. I flew home to LA to see him for what would turn out to be our final visit. On the last day, leaving his hospital room to head toward the airport, I wanted to shake his hand instead of kissing him goodbye. A casual observer might have guessed we were friends rather than father and son.

Sometimes I imagine that my father believed he had won our nearly life-long standoff over his promise that our relationship would never change. Other times, as when I discovered after his death that he'd named me as his successor trustee for the family trust, I wonder whether *I* was the obstacle to growth and development in our relationship. Perhaps we were both at fault. For whatever reason, our understanding of each other was no deeper on the day he died than it had been on the New York night, twenty years earlier, that he asked me who I loved and I answered with a lie.

One thing he hadn't noticed in his last days, as his heart labored and life ebbed, was that the constantly changing dictates of fashion had come full circle, and the hirsute grooming of the 1970s is once again the latest fashion. I don't have distinguishable sideburns anymore. Instead, my hair grows without interruption from a graying crown to a full salt-and-pepper beard. It pleases me to think that my parents would have hated it.

Panic at Twenty-Four Frames Per Second

Dead Birds is a documentary about the aboriginal people of New Guinea. *Behavior Modification* examines early attempts to treat autism.

Orange is an erotic short film shot entirely in extreme closeup in which a man peels and eats an orange. Slowly.

I worked my way through undergraduate school as a film projectionist, screening movies for the university's classes. It didn't pay much, but had other benefits: flexible hours, easy work, interesting subject matter. The only problem was that I was assigned to show the most popular films in the college's library so many times that after only a few months on the job it became impossible for me to stay awake while they were running. At some point I trained myself to fall asleep during the opening credits of these films and wake up just before the loose end of the trailer began to flap against the projector stand.

Color Chromatography demonstrates—you guessed it—color chromatography. *Sirene* is a prescient 1968 Oscar-winning animated short about the destruction of the natural environment. *A Normal Birth* shows a normal human birth in a medical environment; one or two students would faint during each screening thanks to the detailed close-ups. *This is Marshall McLuhan.* I assume no explanation is necessary.

Behavioral Studies In Obedience was a favorite of the psychology department. The sixty-minute film summarized experiments by Dr. Stanley Milgram, a Yale psychologist, in which an actor posing as a doctor was able to persuade some of the study's subjects to administer what they believed were painful, even lethal electric shocks to another actor in an adjacent room. At the other end of the spectrum, the telecommunications and film department couldn't get enough of *Why Man Creates*, an Oscar-winning twenty-five-minute paean to human ingenuity by famed film title designer Saul Bass. I must have shown that movie more than 700 times in the four years I worked for Audio/Visual Services, sometimes four or more per day. The TCF professors would also order older classic feature films for their classes, like *Citizen Kane, Casablanca,* and *Dark Victory.* And two evenings a month the student union would sponsor more contemporary feature films—*Easy Rider, Woodstock, Last Tango in Paris*—in a large hall in the student center or outdoors in the Greek bowl.

This is the point in the essay where you should **SIT UP AND PAY ATTENTION!** Everything I've told you up to this moment has been in the interest of presenting my bona fides, because it's important that you believe I know what I'm talking about. If you're a film buff, as I am, what I'm about to reveal will permanently spoil some aspects of your future film-viewing enjoyment. You can be as certain of that as you are that there will always be a dirt-blackened piece of Bazooka imbedded in the high-traffic carpet under your theatre seat. All you need do to continue enjoying classic films is to read no further. Turn two pages and go on to the next story or essay or poem in whatever journal you're holding in your nervous fingers. That's what I'm advising you to do.

And I mean *now.*

Why am I threatening you—and it is a threat, believe me—with information so disruptive that it merits this warning? My reason may be as simple as the fact that misery loves company. Or you may imagine me as Mephistopheles, the seducer, in the cautionary tale of *Faust* (which has been filmed no less than four times) and you, as Faust, falling prey to my appeal to your obsessive thirst for esoteric knowledge. After all, here you are, still reading after I've advised you to stop.

I have to pause a moment here to enjoy your demonstration of that most human of traits, the presumption that you will triumph where others more knowledgeable and better prepared have failed. What can I do in the face of such determination? How can I deny you what you're willing to risk so much to discover? But I'm not a monster. I've given you an out.

Now I can sense your curiosity beginning to get the better of you at last. Your heart quickens; you feel you must read on. A true film buff, you thrill to the obscure and thrive on the arcane. While viewing Ken Russell's 1969 film *Women in Love,* only you among your friends noticed that sliced bread was one of the props used in a scene that takes place in 1920, eight years before commercial pre-sliced bread was commonly available in Britain. In *Casablanca,* one character holds a gun that switches from one hand to the other or disappears entirely between takes. In *Citizen Kane,* Orson Welles' hand is in his left pocket on one side of a jump cut and his right on the other, all happening faster than you can pop a Junior Mint. These are the kinds of things you search for, and revel in.

But this story has nothing to do with trivia. You can find that stuff on the Internet. I did; you're welcome to it.

By now you suspect I may be teasing you, that I'm dangling my "secret" in front of you as though it were an unreleased clip from Terry Gilliam's last disaster-plagued attempt to film *Don Quixote*. *I may as well forge ahead*, you think, *see what it's about*. Maybe you're so sound of mind that you needn't fear what I might say. Anything is possible. I could be over-exaggerating. But I assure you I'm not. Wouldn't it be wiser to be safe, to heed my warnings to stop? What secret could possibly be worth the risk of ruining one of life's great pleasures? Don't be the Sam Spade of this story. Don't wait until the casualties are piling up before wondering if you've carried things too far. This is your last chance.

And so, as simply as that, your choice is made.

There are just two things you need to know in order to watch a film as a projectionist watches it.

The largest film reel that fits on a 16mm projector (the kind I operated) holds sixty minutes-worth of film. Since full-length feature films typically time out at somewhere around ninety to a hundred and twenty minutes, they're always on more than one reel, and sometimes need three or more.

To achieve a smooth, seemingly continuous film screening, two projectors are used. The first is for odd-numbered reels, the second for even. The projectionist handles the manual "switchover" from the active projector to the one loaded with the next reel.

So, how does a projectionist know exactly when to switch?

Before I answer, here's another question: did you notice anything unusual near the bottom of the first page of this essay? Did anything catch your eye, distracting you for a second or two, interrupting the flow of your thoughts? If not, go back and look now. Do you see the black dot near the right margin about three inches from the bottom of the page? Imagine that from now on, everything you read will have a black circle like this one after the final paragraph of every chapter or story, to signal that you should go on to the next page. In fact, just to make sure you don't miss it, there will be a warning dot two inches above the final one. How long do you think it would be before your subconscious begins to keep a constant watch for that warning signal? Would it distract you from what you're reading?

This is the solution film distributors came up with to solve the switchover problem. A black dot is painted, or a small hole is punched, in one frame of the film ten seconds before the end of each reel. When that frame passes through the projector at a speed of twenty-four frames-per-second, a small white dot or flash appears in the upper-right-hand corner of the screen. This GET READY! warning is followed ten seconds later by another flash: SWITCH! And the projectionist flips on the power switch for machine two, where the second reel has been cued-up at the first frame, simultaneously turning off the power to projector one.

No doubt you're thinking, *A twenty-fourth of a second? That's what all this is about? Big deal!*

I admire your confidence, but yours is the reaction of someone who has never noticed the dots, or perhaps thought they were just random scratches in the film. All that has changed as of this moment. Once you see them, now that you know what they are, you'll always see them. Tomorrow, next week, three months from now, you'll come to the realization that you're dot-obsessed. You feel a nervous anticipation as you watch the last few feet of film roll off reel one, your breath coming short gulps, your nerves tightening, your heart drumming in your chest at the GET READY! signal. It seems too long to be just ten seconds. A panic sets in. Did you miss it? Suddenly, the second flash. SWITCH! You flip the toggles, and you can relax, you can breathe again, and you return to the film with fitful attention, almost ignoring the plotline, impatient with the dialogue, silently estimating, over and over, the interval until the next reel change. And so you'll finally become, like me, an anxious addict, counting the minutes, twitching as you wait for the next visual twang, finding relief—at last—only in a brief flash of white light in a darkened room.

●

I've dragged you to the brink of the abyss, but the time has come for you to take the final step on your own. This is my last instruction to you, one I know that, having come this far, you are unable to resist. The next time you're watching an older movie, keep an eye on the upper-right-hand corner of the screen starting at about the twenty-five-minute mark. I'll bet you'll see switchover dots. And, having once seen them, will never be able to *not* see them again.

Just One Word: Plastics

I'm about to toss a bag of garbage in the dumpster behind my apartment complex when I notice a large, clear plastic jug on top of the older trash.

"Wide mouth, good for spare nuts and bolts," I hear my mother murmur in my ear. "Or maybe it's big enough to hold electrical parts."

"The label says 'salsa'," I whisper back. "It's intended for food."

"Oh, *really*. Sometimes you seem to have no imagination at all, Bud."

My mother abhorred the idea of throwing away anything that might be of use some day, no matter how theoretical the use or distant the day. She's been offering me these *sotto voce* suggestions ever since she died, twenty years ago. They're the reason the shelves in my garage are lined with Chinese take-out soup tubs, boxes that once held organic salad greens, and super-sized peanut butter jars—rows of clear or painted or printed-on plastic containers, all emptied, cleaned, and filled with odds and ends.

My mother was born in 1920, only a few years after plastic was invented, which may explain her fascination with it. She grew up in a largely plastic-free household. In my grandmother's opinion, it was too modern, too mysterious, too quick to melt when absentmindedly set on a hot stove or left too close to the toaster. But in my mother's house, we drank from plastic glasses and ate off of Melmac plates using flatware with two-toned handles made of Bakelite (the first thermosetting plastic), which had been a prized wedding gift.

As the use of plastic became more universal, my mother perfected her talent for peeling a blister pack from its cardboard backing in a way that avoided creases and cracking. She would fix the empty shape with an appraising eye and announce, "I could use this for something." It was a "do not discard" notice to the rest of us—one we dared not ignore. And if she couldn't think of a new use for the item right away, she'd store it neatly with its fellow containers-in-waiting in—what else? —a plastic bag.

Over years, the question of what to get my mother for her birthday always found a thrifty answer on the pages of the Tupperware catalog. My siblings and I were only too glad to assist in her goal of accumulating a complete set, including the salt and pepper shakers and the lettuce crisper. As her collection grew and the acquisition of unique pieces became more difficult, her children inevitably made mistakes in their gift purchases. Protests like, "But this one's *green!*" were tolerated only from those younger than eighteen. Once we passed the age of majority, my mother felt we had the adult obligation not to saddle her with duplicates or triplicates unless she specifically asked for them. But if she wasn't thrilled to receive yet another cake keeper or chip-n-dip set for Christmas, she was gracious enough not to let on.

I pull the salsa jug out of the garbage and heft it in my left hand. I'm thinking, *Electrical parts? Ha! It's perfect for extra sprinkler heads.* And you know what? It *is* perfect.

NB: My friend Alice informs me that the chemical name for Bakelite is polyoxybenzylmethylenglycolanhydride. This seems to be important to her, though I have no idea why—JB

Spring Fever

As I approach the procedure room, the smell of blood fills my nostrils. Ever since I lost a rock fight at age six and stumbled home from school with blood streaming from a gash in my head, my brain sends this warning whenever I'm in physical danger.

From where I'm standing, on its threshold, the room seems more dreary than threatening. Small. Dim. Cold. Walls, cabinets, counters, floor: gray and white. I could be in a medical facility in any town or city or, for that matter, in any country. I can see a small wheeled cart near an examination table in the center of the room. A number of stainless-steel objects in sealed plastic bags—medical tools, I assume—are arrayed on it. They lend the scene an air of aseptic efficiency even though their uses are not immediately apparent. On the top tray is a battered monitor that reminds me of the oscilloscopes that TV repair shops once used to test the vacuum tubes in early receivers. If the room's purpose were less serious, the anachronism would be funny, like visiting the cockpit of a modern jet and finding the navigator using a sextant. The nurse who's led me here stands inside, near the cart and table, and looks back at me in the doorway. She waits with obvious impatience, tapping her pen against the edge of a clipboard she cradles in her left arm.

Is it just me, or are things progressing too fast? It was only two weeks ago that I got the results of the prostate-specific antigen test that's been part my annual check-up since 1990, the year I turned forty. The measured march of moderately-elevated but stable values across a graph now ends with a peak marking the most recent result. It juts into previously uncharted territory like an exclamation point. "No reason to panic," my doctor tells me. "False readings are not unusual, and anyway, prostate cancer is usually a very slow-growing one. We can repeat the test now and every six months instead of twelve, and just watch it for a while."

When the result of the re-test shows an even taller peak, he says, "We could do a biopsy at this point, but the biopsy itself has risks. At any rate, *you* will make the go/no go decision as to when to take the next step."

I get it. The translation: if you die from an infection contracted in the course of a biopsy, it's not the doctor's fault; you're the one who decided to have it done. If you incur the risk and discomfort and the biopsy turns out to be negative, so sorry. Later, I discovered in my research an article explaining that if a man lives long enough, he has a one-in-nine risk of developing prostate cancer. Studies show that treatment doesn't increase life expectancy; men who have a CaP diagnosis usually die of something else. Many medical care strategists think that's a good reason to stop "wasting" money looking for it, to stop doing the PSA blood test. You have to die of something. That's how their logic goes.

The list of effects of advanced prostate cancer is very long and very hard to find, even with the help of the internet. What often goes unmentioned is that when prostate cancer metastasizes, it tends to migrate to the hips, spine, and pelvis, and make the smaller bones as brittle as cinnamon sticks. My logic says I'd rather die suddenly of a heart attack in the middle of the night, in my sleep, than of prostate cancer after years of a lingering, pain-wracked, bed-ridden existence.

Many of these points I will learn only later, after I've had to confront the results of the second abnormal PSA test and the unspoken expectation that I once again will decide what to do next. And I *did* make a decision, though at this moment, standing just outside the procedure room, I question—as I have a thousand times in the last few days—whether it's the right one. Does it bother anyone but me that my decision may have been made in haste, or in a state of almost complete ignorance, confusion, or fear? That, again, is not the doctor's responsibility; I signed a release that says so.

There's one thing I *do* know and that I feel keenly while I hesitate to cross this threshold: if I take another step I will pass a turning-point. I imagine a row of dominoes, carefully set so that if one falls over, it will cause a chain reaction that will topple the rest. Right now, I could simply say to the impatient nurse, "I'm sorry. I've changed my mind," then turn and leave. *Any* other action will set the machinery of standard medical practice in motion without providing a clue as to where the chosen path may lead. Like Dorothy in *The Wizard of Oz,* who abandons the familiar when she steps off the porch of her gray clapboard home onto the yellow brick road, I know I am changing my future. Except I would be moving in the other direction, from the lush, tropical vibrancy of Munchkin Land into the dull black and white landscape of hospital rooms, operating rooms, radiation rooms. In my Kansas, knowledge can bring confusion rather than understanding; false comfort instead of certainty; bondage in place of freedom.

Nothing has changed at the threshold of the procedure room. I'm immobilized by the realization that *any* action I take at this point will affect the outcome, even if I do nothing. The nurse is more impatient than I, but both of us, I think, feel the awkwardness of our positions. I'm embarrassed by my indecision, and angry at myself for being embarrassed. In the end, I can't bring myself to make an unconventional choice. I follow the nurse into the room.

"You can take off your clothes in here," the nurse says, pointing to an open door on the other side of the room. "You can keep your socks on but take off your shoes put on this gown and lie on the table on your side."

Now that I'm committed, my perception of everything slows down. Have you noticed that in movies, TV shows, commercials, when they want to imply that things are happening very quickly, they shoot the main actors in slow-mo with the location spinning around them like they're at the center of a tornado? My thoughts do that now, become sluggish, as though I'm drugged, even though no one has yet come near me with a needle. The nurse's words swirl past on fast-forward, with comprehension approaching zero on my part; I struggle to organize the torrent into sentences and paragraphs that make sense. A poster on the wall near the clock has the headline, "Learn to Recognize the Symptoms of Shock." 1) A state of "daze." Check. 2) Narrowing of attention, check. 3) An inability to comprehend stimuli, check. 4) Disorientation, double-check.

I slow-walk to the small changing room, relieved when I see that it includes a sink and toilet that appear to be stationary. I pee as soon as I close the door, then again three minutes later after changing into a standard hospital gown, opening in the back as instructed. The fabric is rough against my skin and smells of disinfecting detergent. I wonder how many people have briefly worn this gown—and the dozens of others I glimpsed in the closet when the nurse opened it to extract one for me—for similar reasons. The gown is not the uniform I would have chosen for the coming battle. Like most uniforms, it's dehumanizing, a destroyer of individuality. Donning the gown, I become the generic patient, just one more among the ranks of those who have worn it before me.

On the practical side, it gives the urologist ready access to the passageway through which he'll perform the biopsy.

Back in the procedure room, the nurse again stands near the table. "Lie-on-the-table-on-your-left-side-with-your-knees-slightly-bent-would-you-like-a-blanket."

"No, thanks," I answer. I think I got the gist of that word burst.

But why did I say no? The procedure room is freezing. That, and a mix of nervous energy and dread, have set my teeth chattering. My words tremble as they leave my lips. I realize that I'm doing my "perfect patient" act, bargaining for a better test result as a reward for good behavior. That's the kind of irrational deal-making I'm reduced to, the kind more commonly found in a church. I should have said yes to the blanket offer.

The sounds in the room are of the nurse going about her business: she rummages through drawers, tears open the bags of tools, dumps them—CLANG!—on the roll-around cart, all (purposefully, it seems) just outside my field of vision. Are the items she's arranging on the table so frightening that I'm not to be allowed to see them? The nurse, as well, is behind me, and I realize I neglected to take note of anything about her. I've made no effort to remember her face, figure, age. On her character's blank slate, I'm free to superimpose whatever figure I need, and right now I want a short, plump avatar of my mother. Strange. My mother is dead, and we didn't get along for the last fifty years of her life. Still, I want comfort, and I remember how, when I was very young, my mother would hold me on her lap, pat my arm, stroke my forehead, whisper that everything will be okay. Which of these would the anonymous nurse allow if I ask her? I wish I knew her name.

"Woodjew-likkapillo-foururhed" she says.

What's she saying, what's she saying, what's she saying? I chant this to myself, the percussion part courtesy of my chattering teeth.

"Um… sure" I answer out loud. She gently lifts my head to place the pillow underneath. It's not a hug, but it's something.

The door flies open; I hear the end of a loud conversation in the hall. Warm air rushes in and the temperature in the room goes up one degree. I can feel the change on my naked buttocks. Thanks to my position on the table, they're the first thing someone coming through the door would see.

"OK, let's talk next week!" the voice booms. It's my doctor. He sounds cheerful. Why shouldn't he? He will be at the dull end of any instruments he uses. The door swings closed and latches, returning us to dim, frigid isolation.

"Good morning! How are we today?" Brisk walk around front, quick handshake, my grip already tentative, weakened by uncertainty. Then a sigh from the cushion as he settles himself on a rolling stool; the sound of metal wheels as he glides across the floor behind me.

How are we? What a stupid question! We who are possibly about to die salute you. That's how I feel. You'd have to be brain dead not to be terrified of what's going to happen here. Dial back on the cheerfulness, mate!

"Um... fine!" How many people in the room have I convinced?

"Good!" Snap of latex gloves. "I'm just going to start with a digital exam." His index finger is in and out in a matter of seconds.

"Okay!" To the nurse: "I think we'll do eight needles." To me: "This is the ultrasound wand." He's selected a metallic-looking stick from the items on the cart and waves it around where I can see it. *Expecto Patronum!* I want to shout it and see if I can get a laugh, then remind myself that this is probably not a good time to make jokes.

The wand is about an inch in diameter and ten inches long. A cord exits the end he holds in his hand and is connected to the monitor I noticed earlier on the small table. "I'll be using it to get an image of your prostate on this." He pats the ancient-looking box. "It will help me get the needles to the right spots." For emphasis, he works a small button on the wand near his thumb. A thin needle pokes out of the other end, retreats. "Are you ready?"

"Um... I just want to mention that when I get anxious I have to pee."

"You're not anxious now, are you?" The nurse joins in on his laugh; it seems unfair, at my expense, and it's too late now to come back with my Harry Potter reference to balance the score.

Yeah, yuk it up! I don't tell him that I've already peed six times this morning, and it's only 9:00am. Six times in about two hours, the last time now at least ten minutes ago. I do some silent arithmetic and figure I have ten minutes, max, until I'll have to go again.

"Well, this won't take long," he says. "We'll be done before you know it!"

Unlikely, I think.

"Okay, open wide." He and the nurse share another giggle, but, surprise! The ultrasound wand slips in almost without me realizing it. "Okay. When I take a tissue sample you're just going to feel a little pinch and hear a 'snap.' Ready?"

I try to imagine what being ready for this would mean.

There's a click-snap, and I feel a piece of my insides snatched away. I'm shocked at the idea that the needle's tiny hook has punched through tissue walls, membranes, organs that are supposed to be separate from each other. My shoulders and legs begin to tremble, as they often do in high-stress situations. I know that if I don't take some kind of action to stop it, the shaking will become violent. Almost immediately I feel the need to pee.

"That's as bad as it gets." my doctor is saying. "Are you going to be okay?"

There's a metallic shuffling of needles in and out of the handle end of the probe going on behind me. Can I make it through seven more needles without peeing all over everything? I don't think so.

"No. I have to pee," I answer.

"Okay, we're going to be done here in a minute. Can you hold on?"

I weigh the urge growing within me—like a wave building to its break—against my mental clock, which seems to have come to a complete stop. I know he's lying about the "one minute" estimate.

"I don't think so." I feel a flush of shame with my admission of failure, my inability to control myself. Immediately the urge becomes stronger.

"We can't have a wet operating table." Annoyance begins to eclipse his cheerfulness. "Grace, do we have a urinal in here?"

Grace, I think. Of course.

Cupboard doors open and close. I catch a glimpse of a plastic vessel in Grace's hand.

"Don't worry," my doctor says. "She has a two-year-old boy."

I'm too desperate to try to understand this nonsequitur as Grace's chubby fingers reach under the front of my gown and find my shrunken penis.

Grace, Graciella, Gracia mi Salvadora, I chant in my head as my urine streams into the plastic bottle.

The diagnosis comes two days later. When my doctor calls, I'm standing on my back patio, idly gazing down the valley that seems to begin where my feet are positioned on the concrete, warming myself in the weak March sun. Spring always seems to come early in San Diego.

"I want to give you the results of the procedure we did the other day," he begins.

This is going to be bad. He can't say the word "biopsy".

28

"Sorry to give you this information over the phone, but I'm afraid the pathologist found cancer in two of the eight cores. Twenty percent of each of the two cores is involved. All the cancerous cores are from the right lobe."

I realize I'm not breathing. As I look to the east, the sunlight and sparse clouds, like karma-dealing shadow puppets, create changing patterns on the face of the Cuyamacas, the closest mountains. The feverish sun teases the scent of sage out of the winter-toughened leaves of the canyon brush. Fragile, lemon-green shoots carpet the normally powder-dry and odorless soil that a recent rain has turned dark, moist, and fragrant.

I draw a deep breath through my nose as the doctor continues. Suddenly the air feels cooler, almost frigid, and I recognize the metallic smell of danger as the tiny veins in my nose swell with blood.

I have cancer.

Another breath: cold iron. The doctor's voice drones on in my ear, talking statistics, grade, Gleason score. I stare across the valley toward the near hills, wooly with a coat of new green that looks farcically unrealistic in the dry landscape. The next row of peaks is darker; the blues, blacks, and purples like massive bruises, unaffected by the changing sun and clouds. The third row of peaks is faint, hardly discernable; it's difficult to tell where the earth vanishes and the pale blue-gray sky begins.

I wonder if today marks the beginning of my own slow vanishing, of the gradual diminishment I've watched in a lover, then one parent, then the other; the relentless but almost invisible daily wearing away of personality, of vitality, of hope. I wonder what accommodation I'll have to make for the disease. Will my life be ruled by drug schedules, chemotherapy appointments, radiation treatments?

"Do you have any questions at this time?"

I imagine how this topic might be covered in the fifth week of year two of medical school: How to Deliver Bad News. "Explain the situation clearly and completely," the textbook would say. "Give the patient the opportunity to ask questions, though there may not be any during the first conversation."

I look down at my feet again, where large cracks vein the concrete patio like crazing in an old teacup. It looks unstable. I imagine the cracks widening, becoming ruts, ditches, gorges, and struggle to keep my balance, to avoid being swallowed up by them.

I realize that this silence means it is my turn to speak, though I catch the perfunctory tone of the question. He's busy. He wants to move on. Perhaps to his next call. Perhaps to a more cheerful one, one that starts out, "Good news! Your biopsy was negative."

I listen to my doctor waiting, breathing, waiting, and in our individual silences I imagine the sound of one domino falling against the next.

"No," I say. "No questions."

I H8 David Sedaris

think \ think\ *vb* OE *thenken*; akin to OHG denken 1 : to form or have in the mind 2 : INTEND, PLAN 3 a : to have as an opinion : BELIEVE <~ it's so > b : to regard as : CONSIDER <~ the rule unfair>

dif-fer-ent \ 1dif-ernt, \ 2 dif-(e-)rent\ adj [MF, fr. L different-, *differens,* prp. of *differre*] 1 : partly or totally unlike in nature, form, or quality DISSIMILAR <could hardly be more> —*Webster's Seventh New Collegiate Dictionary*

It was 1995, and Apple Computer was struggling. It had suffered through internal power-plays and the forced departure of its remaining founder, Steve Jobs. It had flooded the personal computer market with models based on slight variations of its Macintosh product that were so poorly marketed that a 1996 *Time Magazine* article called Apple "arguably one of the worst-managed companies in the [personal computing] industry." It was losing market share; had considered and ultimately rejected purchase offers from IBM and Sun Microsystems. In 1997, in desperation, Apple recalled former CEO Steve Jobs and charged him with saving the company. What happened next is the stuff of myth and legend, but the short version of the story is this: Jobs not only saved the company but made it one of the largest, richest, most successful corporations in history, largely through the power of advertising.

Think Different. That was the tag line for Apple Computer's history-making 1997 advertising campaign. Controversial, divisive, revolutionary, even irritating when first introduced, its pattern has been imitated so many times that it now feels commonplace. Critics derided the slogan's verb-adjective structure as ungrammatical; supporters countered that similar phrases, like "think hard," were already well-accepted by consumers as proper English. Some senior managers at Apple worried that the slogan might be seen as an attack on IBM; "Think" was the one-word marketing slogan the mainframe computer giant had been using for most of its existence. Jobs responded that the campaign's tag line was not a specific reference to any of Apple's competitors, nor was it about competitiveness in general. It was a statement of Apple's business philosophy: people can change the world for the better.

The campaign that originated in the Los Angeles offices of Apple's advertising agency, TBWA\Chiat\Day, was deceptively simple. It relied on an emotion-inspired atmosphere of solemn-sounding gobbledygook spoken over a series of seventeen grainy black-and-white photographs and film clips of nineteenth- and twentieth-century innovators from social, scientific, political, and artistic fields. One of the agency's significant accomplishments was to actually obtain releases from the estates of Albert Einstein, Martin Luther King, Jr., John Lennon (with Yoko Ono), Buckminster Fuller, Thomas Edison, Muhammad Ali, Maria Callas, Mohandas Gandhi, Amelia Earhart, Martha Graham, Jim Henson (with Kermit the Frog), and Frank Lloyd Wright. A serious-sounding voice-over spoke. "Here's to the crazy ones," the voice-over intoned. "The misfits. The trouble-makers." The spot finished with a black screen, the tag line center-bottom.

Within Apple's corporate offices, there was a good deal of internal ambivalence toward the ad. Jobs reportedly thought the concept was brilliant but referred to an early draft of the campaign as "shit." Later, in a video that captured the speech he made to Apple employees the day the ad was released, he was all praise. He could not have guessed, on that day, that the Think Different campaign would become one of the most influential advertising memes of our time—one that continues to exert its influence today.

I hate advertising. I realize it's an unavoidable component of an economy that depends almost entirely on consumer spending, but over the last century or so advertising has infiltrated our lives to the point where it has become ubiquitous, and so integrated with content that the fine line that formerly separated the two long ago became invisible. Among modern cultures, Americans, in particular, have accepted the stealthy intrusion of advertising into their every-day lives to the point where some experts estimate we are viewing, on average, as many as five thousand ads every day. A January 2007 article in the *New York Times* reported on the phenomenon under the headline, "Add this to the endangered list: blank spaces." The article went on to cite examples of newly-explored advertising opportunities: "Supermarket eggs have been stamped with the names of CBS television shows. Subway turnstiles bear messages from Geico auto insurance. Chinese food cartons promote Continental Airways. US Air is selling ads on motion sickness bags."

If the subject were anything other than commercial advertising, you might think these ideas were intended as a joke. Tell that to the commuters in San Francisco who demanded that a "Got Milk?" ad on their bus shelter stop emitting the smell of freshly-baked chocolate chip cookies.

Everyone alive today was born into the age of advertising. This will most likely be true for our grandchildren and our grandchildren's grandchildren. We have learned our consumer habits and the shorthand of advertising symbols and signals from birth, when our isolation ends and mothers (typically) begin to exercise greater control over what their babies see, hear, taste, smell, and touch. New mothers become the focus of intense marketing, which is how Gerber managed to convince them that manufactured, "scientific" baby food is superior to what they can prepare from fresh ingredients in their own homes. Bonus for mom: no need to spend tedious minutes chopping and straining your baby's food.

What if it were possible to advertise to our children *before* birth? We've seen that advertising abhors a vacuum. Case in point: sometime during the twentieth century—the data in Google's n-gram database suggests a peak around 1943—expectant mothers got it into their heads that playing music by composers like Beethoven, Chopin, and Mozart for their developing fetus would make their baby smarter after birth, thus giving the genius baby a life-long advantage over its troglodyte fellows. It's not clear where this idea came from; I suspect it was driven by constantly-improving recording and playback technologies and devices and a mother's hope that her child will be remarkable in some way. Although research has shown there is no basis for the belief, a steady percentage of expectant mothers continue to subscribe to false science on this topic, feeding sales of specialized CDs and internet-connected "prenatal sound delivery systems." There's no justification for this prenatal retail category other than its snob appeal.

Much of the advertising we're exposed to reinforces cultural stereotypes. Ads for products from snack foods to automobiles feature stereotypical characters that refer back to traditional gender or occupational roles, or purposefully violate them for effect. Men buy cars. Black women cook southern fast food. Housewife avatars sell snack-sized yogurt to real housewives, making it a product that's primarily pitched to women by women. Go ahead; try to find a male in a yogurt ad. I'm sure that Dannon, which makes more than two hundred different flavors, styles and sizes of "cultured refrigerated dairy products"—or "yogurt," as I call it—has done the research to confirm that men generally don't buy their products.

But there's another subtext in most yogurt ads that really puzzles me: why are the women in these ads almost always shown dancing around the room while they eat it? In fact, in TV commercials, women are shown dancing around the room when they're called upon to eat *anything* on-camera. I suspect that foods considered "feminine," like yogurt, are marketed as part of a "healthy lifestyle" (despite the twenty-six grams of sugar in a six-ounce container of Yoplait original), and make you feel so great that, like Ellen DeGeneres, you've just got to dance. Those jitters don't come from too much sugar; they come from happiness.

As vacancies in spaces for traditional advertising become harder to find, we can expect even our definition of advertising to change. Some may remember that the original appeal of the cable networks was the widely-assumed-but-never-explicit promise that a subscriber would pay a monthly fee for the service in exchange for the privilege of not being bombarded by commercials every seven minutes. That tacit agreement between producers and distributors lasted for about nine years. In July 1981, an article in the *New York Times* announced that "The floodgates for advertising on cable are down."

There are still a few TV stations that describe themselves as "commercial free." Your local PBS station is one; Turner Classic Movies is another. But both fill the awkward spaces between one film or program and the next with "announcements" that look an awful lot like commercials. They flog branded products like paid-subscription program guides, accessories (T-shirts, ball caps, coffee mugs), location tours, an annual film festival, and other products and activities. If the sixty-second spot soliciting movie-lovers for TCM's annual Caribbean cruise isn't a commercial ad, I don't know what is.

At this point, you may be wondering what all this has to do with Apple's Think Different campaign. The short answer is: nothing. In keeping with its slogan, Apple's campaign didn't rely on any traditional advertising methods and tricks to get its message across. It didn't show a product in the photos and films and didn't even mention the company's name in the voice-over. From Jobs's point of view, the campaign wasn't an ad to sell computers. "Marketing is about values," he told the small gathering of employees the morning of the day that the 1997 campaign was released. "We believe that people can change the world for the better. We need to show why we're still relevant in this world."

The television and print spots for Apple's campaign ran for more than a year, winning a 1998 Emmy award for Outstanding Commercial and the 2000 Grand Effie Award for most effective campaign in America. More importantly, it re-established Apple's reputation as a counter-culture brand and helped the company recover from a loss of a billion dollars in 1996. Today, in 2017, the company has an estimated net worth of three-quarters of a *trillion* dollars, making it the second-largest company in America (Google is first. Motto of Google's corporate code of conduct: "Don't Be Evil.")

Given Apple's success, it was inevitable that we would see other companies trying to duplicate the lightening-in-a-bottle results of Think Different. It took a while, but in 2009, twelve years after Apple's ad was first introduced, the Sci Fi cable network decided to take a shot with a re-branding effort that included a puzzling name change—to SyFy—and a new tag line: "Imagine Greater." Two words, verb-adjective. The effort was greeted with a mixture of ennui and outright hostility by many industry-watchers, and though it won the Gold Addie at the American Advertising Awards in 2013, a comparison of the network's ad revenue across three years shows that the facelift had virtually no effect on the network's bottom line.

Apple suspended widespread insertions of the Think Different TV and print ads in 2002; the company continues to use the slogan often enough to retain the copyright, most recently on its product packaging. But what interests me about Apple's Think Different campaign is how many times it's been imitated, and to what length a company or their ad agency will stretch an idea to catch some fraction of the profit breeze on which Apple sailed to success. Those imitations have largely fallen flat, sometimes to unintentionally humorous effect.

As research for this essay, I compiled over a period of nearly two years a list of twenty-five advertising slogans that are indisputably imitative of the Apple campaign. I urge you not to try this at home. Think of me as the professional driver on a closed road we're always warned about, the one we're told is driving the car when a vehicle is speeding down a winding mountain road or spinning in slow motion on the Bonneville Salt Flats.

Studies have shown that excessive TV-watching can degrade cognitive function. I think "can make you stupid" was the way the danger was described. I've mentioned that I hate advertising, so you can imagine how painful and dangerous the project was for me. I used a brute force approach in my survey, watching hour after hour of commercial television. Keep in mind that in 2016, the year I completed my research, about a third of the average TV hour was given over to advertising. That ratio is slowly but steadily increasing. A watcher/researcher has to have a quick thumb on the mute button if the goal is to catch the largely inane commercials and avoid as much as possible the tripe that comprises the other seventy percent of the broadcast. My list of twenty-five campaigns is included below, now mostly as a curiosity, which I'll explain in a minute. Again, you may think I made up some of the more ridiculous ones, but I promise you these are all legitimate, corporate-approved advertising campaigns developed by professionals in the field. I would just ask you to meditate for a moment on the last one on the list, intended to market the services of Massage Envy: "Because Everything." Try to imagine the level of desperation that would drive an agency to propose that catchphrase to their client, and the client to buy it.

This isn't the essay I'd intended to write about my hard-won list of campaigns. I'd hoped to produce a humor piece focused on observations about how different the world might be today if Apple's campaign had failed. (I pose that question as I sit at my desk working on a Macbook Air laptop; my i-phone and i-pad are charging on the other corner.)

I will never write that essay. You'll never have the opportunity to speculate along with me as to what the conversation in the Comcast/NBC Universal (corporate parent of SyFy) boardroom might have been when the senior managers were pitched the "Imagine Greater" campaign. I will never finish a devastating indictment of the use of instant messaging, which I consider a civilization-destroyer wreaking daily havoc on thousands of years of human language and literary evolution. I will never have the opportunity to explain my disgust with cute phonetic spellings of product names like Chick-fil-A (which I mispronounced for years, thinking the vowel sound at the end of the word was a short A) and Finast, or other supposed fowl products such as Appateazers and Chicken Wyngz, which, whatever they are, I'll bet have nothing to do with chicken.

That's the commentary I'd begun to outline in my notes: a document so compelling in its reason and insight that it would finally and permanently trigger the voluntary abandonment by my fellow authors of every word that appears in the Urban Dictionary.

Why won't any of this happen? Blame David Sedaris.

I've been a huge fan of David Sedaris for many years, ever since—arriving early for a movie at a local mall—I went into the adjacent Borders bookstore to kill some time and stumbled onto a copy of *Naked*, his third book of memoir-ish short stories. I immediately fell in love with his writing style and his wry, carefully targeted sense of humor, which allows him to escape unscathed from writing about the most horrific experiences. His telling of a story can seem casual, even chatty. Often, he starts one story, then seems to abandon it and start another on an unrelated topic. Eventually he shows the reader that the two stories are related in an unforeseen way, and one ending suffices for both. Since that chance meeting in the bookstore, I've eagerly anticipated the paperback release of each new Sedaris story collection.

One beautiful spring afternoon, sometime after I began work on the career-defining critique of modern culture I've described above, I decided to take a break and download a copy of Sedaris's then-latest book, *Let's Explore Diabetes with Owls*. I comported myself in my most comfortable reading pose—on a lounge chair in my sunny back yard, clad only in boxer shorts, with a box of cranberry walnut oatmeal cookies from Sprouts and a tall iced tea beside me—and, with eager anticipation, opened my Kindle and began to read.

All went well for about thirty minutes. The first story, "Dentists Without Borders," summoned memories of my own experience with dental implants and a smile "bittersweet and drearied with blood." Been there, done that, excuse me if I skip the gift shop as I exit. Then "Attaboy," in which an anonymous neighborhood kid calls Sedaris's mother a bitch and Sedaris fantasizes about how he might be punished should he ever commit a similar transgression. The fantasy includes a "white dinner" during which he's served, in succession, a bowl of paste, then joint compound, and "maybe if I was good, some semen." *Wow*, I thought; *I don't know if I could write something like that, even as a fantasy.* But, then, he's David Sedaris and I'm not.

I turned the page, and my eyes fell on the title of his next story: "Think Differenter."

Maybe you can imagine my reaction. I might have done a spit-take if I hadn't just swallowed my last bit of tea. As it was, a piece of walnut from the cookie I was eating lodged in my throat on a sudden intake of breath, and I began to choke. My face grew hot, but I was shivering. My focus shifted to the specific brain cell that would soon become the center of a whopper of a headache which, if I survived it, would someday turn into Alzheimer's and kill me.

David Sedaris has stolen my story idea, I thought, but of course I knew that was ridiculous. Here his story was, in print; he'd probably tossed it off in an evening after a few glasses of wine while my masterpiece was still an idea in vitro, gradually developing through my excruciatingly slow creative process—one that could end up requiring six months of work to settle on a title. Which was not going to be the same as Sedaris's, by the way, but what did that matter now?

What made the whole situation worse, I realized as I sped through the four-pager, is that "Think Differenter" is not a great story. Resentment surged like bile through my narrowing esophagus as I read his Tea-Party-like rant written in the voice of a redneck with serial wives and children whose names and even gender he can't reliably remember, who measures his life's progress by Apple product releases. It was tedious rather than funny. I was forced to confront the fact that my prospects for greatness had been ruined by a mediocre piece of work from a much-more-talented author. No matter that our subjects and themes were completely different, that he was writing fiction and I was writing non-. I knew no one would ever be able to read my piece without thinking of *him;* the opposite would never be true.

Why can't he stick to the tough stuff? I remember thinking. *Why can't he stick to writing about being fed bowls of semen, and leave the mocking of corporate taglines to those of us with less imagination?*

I had stopped choking, and so sought comfort in another bite of cranberry walnut oatmeal cookie while I planned my next move. Maybe I should read one more story....

"Memory Laps" tells of a teenager's experiences as an unwilling member of the swim team at the poorer of his town's two swim clubs. In many ways it's my story, too, though I didn't stay on my club's team long enough to compete in even a single match. What rings true for me is the yearning for paternal approval, which ends up being lavished on someone else's more athletic son. It's my story as much as Sedaris's, and it's beautifully written. All I could hope was that maybe, someday, I would be able to write something half as good.

I won't say all was forgiven, but.... I counted the cookies left in the Sprouts box. If I rationed them, I would finish the book before it got dark.

An incomplete list of marketing slogans—and the companies that paid for them—that are derivatives of Apple's "Think Different" campaign:

Drive Happy	Alamo Rent-A-Car
Breathe Happy	Febreeze
Deserve Delicious	Coldstone Creamery
Eat Fresh	Subway
Rethink Possible	AT&T
Do Brave	Degree Anti-Perspirant
Enjoy Better	Time/Warner Cable
Be More	PBS
See Impossible	Canon printers
Let's Movie	TCM
Enjoy the Go	Charmin bathroom tissue
Dare Greatly	Cadillac
Wander Wisely	Travelocity
Get Knowing	Credit Karma
For the Greater	National University
Activate Your Within	Trulicity (Lilly)
Never Too Next	Kohler
Wash In the Wow	Downy
Sniff Sniff Hurray	Glade air freshener
Play Delicious	Skittles
More Happy	Pepsi
Work Less Dumb	Quip Software
Get Your Better Back	Zicam
Be More Tea	Lipton tea bags
Because Everything	Massage Envy

Adult Swim

That summer at Boy Scout camp, you were ... what? Eleven? Twelve? Up early every morning, before the pool officially opened, swimming your laps, prepping for the mile swim later in the week. You remember Tony, the morning lifeguard? Eighteen years old, from Baltimore. He'd open the gate for you an hour before he was supposed to. You'd swim back and forth in the unheated outdoor pool, the sounds of the waking camp outside the chain-link fence dulled by the water washing in and out of your ears.

You had the whole pool to yourself, and for an hour or so you had Tony, as your coach, to yourself as well. You'd been surprised when he'd pulled you out of a group splashing around in the pool's shallow end during the first open swim of the week. You're a strong swimmer, he'd said. How'd you like to earn your merit badge this week?

Fact is, you *weren't* a strong swimmer, but you didn't want to disappoint Tony when he'd offered to be your coach. You'd meet him at the wire gate in the morning just before the sun came up, when everyone else was asleep. Don't let anybody see you, he'd said; they'll have my nuts in a vice. He counted your laps while he washed down the concrete deck with a hose, readying the pool for the day's onslaught of teenage boys. If he thought you were going too fast he'd call out, Slow down, Davey! Take a breath every other stroke. Relax. The mile isn't a race; it's a test of endurance. So you slowed down, rolled over half way on every right-hand stroke so you could catch a glimpse of him while he worked. When you sensed you'd reached your goal you'd call out to him, quiet as you could, Tony, how many is that? and he'd pretend he'd forgotten. Sorry, you'll have to start over he'd say just loud enough for you to hear, and you'd stop in the deep end and tread water until the two of you agreed on a number.

It seemed like Tony was always washing down the pool deck while you swam, his thumb over the end of the hose to make a spray. Sometimes when you'd turn your head to steal a breath, you wouldn't see him right away, and you'd raise your chest and interrupt the rhythm of your strokes. Then you'd hear him, on your blind side: Head down! And you'd spend the rest of that lap hoping that Tony didn't think you were some goof-off just wasting his time.

The first lesson had been the best so far. It had been fun to sneak through the sleeping campground, your nerves on edge while you waited for Tony at the locked gate. Once inside, you both slipped into the frigid water; Tony stood with both feet on the bottom while you stretched out, floating on your stomach in crawl position, Tony's open palms supporting you at chest and hips while he coached you on your strokes and breathing. When he finally let you go you swam away with all the He-Man power you could muster. Tony laughed and called out, "Keep at it, camper."

You wished you could be like him—cool, confident, easy in the body he'd honed during his own hours in the pool. Muscled shoulders and triceps; narrow waist. You were embarrassed by your skinny pre-teen physique, your squeaky soprano voice, the few translucent hairs that had sprouted on your upper lip and (this was still your secret) at the base of your dick. Sometimes you'd pretend you were resting, do the backstroke for a lap or two just so you could look at Tony longer, see him watching you. He was only six years older, but you daydreamed about what life would be like if he were your father. One of the guys in your troop had seen him smoking a cigarette in his cabin between dinner and lights out, a rule violation that could have gotten him fired. When he went into town, he'd drive his old '55 Chevy; in camp he'd spend his free time under its hood, tinkering with the car's idle or re-gapping the spark plugs.

One day Tony was standing by the pool ladder at the end of your practice and turned the spray from the ever-present hose on your boney chest as you climbed out. Stop it, you shouted. But you were laughing, too, dancing and leaping on the concrete deck, dodging the stinging bursts of water as he chased you around the end of the pool. Hey, camper, he shouted. No running! You were wearing your old green-and-white striped knit bathing suit—remember it? A third-generation hand-me-down that might have been fashionable at the turn of the last century. It had lost all its stretch; in the pool it billowed around your legs like a jellyfish. On dry land it was a sodden weight that would have fallen to the ground around your ankles if you hadn't held it up by grasping a handful of the limp fabric.

Tony took his thumb off the end of the hose.

C'mere, he said.

No! It's a trick.

No, really, c'mere. I'm not going to do anything.

You kept an eye on the running hose in his right hand and inched nearer.

Come on, Davey! Are you going to do what I say? Get over here. He pointed to a spot two feet in front of him.

You stood where he pointed. He reached forward with his free hand to tease the gathered swimsuit fabric out of your clenched fist. The suit's sagging waistband swooped low across your pale belly. Tony hooked its top edge with one finger, pulled it toward him so that it gapped open, then leaned forward to peer down at the pale, smooth arc of your abdomen as it curved toward the parts between your legs. "Plunkies," your big brother used to call them. Tony fed the streaming hose past the suit's tired waistband; left it hanging there. Cold mountain water washed over your privates, flowed across balls shrunken to the size of chickpeas by the chill, then down skinny thighs to puddle on the spotless deck. Tony stepped back to admire his work. You didn't dare move. This was a new game, and you didn't know the rules.

How does that feel? Tony said.

Fine. That's all you could think of to say. Your thoughts flew back and forth between fear that you'd do something that would ruin the game and fear that if you *didn't* do something in the next few seconds you wouldn't be able to stop it. You and Tony watched each other, unsure what would happen next.

Tony reached forward again, snatched the hose from your waist band, quickly lifted the hem of his white T-shirt and slipped the hose down the front of his own boxer-styled trunks. He started dancing around, yelling jeez that's cold. But you could see that the end of the hose was positioned so that the water was mostly running out the leg hole of his shorts. Only a small part of the front of his suit was wet; just enough to show he had an erection.

I have to go, you said. They're waiting for me.

Sure, Tony said, turned away, shut off the hose, took his time coiling it into a neat doughnut. You were gathering your clothes, putting on shoes and T-shirt, wrapping your towel around your waist. When Tony turned
to face you again, his erection was nearly gone.

Y'know, Tony said, if you ever need help with your other merit badges or anything, you can always come by my cabin after dinner.

We're supposed to do stuff like that—the counselors. We're supposed to help you campers. With your merit badges.

Great, you said. Thanks. But you knew you wouldn't be getting any more help from Tony; that tomorrow morning the chain-link gate would be locked when you came down for your practice; that in a few days you'd swim your mile without your coach shouting encouragement from the sidelines. That was just the way it had to be. Once you'd told your scoutmaster what had happened, once the Sheriff had come and gone and Tony had roared off in his Chevy—cigarette dangling from his lips just the way James Dean would have done it— you knew that you'd never see Tony again.

Parking Signs

BANG! BANG! BANG! The pop and grind of metal-on-metal is not the kind of sound you want to hear from machinery encircling your head. I'm grateful when it shudders and suddenly goes silent, but... Did I break it, or what? If so, it was unintentional. I certainly don't want to go through this more than once.

I'm lying on my back, half in/half out of a giant donut. My imagination conjures a torpedo in a launch tube—a scene from the TV series *Voyage to the Bottom of the Sea*—or the scene in *Star Trek II* where Spock's coffin is about to be shot into space. Even with the earplugs the MRI technician's given me, the sounds from the scanner—like jackhammers pounding away just inches from each ear—is deafening. *All this*, I'm thinking, *just to prove I* don't *have a brain tumor.*

Earlier, before they called me into the MRI "suite," I'd come up with a plan to distract myself from the anticipated unpleasantness by reciting Coleridge's Kubla Khan. I'd memorized the poem forty-five years ago, in the twelfth grade, and it's a point of pride—and evidence, to me, that there's nothing wrong with my memory—that I can still recite it perfectly:

> *In Xanadu did Kubla Khan*
> *A stately pleasure-dome decree:*
> *Where Alph, the sacred river, ran*
> *Through caverns measureless to man*
> *Down to a sunless sea.*

I'd heard stories from others about the panic-inducing claustrophobia of the MRI tube, but no one had bothered to mention the deafening noise—noise that chases the oxygen from the room and makes me dizzy, even while I'm lying down.

Through the speakers in the part of the apparatus near my head, the voice of the technician comes to my ears like a radio transmission from an alien planet: remote, thin, awash with static. "You're doing fine. This next one will last four minutes."

My heart sinks. *There's more?*

I've been warned to stay still, which of course only intensifies my urge to squirm and writhe like an ill-behaved two-year-old. The previous scan lasted two minutes and seemed like twenty. Can I manage twice that? Before I can decide, the machine starts up again, emitting a noise exactly like the one the alien spaceships make in the movie version of
War of the Worlds.

> *Down to a sunless sea...*
> *Down to a sunless sea...*

Dammit! What comes next?

My hands and feet are strapped to the table; I'm reminded of the fetal pig we dissected in high school biology. In the darkness behind the blindfold and a protective face shield, universes being created and destroyed, towers welded together, then collapsing. Terrible beasts— crosses between lions and minotaurs—rampage and roar. Like a youngster who covers his own eyes and cries out,"You can't see me!," only the fact that I can see nothing protects me from the havoc that's been unleashed around me. That, and the on-off voice of the technician traveling to me
on slow waves across empty space.

Another sudden silence from the machine.

"We're almost done," the technician says. "The next is the longest one—seven minutes, okay?"

I get it, I'm thinking. *I'm being tortured. He's mistaken me for someone else, a terrorist, perhaps. If he'd only ask me a question, I'd confess and this could be over.*

The machine revs again. Now I'm in the middle of a drumming circle, the sound amplified a thousand times. The drums are steel; the drumsticks are ball-peen hammers the size of sledges. My fingers fiddle with the panic switch the technician had put in my hand at the beginning of the session:
a rubber bulb trailing a long cord. I tell myself I don't need it, but a primitive voice rising from the place that fear comes from keeps screaming

SQUEEZE THE DAMN SWITCH!

SQUEEZE IT NOW!

NOW!
NOW!
NOW!

Ba-BOOM, ba-BOOM, ba-BOOM, ba-BOOM go the drums, and their plodding stresses give me a pathway back into Coleridge's iambic tetrameter:

So twice five miles of fertile ground
With walls and towers were girdled round...

Saliva begins to pool at the back of my throat. I warn myself not to try to swallow, afraid that, in this unnatural position, my head will jerk and ruin the scan and we'll have to start over. On the other hand, I'm convinced I'm about to drown in my own spit.

And there were gardens bright with sinuous rills,
Where blossomed many an incense-bearing tree

That's when a question worms its way into my thoughts: *How am I going to write about this?*

I want to laugh out loud. In the midst of everything that's going on, can that really be the most important issue? Technicians' reassurances, breathing exercises, Yoga, Valium, ancient poetry—all, it turns out, are for naught. It's the question of how I'll describe this experience to a reader that finally consumes and transports me.

And that's when I realize that everything is going to be all right. At least for now.

Two

So, if it's not a brain tumor, what is it that's causing me to stagger around like a drunk?

Six Advantages of Having Parkinson's Disease
(in the style of BuzzFeed.com)

1. Blame medications for the "sudden" heightened interest in sex
2. Lonely? Need buddies to party with? Take along your hallucinated friends
3. Opportunity to work the lyrics for "I Won't Dance (Don't Ask Me)" into your conversations ("My head won't let my feet do things that they want to do...")
4. More data points to ponder in connection with the phrase "Lifetime Warranty"
5. It's unlikely you'll ever wear out your favorite shoes
6. It's incurable, so you don't have to bother worrying about that.

Three

My sister, only thirteen months older than I, died from the effects of dementia in 2012. We were very close, even while living three thousand miles apart, but I only saw her twice during her illness, which seemed to progress at the speed of light. She was smart, adventurous, beautiful. The last time I saw her, she was unable to put together a complete sentence during conversation. I wondered whether her sudden illness and rapid decline should trigger concerns about my own health, but clung to the facts that, unlike Rebecca, I had never been a heavy drinker or drug user.

The chemical process that's expressed in Parkinson's disease is not well understood. It's known that the disease is caused by a die-off of the dopaminergic neurons that carry messages from the brain to the rest of the nervous system. But it's not known *why* these neurons die. Answering that question is the focus of hundreds of continuing research efforts around the globe. They are joined by private and governmental foundations who are engaged in the fight as well, seeking short-term solutions that will improve quality of life for PWP.

Doctors tell their patients that, on average, they have the same life expectancy as the general population. That statement may forestall a difficult conversation, but I doubt its truth. The most common causes of death for PWP are aspiration pneumonia—an illness caused by breathing contaminants into the lungs—or falls due to poor balance. One current theory suggests it's activated by a combination of genetic mutation and exposure to certain types of chemicals. Another speculates it's a result of taking a blow to the head. Still others blame wheat gluten, red meat, and cow's milk. "Leaky gut" is a new one. I don't know which, if any, of these are the culprit, but I do know this: my family—at least on my mother's side—has a wretched legacy when it comes to brain disorders. A method for measuring the effects of Alzheimer's disease was established in 1968, just in time for it to be listed as the cause of my grandmother's death. Her only son and a daughter (my uncle and aunt) followed in her footsteps. My mother died after a three-year struggle with ALS, which, like Alzheimer's and Parkinson's, is a neurodegenerative disease.

Four

My life is over.
That's the first thing most people think when they're diagnosed with Parkinson's disease. But don't be too quick to jump to a conclusion.

It's hard to ignore words like "degenerative," "progressive," and "incurable," especially when they're linked to the phrase "brain disorder" and noted in your health record. We've grown accustomed to thinking we live charmed lives, many of us—enjoying the fantasy that our gym-worked bodies will last forever or, if they show signs of failure, that medical science will be able to fix them. Despite the constant handwringing over obesity rates, heart disease, and diabetes, we hear every other day about a seventy-year-old who's just biked cross-country to raise money for some charity, or an eighty-four-year-old who's launching a new career designing high-end wallpaper. For those who can remain healthy, the future is still full of potential. We may outgrow the youthful belief in our own indestructibility, but aren't we the generation that, better late than never, is supposed to be constantly reinventing ourselves, continuing to eke meaning out of our lives into our third or fourth childhood?

That was my expectation three years ago. At age sixty, I chafed under the "senior" designation some wanted to slap on me, but secretly enjoyed the discounts at restaurants and amusement parks. I was strong and healthy (or so I thought), with a good wit and an ambitious heart, taking my time to identify new worlds to conquer. I retired early, took a writing class, and actually began to have some modest success as an author. I got certified as a Personal Trainer, just for the heck of it. I made plans to hike mountain trails I'd always wanted to explore but never had time for. I moved from one coast to the other. I began to think about going back to Europe for an extended stay. Then, gradually, I began to notice that I couldn't taste my food and was having trouble swallowing. I felt exhausted all the time. I couldn't walk a straight line. A journey down my hall at home felt like walking down the aisle of an airplane being tossed by turbulence. In the gym, my left side felt weak; my time on the cross-trainer was torture.

I can admit that, since my diagnosis, every account I read about a high-achieving oldster triggers a stab of resentment. Why them and not me? I'm jealous of others' accomplishments; I know I won't be riding my bike across the country at age seventy, or even next year. It's possible I won't even *live* to age seventy. That was always the case, of course; but until now I didn't have a specific reason to worry about it. In my mind, I had all the time in the world. That's the thing that angers me the most: the *untimeliness* of it all. It's like living the plot of a Lifetime tearjerker.

Five

Parkinson's can make you doubt everything you see, hear, think, and feel. It undermines your self-confidence, your belief in the integrity of your own actions. When some household object ends up in the wrong place, you wonder guiltily whether you're the one who put it there, even though you don't remember touching it. Joints and muscles gradually become stiffer, making it difficult to hold a fork, brush your teeth, or turn over in bed. Many of us have seen the telltale tremor in a stranger's hand, but tremor can also occur in feet, arms, legs, jaw, or tongue, or internally, invisibly. Hoarseness and difficulty swallowing are often early symptoms. Poor balance increases the risk of falls, as do environmental hazards such as dim lighting and uneven surfaces. You trip over throw rugs. You sweat excessively, drool, and develop skin conditions. Insomnia is common, as is "active dreaming" (thrashing about in your sleep) and profound exhaustion that can be debilitating. I know this from personal experience.

In my case, it's the potential for cognitive changes—memory loss, alterations in personality, hallucinations—that I dread most. What are we if not a lifelong accumulation of our memories, experiences, and friendships? Who am I when those are no longer available to me, and disappear one by one, day by day? Life can become a quagmire of self-questioning and diminished confidence. Is the dark silhouette that I catch in my peripheral vision slipping away around the corner of the garage really there, or is it a hallucination? Is the garbled question from my spouse— "Did you put the peanuts in the laundry basket?"—really what he said? Can I recall why I came into a room without facing the shame of retracing my steps to see if something along the route will remind me of my purpose? At times, I adopt silence as the wisest tack, not wanting to embarrass myself or others with "crazy" questions, thereby suffering another loss through my silence. And what about my dream of being a writer? Can I still write something that makes sense to a reader? And if so, for how long?

Six

Parkinson's experts will tell you that the disease is not fatal. That may be literally true, but I think the claim side-steps the question. If I were to trip and fall and, later, die as a consequence of sustaining a fracture of a hip or shoulder; or because I'm unable to safely navigate a throw rug; or because I'd contracted a fatal virus while in the hospital,

Parkinson's would not be included as a potential culprit in any of these three outcomes. Yet it could easily be the root cause.

The federal government has a lot of data on aging and life expectancy. The Social Security Administration's calculations say that the average life expectancy for all males currently age sixty-five is 88.4 years. The Centers for Disease Control breaks the data out by race and state of residence in addition to age and gender, and predicts that a 65-year-old white male Californian will live 22 more years (to age 87), 15.5 of them healthy years. It's difficult to make a meaningful comparison to those with Parkinson's, partly because there have been few investigations. A Norwegian study, published in 2012, followed 230 Parkinson's patients of various ages for 12 years and calculated an average life expectancy of 81 years. But of the patients studied, only 19 were still alive at the study's 12-year mark. A 2002 study by doctors at Washington University in St. Louis found that only a third of Parkinson's patients of various ages were alive six years after diagnosis. If I were in the two-thirds contingent, that would mean I would be dead at age 69, a far cry from 87 or 84.

Who wants to live out the modern version of unhealthy old age, anyway? Bedridden, possibly demented, in pain, forced to watch daytime television. On the other hand, I'm amazed by people like physicist Stephen Hawking, who lived 76 years and wrote eight books while suffering from ALS, the same disease that killed my mother in three. Of course, as a world-famous scientist, he had access to a lot more resources than most of us, but all the technical and human assistance in the world can't alone make life worth living. There has to be something else, and I suspect the something else is that, until the moment he died, he seemed to still possess his full mental powers. He could reason, remember, converse. He could express himself. He could create.

There have been quite a few famous people who've had Parkinson's Disease. I thought the earliest one I was aware of was Kathryn Hepburn; then I found out that she had something different. I thought the latest (revealed posthumously) would be Robin Williams; then, while I was preparing this manuscript, Linda Ronstadt and Alan Alda revealed their diagnoses. But there are tens of thousands of anonymous sufferers for every well-publicized case, people who struggle every day to maintain their ability to walk, eat, sleep, speak, think constructively. I am one of them.

Some doctors argue that there is no such thing as a good way to die; any way it happens, you're dead. This is black and white, dichotomous thinking. I've seen a spouse die of AIDS, a mother die of ALS, a father from congestive heart failure, a stepmother of pulmonary hypertension; their deaths were all different from each other's. If I were given the chance to choose, I would choose a heart attack in the middle of the night. I don't really even care at what age. Why not tonight, when I've just eaten a delicious meal at the end of a beautiful summer's day, am in full possession of my faculties and in my spouse's arms, rather than six or ten years hence after having suffered the personality-robbing progression of Parkinson's? If I could plan it, schedule it, that's the way I would do it; the way that spares me and my loved ones as much suffering as possible.

But in case that doesn't happen, in case I end up feeling my history, which is what makes me *me*, draining away, making a slow disappearance, I've made a list of the things I hope others will remember for me.

Seven
500 Things I Don't Want to Forget

1. I lived the first six years of my life in Tarzana, California—named in homage to Edgar Rice Burroughs, on whose estate the town was founded. Burroughs was best known as the author of *Tarzan of the Apes*, which was the basis for the movies my sister and I would watch on TV on Saturday mornings. I thought it would be nice to have Jane as a sister, but I longed to be carried away in the arms of Johnny Weissmuller, a former Olympic swimmer who played the scantily clad, smooth-muscled hero in twelve films.

2. I was the only sibling that wasn't allowed to hold my infant baby brother when we came home from his christening. I pitched a fit on the day like a little brat; soon enough I didn't want anything to do with him; later we became friends again. He travelled from San Francisco to New York to attend Ralph's funeral—the only member of my family to do so.

3. We used to see Roy Rogers and Dale Evans in church every Sunday.

4. When I was seven, my favorite TV show was *Zorro;* later I liked *The Honeymooners* and George Burns and Gracie Allen.

5. I used to be a bully: at age eight, after we moved to San Diego, I got into a rock fight after school and one kid managed to bean me squarely on the head, causing blood to gush all over my new pale blue corduroy jacket; after that, I never bullied anyone again.

6. When I was eleven, I was molested by the swimming counselor at Boy Scout camp. When I was 20, I was assaulted again during a European trip. I could go on, but I don't want to test my believability in your eyes.

7. Concord Grape was my favorite kind of jelly, but I only use ketchup on my peanut butter sandwiches.

8. My family went on a camping vacation every summer, and in 1964 we drove from California to New York to go to the World's Fair.

9. I hitchhiked through Europe with my sister for three months during the summer between my freshman and sophomore years of college; one night, while we slept in our tent in a campground near Hamburg, Germany, someone sneaked into our campsite and stole everything we had.

10. I never cut my fingernails until a couple of months after I graduated from high school; up to that point, I bit and tore them under the pressure of being what today would be called a nerd, but back then I was called a faggot.

11. I didn't get drafted into the Vietnam War because I drew a high lottery number in 1970 and gave up my student deferment for a year, knowing it was unlikely I would be called up.

12. My favorite TV show in the late sixties/early seventies was *Rowan & Martin's Laugh-In*.

13. In my fourth year of college, I changed my undergraduate major from history, economics, and political science to design for theatre.

14. My father, born and raised in Spring Valley, New York, moved three thousand miles to get away from his family. I moved three thousand miles back the other way (to Boston) for the same reason, and to attend graduate school; after grad school, I moved to New York City.

15. My siblings and I climbed Mt. Whitney together while we were all in California for my dad's second wedding.

16. I met my first lover five years after moving to New York.

17. Until I met Ralph, I hadn't taken a vacation in ten years; during the next five years we travelled together to Puerto Rico, St. Maarten, The Dominican Republic, Key West, California (for him to meet my family), Hawaii, and Grand Cayman.

18. The last job I had in the New York theatre was as a milliner for Franco Zeffirelli's 1984 production of *Tosca* at the Met; my name appeared in the program for the next twenty-five years every time the company revived the production, even though my total contribution to the project had been to make a dozen nun's wimples for the chorus in Act 1.

19. Weary of being poor, I managed to get a job at Merrill Lynch in 1985 as a programmer trainee, shortly became a manager, and, for the next 23 years, made it my life's work to shepherd the careers of my employees; I left Merrill as a Director, managing a group of 150 employees and consultants.

20. Ralph and I exchanged rings on Christmas Day, 1989.
    He died of AIDS on December seventh the following year.

21. As part of her campaign for the US Senate, Hillary Clinton marched in the 2000 NYC Gay Rights Parade; when she and her secret service contingent passed my viewing spot at 34th Street, I stepped off the curb and fell in line behind her, walking the rest of the way down Fifth Avenue to the Village amid constant cheers from the crowd.

22. I met my current husband in 2000 through an Internet ad on Love@AOL; in 2003 we entered a Vermont Civil Union even though it had no legal standing in New Jersey, where we lived.

23. In 2013, once again living in California, I married John Castell at the San Diego County Administration Building on the tenth anniversary of our Civil Union, a few days after the US Supreme Court declined to review a lower court ruling that California's prohibition of gay marriage violated the US constitution.

And so on. A life in numbered bullets.

How many more memories, even now, are lost? Here's something funny: at times I can't even remember the name of my best friend of thirty years, or the name of the disease that afflicts me. They say the brain can develop new pathways when the old ones are destroyed, so I've become diligent about creating mnemonic devices whenever I have trouble remembering something. "Parking Signs," for some reason, comes much more easily to mind than "Parkinson's," and that's how I remember the name of my disease. Still, such tricks are only a stopgap. I'm terrified by the idea that I could eventually forget everything that's ever happened to me, everything that's made my life worthwhile.

Eight

Memory Games: A Story

"C'mon, what was her name?" Danny says. He's staring at me with that lost look—lips puckered, eyes darting about. It's a look I've grown accustomed to over—what's it been now? *Years* since his spotty memory has developed gradually larger holes.

"You know—the one who sings 'Broken Glass.'"

I breathe through my own moment of panic; I always feel it now whenever anyone asks me about a name. I try to concentrate, but the parade of people shuffling around the day room is distracting, annoying. Why can't they sit down and shut up? Jabber, jabber, jabber, talking to themselves. I can't think….

Poor Danny. How can anyone stand to live in this place?

Wait…. This is weird. For some reason, I already have a moronic divorce set up for this one. "Moronic divorce" is what I call the connections I make to help me remember something, especially names. Everyone else says "pneumonic device," but that's no fun. I've tried to teach Danny how to do it, but I guess he thinks it's easier to just ask me every time he needs to recall something.

This is the way it works:

"Walking on Broken Glass" > broken crystal > Lenox crystal.

"You mean Annie Lennox?" I say to Danny.

His features relax.

"Yeah, that's her. Annie Lennox."

"What about her?"

"I don't know. You're the one who brought her up."

"No, I didn't."

Or did I? If I hadn't already been thinking about her, why would I have a divorce ready?

The plastic upholstery squeaks as Danny sinks lower in his armchair, going into sulking mode.

"You always do that to me," he says. "You always turn things around, like *I'm* the one that's losing it."

I turn back to the TV screen, where Turner Classic Movies is showing George Cukor's excellent 1939 film, *The Women*. The actress playing Mary Haines is doing that tearjerker speech where she tells her young daughter that she's separating from the girl's father, but now I can't get the image of Annie Lennox out of my head—the bright-orange, close-cropped haircut she had on the cover of the "Touch" LP. It's funny. Annie's hairstyle must have seemed as outré in 1983 as the one this actress was sporting in 1939. Masculine. Aggressive. What's her name, again?

I stop short and steal a glance at Danny. He appears to have forgotten his sulk, is back to watching the movie with slack-jawed concentration. I have a minute to work this one out.

But I don't need a minute. When I think about it, this one is easy, like this:

"Annie Lennox hairstyle" > abnormal shearing > Norma Shearer.

"I love Norma Shearer in this role," I say.

"THAT'S the name I was looking for," Danny replies, satisfied.

I love that guy. He never remembers an argument.

"Hey, Danny Boy, I hate to say it but I'm gonna have to go. I'm a little tired, and I've got a bit of a drive to get home."

Danny says nothing, but a smirk brushes the corners of his lips.

"What's so funny?"

"Yeah, you've got quite a drive," Danny says. "All the way up to room 326."

"What are you talking about?"

"Jesus! Do we have to go through this every friggin' day? When are you going to get it through your thick skull that you don't have a home? THIS is your home. This is where you live."

Before I can respond, I see Chas [Sonny and Cher > Chastity Bono > Chas], the dumbest of the staff of dumb attendants, coming toward me with another guy I don't recognize, both dressed in scrubs.

"And this," Chas is saying, "is our star resident, James. Hey, Jamie. How you feelin' today?"

I despise nicknames, so I ignore Chas and turn to Danny. "Don't talk to him," I say.

Danny decides to hide by turning himself into a dog.

Chas: "Oh, so you've got your friend here with you today. Hey, Danny!" he says, waving vaguely to my left, my right, over my head like Danny's some kind of angel or something, hanging in mid-air.

"Don't say a thing," I whisper to the dog. "Don't say a friggin' word."

Nine

A few days ago, I found a letter I hadn't seen in years. It's from my mother, sent in June 1982, when she was about the age I am now, and two years into her struggle with Lou Gehrig's disease. She wrote it on a second-hand IBM Selectric typewriter my father had purchased to facilitate conversation, but it was torture to watch her use it with her hunt-and-peck approach, slowed even more by her poor eyesight and enfeebled hands. I can't imagine what the effort cost. It's the last letter I ever received from her.

> DEarest Jim,
>   Thank you for your morst inform-
> ativeletter   in a long time.
>   I'm tal k as well   now,as I CAN EVEN
>   YOUR dad has trouble understanding   me.
> My tongue muscles   aregettingla zy.
>   my knees   are   alo not holding up well.
>   I Read , in   Guideposts
>   I read an artical called
> " Imaging"   THE JIST OF IT WAS THIS.
> you   in your mind what you would
> likeptotbe, then you pray & te-
> ll   theLordI told Him   Ididn'T want to be la-
> ze. the next morning when I woke up my left handwhi-
> habeen swollen & mishapen for 2 years was
> normal size &my fingers were straighter than they had been
> in at least   2 yrs.
>   now, what do you think of that? My strength
>   hasn T returned yet, but theropy is
>   working on it.
>   Love
>   mother

She died nine months later, bedridden and able to communicate only by answering basic yes/no questions using eye blinks.

Ten

The immediate family gathered at my father's house near Santa Ana for my mother's funeral. Several of us had travelled from the east coast for the event, others from places nearby. It was the first time in a number of years that all of the living family members had been together. Even those who lived only a short distance away came prepared to stay overnight. It was like a grown-up slumber party that went on for three days, full of laughter, camaraderie, and reminiscences. On the fourth day, people began to make motions to leave; my sister had to return to Florida, my younger brother and his family were headed back to San Francisco, and I myself had a flight to New York later that evening. When everyone else decided to see my sister off at the airport, I stayed behind to pack. As each group left, I grew more and more anxious; the warm feeling of being surrounded by my family began to dissipate. Finally, the front door bumped closed and I was alone in the silent house. I sat down on the stairs and began to weep, overwhelmed by what felt like sudden abandonment. *Remember this lesson,* I told myself. *Life is ultimately about leaving or being left.*

I resolved at that moment that I didn't want to be left, didn't want to be one of a slowly thinning group of mourners at a string of funerals. I still feel that way. I have no children or grandchildren to worry about, and my spouse is well provided-for. He's also sufficiently younger than I that I can hope he will find other companionship once I'm out of the picture. I'm sorry that—if my plan works out—he'll have to deal with losing me, as will any of my surviving siblings, but what's the alternative? I can't bring myself to contemplate living without them.

Eleven

So, what's next? I don't know, but I'm not going to sit around and wait to die. Although none of the current Parkinson's medications will slow its progression, there are things that seem to help. Vigorous daily physical exercise (building those alternative pathways) is one. And there are meds that help with some of the symptoms, though most of them come with their own undesirable side effects. I've met people with Parkinson's who were diagnosed as long as eighteen years ago and are still doing well. I try to model my lifestyle on them, hoping some of their... luck? best practices? health maintenance routines? social reinforcement? dietary practices? will rub off on me.

I have a guitar someone gifted me twenty years ago. It looks brand new; I fiddled with it a bit when I first got it, then put it away, thinking

I would pull it out when I had more time for it. Eventually I put "learn to play the guitar" on the list of things I planned to do in retirement. Have I waited too long? Will my stiffening fingers and unreliable memory make my attempts to master it a useless, frustrating exercise?

Those are just two more questions I can't answer, but this I do know: right now, I'm late for a guitar lesson.

Sandman

While I lie on the sand, my eyes drooping toward an early-afternoon doze, the warmth of the sun barely manages to pierce the cover of gray clouds—clouds that I would, finally, decide were the exact color of your eyes—and waves from the vast Atlantic roll toward Cape Cod, so far from their gale-driven origin that they break at last, puny, weak, on this spit of sand the Pilgrims named Provincetown, continually advancing and then retreating a little less each time (tide coming in!), chasing the sea birds up the beach and making way for them again, back and forth, the gulls screaming in celebration as they swallow small crabs they've plucked from the wet sand, and I, of course, resting on my blanket above the high tide mark, recognize the genial breath of fall rustling through the hair on my chest, now gone almost white, just as it would, later in the season, shiver the leaves of the ash trees at home (the rustling, the shiver, the breeze that hardens nipples with its chill, reminding me of the years when I could carry it off, the legal nakedness, whereas today, at this age, I would never have the confidence to try, but opt instead for running shorts and a now-doffed T-shirt that shows, despite my best attempts at regular exercise, that I possess every attribute of the Buddha except his posture and divinity) and then aware, suddenly, of you standing there, announced only by the fact of your shadow falling across my closed lids, nothing but a silhouette at first with the sun and clouds behind you, and confusingly out of place in your dark suit (until I make out the four gold stripes on your sleeve and realize you've arrived early for the airline pilots' convention the coming weekend), you saying, "I seem to be overdressed," asking if you can borrow a corner of my blanket, and moving, without waiting for an answer, to take off your jacket and place it neatly on an un-sanded patch, to reach down and slip off your black leather shoes, to undo your tie and the buttons of your white shirt, and I, made speechless by this turn of events, can only watch with mouth agape and damn the sun in my eyes (would it be rude to put on my sunglasses?) as each button gives way and your shirt falls open to reveal the hairless swell of your chest, the furrowed rows of your abdomen (sweat from confinement in the wool coat, glistening) until the whole shirt is finally free, tails out, and as you turn away to shrug it from your shoulders I first catch sight of the tattoo that completely covers your back, and my breath leaves me, I gasp, amazed at each individually articulated and shaded feather, so exquisitely rendered in sepia and charcoal and olive and gray inks that they appear to flutter in the on-shore breeze, and I begin to fear the wings they comprise will unfurl at any moment and carry you away (whether to heaven or hell I cannot judge; it was Malthus, I think, who argued that physical and moral perfection are indivisible), but instead you add your shirt to the pile on the blanket, and begin to unfasten your slacks, and when they slip below your buttocks (lovely in their own right, inspiring poetry) you snatch at them to prevent their collapse onto the sand, though not quickly enough that your black briefs and their woven waistband aren't momently revealed, the waistband reading, simply, "GUARDIAN," and I burst out laughing at what seems to have become low comedy, and cry out—my first words to you—"That's a good one," at which point you turn to me (carefully folding and stowing the last item of your uniform), a quizzical look on your face, the word play then forgotten as I catch my first full look at you, the black briefs, your short dark hair against the pale, milk-white purity of the un-figured areas of your skin, all of this somehow more seductive than nakedness would be (though doubtless your nakedness would be perfect, too): the way your cock and balls are gathered, the way they thrust forward in a wad against the thin, dark cotton—a sight from which, I must admit, I cannot turn away—and you, seeing my stare, ask, "Do you want to touch it?" and I, my mouth dry all at once, timid in the face of such a brazen invitation, cannot reply, but as I move to reach across the space between us my hand is suddenly feeble, my arm (terrible timing!) powerless, trembling so I cannot even lift it; embarrassed, I look into your eyes and confess—the first time I've done so—"I'm dying," and you hold my gaze, take my weakened hand and press it to your groin, and answer, "We're all dying, some of us are just going about it faster than others," and while you keep my nervous hand trapped in yours I can feel the confusion of parts beneath my palm slowly shifting to the rhythm of my pounding heart, organizing themselves for their neglected purpose.

Have I fainted, or have I slept? You are gone when I look for you, though I only turned away for a moment; your corner of my blanket empty, except.... Is it a black sock I see half-buried in the sand? I don't investigate, not because I lack curiosity but because—even if I were sure it's yours—I don't need a glass slipper to remember your embrace.

Twist and Shout

As soon as you knew anything you knew it was wrong but not *why* it was wrong, when it seemed to come so naturally, unbidden, this yearning for the touch of another boy; you would play with your sister's doll house and when your father saw you he would say to your mother "he's too old for that" and you would think *what? What am I too old for?* and your mother would say "relax, he'll grow out of it," and you'd wonder what it was they expected you to grow out of, whether it would be like a pair of blue jeans that one morning would just feel too tight; the fact is that you *didn't* grow out of it, you just learned to hide it better, until one day when you and your father were going someplace, just the two of you, he asked you what you wanted to be when you grew up and you said, "a girl; I want to be a girl," and he pulled the car over and told you to get out and said, "I am not going to raise a faggot in my house; you think about that while you're walking home," but you didn't have much time to think about it because ten minutes later you saw your mother driving slowly in the other direction, like she was looking for something, and when she saw you she turned around and brought you home in the car and told your father not to do that again, and though their argument continued behind their closed bedroom door the only thing you heard clearly was the word "gay."

On snow days when school ended early you'd sit on the couch with your mother and sister, eating popcorn you'd made in the microwave, and watch old movies on the Early Show with Johnny Downs and argue about which stars were, well, *you* know; except that instead of "gay" you'd say "twist," as in "I read somewhere that he's twist," or "I think everyone in this cast is twist," and you'd all watch closely, looking for clues when Rock Hudson or Cary Grant or Tyrone Power or Dirk Bogarde or Lawrence Olivier or Marlon Brando or Montgomery Clift or Alec Guinness or Randolph Scott or Farley Granger or any of the dozens of others were on the screen about whom you thought, *is that what* they *are, too?* Because, you weren't sure, but there was just something about them, their faces, the sensitivity around their mouths and lips, the blackout draperies deep within their eyes that, like a nictitating membrane, would snap closed to cover their deepest feigning; and you protest saying "No, it shouldn't have to be this way, there should be no obscuration of the truth, not with all of us in the same boat, with all of us feeling the same feelings, hoping the same hopes, wishing the same wishes, dreaming the same dreams, facing the same illnesses, and finally, when you work up enough courage, finding in the touch of another boy (now a man, like you) the strength to say, "I love you;" and about whom you can say, "I love him," without fear of consequences.

My straight friends will say, there! are you satisfied? and I'll say, No, I'm not, because marriage is a civil matter and all the religious hoopla is just hoopla and nothing more; I'll be satisfied when it's taken for granted that all people are created equal and endowed with certain rights, and that among these are life, liberty, and the pursuit of happiness, an amazing phrase to put in a nation's founding documents, "the pursuit of happiness:" language so simple, so unprepossessing, so straight-forward, it is a phrase its authors think everyone will understand, and yet we get bogged down in equivocations like "it depends on what the meaning of 'is' is," we discover that making a cake is speech (surprise, strict constructionists!) and—regarding that all people are created equal thing?—it turns out that some are more equal than others.

So it goes to the Supremes not once, not twice, but three times, and those of us created equal lose our patience and the Supremes say Wait a minute! We don't want to rush into anything; let's think about it for another decade or so, and God bless 'em, they *do* waste another decade and they finally fall into the whole thing bass-ackward, by default, really, and decide I can get married.

But this is what bothers me: almost every case affecting marriage was decided by a *one vote* majority, thus by *one* person in this country and if that *one judge* had voted the other way I might still not have the right to be married to the person who in every other respect is my spouse of twenty years.

This is when I'll be satisfied: when I am no longer called uppity and selfish behind my back because I want my marriage to be recognized as being just as valid as anyone else's. When I'm no longer told I don't know my place, and that what I'm asking for isn't equality but "special" privileges because what I'm demanding is inconvenient; when I can walk down the middle of the sidewalk at noon holding my husband's hand, and no one does a double-take, no one feels they must shield their youngster's eyes from that horrible, disgusting sight, no one tells me to stop trying to recruit young children to my "lifestyle," or that I'm violating the Christians' constitutional rights because I have the affrontery to ask them to make a cake for my wedding (but don't they run a bakery?) Now, I know you all are prone to ask, when you have to make a decision, what Jesus would do. My answer is this: Jesus would put on a hairnet, roll up his sleeves, tie an apron around his waist, and make us a cake. Because he's JESUS, for Christ's sake!

Being Carol Channing

Ars longa, vita brevis. —*Hippocrates*

From my second-floor vantage point in one of the aging brownstones lining 14th Street, I watched a long, black limo maneuver into a parking spot that looked less than a foot longer than the car itself. It was eleven o'clock, precisely the appointed time. Few passers-by took notice; limousines were still quite common on the nearly bankrupt city's pothole-strewn streets, though perhaps more so on Wall Street or Fifth Avenue than in Chelsea. Nor was there evidence that anyone on the crowded sidewalk recognized Carol Channing when the driver opened the car's rear door and offered her his arm. Maybe they were oblivious, or maybe her star had already dimmed too far for that.

Even from thirty feet away, looking down at her at an acute angle, I could see her hesitation, her questioning glance at the driver as she took in the situation. The driver shrugged his shoulders, a universal gesture that could mean many things. In this case it meant, "Yeah, two-fifty west fourteenth—this is the address you gave me, lady."

Carol Channing was sixty-two years old that day in December 1983 when I met her at The Studio. She was about to go into rehearsal for *Jerry's Girls,* a new musical revue featuring the songs of Jerry Herman that was scheduled to open in Palm Beach in two months and had come for costume fittings to the small theatrical costume company where I worked. She was accustomed to having her gowns made at one of the better-known, up-scale ateliers in the theatre district, where she was treated like the Broadway star she had been. But as she gazed up and down 14th Street, her eyes finally coming to rest on the sign in the front window of the brownstone's parlor floor, it was brought home to her once more that her fortunes had changed. The massive, limestone-clad *beaux arts* office buildings on three of the corners of the street's intersection with Eighth Avenue had been built decades ago by banks flush with borrowed cash. Now empty, they served as reminders of the neighborhood's former glory and sudden decline. Few remembered 14th Street as part of the fashionable shopping district that had once, long ago, earned the nickname "The Ladies' Mile." Macy's department store had followed the northward migration as it moved from 14th and Seventh—where, when I arrived in the city in the 1980s, one could still discern the Macy's name in flaking white paint on the red brick—to Herald Square, chasing the stock market millionaires and robber barons who had built their mansions in "the country," as they called it, meaning the open acres of Fifth Avenue that fronted Central Park. The brownstone townhouses that lined 14th Street had subsequently been broken up into tenements that housed the immigrants that poured into the city, and the street-level shops had been converted to bars or stores selling cheap ready-to-wear tailored to the taste of each wave of new residents.

Standing on the street, buffeted by the winds off the Hudson River three blocks to the west, Carol told herself that she was doing this for Jerry, out of friendship and gratitude for the part he had played in making her a star with his music and lyrics for such shows as *Gentlemen Prefer Blondes, Mame,* and her best-known role, Dolly Levi in the original 1964 Broadway production of *Hello, Dolly!* She had lived off that hit and its revivals for decades, but the truth is that for the last eight or ten years her career had been kept alive through television, doing guest shots on *Rowan & Martin's Laugh-In* and *The Love Boat.*

In the few seconds it took her to cross the sidewalk from the limo's door to the Studio's vestibule, Carol adjusted her expectations. The Studio was obviously, as I've said, not a fancy place, but it had its part to play in the New York theatre world. Its creaking floorboards, worn smooth by the feet of thousands of off-Broadway hopefuls, had earned their place honestly. If you were a young, unknown designer trying to do a show with a three-figure budget—and *that* paid in subway tokens—the Studio would likely be your only bidder in the five boroughs.

I was the Studio's milliner and "special projects" creator, responsible for making the hats, shoes, armor, wings, masks, and so forth that the shows required—items that were worn by the actors and therefore considered costume, but whose raw materials were wood, piano wire, plastics, industrial felt, woven straw—you name it. I liked the isolation and solitude of my second-floor aerie. The costume designers would hang out with the first-floor workers, who plied their craft with fabric, needle, and thread; my tools were saws, rivets, and glue guns. Visitors to the second floor never knew whether they would find me wielding a blowtorch, immersed in a cloud of noxious solvents, or brushing the eighteenth coat of tinted latex paint medium onto a felt crown covered with metallic foil to give it the deep, burnished look of real metal. Most designers were more than happy to outsource these headaches. And that's how I came to be hired to make several hats for Carol Channing to wear in the world premiere production of *Jerry's Girls*.

I can only imagine Carol's impression the first time she climbed the short flight of steps to the parlor floor and passed through the front door of the Studio, which opened directly onto the workroom. I assume she would have immediately recognized the bohemian vibe of the place: the receptionist's desk made from a wooden door laid across two filing cabinets, the drooping philodendron strung across the front window, the clumsily knitted afghan tossed carelessly across the banquette in the waiting area. It all seemed so familiar. *After all*, she might have thought, *we're only two blocks from the Village*. She sat, remembering, sipping from a cup of chamomile tea while she waited to be called to the fitting room, the years when she was just another kid— a newcomer bitten by the theatre bug—trying to make it in New York, doing stand-up with Zero Mostel in a Village club not far from where she was at that moment. What was its name? She couldn't recall. Or doing a stint at the black-owned Café Society on Sheridan Square, where she was fired for doing an improvised imitation of Ethel Waters. Perhaps she remembered, in her halcyon days, heading downtown by cab to the Five Oaks at Grove and Bleeker after curtain calls for whatever Broadway or off-Broadway show she was in, and singing at the piano with Judy Garland or Kathleen Battle 'til three in the morning.

Betty, the Studio's manager, materialized at Carol's elbow, speaking through a fit of smoker's cough and throat-clearing. "Miss Channing, sorry to keep you waiting. Would you come with me, please?"

Carol followed Betty past the stacked scrap-fabric storage bins that lined one wall, swatches of their contents echoing the rainbow-colored samples of the thread and notions that filled rows of low metal cabinets. Above three plywood-topped cutting tables, large white paper globes covered the bulbs that hung from the ceiling on long wires. Groups of sewing machines, each designed for a different and (to Carol) esoteric function, dominated the center of the workspace. The Studio was busy that morning, and as they moved through the room Carol would have had difficulty making sense of Betty's small talk over the din of the workers' conversations, the clack and scrape of scissors against the wooden cutting tables, the quick alternating whir and silence of the industrial sewing machines, and the background drone of the news reader's voice on the radio, tuned to WNYC. She and Betty were nearly at the back windows when—this couldn't be right, could it? — they came to an alcove that was about the size of a large refrigerator, separated from the rest of the room by a dusty curtain. They had, indeed, arrived at the Studio's fitting room.

To a performer of Carol Channing's experience, signs that the show's producer was cutting corners financially had been obvious for some time. The neophyte costume designer (a producer's brother or nephew?), the planned premiere in Palm Beach. Now she had been sent to 14th Street, of all places, for a costume fitting. To a less-determined actor, it might have seemed insulting. After all, Carol was a Broadway star, had been a professional actress and comedian for more than forty years. She'd been the lead in a half-dozen original musicals and in a similar number of movies. She'd played Dolly Levi for three years in the 1964 Broadway production of *Hello, Dolly!* When the show's original cast album was released, it temporarily knocked The Beatles out of the number one spot on the music charts. *Jerry's Girls* was opening about as far out of town as one could get without leaving US territory, but it offered the eventual possibility of a new Broadway hit. Carol was determined to make the most of it.

She was scheduled for two costume fittings that day; both were accessorized with a hat. Betty had instructed me to stay out of the way until summoned to the fitting room. When a runner was sent upstairs to fetch me, I gathered the headgear and made for the fitting room.

For a moment, let's leave me carefully picking my way down the narrow stairs of the Studio's vestibule, balancing a silver lamé turban for songs Carol was doing from *Mame* in one hand and a flowery wide-brimmed model for the "Put on Your Sunday Clothes" number from *Hello, Dolly!* in the other. I was nervous about these fittings; many actors are particular about what they will agree to wear on their head or near their face. This was the first time Carol and I would meet in person; if we got off on the wrong foot it could be a disaster for me. Carol still had enough clout—and I was new enough to the profession—to scuttle my design career with one critical comment. In that vein, there was something about Carol that I'd had to discuss with David, the costume designer.

68

According to the measurement chart her publicist had sent over, Carol's head size was twenty-six inches. As a milliner, I knew that the average circumference of an American woman's head is between twenty-one and twenty-two inches. Even men rarely have heads larger than twenty-four. The information on the chart had to be a mistake.

"Here's what I was told," David said. "Carol's head measurement is actually twenty-two, but she has all her hats made for a head size of twenty-six inches."

"I don't get it."

"Well, think about her facial features. Her eyes, her mouth—they're rather large, and her makeup makes her features look even larger. Her voice and her stage personality both have a sort of 'baby doll' quality to them that she thinks of as her trademark. So, what's physically distinctive about a doll—or a child, for that matter?"

I hated it when David adopted this pedantic air, as though I was his student, especially since I was two or three years older than he. "The head's out of proportion—too large for the body," I said. "But how is making the hat too big going to achieve that look? It's just going to slide around on her head."

"Oh, the hats will fit," David said. "All of her wigs have four inches of padding in them."

I took another moment to absorb this new fact. The idea of a woman in her sixties trying to pass herself off as a child might seem a little Baby-Jane-ish to some; I thought Carol's way of achieving it unique and clever. Remember—we're talking show business. It was more common than not for a performer to pad here, cinch there, lift these, dye that. At least Carol's edits to her natural appearance, as far as I could tell, hadn't yet extended to plastic surgery.

Arriving at the fitting room, I stowed the "Sunday Clothes" hat on a nearby table and peeked between panels of the bulging curtain. There, a serene sixty-two-year-old idol in the midst of a crowd of officiants, stood a barefoot Carol Channing, star of stage and screen, in her pantyhose and bra.

Clearly, I was early. I immediately bowed back out, but my quick glimpse had been enough to impress. Her measurement chart said she was five-nine, so I'd expected her to be tall. What the chart couldn't describe was how much of that five-nine was leg. She had a dancer's proportions, gams trim and strong, ready to strut, kick, or tap—whatever a script or score called for. If this show business thing didn't work out, I could imagine her as a senior division hurdler, or the cleanup runner in a 4X100 relay. And if her shoulders stooped a bit in repose, I had no doubt she could still throw them back and belt out a song or six.

While I waited my turn near the fitting room, I listened to the conversation inside, hoping to hear a longer sentence, or maybe a snatch of song, in her distinctive voice. There was something intriguing about that voice: low-pitched but nasal, full of gravel and lazy Southern rhythms that didn't jibe with her West coast childhood, a diction that often sounded like she had a mouth full of spit and no time to swallow, a tendency to draw out her vowels until you might have thought a siren was going off. It was mesmerizing, a voice that had been mimicked a million times and had launched a thousand drag careers.

Betty's impatient bray interrupted my reverie. "WHERE'S THE HAT?"

I jumped up to peek behind the curtain once more. Carol was now fully dressed for her *Mame* numbers: a coat-dress in a late-twenties/early-thirties style, all silver lamé and sequins. The turban I held was of the same fabric, intended to be worn without a wig, and so was padded out to twenty-six inches.

The moment I placed the turban on Carol's head I knew it was wrong—*very* wrong—and the wrong-ness had nothing to do with the extra four inches of padding. I saw that I'd been too sanguine in my approach to the turban's challenges. Suffice it to say that, on her head, the puffy, glittering object I'd created for her made her look as though she'd just undergone brain surgery in a particularly swank hospital. I should have withdrawn the turban immediately when I realized it wouldn't work; instead, I watched, fidgeting awkwardly while David poked and tugged at the bastard lump, pinching it on one side, stretching it on another, trying anything and everything to make it look less awful; he succeeded only in prolonging my embarrassment. Flop-sweat was dripping down my arms when he finally gave up." I think… we'll have to re-work this," he said quietly.

You're telling me, I thought.

Betty shot me a look that I guessed would translate to something like *Watch it, buster. You're on thin ice!*

Carol said nothing, but as I exited the fitting room shedding a trail of silver sequins, I thought I saw her smile with grim relief.

One down, one to go. And it better be good. Extra good. Super good. I was pretty sure my job depended on it.

The outfit for "Put On Your Sunday Clothes," from *Hello, Dolly!* was up next, a girly, four-layer circle skirt and blouse in semi-transparent peach tones. The hat that went with it was a confection of lace, ribbon, horsehair, and silk roses; it was—if I say so myself—beautifully executed. It was of the type referred to as a "picture hat" because of its frequent appearance in portraits by eighteenth- century artists like Thomas Gainsborough and Joshua Reynolds. In such "pictures," lavishly dressed young women are shown carrying rather than wearing the hat; its wide brim protects from the sun but casts nearly impenetrable shadows on a model's face. The same thing happens on stage, but the problem can be turned to a great advantage by an actress who knows what to do with a prop. Bette Davis, for example, as Charlotte Vale, a woman just released from a mental facility, appears at the top of a cruise ship gangplank in *Now, Voyager* wearing an *haute couture* picture hat designed for the movie by fashion designer Orry- Kelly. Bette tilts her head one way and then another, repeatedly hiding and revealing her eyes to the camera, telegraphing her character's shy vulnerability.

When I was again summoned into the fitting room, Carol was wearing the "Sunday Clothes" outfit, complete with padded blonde wig. I elbowed my way in through the crowd and positioned my picture hat on Carol's head as David had drawn it: tilted slightly back, the bunches of pink silk roses cascading down the right-hand side of the hat's crown.

"Awwww, it's lovely! *Just* luuuuv-ly!" Carol drawled. She grasped the points on the brim where it passed above her ears and, lifting slightly, twisted the hat ninety degrees before crushing it back down onto her freakishly large head.

With that simple action, Carol performed a feat of magic. The result so surprised me that I could only stand and stare at her in the mirror. She'd taken my hat—pretty enough, one that could have graced the head of any of a hundred actresses—and made it uniquely her own, simply by turning it so that now, as it sat on her head, the roses trailed across the *front* of the hat. By making that instinctive personal adjustment, she had imbued it with a sort of *Carol-Channing-ness* that I was sure would be apparent even when it was no longer on her head. I could imagine someone coming across the hat on a table in a dressing room in a theatre anywhere in America, and stopping to say, "Oh, is Carol Channing here?" Her alteration had made it a hat that clearly could belong to no one but her.

This is greatness, I thought. In that moment, I understood for the first time the mercurial properties that turn a normal human into something we call a "star." It's more than personality; it's an amalgam of looks, speech, humor, talent. Today we would describe it as a "brand," but that concept is too tawdry, too demeaning of the life force that was Carol Channing. She had refined every aspect of her invented self, until she *owned* everything around her: her physical abilities, her environment, her audience, her destiny. Sure, it didn't last forever. So what? While it lasted it was *alchemy*. It was *power*.

Carol started with her distinctive child's voice and her artificially large head, added a Monroe-like willingness to be silly and a loose-limbed, free-wheeling dance style reminiscent of Ray Bolger, and molded a legend that was still going strong when most performers her age were planning their retirement and clipping coupons. She changed everything she touched, every room she walked into. Sure, she had to have something to work with. She needed the toad she would turn into a handsome prince; the base metal from which to spin gold. But give her those things and then stand back, baby! It didn't matter that her show was opening in Palm Beach and not on Broadway. It didn't matter that she was sent downtown for a costume fitting, or that those fittings took place behind a tattered curtain in a dusty alcove on 14th Street. She was a professional actress, by God, and she knew a dozen gracious but unambiguous ways to make sure you didn't forget it.

By the time Carol left The Studio that day to slip back into her limo and head uptown, she had taught me something about the theatre and the people who work in it—the desperate, grasping, frantic struggle that's the "business" part of show business. I judged the professionalism of every performer I met from that day forward by her example.

Carol never made it to Broadway in *Jerry's Girls*. Nor was she ever again cast as the lead in a new Broadway musical, though she did star in one more revival of *Hello, Dolly!* She continued to perform regularly into her seventies, mostly at benefit concerts and on television doing voice-overs for animated characters. I made several more hats for her personal collection, all to specifications that continued to play with the illusion of a twenty-six-inch head. Carol died in January 2019 at the age of ninety-seven.

My own theatre career lasted barely a full year after my first meeting with Carol, done in by exhaustion and my doctor's warnings against those clouds of solvents and other toxic chemicals I'd been soaking up during my five years working in The Studio's craft room. (I often wonder if they were the cause of the Parkinson's disease I was diagnosed with forty years later.) Then there was the realization that I'd built a career on particular skills that weren't needed often enough to provide me a regular income. When I imagined the likely shape of my future, all I could see was thirty more years of the same struggles. At age thirty-six, I made the decision to leave the costume business and start a new career from scratch.

I did manage, however, to depart on a high note. The last production I worked on before leaving the theatre forever was Franco Zeffirelli's 1985 staging of Puccini's *Tosca* for the Metropolitan Opera. It's the Met's policy to re-print all the creative credits from a production's premier program every time the sets and costumes are used. Zeffirelli's version of *Tosca* was among the best-loved of the Met's productions; it was presented many times—more than two hundred, in fact. And for all those performances, for twenty-three years, I was listed in the *Tosca* program as a member of the creative staff. For those of us who are *not* Carol Channing, that's about as close as we'll ever get to immortality.

A Letter to Anna Bell

Ed. note: A letter found among the papers of Miss Anna Bell, a suicide.

My Dearest Anna,

I would give everything I have of value, perform any deed of penance, endure any public condemnation heaped upon me if, by doing so, I could remove the necessity of writing this letter. When I think of you and of the happiness we've shared over the last several months, and how that joy, at a stroke, has been replaced by wretchedness, I must inveigh against whatever power has wrought this transformation. I had almost convinced myself that our idyll could continue forever. Certainly, that is what I wished and prayed for. But alas! My wishes have been thwarted; my prayers unanswered. Indeed, I am left even without hope, which has fled like a mockingbird startled from its hidden home among the greening cobs, all chatter and flap. The gods do not grant lasting happiness to men like me!

I do not weep for my own cruel fate, dearest, but for the dishonor that must inevitably flow from my heretofore hidden crime, blackening your own sweet innocence. The letter you hold in your delicate hand is my self-indictment, judgement, and condemnation. Even the wind and trees that ring the fields where we've walked together, enjoying each other's company, take up the verdict and murmur it unceasingly: Guilty! Guilty! Guilty! If only there were something I could do or say that would shield you from having to share my misery! I would gladly do it ten times if I must, even ten times ten. But I fear it is not to be. At best I can apologize to those I have injured—you, most of all, my dearest—even though it's certain that redemption is impossible. Yet I swear with my whole heart that whatever pain my acts have caused was unintentional and completely without malice. Indeed, I am convinced that the consequences of my behavior were accidental, perhaps even the result of a mistake. In fact, I could not live with any other possibility.

Last night I discovered where the man I had murdered was buried. I doubt that you can appreciate the shock and horror that accompanied this revelation, though in some respects it must be similar to what you feel upon receiving this news. You know, dearest Anna, that I am the gentlest of men. I flee confrontation or violence, am shy among the denizens of the street, and avoid all public argument and debate. If there is something pre-existing in my nature that has made me the criminal, I now suspect myself to be, I know nothing of it.

I must admit I had almost forgotten about my victim, had finally begun to feel that I could go about my business without the burden of guilt and depression that, until recently, had colored my every waking hour with self-loathing and made me question my own sanity. I had almost managed to return to a normal life, had begun to imagine a future for the two of us….

Now, I must drive those thoughts away. Any possibility other than the hell I am living has vanished entirely, a mirage in the desert. I can no longer keep my story from you, dear Anna, even if it means that your thoughts of me, which once turned so tenderly to an admiration of my character, will henceforth be filled only with contempt and repulsion.

But let me start at the beginning.

It all began about a year ago, at a time when I was experiencing unusually vivid dreams. I often woke from such dreams with one foot still firmly planted in the imagined world, absolutely convinced that what I had just dreamt was real. Usually the incident was trivial; I forgot these delusions within a few minutes, and my anxiety over a missed train or my failure to acquire a mutton chop for dinner soon turned to vapor.

On one particular morning last year, however, I awoke with the firm conviction—nay, I must now call it knowledge—that I had recovered the memory of having murdered someone. Bound and immobile in the bed's twisted, sweat-dampened sheets, I waited for the dream's images to dissipate in the gloomy June morning, overwhelmed in turn by feelings of sadness, terror, and guilt. Alas, my wait was in vain. Desperate, hoping to force forgetfulness, I willed my mind to wander. I studied the pattern of blown roses on the thick window draperies; the dancing light and shadow on the ceiling, reflected through an open door from windows in the next room; spots on the carpet where an unknown substance was slowly bleaching the forest-green threads to the color of a tobacco stain. Everything made me think of violence: the crimson roses became splashes of blood; the flashing light was the reflection from a brandished knife; the powdery spots, undoubtedly residue from some poisonous compound. My recall of the nightmare would not fade.

In spite of my discomfort, I felt fortunate that I had not dreamed of the murder itself. As you know, Anna, I am squeamish about such things, and cannot bear to see reports of even the most common violent crimes in newspapers or scandal sheets. In my dream I knew only that the murder had taken place, and that I, the perpetrator, had suppressed the memory of it until that morning. Who, where, how, when, why—these all remained a mystery.

I've had persistent dreams before, but never one this powerful, this real, and I had always been able to prove them false. But the murder dream… how was I to assay its pretense to reality? I had never seen the face or body of my victim, nor heard him—I was sure, for some reason, it was "him"—give voice to any plea. He might have been a stranger; someone I had never seen before. How could I prove to myself that I had not murdered someone when it felt so real, and yet so many details of the imagined crime were missing? When the only evidence that it had taken place was a strong conviction resulting from a dream? It has been posited that suppressed memories can be uncovered through hypnosis. Is not it then likely that they could also emerge during the course of a sound night's sleep? Is it not at least possible that these memories were of real events?

I managed to arrive at my office on time—though I must have appeared nervous and disheveled to my co-workers—and spent a busy morning wrestling with customer account ledgers. Once I was able to put my mind to it, the tedious work in my quiet cubicle induced a state of ataraxia powerful enough to persuade me that I had, indeed, imagined the event. I began to examine the other side of the question: after all, what evidence did I have of my guilt other than a dream?

But as the days, weeks, and months passed, I felt no final release from guilty thoughts. The more I pondered, the more my entire understanding of morality teetered on the brink of abandonment. I wondered whether the mere fact that I'd had this dream, in and of itself, suggested an evil temperament. Can one man be born intrinsically good, while another is congenitally evil? "Judge of your natural character," Emerson wrote, "by what you do in your dreams." Could my "natural character" include an evil tendency? Even toward as high a crime as murder?

I decided to visit my physician, Dr. Gutmann, to seek respite from my obsession with these thoughts, either through the talking cure or, if that failed, a draught or powder that would at least allow me to sleep undisturbed. But when I told him my story, he brushed my concerns aside.

"My dear chap," he told me, "you are interpreting your experience much too literally! You must remember what Dr. Jung tells us: dreams are symbolic in order that they cannot be understood, in order that the wish, which is the source of the dream, may remain unknown. I would be much more worried if you had dreamed that this mysterious figure was seeking to murder you; that dream would be evidence of compensation for your own murderous urges. No, no," he said, "you must forget about this dream; it is not something that should concern you!"

I left Dr. Gutmann's office quite dissatisfied, despite his assurances. I still hoped to prove to myself that my experience was merely a symbolic manifestation of subconscious conflict, and that the proof would allow me to reclaim some level of normalcy.

I was not to be so lucky. More weeks passed; a resolution eluded me. I began to resist the nightly slow drift into sleep. I knew that, once my sub-conscious mind took control, there could be no way to avoid the possibility of dreaming, and I feared what would be revealed to me through that portal. In my unbalanced state, I thought it at least as likely that new revelations would damn me as save me. Each night I paced from room to room, desperate, repeatedly consulting the clock on my mantel, begging the morning to arrive before I lost consciousness. I left the lights blazing and avoided the bedchamber, afraid that, in my exhausted state, I would collapse onto the bed and be lost to the Oneiroi. Each morning I awoke to find myself splayed across a sofa or curled-up on the floor where I had fainted into a stupor during the night. Blessedly, I did not dream.

During the day there was no respite. I suffered from a constant biliousness in my stomach that no digestive could cure. I searched my looking glass each morning, watching my hair fade from auburn to gray; the sagging skin under my eyes darkened to the color of bruises. A miserable creature began to emerge from my reflection, as if through reverse metamorphosis: carefree moth to cowering grub.

Eventually, dearest, I'm afraid I was left with little choice in my search for resolution. Like historical and fictional monsters before me, I resolved to plumb the darkest recesses of my soul, embracing the worst aspects of what I had come to see as my criminal personality. Acting on this impulse, I soon found myself obsessed with the speculative study of circumstances under which I might, in fact, commit a murder.

Looking back upon that period, my complete absorption in this topic must have seemed like a form of madness to anyone who knew me. I sensed that danger and began to keep entirely to myself but for the intercourse that the activities of daily living required. I lived in fear of questioners, of anyone who might ask me to explain my obsession with texts relating to madness, murder, manslaughter, punishment, and penance.

I will not exhaust you with the details of my many discoveries. Suffice it to say that "derangement"—the one condition under which I could imagine myself committing an act as shocking as murder—is treated by the law somewhat differently than other categories of crime. The law even has a different name for murders committed under one of these conditions: "homicide," which the law defines as "the killing of one human being by another." How dry and unemotional! It sounds almost polite: "Forgive me, sir, but I am forced to be rid of you via homicide."

I seized upon this discovery as a drowning man would a piece of flotsam. If I had indeed killed someone, whether under derangement, necessity, or duress, who could morally accuse me? Perhaps it had been self-defense, against which no one could argue. It occurred to me that it was even possible the killing had been a heroic act, perhaps in aid of some helpless creature. The incident had apparently remained unnoticed by the outside world. I had not been visited by the police; my presumed victim remained unknown. These were mysterious elements of the case, to be sure. Nevertheless, my new understanding of the crime gave me respite from my fear of sleep. At last, I could imagine an eventual reconciliation between my troubled mind and spirit.

And as more days passed without further dreaming, I did begin to put the experience behind me. I no longer avoided sleep but awoke from each successive dreamless night a bit giddy, as though I had emerged triumphant from a harrowing experience. The daily confrontation with the monster in my looking glass eased; as my conscience lightened, so did my spirits and demeanor. My countenance flushed with the roseate glow of rediscovered vigor. My shyness began to fade, and I felt more confident, an enthusiast for life and living!

It was at this point that I first met you, Anna, my dearest, my sweet! I will never forget the day you knocked shyly on the open door of my tiny office. I raised my head and beheld your beauty for the first time. Your lovely eyes, corners crinkled in what I would come to think of as their customary near-sighted squint, peered at me from behind wire spectacles. When you introduced yourself, I made some weak joke about "a kingdom by the sea;" you, charmingly, smiled at my poor attempt at humor. It is true that your hair was unkempt, and that your jumper had a dab of jam on it from your morning tea and toast. Still, I was entranced. I heard nothing of your question about a customer account (Smith? Brown?) but stared, transfixed, imagining my finger as the engine of transportation that would carry that sweet dollop from your spoiled dress to my suddenly famished lips!

O, happy day, and happy those that followed it! Never shall I forget the lovely hours we spent in the fields outside the village, your head in my lap as I read you poetry, you taking the part of the maiden who "lived with no other thought than to love and be loved by me." Whatever my fate, I want you to know, dearest Anna, that these last several months with you have been the most blissful I have ever known.

You may rightly wonder why I have never before spoken to you of the events described on the pages you now hold in your hands; why— until now—I have never revealed to you, my closest friend, these terrible thoughts and dreams. Suffice it to say that I allowed myself to believe that I had put them all behind me and hoped to share a life with you free of the burden of my history of crime. What must you think of me now? With what hatred and contempt must you regard me? I only hope with all my soul that you will forget me, that you will soon find comfort in the companionship of a better man.

You will never see me again.

But I feel I cannot leave you without some sort of explanation, some narrative that will help you understand what has happened....

Last night I dreamt of the murder again, and this time the dream showed me where my victim is buried. How I wish it were an unfamiliar place! How I wish it were unrecognizable, an obscure spot in a foreign country to which I've never travelled, rather than the grassy hill behind my home!

I awoke early this morning in a state near panic. My dyspepsia had returned. I leapt out of bed and was sick several times in quick succession. I splashed cold water on my face, but when I raised my head to regard my own wretched image, I did not recognize the miserable man who stared back at me from the glass. Like Dorian

Gray's portrait, my reflection told the tale of every misdeed I had committed, every instance of cruelty I'd inflicted on others. All the fears that had once kept me in agony came rushing back; every rationalization and equivocation I had mastered was, in a moment, rendered ridiculous. I am seized by a deep sense of hopelessness more complete than any I have known!

What am I to do? In my mind there is but one honorable outcome. Guided by my dream and its attendant visions, I must try to return to my victim's murdered body. If I am utterly unsuccessful, I will immediately take it as proof of my innocence and reclaim my happy life with you, my dearest. In any other case, I will have to accept that I am the true perpetrator, the villain who has committed this terrible crime: I have imagined nothing.

If I confirm the worst, there will be nothing for it but for me to flee—to another town, another parish, another country. It grieves me to say so, dearest, but there is nothing else I can do. Shall I otherwise go to prison, to languish there for the rest of my life whilst you are free and yet condemned to suffer the vicious derision of common gossips? As much as I yearn to return to your arms, I fear that such an improper conclusion would only ruin your reputation and call my own as a gentleman into question.

I have given this letter, which tells everything I know, to Dr. Gutmann, whom I trust implicitly. I have asked him to deliver it to you if I do not return to claim it from him by this evening. That will allow me several hours in which to thoroughly search the location identified in my dream, to either discover the body of my victim or, if I am unsuccessful, return to the good doctor, retrieve this letter, and resume a normal life—secure in the knowledge that I am not a criminal.

You cannot imagine how my heart is broken by the possibility we might never again see each other. But I implore you, dearest Anna, if that is to be our fate, do not to try to follow me!

I have abandoned my home, my name, my country. And should you manage to find me again, I could never let you go.

Piercings: A Dream Poem

My lover came in from weeding the cactus garden, blood running in small trickles down bare forearms. Fine spines clung to punctured skin.

Even Jesus was pierced only five times while he was on the cross, I said. What are you trying to prove?

Nothing, he said. And besides, I'm not like Jesus, here to save humanity. I'm like the blades of grass that are stepped on a thousand times and respond by growing greener.

Scents Memory

"Those pancakes are burning! Can't you smell them?"

In fact, I cannot, as my mate well knows—no more than I can garlic cloves sizzling in hot sesame oil or spice cake just out of the oven. Ditto the Mexican marigolds in the garden, their foliage bruised by a tossing wind, and the cold, wet-cardboard smell of a rare rainy day. As well the cedarn atmosphere within a stand of redwoods—which was my favorite fragrance—and the aura of heat blowing in from the east: a Mississippi of air.

I savor all of these now only as memories. My sense of smell began to fade about a decade ago, a sign (I found out later) of progressing Parkinson's disease. Because it's so closely linked, my sense of taste has been crippled as well. These were losses so gradual and unobtrusive that I didn't even notice them until both senses were quite gone. Now I can detect only saltiness, sweetness, or the burn of capsaicin (which is the source of the heat you feel when eating chili peppers, and which I'm not even sure is a flavor). Any other smells and tastes I relish come to me as figments, as brain-invented conjures with no other basis or cause, and in the most incongruous situations. Lingering in bed in the morning, dozing and waking in short cycles, I'll catch the salty splash of bay water and the sinus-stinging smoke from cheap gas churning in the violent wake of the ski boat my family had when I was a teenager. Working the odorless decomposed granite that answers for soil in my vegetable plot, my mouth waters from the smell of popping corn and the taste of hot chocolate.

It's hard not to be bitter over what I've lost: two-fifths of my interface with the world (though, being honest, I bet we'd all find it easier to live without taste and smell than sight and hearing). I try to focus on and be grateful for the mechanism, whatever it is, that still allows me to relish the greasy aroma of fat rendered from browning bacon and the sharp, astringent perfume of newly-mown grass, even if the former finds me deep within the reference stacks of the public library and the second while driving across the desert, where there's not a green leaf within a hundred miles in any direction.

But most of all I treasure the odd, disorienting moments when my senses suddenly return, and I breathe in the rancid incense of the week-old garbage I'm carrying out to the bin. Seconds later, my burden is again odorless, blank as ice, and my memory book one glorious, fragrant chapter richer.

Superman, Too

Okay, so I shouldn't have been walking down DeKalb Avenue at night. It had been only a month since I was robbed at gunpoint along the same route at about the same hour. Just like last time, two men (I could tell by the heavy slap of their half-laced sneakers against the blacktop) dropped into lockstep ten feet behind me on the otherwise-deserted sidewalk bordering Fort Greene park. It took all my willpower not to break into a run; I knew that's what they expected. Then the thrill of the chase would take over, a situation tailor-made for bad decisions.

The longer I kept a slow pace, disrupting the narrative they had told each other to gin up their courage, the more likely it was that a witness would stumble into the scene and spoil my would-be muggers' plan. I felt the tendons in my neck ratchet up, tight as guy-wires, as I counted down the nine blocks between the subway station and my apartment, following a trail of broken street lights.

Fort Greene was one of the shabbier neighborhoods of New York City back then. A few students and artists, attracted by the low rents, had established outposts among the permanent poor majority, united only by the challenges of living hand-to-mouth. I was lucky to have scored a one-bedroom for two hundred a month, but I had no friends among my neighbors. My pale skin marked me as an outsider; I glowed like a firefly when I walked home after dark.

That second time I was followed on DeKalb Avenue, the two men dogging my steps remained a respectful three paces back, and began to punctuate our synchronized footfalls with a murmured drumbeat: "Hey, Superman! Hey, Superman!" My shoulders sank back into place as I relaxed. They were just fans, the incident another case of mistaken identity.

People are always telling me I look like someone else, usually someone famous. It became an almost daily occurrence in 1980, the year I finished graduate school and moved to New York City. That was also the year the movie *Superman II* was released. Christopher Reeve— to whom, I'd been told repeatedly, I bore a striking resemblance—

reprised his role as the mild-mannered hero. I was working off-Broadway as a set and costume designer at the time and knew a few of Chris's friends through work at the Circle in the Square theatre. Even they would sometimes do a double-take when they saw me backstage or at an opening-night party. At first it was fun to share Chris's fame, signing autographs and making up anecdotes to entertain his fans. I figured it was a harmless deception. But with repetition, the encounters became more and more annoying, and when I'd correct would-be star gazers, they'd insist it was *me* who was mistaken. They were sure they had me pegged, and that I was selfishly denying them the thrill of a chance encounter with fame.

I hated traveling in the screeching, graffiti-splashed coaches of the City's subways, especially in the summer. It seemed ignoble to descend into that humid, sweating, underground world where the only scenery was lighted track switches and the strobe-like snapshots of fellow New Yorkers glimpsed through the windows of trains going in opposing directions. Identity challenges were more frequent in the reeking tunnels, where the wait for a train could seem interminable and boredom would eat away at civility. The outcomes were determined by my capricious mood. I'd try logic— "Don't you think Chris Reeve can afford a cab?"—but logic would fail about 99% of the time. Simply put, it was nearly impossible to convince an excited fan that it wasn't Superman's foot he had just stepped on or Chris's lap into which he had sloshed hot coffee. Shouting over the din of trains going uptown when you were going down or express to 96th Street when you were headed to West 4th, inevitably devolved into an exchange of insults that would end only when a number 3 train toward the World Trade Center showed up or one of us would let fly the classic New York argument-killer: "Hey, fuck you, asshole!" Other times, perhaps when the weather was cooler, I would cheerfully autograph the T-shirt, tourist map, or bare breast that was thrust at me before sending a happy fan on their way. I always signed those ersatz keepsakes "From Superman;" I never forged Chris's signature. I couldn't. I'd never seen it.

In 1983, just as my unwanted celebrity began to subside, *Superman III* was released, and I was thrust back into the public eye. I was approached at a party by an older woman who confided behind her raised palm (thus foiling any lip-readers in the room), "You know, you look very much like a famous actor. But you must get that all the time."

I was in a good mood, helped along by a couple of vodka and cranberries. "Yes," I smiled. "I'm afraid I do."

"It's amazing," she continued. "You look exactly like a young Jimmy Stewart."

There was no Internet back then, but in the New York Public Library's picture collection I found movie stills of Chris Reeve and Jimmy Stewart (from his *Grapes of Wrath* period). Laying them out beside my driver's license, I searched for the resemblances that their fans so easily intuited. I just couldn't see them.

Over time, the list of actors I was mistaken for changed, became shorter and more diverse. I wasn't sure how I felt about being mistaken for Matt Damon, until I found out he's twenty years younger than I. Ray Liotta was a different story.

"Are you kidding?" I protested. "*Ray Liotta?*" While my blind date nursed a third Appletini, I excused myself to use the restroom. I stared at my image in the mirror's dirty glass, and realized he was right. There was Ray, peering at me from my own deep-set eyes, sporting *my* high cheekbones, square jaw, and receding hairline.

Local sightings of me as Ray, Matt, or Chris have tapered off over the years. There was a brief flare-up in 1995 when Chris fell from his horse at an equestrian event and suffered a spinal injury that made him a quadriplegic, and another when he died of heart failure in 2004. On each occasion, the media dug up old stills from the *Superman* franchise, and sightings of me as Chris surged, despite the obvious fact that I was neither wheelchair-bound nor dead. For most fans, it didn't matter.

My spouse and I now live far from New York City, among the dry brush and bare hills east of San Diego. There are few autograph hunters here, which is fine with me. No one expects to run into Jack Nicholson at the weekly farmer's market in La Mesa, nor catch sight of Ryan O'Neal at the annual Mother Goose parade in El Cajon. No one, it turns out, except our plumber, Ivan, whom we see rather frequently. It seems our home has a septic problem that stymies him.

"I know that house," he'd told me the first time I called him, three days after we'd closed on the property and moved in. His voice took on a tone Ahab might have used when describing Moby Dick. "You realize you're on private septic, right? You can't flush any paper except TP. Nothing but TP." He repeats this caution in a forbearing tone at the end of each visit, as if to a child, as though the whole situation is my fault.

Now he's at the house for the fourth time in as many weeks, working a plunger in my backed-up toilet. He doesn't seem to be in a hurry to solve the problem. "You know what I think?" he asks. He's taken a break from plunging, is squinting at me with one eye closed, as though blocking the third dimension of perception will instantly reveal my true identity. "I think you're some movie actor living out here on the down-low."

I imagine I hear the crash of subway car couplings in the far distance, catch a whiff of ozone and body odor, but I'm determined to keep my temper. "Maybe I remind you of someone on TV." I can feel my resolve slipping. "Or maybe I look familiar because I've had to call you out here four times this month. Aren't you supposed to be able to *fix* this?"

He ignores my question but switches his squint from one eye to the other. "No," he says. "It's not TV. That cuts out a couple miles east of here. Internet too. I don't get any of that out at my place. But... I know I've seen you *somewhere.*"

He goes back to roiling the contents of my toilet bowl, staring at me with squinted lids, and tries once more. "Are you *sure* you're not famous?"

That's when it comes to me: pure inspiration. I realize I might be able to turn this whole thing into a win for both of us.

"OK, you got me," I say. "But you have to promise you won't tell anyone. Ever." I wait while he struggles with the idea that his suspicions could be vindicated even as his bragging rights go out the window. His "inside scoop" will be useless. I press ahead to close a bargain before he comes up with a way to weasel out of it.

"How about we seal the deal with—wait, let me think, let me think.... I've got it! How about a discount on the plumbing work?"

He considers it. "Tell ya what. I'll trade it for an autograph. Your *real* name, though."

"It's a deal!" I say. "I'd shake hands, but..." I'm eyeing the spattered glove on his right hand.

"No worries." he removes the glove, hands me his baseball cap, and takes a felt tip marker from his pocket.

I flatten his cap against the edge of the sink to compose my dedication. "To Ivan, Best Plumber this side of Krypton," I write. "Best wishes– George Reeves." I'm guessing Ivan, living off the grid, will never know the difference. And Chris? Well, after all these years, I figure he deserves to rest in peace.

Love Stinks

Toilet, WC, john, lavatory, water closet, latrine, commode—these are some of the English-language synonyms for "toilet" listed in the crowd-sourced reference *The Power Thesaurus.*

Bog, can, dunny, loo, potty, privy, throne, cloakroom, comfort station, convenience, head, restroom, washroom, gong, lavabo, House of Lords, petty, netty, bench-hole, cludgie, gents, ladies, pissoir, crapper, powder room....The book claims 293 of them, which is not surprising given the importance of that appliance to maintenance of an orderly life.

But if you want to talk toilets, the Mallard ADA EL made by Zolo is my first choice. The website ToiletsThatWork.com gives it 9.5 points out of 10 overall, and 9.7 on its flush alone. Tony Cherish, a San Francisco plumber who tests toilets in his own home and publishes his evaluations on the internet, gives the Mallard a perfect 5 hearts out of a possible 5. People love this toilet.

And why wouldn't they? Web testimonials praise its G-Max engineering, its superior QA during manufacture, its unique double-suction effect, and its ability to swallow an entire roll of toilet paper in one flush—this last feature demonstrated in a dozen or more YouTube clips. The Mallard is listed at about twice the price of a standard toilet, but if you, like me, want your goodbye-bye to whatever you leave in the can to be a permanent one, the Mallard is the right toilet for you. And if you choose to add the soft-close seat, the whole package represents pure modern mechanical engineering perfection.

I have a long history of struggle, often fruitless, with the molded clay appliance Americans know as the modern toilet. To read the ads and watch the commercials, one might be excused for thinking that we live in a wonderland of miraculously efficient, beautifully designed toilets. The truth of the matter is somewhat different: I have wasted untold hours, with a plunger as my weapon, trying to hurry-along the contents of my toilet bowl with repeated pushes of encouragement. Which is why I looked forward to installing a Mallard when I remodeled the closet-sized bathroom in my 200-square-foot, fifth-floor walkup on West 49th Street in New York City. But I'm getting ahead of myself. Let me start at the beginning.

It had been a long trip for me from the quiet parochialism of my southern California up-bringing to co-op ownership in the vital core— if not the best neighborhood—of the greatest city in the world. I'd approached New York cautiously, content at first to dream of it from a distance while I finished undergraduate school three thousand miles away in San Diego. I spent my vacations here, where I knew no one, seeing movies and shows, riding the Staten Island ferry (twenty-five cents!), walking up and down the avenues, guidebook in hand. I devoured the novels and films that used the city as their backdrop, from *Rosemary's Baby* to *Manhattan* to *Do the Right Thing*.

Leaving San Diego and its small-town vibe, I'd inched my way cross-country: graduate school in Illinois (where I switched my focus from architecture to set design, having finally realized that the day-to-day job of an architect is too dry and technical for my taste), a year in Boston, a corporate job designing trade show booths for a New Jersey company based in Trenton. From my firm's Trenton office tower, I could imagine I saw the ragged tips of New York's skyscrapers on the smoggy horizon. In 1979, a year after taking the Trenton job, I finally got a call from a mid-town Manhattan landlord with whom I'd left an apartment application. That same afternoon I quit my job, put an ad in the paper to sell my battered '67 VW Fastback, and started to pack. It was time to begin my life as a New Yorker.

"Hell's Kitchen" is how most people refer to the area of Manhattan between 34th and 56th Streets west of Eighth Avenue. No one knows for sure how it got its name. Some speculate that it's a reference to the blacksmith fires that glowed late into the night in the nineteenth century carriage horse stables that lined the streets along the Hudson. Others say that it was the moniker given a single notorious tenement on the corner of 54th Street and Eighth Avenue and later applied to the whole district. Those invested in the gentrification of the neighborhood prefer to call it Clinton, a reference to DeWitt Clinton Park near 52nd Street and Eleventh Avenue, named after a nineteenth-century New York Governor.

Early historians describe an area of farms and streams. Later, as the city spread north, it developed into a warehouse district controlled by Irish gangs and famous for its danger, filth, and lawlessness. During Prohibition, it was a center for gambling and rum running, aided by proximity to the long shoreline of the Hudson River. Whatever the origin of its name, it remains today a neighborhood of tiny, un-renovated brick tenements, limited (as are 95% of all New York buildings that depend on the city's gravity-flow water supply) to five stories.

By the time I was given the opportunity to buy my studio on 49th Street, Hell's Kitchen had long been a mostly Puerto Rican neighborhood, about ten blocks south of the tenements that provided the backdrop for the movie *West Side Story*. The poor would always be displaced by someone who could afford one dollar more in rent; that's the way we would claw our way to the top. I admit to being part of the invading demographic. But what did those who would eventually be displaced want? Should I have said "no" to a reasonable price, the convenience of a mid-town location; a well-funded maintenance account? I was exactly the kind of new buyer developers needed to bring the nearly-bankrupt city back to life—young artists, musicians, and other skilled workers drawn to the cultural center of America. Blame the theatres, music halls, and art schools. Blame the painters, sculptors, writers, architects, set designers, costume designers, fashion designers, interior designers, dancers, actors, dancers who can act, actors who could dance, all of us flinging ourselves naively into the dog-eat-dog stew of the vital city, looking for our share of fame, all of us dreaming big.

My apartment is, as I think I've said, a walk-up, and there have been many days I've wished for an elevator. But, despite the high school mid-block and the drug dealers on the corner, the street is clean and quiet for the most part; any petty annoyances or inconveniences are more than made up for by my slivered view of the Empire State Building and the thrill of living in New York. My building has four studio apartments per floor that share a common stairway, and a shuttered storefront a half-flight down from the street. I assume the layouts of the apartments are identical, half looking out to the street, the others overlooking a weedy dirt garden in the back. All have a window in the bathroom that opens onto an airshaft that provides cross-ventilation during the steamy summer months.

I've been in many New York apartments, some bigger than mine and some smaller (not surprising in a city where the housing code allows a landlord to call any space with a window a bedroom, even when it can't accommodate so much as a twin bed). My studio felt a little claustrophobic at first, but I soon got used to it and eventually came to enjoy its spare efficiency. I never thought about what it would be like to live in that space with another person, let alone the eight or ten who crammed themselves into it during the building's tenement years.

My building is blessed with a floor plan that allowed room for a combination tub/shower in the bathroom; many tenements in the district don't have this twentieth-century innovation. At the time the tenements were built, many New Yorkers—especially the poorer ones—used the elaborate public bathhouses that dotted the city, their fanciful Roman Revival facades and tiled interiors accessible at the cost of a nickel. Most were torn down long ago, with notable exceptions like the Continental and Asher Levy. As enthusiasm for public bathing waned, landlords began to install bathing facilities in their apartments. Showers were not well known outside the homes of the wealthy; for ordinary New Yorkers bathing required a tub, and in nineteenth-century buildings the only space large enough to accommodate a tub was in the area used as a kitchen. The arrangement is inconvenient but encourages the residents' creativity in devising "dining tub" solutions for dinner parties they don't have room to host anyway.

My kitchen area consists of an under-counter refrigerator that has just enough room for a carton of milk or juice and (when it's not frosted over) a tray of ice cubes in the freezer compartment; next to that is a narrow sink and a compact four-burner gas stove. A floor-to-ceiling partition separates the cooking/eating area from the working/sleeping area. To preserve floor space, my bed is pushed into the corner against the outside wall under one of the two windows that overlook the street. A tall chest of drawers, a drafting desk, and the kitchen table with its four canvas director's chairs are the sum total of my furniture.

New York is, with few exceptions, a city of small apartments; this partially explains the abundance of coffee houses, restaurants, and bars. No one has enough room at home to invite guests over. But who cares? Being outside in New York is exhilarating, and a walk from Central Park down through mid-town or from Chinatown to Wall Street can be a voyage of discovery. I don't apologize for the fact that I saw New York through rose-colored glasses. I still do. To me its massive skyscrapers are like crystals growing straight, tall, and dense from a mineral-rich twenty-three-square-mile chunk of Manhattan schist that has broken off of the eastern coast of New Jersey. The whole history of western architecture is on display here, told through crenellated crowns, spires, tiles, and gargoyles. Consider the neo-classical columns of the public library; compare Phillip Johnson's post-modern interpretation of the same design elements for the AT&T building (since sold to Sony). Everything is extreme style writ large: Cass Gilbert's neo-gothic Woolworth building renders Victorian aesthetics in stone; Thomas Lamb's Egyptian Revival Temple up on 70th Street imagines what a pharaoh might have ordered up if the ancients had known about steel. Everywhere you look there are strange allegorical figures in three dimensions: heroes, villains, saints, demons, captains of industry. The known and unknown. Statues representing Time, Courage, Knowledge, Death, surrounded by chiseled aphorisms and mysterious glyphs suggesting the supernatural. It's the *excess* of it all that's so thrilling, a general exuberance that, in contrast, reinforces the intended simplicity of the blunt-topped International-style buildings. Look up from the sidewalk, and one is immediately intoxicated by variety of style, as I've been my whole life, from the moment I first arrived.

I managed to survive in the world of the theatre for five years, constantly scrambling for work as a scenic artist while earning minimum wage for drawing floor plans and elevations for other designers. Sometimes there were three or four days of set painting at a studio in Long Island City, or a gig as a stylist for one of the TV ads being filmed around town. I never made enough money to honestly call it a living; it was tough competing with designers that would work for free just to have a New York credit on their resume.

I figured five years were enough; I had given it a fair shake. When I looked ahead, I saw that things were unlikely to change. I wasn't going to be rich or famous. I hated not knowing when I would earn another fee, or how much it would be. I hated never having a vacation other than the forced ones I sweated through during jobless periods. I was sick of it, and I took the out that thousands of others had; I became a computer programmer.

Of course, it didn't happen just like that. It took two more years of NYU extension courses, working during the day, attending school in the evening, often leaving work to go to school and returning to work at nine or so, after class was over, to work into the night. But it paid off: I was hired by a financial services firm to work on their back office systems—margin, bookkeeping, client statements. It was boring but steady, well-paid work. A steady job gave me financial stability and, with my experience living frugally, allowed me to accumulate a nest egg.

When my building went co-op, I had just enough cash to make a down payment and saddle myself with a mortgage at the peak of the New York City real estate market. The apartment badly needed an update, especially in the bathroom, but I figured I could put my construction skills to work so that my out-of-pocket would be limited to materials. I knew I was unlikely to recoup my investment in home improvements should I ever want to sell. But, what the heck? You have to take some risks, and in the meantime, I could look forward to some high-quality bathroom time.

It was a splurge to spring for the Mallard as part of the reno. In a nod to economy, I had decided—after re-plumbing everything within the walls—to save and re-install the 1940s-era tub and sink. So, my state-of-the-art toilet was my pride and joy, the centerpiece of my beautiful new bathroom. As with anything that's new and expensive, I was overly anxious about scratching it or getting it dirty, and the first few weeks after I installed the porcelain masterpiece, I was reluctant to use it for its intended purpose. When I was in the apartment, the soft white gleam of its Sani-gloss finish would beckon me and I would find myself standing in the bathroom doorway admiring its exquisitely pure glow. I couldn't bring myself to defile something so beautiful, so perfect, so otherworldly. When nature called, I would sidle reverently past the glowing throne to piss in the bathroom sink. I sought to take care of other needs while I was at work. A couple of times I missed that opportunity and had to hotfoot it downstairs to that rarity of rarities, a twenty-four-hour public restroom; this one conveniently in the *bodega* on the corner of Tenth Avenue. I think you get the idea: I went to a lot of trouble to keep my prize possession in its spotless new condition, at least (I reasoned with myself) for a little while.

Imagine my surprise then when, after about a week of proud new toilet ownership, I lifted the Mallard's soft-close seat one evening to admire the perfection of the bowl interior and noticed a small object sitting in the three inches of fresh water at the bottom. It was round, metallic, and appeared to be about three-eighths of an inch thick—about the size of four quarters stacked on one another. Without thinking I quickly reached in to remove the profaning item. When I had dried it on the nearby hand towel and had a chance to examine it, I realized it was a small, inexpensive tin compass—like one you might receive as a prize in your cereal or in a box of Cracker Jack—that had been lying face down in the Mallard.

I placed the compass on the birch veneer of my small kitchen table and sat in one of the director's chairs to study it. There were several things that puzzled me. First, of course, was the question of how the compass had made its way to my Mallard. I knew that *I* hadn't dropped it in, and the reasonable list of other potential defilers was short: there were none, as far as I knew. My super had a young boy, about the right age to be carrying around a toy like this one; but Javier rarely accompanied his father to my apartment. Besides, I hadn't asked the super to do anything for me since he let in the inspector for the final OK on the reno, and I had never known him to enter my apartment without being asked. I guessed that the compass could have *backed up* into my toilet from someone else's apartment, maybe as the result of some sort of plumbing problem in the building. But that was highly unlikely: I was on the top floor, and the laws of physics required that the foreign object, to end up in my toilet, would have had to come from somewhere *above* my bathroom. And besides, if that had been the cause, wouldn't there have been something more than just the compass in the spotless bowl? Wouldn't there have been—it's difficult to put this delicately—some other evidence of a clog?

This is where the story becomes a little weird. In fact, it makes me uncomfortable to continue telling it in the first person, knowing what's coming and what you might end up thinking of me. You could end up thinking I'm crazy, for example, and my story the product of an over-active imagination. More on that later. For now I just wish I could tell it in a more detached way, one that didn't make me seem insane. If only that were possible.

"What would you think if you found something in your toilet that didn't belong there, and you ended up falling in love because of it?"

"What would you think if you found out your lover wasn't human?"

See what I mean?

As I sat at the kitchen table, staring at the found object and speculating silently on its unlikely, inexplicable journey, a strange thought occurred to me. At first, I rejected it as absurd. But the longer I thought about it the more convinced I became that the compass was a message intended specifically for me, a wish or request embodied in a tribute object. A prayer, if I could call it that.

How it had arrived in the bowl of my pristine Mallard was still an open question, one I was unable to answer. But the *why*—well, there was the magnificent porcelain artifact glowing softly in the dim light from the bathroom's air shaft. What was there to limit speculation? After all, it's become quite common to hear of people discovering images of the Virgin Mary in everything from salt stains dripping down the concrete walls of a Chicago expressway underpass to the caramelized starches on the broiled surface of a grilled cheese sandwich. This wasn't a common case of Pareidolia, but if people are willing to pray to salt scum and a piece of toast, why couldn't my virginal toilet be a conduit to the supernatural? I'd received a gift from someone, or some*thing*. How was I to decode the offer it implied, and let the giver know that I understood a conversation based on the exchange of tokens? In fact, it turned out that *I* was the one who didn't understand, but I didn't know that yet. I stood up, walked the two short strides to the sleeping area at the other end of the studio, and pulled open the bottom drawer of my bureau. This was where I dumped all of the detritus—receipts, brochures, admission tickets, etc.—that accumulated from my infrequent travels out of the city. I rummaged through the drawer and, in a small collection of road maps, found one from Vermont that I thought would be the perfect response to a conversation that began with "compass." I hastily rolled the map around the tiny compass and fastened the bundle with a rubber band that had previously held a bunch of fresh cilantro. I didn't want to stop and think, afraid that if I delayed, I might realize that what I was about to do was entirely mad. I moved quickly into the bathroom, dropped my bundle into the Mallard, and pressed the flush lever.

With a roar of G-Max power, the small package disappeared. I knelt in front of the toilet for a few moments, watching the water level rise in the bowl as the tank refilled, admiring the efficiency of the cleansing rinse action that sprayed water in a freshening sheet from under the rim. Even when the cycle had completed, and the Mallard had returned to its silent reverie, I waited attentively on my knees for several more minutes for… What? Was I really expecting a thank-you note or something? Then I began to wonder whether flushing the rolled-up map had been a smart thing to do. Sure, the Mallard was supposed to be able to handle objects of its size and shape, but why test it in a situation that was beginning to seem silly the longer I thought about it. Soon realizing that it might be quite a while before I received another message from the liquid beyond, I wandered wearily to the other end of the room to fall into my bed and then to sleep.

When I awoke the following morning, the day seemed full of promise; I scrambled out of bed and rushed into the bathroom to peer into the serene puddle at the bottom of the Mallard. Nothing. I'm not embarrassed to say I was disappointed. I carried out my weekday work preparations with an air of dejection. I briefly considered calling in sick. My faith in magical thinking was taking a serious drubbing, and I didn't like it. I wondered if I was slipping back into an old pattern, one for which my friends had roundly criticized me: "Did you *really* think you'd find a serious boyfriend by being a pen pal for someone in prison? I mean, this guy's in for *murder*, for Christ's sake!"

I looked at it another way: as a single, not-particularly-attractive fifty-five-year-old queer, I had little left to believe in *but* magic. After all, hadn't I already become, by virtue of my age, invisible to most other gay men?

I finished dressing while I stared at my reflection in the bathroom mirror, noticing as I did every morning that my reflected image always ties his tie backwards, and that it takes him several tries to get the tails the right length. The threads were separating and beginning to fray, the red silk grimy in the segment of tie that always ended up in the four-in-hand knot. I made a mental note to make my next tie a clip-on. While I struggled with my tie, my tongue worked at dislodging a soggy corn flake that had wedged itself between two of my molars, upper left. I continued to turn the problem of the Mallard over in my mind. Was it possible I had misunderstood the rules for conversations with the realm on the other side of the watery portal that was my toilet? Perhaps it was my turn to make a request by sending along my own amulet. It was worth a try. But what of sufficient value or meaning did I have to offer?

Then, inspiration! I suddenly knew what it should be. I trotted the four steps to the bookcase that held my stereo, the bookend for a row of LPs and a collection of old theatre programs arranged in alphabetical order by year. I ran my fingers across the slick covers of the pamphlets as through a Rolodex. There it was: *Tosca* at the Met, 1985. The Zeffirelli production, with Domingo and Behrens. I carefully withdrew my torn ticket stub from the program. I was going to have to hurry if I hoped to make it to work on time.

I extracted an unused Ziploc bag, sandwich size, from a kitchen drawer and slipped the ticket stub inside. I sealed, unsealed, and resealed the bag several times, testing to make sure water couldn't find its way inside, and dropped the newly waterproofed fetish into the Mallard's bowl, where it floated placidly. Acting fast, before I could change my mind, I pressed the handle and watched the ticket stub disappear in a rumbling torrent of raging foam. Whatever happened now, I felt that I had given it my best shot: I had offered a prize worthy of even a petulant god. I hurried out of the apartment and made it to the subway just in time to catch the 8:47 "E" train at Eighth Avenue.

I won't bore you with the details of my workday; suffice it to say it was one of those during which my eyes seldom strayed from the clock, which only made the passage of time virtually imperceptible. As 5pm neared I fidgeted at my desk like a distracted schoolboy waiting for the dismissal bell to ring. At 4:58 my friend Nate prairie-dogged over the wall of the cubicle next to me.

"You wanna get a drink at Friday's before you head home?"

"Can't. I've got something I need to do tonight."

"Oh, big evening, huh? You know, *Project Runway* doesn't come on 'til 9. We could hang out for a couple hours, maybe watch it at Uncle Charlie's."

"Sorry. See ya tomorrow, Nate!" I replied, hurrying out. I didn't want any delays, not that night!

Say what you like about New York; it has great public transportation. While tempers erupted on the gridlocked streets above us, I and a few thousand other straphangers were whisked from Chambers to 49th Street in a mere fifteen minutes. It would have been even faster had I been able to bring myself to get on at the World Trade Center station, but I couldn't do it; not yet.

I half-jogged the two cross-town blocks from the station to my apartment, past Worldwide Plaza and across Ninth Avenue. I must have looked like an idiot flapping along with my virtually empty briefcase and unnecessary raincoat flying here and there in the wind of my own momentum. By the time I reached my building's stoop I had to stop at the bottom of the stairs to catch my breath. For the umpteenth time I wondered about the wisdom of buying a fifth-floor walk-up at my age. *I'll be lucky if I get three years out of this place*, I thought.

I took another breather at step seventy-five, outside my apartment door, while I rummaged in my briefcase. How is possible to lose a ring of keys in an otherwise empty bag? I finally found them and, with trembling fingers, fit one into the first of three locks. By the time I got the door to the apartment open my heart seemed to be beating only spasmodically, and with booms that I was sure were audible in the cramped room. I forced myself to slow down, placing my briefcase on a director's chair and draping my coat neatly over its back rather than just flinging them both in the general direction of the bed. I pried open the knot that had become a noose during my eight hours at work and heard the crack of more threads breaking as I tugged on the knot to give myself a little breathing room. It was time to buy some insurance against frustration.

"There's probably nothing there," I said out loud. The phrase echoed, even in my small apartment, and reminded me of every Christmas morning I could remember: the atmosphere as heavy with the chill of potential disappointment as the heat of anticipated delight. It's a good mantra with which to chill one's expectations and helps me feel more grateful when whatever I find under the wrapping paper is more modest or less exciting than imagination may have led me to expect. In this case the package to be opened was the sparkling Mallard, which I could already glimpse through the half-open bathroom door.

I affected a casual saunter—for what audience, I don't know—as I moved the two steps to the doorway, pushed open the door, and flipped the light switch. The fluorescent bulb flashed once, paused, then two more times before it finally steadied; each flicker reflected in the Mallard's polished surface was like heat lightning flashing across the sluggish Hudson on an August evening: ominous and insistent. I bent at the waist and inserted my right index finger under the lid and seat and lifted. A shadow—the silhouette of my head—darkened the bottom of the bowl, but I was almost certain I could see something there. I sank to a squat to move out of the light and looked again. There was definitely something there: dark and flat, in what looked like a plastic envelope.

It was a moment of Truth, capital T. I knew that if I retrieved the object and was able to correlate it to some part of my ticket stub, it would shake my understanding of the universe and change my life forever. On the other hand, history and mythology are rife with the stories of mortals that have meddled in divine business to their rue. Sometimes it's really not a good idea to toy with things we don't understand, and in this case, I had no idea whether the object at the bottom of the bowl was tainted by heaven or hell. I had only to raise my left hand and press the flush lever, and this allurement would disappear as surely and swiftly as the Red Sea had swallowed Pharaoh's armies.

The water was like ice, making my finger-bones ache as I gingerly withdrew the package from the bottom of the bowl. I carried it to the table by one corner and laid it carefully on a dish towel to soak up any water clinging to it. I switched on the overhead light and sat down for a thorough examination of the bundle. "The First Epistle of Khonsu to the Clueless," I mumbled as I leaned closer.

The first thing I noticed, with some satisfaction and little surprise, was that what I thought was a plastic envelope was, in fact, the same sandwich bag I had sent in the other direction. I also thought I could see my ticket stub through the plastic that had become cloudy from exposure to water. But what was in there with it? I began to pry the zip closure apart with tiny, deliberate movements. When I was finally able to slip the contents out of the bag, I saw that it consisted of a packet of small pages folded in half. When I unfolded it, my heart began to pound once again. It was the *Stagebill* for the production of *Tosca* that matched my ticket stub.

I was so astonished that I sat back in my chair with an audible huff and stared at the items in front of me for some minutes. A suspicion began to grow that propelled me up out of my chair and across the room to my collection of programs on the bookshelf. *I* had this program. What if someone—who, or why, I couldn't guess—had entered my apartment after retrieving the baggie I had offered that morning and simply added my copy of the program to it? My fingers flew through the collection until I came to the program's assigned place. It was there. I pulled it out and returned to the table. I placed the two pamphlets side-by-side and began to leaf through them in tandem. The first twenty pages were ads and articles, but my new acquisition seemed to be authentic: it matched my own copy exactly. Until I came to the title page announcing the opera.

Like mine, the creased *Stagebill* listed the name of the opera, the composer, the librettist, the director, the conductor, and the designers. When they're of sufficient status, as they were here, a few of the star performers are listed on this page, often with their photos. The title page in the folded program was for the same 1985 *Tosca* at the Met, but it didn't match mine. In styles ranging from spidery to bold and with what was obviously three different pens, it was autographed by Placido Domingo, Hildegard Behrens, and—just for good measure—Cornell MacNeil, who had sung the role of Scarpia in that production.

What was I supposed to make of this chain of events? Stunned into incoherence, my mind retreated to conceivable details. *What a shame* (I remember thinking) *that they folded the program. Maybe I could flatten it with a warm iron.* But shortly I became aware of a voice in my head: *Oh, my God, you fucking idiot! You're fucking communicating with someone through your fucking toilet!*

I was on my feet again, pacing the apartment like a wild man, trying to absorb the meaning, the *possibilities* of meaning, of what I had discovered. The room had never seemed so small. I needed to run, to shout, to wave my arms and wail like a banshee. Instead, I crossed back and forth, from one end of my apartment to the other, in five strides. Again. Again. Later I would think that, if only I had been able to work off my excitement in a reasonable way, if only I had run out of my apartment, down the stairs and out onto Tenth Avenue—where they're used to seeing lunatics in the street—and walked and howled until I was capable once more of rational thought, maybe, *maybe,* I wouldn't have done what I did next. But in my fevered, un-exorcised state it was useless to try to think rationally. I was like a gambler on a winning streak: I felt that the only logical thing to do was to double down immediately.

How did the next idea come to me? I honestly can't remember. It may have been this simple: on my next trip to the bedroom end of the apartment I threw myself on my unmade bed and began to roll and thrash, hoping the deranged bedclothes would absorb some of energy that seeped out of me through my skin and clothing and scented the air in the room with what I could only imagine to be the smell of brimstone. As I rolled to the side of the mattress that wasn't against the wall, I looked down at the floor and noticed the short stack of magazines protruding slightly beyond the edge of the bedframe. When I reached down to tug on the pile, it slid easily across the floor's asphalt tiles.

There, on the top of the pile, was the latest *Unterpantz* catalogue. The cover model clad in nothing but a conservative white cotton fly-front brief, his thumbs hooked enticingly in the waistband, gazed up at me with a look of mocking indifference. I stared back, mesmerized by his otherworldly anatomy and the insane plan that was already beginning to arrange itself in my head. I snatched up the booklet and carried it back to the kitchen.

Sitting again at the table, I arranged four items in front of me: my ticket stub, the two Tosca programs, the underwear catalogue. *You must be crazy!* I told myself. *You should get help now! There's got to be a twenty-four-hour crack-up hotline or something you could call. What you're considering is lurid, perverse!*

And yet...

Wouldn't I have been a fool *not* to grasp at what I believed would bring me happiness, no matter how bizarre the path to its achievement? After all, it was my *faith* in what I was about to do that made me the potential target of ridicule, not the act itself. I wasn't doing any harm, or so I thought; my actions were more those of a kook than a psychotic. It's all well and good for you to sit in judgment of me now— or as you will, perhaps, when my story is finished, the outcome known and my damnation certain. But wouldn't many among you have leapt at opportunity just as I did? How many, alone in your tiny apartments in the cold, miserable heart of a friendless city that won't return your adoration, would have been able to resist a chance to change your fate?

I began to turn the pages of *Unterpantz*, paying equal attention to models and product. Now that I looked carefully, I realized that almost all the models appeared to be in their mid-twenties or so, really too young for a real romance with an older man. But this was *fantasy*, wasn't it? Everyday, rational considerations need not apply. Still, I wanted to send a considered, *specific* message; the possibility for misinterpretation had to be avoided at all costs. My choice from the catalogue would be all my correspondent knew of my personality. It mustn't be outlandish, like the styles made out of something meant to imitate leather, or with see-through panels or rows of straps where there should be fabric. But it shouldn't be too conservative, either; I don't really find anything sexy in boxer shorts, for example—neither the traditional ones nor the more contemporary knit boxer. Maybe something like the Klavin Kleene Bold, page eight: classic, tasteful. But then again, the elastic waistband is woven with the designer's name in inch-high letters, repeated as it circles the model's waist. How obnoxious! If I want to read a billboard I can walk over a couple of blocks to Times Square! What about the Myles High Lo-cut Brief, page twenty-three: simple, chic. But wait! It doesn't come in white. And the model looks Hispanic. No good. I wasn't about to sign up for that brand of drama.

With that thought in mind, I started scanning the catalogue for models rather than style, and soon realized they were mostly white-bread mongrels: boys from the suburbs who had managed to build up a little muscle and thought their girlfriends would be turned on if they flashed their packages in a magazine or video. There were a couple of black guys, but not for me; the black guys who look like that always want to be on top. Germans, Swedes, likewise no-can-do. An Italian is what I needed: dark, pliable, endlessly amorous, noble-seeming but with simple needs; a descendent of men that, over millennia, have labored like mules for popes, emperors, and dictators and have the work-hardened bodies to prove it.

Like this one, page fifty-two, in the RoxSox Racontour Basic Brief. Black hair longer than most, flopping casually across one eye as he peers from under a slash of dark brows. No need for the gym-rat buzz-cut to look masculine. Beard stubble just at the three-day length, I'm guessing; though, who knows? I've met Italian boys who have to shave twice a day if they don't want to flay your skin with their stubble when they go in for the smooch. Olive skin, good physique, but doesn't look like he has to work for it or, at any rate, like he did. And the brief: simple, white of course. Maybe a little too stylish, but Italians of either gender take naturally to style. They look great in something that would look like a costume on anybody else.

But as I examined the small catalogue photo more closely, I spotted a problem. It was hard to see because of shoddy lighting and the dark background, but I was pretty sure I could detect the faint suggestion of a tattoo on the back side of Cesar's right upper arm, running vertically along his triceps. (I'd decided to call him Cesar, at least until I learned his real name, in tribute to his obvious natural superiority.)

I despise tattoos of any kind, in any place, no matter how well executed. That's simply a fact, one some of my friends frequently challenge me to defend. I consider tattoos an affront to the beauty of the unsullied human form; a permanent defacement. They are a sign of descent from a state of grace to the aboriginal, from sophisticated to primitive culture. Can you imagine looking up at the ceiling of the Sistine Chapel and seeing a "sleeve" of tattoos on Adam's left arm as he reaches toward God to receive the spark of life? I rest my case.

I would have to find a way to reverse this act of vandalism on my Adam, my Cesar. I had to cut out the photo anyway, so as I snipped along the left side of the image with my kitchen shears I swerved in just slightly and nicked the edge of his right arm. The tattoo was excised in one bloodless stroke.

Now I had my wish object; what could I offer in tribute? I briefly considered cash but realized that might be misconstrued on the other side of the Mallard's gateway. Cash is what's called for on Eleventh Avenue by the convention center, or in the Village among the trucks along the piers. Definitely not appropriate for an offering to whatever or whomever was speaking to me from the Mallard. Rummaging through my odds-and-ends drawer once again, I pulled out a couple of drink coupons left over from an ill-advised outing to Fire Island last summer. I remembered how, under the influence of a contact high acquired in the men's room of The Ice Palace, I barely escaped being plundered by a group of leather queens by falling, fully clothed, into the pool—using the incident as an excuse to take the last ferry back to Sayville. The unused chits wouldn't really set the tone I wanted either. Suddenly my eye was caught by a small, square, cardboard jeweler's box at the bottom of the drawer.

I had travelled through some period of years in the arc of my life during which I was repeatedly prospected by the women in my office as a potential husband—not for themselves, certainly, for their own standards were (so they believed) far higher than I could hope to satisfy—but for their unmarried sisters, cousins, and friends who were approaching spinsterhood. According to their understanding, any man who arrives at a certain age, say between thirty and forty-five, without having married is considered to be a charity case that just might be willing to settle for one of the less favored of the female gender. In order to forestall intrusive assays by would-be cupids or, more accurately, Aphrodite, I had taken to wearing on my ring finger a plain gold band I had picked up for five dollars at a kiosk in a New Jersey shopping mall. This simple deception rendered me instantly invisible to the relationship sharks circling the office pool while—as I discovered quite by accident—making me immensely more interesting to certain patrons of The Monster, a gay bar in Sheridan Square that I visited infrequently on my way home from work.

In those days, before gay marriage, the sight of a wedding band on a man's finger was the imprimatur and guarantee of hetero masculinity, even if that man was currently draped drunkenly across the piano in a gay bar, singing tuneless versions of songs from *Cabaret*.

Hunters among the crowd would circle him one at a time, patiently gathering tidbits of his story before meeting back at their table to compare notes and concoct a seduction scenario. Is it any wonder my visits were rare?

But rare doesn't mean never. I'm not proud of it, but I did on occasion extend my role-play to dates with the more attractive or entertaining suitors. We would always adjourn to his place (after all, as I explained, I supposedly had a wife at home). I would play the role of the somewhat dull, sloppily overweight New Jersey husband excited to be exploring a brave new world. Inhabiting such a character allowed boundless opportunity for stupid, insensitive acts, all excused by my *inamorato* because of the hetero entitlement symbolized by the narrow gold band on my finger. Sometimes I would even meet my "mistress" for a second or third time. It was particularly fun to arrange a meeting at one of the many no-tell motels that dotted the nearby suburbs, completing our transaction to the accompaniment of headboards banging against adjacent walls like the snare drums of an army on the march. It seemed like the whole world was lost in sex. Eventually, of course, I would tell a heartbroken story about why we had to break up: my wife was suspicious, my children were sick and need my complete attention, my job was being transferred to another city. The only disadvantage of my story—other than the fact that it was a complete lie—was that after one of these affairs I had to avoid The Monster for a while.

I no longer wore the gold band at the office, having passed through that age-defined period of marriage vulnerability and entered the life phase in which interested observers, if any, assumed my bachelorhood to be confirmed by choice. Still, I initially rejected the wedding band as an offering to the Mallard, influenced by my knowledge of its original purpose: I certainly didn't want to imply that I was married. But there are certain associations with a wedding band that made it perfect for what I had in mind. I'm thinking of sincerity, seriousness, sentimentality. If I could be sure it would be seen on the other side in the spirit in which it was offered....

I really didn't have anything else. I quickly assembled my package as I had before, the catalogue photo and the ring (without the box: more casual, conversational) in a new waterproof bag, and prepared to send it on its way.

It was now after 8pm. Darkness had fallen outside, and there was no natural light in the bathroom as I carried my prayer bundle toward the door. The fluorescent light still hummed and flickered occasionally, though it seemed dimmer than before, as though starved for electricity. Perhaps it was my imagination, but as I approached the Mallard I sensed a shadow that wasn't cast by anything in the room. Whereas earlier it had radiated efficiency, wholesomeness, even warmth, the Mallard now had a cold aura of peeved annoyance. I gently lowered my packet into the water at the bottom of the bowl, as before; but this time a roaring, watery froth and flume erupted violently almost before I touched the handle, as if my offering was being snatched away in a fit of pique. When the foam subsided, the packet was gone; but as I lingered a few moments I thought I could hear a distant, responding cough or gurgle echoing through the building's old pipes.

How long would I have to wait this time? Given the scope and effrontery of my latest request, I imagined it would certainly take longer than the last one—possibly forever. Had I known the true value of my request to the "other side," I would have been more impressed by my own *hubris*. Perhaps the more reasonable question would be to ask how long I was willing to wait before abandoning the experiment? I was pretty certain I could expect nothing that night but knew I wouldn't be able to bring myself to leave for work the next morning, a Friday, if I hadn't received a response. I decided to call in sick, leaving a message on my manager's work number, reasoning that the excuse that gave me a long weekend would be more plausible if I didn't wait until the last minute. That taken care of, I stripped down to my white T-shirt and boxers (I said they're not sexy, not that they aren't comfortable!), turned off the lights, lowered the shades over the two street-side windows next to the bed, and positioned myself for sleep.

It was still barely 9 o'clock, and I'd had no dinner (though I didn't really feel hungry), so it's not surprising that sleep did not come right away even though I was exhausted by the evening's excitement. From the windowsill closest to me, I picked up the remote for my thirteen-inch Sony TV that sat on the bookcase opposite the foot of the bed. Perhaps it was an ill-advised choice, but I landed on the local PBS station, which was showing *Nosferatu*—the silent 1922 German version of the Dracula story, with Max Schreck as the vampiric Count Orloff. It's my favorite version. I turned the volume down to eliminate the contemporary score (the original has been lost) and eventually drifted off to the flickering images of stacks of coffins and a dark, malevolent stranger.

It was just before dawn—about 5am I would guess—when I was awakened by a change in the atmosphere of the apartment. Maybe you've experienced what I'm talking about: being aroused by an awareness in your unconscious mind that something has happened. It's not as simple as hearing a noise, feeling a rise or lowering of air temperature, or a change of lighting sensed through closed lids, although any or all of these could be part of it. Whatever the cause, you wake suddenly, every sense alert, blood surging through a wildly beating heart.

I lay still in the dark room, listening. The TV was still on, and I recognized the stage set and PowerPoint slides for the self-help, touchy-feely, I'm-so-much-more-spiritually-advanced-than-you-are lecturer striding back and forth and flourishing his laser pointer. I felt for the remote among the folds of my blanket and switched the set off, triggering a "click" that sounded much too loud in the room that was otherwise silent but for my own breathing and heartbeat. As I slowly awoke to the atmosphere in the room, I could sense water nearby. Not a drip, more like a slosh. Yes, that was it: the subtler, almost undetectable sound of water moving back and forth, like the tiny laps of what had once been waves against the sandy shore of a protected cove, or the barely audible response of pond water to the slow sway of a carp's tail in a decorative pool. Occasionally a splat! of a small amount of water falling from a height.

I had enough sense to consider the most likely causes first: the airshaft window was open, and it was raining; I hadn't turned off the water in the sink completely after brushing my teeth. But even as my mind ran through the possibilities, I knew none of them were the cause.

I sat up and swung my legs over the side of my bed so that my feet rested on the floor, startled by the film of cold liquid that wet my bare feet. I never thought to turn on my bedside lamp. Still disoriented, groggy, shivering in my skimpy clothing despite the late-summer warmth, I began to feel my way in the dark toward the closed bathroom door. I reached instinctively for the kitchen towels as I passed the stove, laying them on the floor ahead of me to create some traction on the slippery tiles. I unlatched the bathroom door and reached through to find the light switch.

In the initial strobes of the faltering fluorescents, everything at first seemed normal but for the somewhat dirty-looking water on the floor. A glance at the dully gleaming Mallard gave no hint of anything amiss. As the light steadied I realized that the bathtub was the source of the water; it was full to the brim with a brownish-gray, somewhat foamy liquid that was sloshing slowly back and forth—the noise I'd been able to hear from my bed—in small waves that crested at each end of the tub and splashed over the edge onto the floor. But what stopped me in my tracks—I even choked out a strangled yelp—was the sight of a human hand gripping the tub's rim.

Have you ever experienced a moment of emergency when you can't seem to make yourself move? Perhaps your mind is so boggled that it loses the will to control your limbs, or maybe the urge to rush to the rescue is exactly as powerful as the urge to flee, and the conflict renders you motionless as a statue. For whatever reason, I stood stock still in the bathroom doorway for far longer than I should have. When I finally took two rushed strides to the side of the bathtub, pulling more towels from the racks on the wall as I went, I tried to peer through the murky whatever-it-was—certainly not water, as it was filling the small room with an acrid odor like that of nail polish remover—to see what form might be attached to the hand and wrist, even as I gripped that hand firmly and pulled upward with all my strength. Meanwhile, the rational part of my brain was trying to organize the steps for rescue breathing for a drowning victim.

The forearm emerged from the scum, then the upper arm, then a shoulder. Already the musculature, the square jaw, the beard stubble told me the figure was male. The side of the neck, the side of the face, the head now emerging, bent back at the neck and hanging limp, dark long-ish hair trailing back into the muddy liquid to mingle with the sludge. I realized I wasn't going to be able to drag his whole body out of the tub by pulling on one arm, but if I slacked off to change position his head would slide under again. On the other hand, he wasn't choking or sputtering. He didn't seem to be breathing, either; he was probably already dead. With this thought I immediately felt a sense of relief. If he was already dead, there was nothing I could do that would harm him further. Whether I helped or didn't help made no difference.

I quickly walked my grip down his right arm to keep him from sinking as I dropped to my knees beside the tub. I reached across to where I assumed his other shoulder would be, hidden under the muck. With a hand under each arm, I was able to wrench his entire torso above the oil-slick surface and pull it toward me so that his head, shoulders, and arms, still limp, hung over the near edge of the tub.

Now that his face was safely above water, I collapsed backward, breathing heavily from the exertion of shifting a dead weight even a short distance. I knew I should probably be starting CPR, but it wasn't do-able with him in this position, and I knew I wasn't capable of getting his whole body out of the tub by myself.

I had a few seconds to decide what to do. Half of me hoped he had already expired; it really would be the simplest outcome. I'd made an effort to save him, whoever he was. I could call the police at this point with a clear conscience and make a credible claim of ignorance as to how he had entered the apartment—most likely through the open window to the airshaft, I would guess. The police would send someone to pick up the body, there would be some questions, and it would be over. Certainly, if I did anything other than call for help at this point, I would have to answer for my actions. But as the seconds ticked by, each story that ran through my head sounded less and less plausible. Did I really expect anyone to believe that a strange intruder would enter my apartment just to drown himself in my tub in some kind of chemical stew? And then there was this: during the struggle to raise his head above the surface of the fluid, I had briefly grasped his left hand, on the third finger of which the intruder was wearing something very much like my gold wedding band. It didn't demand notice in the rush of an emergency; plain gold bands are common enough as men's jewelry. But I found myself thinking of it now as more than a coincidence.

It was time to act, but I needed help. I stood and leaned over the tub, fishing with my fingers for the drain between the stranger's knees and hoping I didn't encounter anything too disgusting. I brought up a handful of what looked like common mud but smelled like a dead animal. I threw it in the wastebasket. I was glad to see the level of liquid in the tub begin to drop almost immediately. Satisfied that my visitor's head would not submerge if he slipped back into the tub, I returned to the kitchen, flipping on lights as I headed for the apartment's front door.

I shared the stair landing with three other apartments but knew only one of the residents well. Eduardo was a renter who had managed to hang on to his lease when the building went co-op. I knew he wouldn't be up at this hour; the sun wasn't yet above the horizon. But there was nothing for it. I'd have to try to wake him and try to do it without waking the rest of the building as well.

I pounded on his door with the softer surface of my fist. "Eduardo! Eduardo, are you in there?" I stage-whispered, imagining a configuration of my lips, tongue, and teeth that would send my voice through the steel-clad door directly to my neighbor's ears, without waking the other occupants.

There was the muffled "mumpf" of someone coming out of a sound sleep.

"Eddy, come to the door! I need your help!"

A groggy voice: "Wha? What happened?"

The seconds were still ticking away. I got louder, sharper. "Eddy, open the door! Please! I need you!"

Shuffling steps on the other side of the door. *Hurry up! Hurry up!* I heard Eddy fumbling inside with what New Yorkers call a "police lock," a metal bar that fits into an anchor in the floor about three feet away from the door; the other end fits into a bracket in the center of the door itself. It's designed to prevent bad guys from forcing their way into your apartment with a battering ram and murdering you in your sleep. Maybe the locks had saved some lives; in the current situation I imagined it being the cause of losing one, and silently cursed the clumsiness of both the device and its operator.

Finally, the door clattered open. Eddy glared at me from his threshold, standing in bare feet and wearing a thin robe that he hadn't taken time to tie closed, rubbing an eye with one fist and gripping the smaller end of a baseball bat with the other. *He stopped to put on a robe?* I must have been a frightening specter in my boxers and a T-shirt half-soaked with filthy water, and smears of black sludge on my arms and legs.

"Hurry!" I begged in a whisper, grabbing his unencumbered arm at the wrist and trying to drag him toward my door. How many minutes had passed? There was a moment while I watched him make a sleepy choice whether to hit me over the head with the bat or allow himself to be dragged wherever I was taking him; was relieved when I saw his eyes clear and he stepped forward, dropping the bat on the landing with a clatter that I was sure could be heard down to the first floor. I guess my outfit, too informal for social calls, had convinced him there was an emergency.

I dragged him toward my bathroom, gibbering words like "accident," "slipped," "knocked his head," hoping the confusion of the early morning would mask the improbability of the story I was spinning. When we got to the door of the bathroom Eddy stopped short and stared at the filthy scene.

My visitor was exactly as I had left him, but now I saw the situation through Eddy's eyes. Scummy liquid and dirty towels covered the floor. The figure in the tub, who appeared to be dead, was streaked with the same black goo that was smeared on my shirt and bare arms; his lower half, now visible resting in the muck left behind by the draining water, was even filthier. It must have looked as though the two of us had been mud wrestling in the tub; certainly the "slipped in the shower" scenario I had been trying to spin couldn't explain the mess. It had to have been obvious to Eduardo that I was making my story up as I went along. What he didn't know is that I was doing so to protect him from the truth, which in this case was so much stranger than any fiction I could dream up.

I watched his face while he made another decision, sure that "accessory to murder" was one of the thoughts I saw flit across it. When his expression softened, I knew he was going to help me, but as I followed his gaze I froze with shock once again. Eddy was staring at the figure's groin, where a pair of white cotton briefs had, in spite of the muck, turned virtually transparent from their soaking, thus revealing in great detail what they had been designed to hide. But I was shaken by a different realization: I was pretty sure I recognized his dirt-caked underwear as the RoxSox Racontour Basic Brief.

"Where do you want him?" said Eddy.

We managed to wrestle the body over to the bed and flop him on top of an old sheet I had quickly spread over the clean bedding. I pressed a twenty into Eddy's hand and hustled him toward the door, then decided I'd better add another when he raised one eyebrow and resisted my push at the threshold.

"Eddy," I whispered from my doorway as he headed across the landing back toward his own apartment, "Don't mention this to anyone, OK? He'll be fine—it was just an accident, a lovers' quarrel." I ha-ha'd nervously. Eduardo knew I didn't have a lover.

He turned to me, then glanced down at the forty bucks in his fist. "Sure. Let me know if you need any more help."

I stood at the foot of my bed and simply looked at the stranger for a while. I no longer feared he was dead; I had noticed a rapid flickering of his eyeballs under his closed lids while we were moving him, as one's eyes are said to move while dreaming, or as you can observe in a child who's only pretending to sleep. I still didn't know how he had survived what surely was at least several minutes submerged in that fetid liquid. But now, lying unconscious on the bed on his back, positioned as Eddy and I had left him—his right leg bent slightly at the knee, his left arm flung carelessly over his head—he would have appeared the prototypical image of the peaceful sleeper if it weren't for the dirt slowly drying on his skin and hair and the cold, pale, blue-green tone of his skin.

He was handsome—there was no doubt about that, even through the grime: strong features, a well-muscled torso. His nose was Roman, starting high between his brows and running straight and true toward his lips, which were full without seeming feminine. His brow was dark above deep-set eyes, where his lids were fringed with long, delicate lashes that gave his face a sensitivity it wouldn't have had otherwise. Cheek and jaw were covered by dark stubble that looked as dangerous as a wire brush, especially in contrast with the fragile, almost translucent quality of the skin underneath.

It was the skin that seemed wrong, so unnatural, too fragile for the job it was asked to do; more like the skin of a newborn than an adult. I feared that, if I touched him, his skin might stick to my fingers like the top layer of a baklava and come away from his body when I withdrew my hand. Or maybe that's not right; its texture looked spoiled rather than crisp, reminding me of a purple-white streaked heirloom tomato I had seen once that was rotting from the inside out, the way tomatoes do, almost retaining their unblemished appearance until, at the gentlest touch, they burst in your hand with a gush of reeking, putrefied innards. It seemed impossible that the stranger's skin held together over his strong neck and muscled shoulders, chest, and arms. The plane of his pectoral muscles crested, then dove to his stomach as if over a cliff, then further down across his ridged abdominals and over the foothills of his obliques, which formed a perfect arrowhead pointing straight to his groin as they slipped beneath the waistband of his briefs. As is the nature of an eddy in a stream, the underwear had collected a large amount of the dirt that had been left in the tub when it drained. His thick thighs with their curving sinews emerged from the leg holes of the muddy underwear, flowing toward the angles of his knees and ankles like the exposed roots of an ancient tree.

Beautiful as this creature was, I realized as I looked around my apartment what a near-fiasco his arrival had been. Beyond the filthy, unconscious figure sprawled awkwardly on my bed in a mess of dirty sheets, damp and muddy towels were scattered across the floor between puddles of sludge. The bathroom looked like the set for a disaster movie (except for the Mallard, which appeared as pristine as ever and nearly thrummed with phosphorescent self-satisfaction). And I myself was still wearing the muck-smeared T-shirt and boxer shorts I had been sleeping in when the whole incident started. The frantic string of events that had been set in motion by my discovery were over for the moment; I needed to restore some normalcy, some order.

For once I was grateful the apartment was small. It took only a few minutes to wipe the floors from one end to the other. The bathroom took a bit more effort but was soon made presentable; a thorough cleaning would have to wait for later. I knew I should take a shower to get rid of the brown sludge stink that I imagined lingered on my skin, but I couldn't be out of sight of my visitor for that long; I didn't want to miss any movement or change in his demeanor. I gave myself a sponge bath with a facecloth, applied some deodorant, and put on clean underwear, T-shirt, and walking shorts.

Now what? There were no further signs of life from my mud-smeared visitor, who still lay in a foul nest of dirty sheets, the last evidence of his unconventional arrival. I realized that I could probably wash him the same way I had cleaned myself, and it would be a lot more pleasant for him, when he awoke, to find himself somewhat clean and in a tidy bed rather than in his current state. It would be more pleasant for me, too, and would give me something to do while I waited.

I filled my pasta pot half full of warm water at the kitchen sink, fetched a clean facecloth and my bar of French lavender soap from the bathroom, and sat on the bed near his shoulder. His trip from tub to bed, with Eddy at his feet and I at his head, had been a pretty bumpy one as we navigated through doorways and past furniture; I was pretty sure he was not going to be awakened by a sponge bath. Still, I hung back. I'd never had contact with him while I was in any state other than panic. Now, to deliberately choose to touch his reeking hair (clogged, as it was, with clumps of tub muck) and pale, tissue-delicate skin (which I still found slightly revolting) while he was unconscious seemed to shift the tone of our interaction from supportive to invasive.

It had to be done. I touched him gently at first in neutral spots (wrist, shoulder) and brushed the damp hair away from his eyes. When, as expected, he didn't react, I grew bolder, lifting the entire length of his arm and letting it drop back down on the bed, grasping his ankle and shaking his limp foot like a rattle. I discovered that it peeved me to see him just lying there, silent, betraying not the slightest awareness of my presence. He was like a marionette that had been tossed carelessly on the bed, awaiting the puppeteer who would make real this simulacrum of a living thing.

I wished he would wake up. All the waiting had become tedious, and I realized that, without any conscious decision on my part, my prodding and manipulations were becoming more abusive than helpful. When I grabbed a knot of his hair and slapped him hard across the face, the smack of my fingers connecting with his cheekbone shocked me out of a reverie and back to the task at hand. I soaped the facecloth and began to wash the brownish shadow from his deep-set eyes and their fringe of lashes. I was relieved when the rough cloth didn't tear his skin; the more so as I discovered the tenaciousness of the dirt that had dried in the tiny crevices of his ears and nostrils. Moving on to the broader planes of his body, I used long strokes of the wet cloth to sweep the mud from his neck, chest, shoulders, arms and hands, where fine, pale hairs caught specks of dirt near their roots, lifting each as one would when bathing a baby or, more similarly, a corpse.

It was heavy work. The cloth had to be rinsed frequently and the pot refilled with clean water. He was a dead weight I had to roll back and forth along the horizontal axis and lift along the vertical. I was sweating as I moved down his torso and reached the waistband of his briefs.

The logical and practical thing would have been to immediately remove them and continue the washing process. But with the stranger still unconscious, that would be a further violation—one that would be irreversible, as I didn't see a way of removing the briefs without cutting through the waistband. I doubted I could wrestle them off of him in one piece. Would I be able to explain my actions to this visitor when he finally awoke and found himself naked? Was there a possibility that my effort and intentions could be misinterpreted?

I stepped back to assess my current situation. There was a strange man, dressed only in his underwear, lying unconscious on my bed. I had no idea how he had entered my apartment or why he ended up in the tub, immersed in some foul liquid. I didn't know where the rest of his clothes were, or what had happened to put him in his current physical state. I was unqualified to determine whether he had internal injuries, though it seemed to me more likely than not. It was entirely possible that he was severely injured, perhaps in a coma, and needed immediate medical treatment. He hadn't stirred or given any sign of life other than the flickering of his eyes behind closed lids for at least an hour now. And yet what was I doing? I was washing him down with scented soap and debating with myself whether to remove and destroy his underwear, the only clothing he had (as far as I knew).

Why hadn't I called 911? Why had I sent Eduardo away with a handful of bills that were obviously given for no other purpose than to buy his silence? What was I afraid of, or trying to conceal? Did I really think the magnificent creature lying helpless in my bed had been sent to me by whatever was speaking from beyond the Mallard's watery portal? Did I imagine he was going to be—for want of a more specific term— my boyfriend? I shifted my examination to my own pudgy, middle-aged body, experiencing the familiar cringe of distaste. I couldn't help but focus on how my sweat-dampened T-shirt emphasized my sagging chest, or how it clung to the bulge of my stomach above the low-slung

waistline of my shorts. I couldn't even see my own feet or meager
calves and thighs without effort. I had an indelible image in my mind of
the reflected profile I had glimpsed in a thousand chanced-upon
mirrors and store windows, where I recognized in my posture the lazy
S-curve of middle-aged despondence: rounding shoulders, flaccid
stomach, a body weighted down with age and failure. I drew myself up,
pushed my shoulders back, clenched my abdominals beneath the flab;
but no amount of "sucking it in" was going to refute what I had seen in
those mirrors. Did I really think Cesar was going to be attracted to me?
Confronted with his physical near-perfection, I realized—as I had
many times before—that my attraction to the ideal male form wasn't
simple admiration but envy: I wanted to *be* the person I admired as
much as I wanted to possess him. I desperately wanted to inspire in
others the kind of obsessive desire I felt for the still figure splayed
across my bed.

My actions during the events of the morning had not been
reasonable or rational—I know that now, even if I'd deluded myself at
the time—and couldn't be misinterpreted. The worst possible
conclusion would be the most accurate one: in failing to seek medical
or other help for this man—if that's what he was—I had, for all intents
and purposes, made him my prisoner, stripped him of his freedom of
movement, made him subject to my questionable decisions. I had taken
advantage of his helplessness while he was physically unable to express
his approval or objection. If I took the action I was now contemplating
I would make it worse. The only excuse I had for these thoughts was
this: I knew with absolute certainty that he had been sent to me, and I
intended to keep him.

There was a reason he was there, connected somehow to the
offering I'd made through the numinous Mallard. And I had
approached the whole affair with such purity of heart, such a generosity
of spirit, how could it all end with an unconscious body lying on my
bed? There had to be something more that was supposed to happen
between us, me and this pale-fleshed young man. Wasn't he wearing my
gold wedding band (which I'd examined closely when I was washing his
hand) on his finger? Wasn't he wearing the RoxSox Racontour brief I'd
admired in the catalog, identifiable even in its sad, filthy state? And
what about the swollen, scuffed area of skin over his right triceps
muscle—the only place on his body with anything resembling a normal
skin tone—that I'd also noticed while bathing him. Wasn't that exactly
where the tattoo that I'd excised from the photo would have been? No,

it wasn't possible that these were all coincidences. I was certain this was Cesar; he had been sent in answer to my prayers, and therefore nothing I might do to fulfill our destiny could be improper.

I went to the table and found my kitchen shears where I'd left them the night before. Returning to the bed, I quickly slipped my left index finger under the waistband of Cesar's briefs at the spot where there was the least amount of fabric, a point low on his left hip. Pulling the fabric up and away to keep plenty of space between the shears and his skin, I slid the scissors into position and cut. To minimize damage to the underwear, I'd decided to cut just one side so the brief could be removed by dragging it down Cesar's right leg. His body, still lying mostly supine on the bed, was now fully naked.

If you do an internet search for the phrase "Love is in the details," you'll find that Oprah Winfrey is credited with originating the phrase. A similar aphorism, "God is in the details," is credited variously to Mies van de Rohe or Nietzsche, or described simply as "an old German saying." Whatever the idea's origin, I have, at times, found myself in the grip of a passionate "love" that arose from something others had not even noticed. I put "love" in quotes because it's not the right word; "fetishist" is the closest I can come in English. The specific arrangement of a freckle relative to the corner of a bottom lip on the face of a stranger, for example; or a disorderly trail of dark hair that runs down a man's lower back and disappears into his clothing at the waist. A slightly-built, unusually small work colleague once brought something to my desk that he wanted advice on. I was useless to him as a critic and, once he left, couldn't recall what we had talked about. I had watched, fascinated, while he pointed to one area of his presentation after another with a tiny, perfectly manicured index finger. It was all I could manage to resist the urge to seize his hand and cover it with kisses; explore the mysteries of his cupped palm with my tongue; enclose with my lips each digit, sucking on it in turn. At such moments I can be said to be present only in the corporeal sense. Otherwise I have no thoughts—none, at least, that I can recall when I emerge from my trance—and no awareness of place or time.

The naked human body presents many such opportunities for study and observation. In its holes and hollows, in its plains and peaks, there's enough to occupy the careful observer for weeks at a time. Such was certainly the case with Cesar, whose complete details I had just uncovered—or so I thought. I examined him once more then, as he lay naked on my bed, seeing his complete-ness for the first time. Without the distraction of what were once his white briefs, I could finally appreciate the exquisite nature of his form on my own terms, without interference or the need to ask permission. Having gone so far in my violation of his privacy and disrespect for his basic human rights, I had nothing additional to lose by going further, which I had every intention of doing.

First, though, I wanted to take a few minutes to look around me and take note of the small details I instinctively knew I would want to remember on some future date. I noted the muck that still coated the floor of my apartment. The dirty, tangled sheets that covered the bed I've already mentioned. Whatever foul-smelling fluid it was that had supported Cesar's incubation—if, in fact, that's the correct way to describe what he had been through—had either drained away somewhere or had formed small puddles at low points in the uneven floor. I caught sight of the Mallard through the open bathroom door; it appeared to have been untouched by the events of the last hour.

I stood back to admire my work. The sun had risen far enough to steal through the wall of high-rise apartment houses along the East River, and slanting bars of unfocused morning light leaked around the edges of my window shades to stripe the bed blanket with slashes of color. The sounds of morning, too, floated up five stories from the street, even through the closed windows: the clip-clop of the carriage horses heading to the park from their stable on Eleventh Avenue, the incessant honking of cabs, the high-pitched screams of children playing tag on the crowded sidewalk as they headed to school for a hot breakfast. As I watched Cesar slumber (for want of a better word), I couldn't help thinking *this is our first morning together.*

Suddenly, I lost my desire to see him naked. He seemed so trusting, so completely relaxed as he lay on the bed; I even imagined that I saw the hint of a smile on his lips, as though he was having a pleasant dream. I couldn't take advantage of him, even if he *had* been sent to me as a present, with implied permission to do with him what I would. I leaned across his chest to reposition his damaged underwear. I figured I could find a needle and thread somewhere with which I could effect an emergency repair.

But there was still one discordant note in the tableau I'd created. The hair on Cesar's head, which I had thought could wait to be cleaned until I could get him into a shower, was still matted with goo from the tub. With no evidence of imminent change in his condition, I realized there was nothing for it: I would have to tackle his hair as he lay there.

I gathered a couple of the already-dirty towels and one large clean one, another fresh pot of warm water, and my own hairbrush. I sat on the bed with Cesar's head resting on the dirty towels in my lap and used the saturated washcloth to drip water through the curled strands at his hairline. There appeared to be a layer of dirt just behind that edge, on his forehead, but no matter how diligently I scrubbed with the cloth the dark color of his scalp remained. As the hair became wetter and less muddy, it separated into groups of strands through which I began to discern a geometry in the shapes of darker color.

I stopped washing for a moment to consider what I had discovered. I was beginning to suspect that my snipping of the catalogue photo had not eliminated all of the tattoos from Cesar's body. I had heard stories of kids who, in the unbridled, careless enthusiasm of youth, had shaved their heads and gotten scalp tattoos spelling out "fuck you" or some other clever phrase. Later, upon discovering the (mostly financial) advantages of conforming to society's conventions and expectations, they allowed their hair to grow to hide their indiscretion and took jobs in the industries they used to despise. But the tattoo was still there, waiting to be revealed by a receding hairline or discovered by someone like me.

I was angered and disappointed to think that Cesar might have succumbed to this childish, cultish fad. What message had he thought so important that he had it tattooed on his scalp? I had an impulse to snatch up the shears that now lay on the nightstand and cut the hair away from his forehead; fortunately, I rejected the idea as too invasive, even for me. I moved from under his head to a position where I could more easily pick through the threads of his hair. There was a vertical line near the center of his forehead which, as I pulled the strands of hair to one side, then the other, I could see was connected to a downward slanting mark at its top end. *It's an M*, I thought. I worked toward his left side next. Another vertical line but intersected by three horizontal bars—an E. further to his left, another vertical line, this time without any intersecting bars. An I? MEI? *What word ends with MEI? Something Japanese….* Wait—there *was* a bar, at the very top: a T.

"Met," I whispered.

A sudden and violent convulsion wracked Cesar's body and I jumped back in a panic. What little color had been in Cesar's skin quickly began to drain from it.

I didn't know what to do. It was obvious that something had happened to suddenly change Cesar's condition for the worse. Could it be connected to the word or words written indelibly on his scalp? Is that why they were concealed? I had to find out, and quickly.

I moved back to the side of the bed and began to search through his hair again. Desperate for a clue, I ran through the territory I'd already covered to make sure I hadn't been mistaken. No, the letters were definitely M-E-T. Was there anything on the other side of the M? I frantically searched through the strands flowing from his scalp. His skin was growing cold. Three bars: another E. Anything else? I didn't see any further traces of ink stain. E-M-E-T? What did it mean? A name?

I leaned close to Cesar's ear and twitching body and, in a voice fractured by tension, took my best guess at pronunciation: "Emet, wake up!"

Cesar's eyes flew open and stared into mine. They were the color of old honey.

"Hello, Michael," he said.

***

This isn't the end of my story, nor of Cesar's. But it *is* the point at which a prudent narrator, sharing this story as an after-dinner tale for the edification of friends, might excuse himself to use the restroom, duck out the exit, and disappear. To stay would almost certainly be to run the risk of being labeled a fantasist at best and a liar at worst. To dwell on the lugubrious specifics of what would turn out to be a relatively short love affair between Cesar and me would be to re-tell an all-too-familiar story of initial passion, eventual disappointment, and ultimate abandonment, and to draw it out beyond the point at which it's of any real interest. Likewise, to reintroduce the supernatural aspects of the narrative—which is to say, the religious aspects—would run the risk of giving unintended offence to believers and what might be seen as mocking succor to those in doubt.

I suppose I could provide one or two additional clues for those among you who refuse to be satisfied with only as much as I'm readily willing to share. First, remember that names are the easiest "facts" to change in any story. Of course, my visitor's real name was not Cesar, but neither was it—and this may surprise you—EMET. It was Herschel. I wouldn't go around saying "EMET" out loud, though; the consequences may surprise you.

It took me only a week or so of sharing my small co-op to realize that I was never going to be able to ignore the pronounced lisp in Herschel's speech, nor could I overcome my irritation over the fact that

Herschel's intellect had the approximate sophistication of a potato. I felt I had been misled by the exchange of *Tosca* programs; Herschel didn't know the difference between an aria and a police siren. I was baffled by his penchant for taking long baths in a tub full of cold, almost freezing, water. It seemed out of character, given the way he was brought into the world.

Then there was the issue of Herschel's skin. The slightest friction would cause him to lose layers of that fragile, pale green film that seemed always to be wet. In spite of his frequent bathing, Herschel never seemed to smell fresh; he always had a lingering air of sourness about him, and eventually I had to face the fact that Herschel was spoiling, like week-old lettuce that's under-refrigerated. Times being what they were, gossip had it that whatever was wrong with Herschel was the result of him being HIV+, which was simply not true.

I got a call from Nate one morning to tell me that he had heard that Herschel was dead. I hadn't seen him for about eight weeks at that point—not since he and Nate had starting dating. Nate described it as a freak accident, that Herschel had been heading home on foot late one night after an evening spent at several Lower East Side clubs, where other patrons had complained that he smelled bad. Outside one club, he was confronted by a group of exuberant twenty-three-year-olds who, not knowing how fragile Herschel was, picked him up and dropped him in a garbage dumpster that had been left on a side street. Herschel was too weak to climb out, and no one heard his calls for help, if he'd made any. Nate said he suspected Herschel had ended up in the Fresh Kills landfill on Staten Island.

I had a falling out with my neighbor, Eduardo, when I learned that he and Herschel had had a brief affair a couple of weeks after Herschel arrived. It was a one-night stand; Eduardo confessed to me (once we were talking again) that he couldn't stand the way Herschel had smelled.

"Can I tell you something," I said, "and you promise you won't laugh? I think Herschel had an expiration date."

"Well, of course...I mean, don't all boyfriends..."

"No, that's not what I mean. I mean he literally had an expiration date. Did you ever notice the string of numbers tattooed on the bottom of his right foot? That's what I think they were. There was never a chance that Herschel was going to stay with me long-term. That had been determined by someone—or something—long before we even met, maybe years ago."

"Wow. If that's so," Eduardo said, "You have the worst luck with love of anyone I know."

"Love? Don't talk to me about love. As far as I'm concerned, love stinks."

A Short Lesson in Greek

You're three hours into it—the bus ride from Athens to Igoumenitsa—with four hours to go. As far as you can tell, you're the only foreigner on the bus. The other passengers have been gawking at you the whole time; they'll gawk for the whole seven-hour trip. Maybe it's because tourists don't normally ride this bus; once clear of Athens, you'd swear it's stopping at every cross street. Or maybe they gawk because you look like someone who's life has nearly reached bottom and you've forgotten how to bounce. Like somebody who's spent the night on a bench in the bus station, policing for half-smoked butts to get through it all.

They all look the same to you. their faces swim in and out of your field of vision. You glare back at them. You don't even have to think about it to realize who they remind you of. It's Androu. Man, woman, child—they're all Androu. Even the two chickens in a cage on an old woman's lap remind you of him. They turn their heads from side to side in sudden, jerky movements, studying you with one eye, then the other. You shift in your seat, trying to find a position where you don't have to look at anyone, where the ancient steel springs don't feel as though they're burrowing into the flesh of your thighs. I'll bet they can smell him on me, you think— his oily sweat, the slow-drying residue of semen on his clothes. Maybe it's *your* sweat they smell. So what? You're guessing no one on this bus has had a good wash-up this week.

What are you staring at? That's what you want to scream. WHAT THE FUCK ARE YOU ALL STARING AT? But you don't speak Greek, and you'd bet a million bucks none of them speak English.

I think we have something in common. That was what he'd said. His voice was soft, heavily accented, confident. You realize now that he must have had the whole thing planned before he ever spoke to you. He probably had someone to teach him the ropes. Choose the foreigner, the one who's alone, they'd tell him. A tourist, obviously.

And you played along, thinking you were so—what would you call it? *Cosmopolitan.* There's a good Greek word.

He may as well have been Tony, you say to yourself.

Wait, where'd that come from? You haven't thought about Tony in years. You remember that first summer at Boy Scout camp? What were you then—eleven? Twelve? You were up every day before the pool officially opened, doing endurance laps, prepping for the mile swim later in the season. Tony was the morning lifeguard, eighteen years old, from Baltimore. You remember? He opened the gate for you an hour before he was supposed to. You swam back and forth in the outdoor pool's unheated water, the sound of campers outside the chain-link fence dulled as it washed in and out of your ears; you reveled in the luxury of having the whole pool to yourself. Tony counted your laps while he washed down the deck with a hose, his index finger half-covering the nozzle to make the spray stronger. When you'd been swimming for an hour or so you'd call out to him after every few turns, Tony, how many is that? and he'd pretend he'd lost count. Sorry, you'll have to start over, he'd yell back, and you'd stop and tread water until the two of you agree on a number.

If only Tony could have been satisfied with that. The adolescent roughhousing with the counselors, no one reading too much into the sexual aspects of the play. No one worried about the occasional crotch grab or the frequent "pantsing" battles that took place in the pool, started by one troop and prosecuted by another until everyone had the chance to display their wares.

Then there was the morning Tony was late opening up, and you stood shivering outside the gate while you waited for him. You knew he would come. When he finally arrived, he was barely dressed. He was wearing his tennis shoes, but the laces weren't tied and, as far as you could tell, he didn't have his socks. The waistband of his jock strap was clearly visible in the V formed as a result of his white shorts being un-zipped half way, the loose ends of his belt dragging on the lightweight fabric. His T-shirt was wadded-up in one hand; he looked tired and out of breath. And *angry.* You'd never seen him angry before. You kind of tip-toed as you went about preparing for your workout, and when you called out to ask him how many laps you had left he didn't answer.

Finally, as you were toweling-off, Tony called you over to where he was washing down the deck. You thought he was finally ready to play some of the special games the two of you had devised during his long hours supervising the camp's pool, but his conversation headed off in a new and unexpected direction.

C'mere, he said.

No—it's a trick, you said.

No, really, c'mere.

You kept an eye on the running hose in his right hand and inched nearer.

Come on, Davey! Get over here. He pointed to a spot two feet in front of him. I'm not going to hurt you.

You were uncertain what to do. He'd never spoken to you before with the annoyed tone you detected in his voice. You stood where he pointed; he reached forward with his left hand and teased the extra folds of your ancient green-striped knit bathing suit out of your clenched fist; the bedraggled knit swooped low across your belly. He pushed six inches of the streaming hose down the front of your suit, left it hanging on the useless waistband. Cold mountain water rushed over your bald genitals (your father called them plunkies, remember?), flowed across balls shrunken to the size of chickpeas by the chill, and from there ran down the inside of your skinny thighs to puddle on the spotless deck. Tony stepped back to admire his arrangement; you dared not move. If this was a new game, you didn't know the rules.

How does that feel? he said.

Okay. You were unable to come up with a better answer on the spot; you didn't know what Tony wanted. All you knew was that you didn't want him to take the hose away; the rush of water, cold as it was, still excited you. You felt your dick beginning to stiffen and jerk.

When you gonna get some hair down here, Tony said, stretching your suit's waistband well beyond its remaining capacity and leaning forward to get a good look. Shit, my *sister's* dick is bigger'n yours.

Yeh? you said. Her beard's probably longer and darker too. Then the two of you just stood there and watched each other, neither of you moving, neither of you knowing what would happen next.

I have to go, you said, finally. They're waiting for me.

What if you hadn't gone? What if you'd decided you were going to stay—stay with Tony, I mean. Y'know, like he told you, the first summer of camp, that if you ever needed help with your merit badges or anything, you could come by his cabin after dinner. They're supposed to do stuff like that—the counselors. They're supposed to help you. With your merit badges.

The bus hits a pothole and you're temporarily airborne, then come down hard on your aching tailbone. FUCK! That's going to leave a bruise. It does bring your attention back to the current problem, though.

You have to admit you've been a little directionless for the last couple of years. Initially, everyone was supportive when you said you wanted to take some time off before starting college, but after you'd missed a couple of deadlines for reenrollment, they began to drop hints that made it clear they thought it was time for you to move on. You were idly paging through other applicants' profiles on LinkedIn, the career management website, hoping to stumble across the magic bullet that would make your applications irresistible to college admissions committees, when you realized there *was* something in your background you might be able to leverage. There seemed to be a lot of people— nearly 200,000 in fact, once you'd run a search—who claimed in their profile to be an Eagle scout. You weren't sure whether, at that great a number, it still represented an advantage over non-scouts, but then you had to remember that the database is international. The 200,000 gleaned from the search might represent less than ten percent of the site's subscribers.

You'd never made it to Eagle; you'd quit scouting at Life, one level below the ultimate prize, for reasons you really didn't want to explain. But when you added in a few of the extra merit badges you'd already earned, you realized that you were within striking distance of Eagle if you could focus on the task for the rest of the summer. You didn't have the Citizenship in the World badge, one of thirteen core badges that were required in order to be promoted, so that one was definitely "in." Maybe, since you'd been out of the process for a while, you could start with a couple of easy ones, like Dog Care and Cooking, then end with a flourish by finishing Citizenship, tying it in with your planned trip to Greece. What better background for your final report than the Parthenon in Athens. You would have only one shot at it, though. You'd turn eighteen in late August, and you'd no longer be eligible to earn merit badges.

So, that's how you happened to be in Greece, in Athens, touring its acropolis. From one perspective, its steep slope could be any indistinct jumble of rocks and boulders. You know better. Even in ruins, if you shift your perspective slightly you can discern the traces of nobility in the pick-up-sticks pile you're resting on. Thanks to having done your homework for the merit badge, you're able to reconstruct in your mind's eye, one pillar at a time, some of the smaller temples. The limestone boulders give back the warmth they've soaked up during the August day. Actors are running through a late-afternoon rehearsal of a tragedy in the theatre of Dionysus, just below. Let's say it's *Oedipus Rex;* it doesn't really matter. Sightseers, a mix of locals and tourists, stop for a minute, drawn by the flurry of activity, then grow bored and wander away. It's hard for you to stay awake with the warm boulder against your back and the sound of the actors droning away in Greek.

You must have dozed off behind your sunglasses, because the next thing you know this guy is standing nearby, talking to you in approximate English about the two of you having something in common. You don't have a clue what he's talking about; he's obviously not American. He's older, Greek, dressed neatly, like an office worker rather than the typical poor-student-touring-Europe-for-the-summer T-shirt and jeans *you're* wearing. But you play along. Maybe this nosy little Greek can come up with something interesting to do.

So Androu, which is how he introduces himself, has moved his perch to the same chunk of rock you've been occupying. He's chattering along, telling you his story about being an instructor at the University, claiming that at first he'd thought you were one of his students. He probably notices you're losing interest. He turns to face you and asks whether you know who Socrates was. Sure, you say— allegory of the cave, and all that. Well, no he says, that was actually Plato, one of Socrates' students. But Socrates met with his students right here, in the woods at the bottom of this hill. Philipapou, it's called. Then he asks if you'd like to see the exact spot.

Why not, you say. It doesn't sound all that interesting, but it's better than listening to more of the broken English version of his life story. Besides, you've got nothing better to do while you're waiting for the tourist bus that will take you back to the hostel. And if it turns out he really *is* an instructor at the University it might be fun to have a free local guide while you're in Athens.

The sun is low in the sky; its weak light is almost completely lost as the two of you enter the forest. You stumble along the narrow path, trying to keep up with the sure-footed Androu, who seems to know the route by heart. At one point he pauses and wraps his left arm around your waist. You push him away, say What the fuck? and he says, Keep me this way. It takes you a few seconds to figure out he means hold on to him, but you're not sure whether he's offering stabilizing support or something else.

Maybe you're being over-sensitive, having had to deal with memories of Tony coming to the fore. You've seen small conversation groups of Greek men in the city's squares and plazas, standing around with their arms draped across each other's shoulders. Androu seems just as casual; he repositions his arm and says This is the way we do it—friends!

You begin to wonder whether any sightseeing is actually going to be possible under the quickly darkening skies.

Are you sure you know where you're going? you ask. No response. You walk a bit farther.

You know, you say, I think I've done enough sightseeing for today. Androu is silent, but he releases his hold on your waist. Suddenly, you're weightless. In the utter blackness of the night, you can't tell up from down. You begin to suspect you've made a big mistake.

You feel more than see Androu swivel around, mid-sentence in his lecture on Greek philosophers, and pin your arms to your side. At first you think he's going to try to rob you (Ha! Your pockets are empty). Now that you're face to face, Androu mashes his thin lips against yours and you gag as the fat slug of his tongue tries to press past your teeth. His breath stinks of acrid Greek herbs, stale cigarettes, and the pungent remains of the glass of retsina he'd consumed earlier—all vinegar and rot. You find he's surprisingly strong for the short, aging, overweight, college-lecturer type he claims to be. You're seventeen, almost six-two, and even at the end of a summer of scrimping on food on an already-meager travel budget, you should be able to escape his grip. As it is, the two of you are at a standoff. Then he pushes you backward; you catch your heel on an exposed tree root and sit down hard on your butt, collapse onto your back with Androu on top of you. He presses his new advantage, covering your face with drooling kisses, the fingers of his right hand scrabbling under the hem of your T-shirt at the fly button on your jeans as he dry-humps your leg. GET OFF OF ME, ASSHOLE! you yell, thinking you'll scare him away if you make enough noise.

The situation starts to feel more dangerous; you wonder if anyone will come looking for you if you don't come home, back to the hostel. You give up your yelling; you figure it's pointless since Androu makes no attempt to stop you. You're struggling with this little shit, he's groping your crotch, still holding you down with the weight of his body. All you can think about is getting away, but that conscious thought is contradicted by some pea-size gland in your brain that begins to leak its will-weakening steroid into your bloodstream. You're getting a hard-on.

You try again to roll away, infuriated by your body's betrayal and the knowledge that there's nothing you can do about it. Androu senses what's happened, recognizes the surrender that's communicated through almost imperceptible shifts in your breathing, the surface tension of your skin, your heartbeat. He gives up his effort on your fly, slides his whole hand down the front of your jeans.

This is the first time a stranger has touched your dick, and the sensation flashes through you like the recoil from a blow to the head. Every part of you is pulsing, each pulse pushing you closer to the loss of control that you fear and desire at the same time. From a disembodied distance, you watch yourself grasp Androu's swelling, unrevealed cock. You want to see it, this truncheon with which he would murder your innocence; you want to test its hardness, tease yet more stiffening blood into its flesh. Your climax comes almost immediately, and when it does you aren't looking at Androu; you're looking off into the darkness and disorientation of the woods.

Once again Androu slides his hand once more down the front of your jeans to find the hot puddle there, satisfying himself that your reaction was real, if brief.

You feel sick, scared, out-of-control; you're looking for a way to act out your rage. You want to smash Androu's soft, slobbering lips with your fist, break his pawing fingers with your own hands.

Your chance comes the next time he draws a breath. You punch upward as hard as you can with your free arm, catching him just under the chin.

His grip loosens entirely as the punch lands; he cries out and brings his hands up to protect his face. When he rolls to the side, you follow up with a hard slap to an exposed cheek. It feels good; you're tempted to hang around and hit him some more. Instead, you find your footing and make a quick decision to stumble-run as best you can down what you hope is a trail, going farther into the woods, figuring Androu won't follow toward the possibility of another blow. You trip, tumble, tear your shirt when it snags on a stump, lose a sandal thrashing through brush that seems to have sprung up specifically to block your way, then, a few steps later, losing the other one. After a minute, you stop to listen for clues as to what's going on behind you.

You can hear Androu calling your name in the distance. Da-veed! Da-veed! Don't run away. Come home with me—I'll make you some hot chocolate!

Yeah, like that's going to happen. What kind of rapist offers his victims hot chocolate? Sounds like the plot of a bad Tennessee Wiliams play.

So, that's how you ended up on the bus to Igoumenitsa. By the time you found your way back to your hostel, you'd missed curfew and were locked out. Shoeless, with only the torn and filthy clothes you were wearing, you couldn't present yourself at a hotel even if you had the money to pay for one. You'd always looked down on people sleeping on public benches or in the bus or train station; now those were the only places you could think of to go. Not that you slept. You re-played the events of the evening in your mind over and over, trying to understand what had happened. You found a toothbrush someone had left on the sink in the restroom and tried to scour away the taste of oregano and stale cigarettes. With wet paper towels, you rubbed at the dried semen spatters on your jeans, the dirt on your T-shirt. Your feet were cut and bleeding, but you could tell, in the fluorescent brightness of the restroom, that the injuries weren't serious. You used a roll of toilet paper to clean off dirt and blood as best you could; the makeshift bandages need only last until you could retrieve the First Aid kit you'd left in your backpack in one of the bus station's lockers. You were waiting outside the door of the hostel when they unlocked it early the next morning. You changed clothes, packed up, and paid your bill; you didn't even argue with the desk clerk over having to pay for the night you'd been locked out. The other men in your dorm reported that you seemed to be fixated on three sentences that you muttered to yourself over and over: I hate Athens. I hate Greece. I have to leave— immediately.

So that's pretty much where I lost track of you again. When I went to fetch you from the hostel, ready to try to introduce myself again, you'd already left. One of the other travelers told me you'd said something about heading toward Otranto. On the off chance he was right, I bought the last ticket for a seat on the only bus that travels there (though once it left Athens proper the driver seemed to ignore every traffic rule—especially those governing maximum number of passengers on buses). We made it to Otranto by the afternoon of the following day, but I still had not found a private moment to introduce myself as your coach for your Eagle Scout project. I guess I figured you would notice the large Boy Scouts of America emblem embroidered on the flap of my bag; if you did, you ignored it.

At the edge of the port, you hoisted your backpack and stuck out your thumb. You must have found a ride almost immediately; when I returned to the bus after claiming my duffel at customs, you had already disappeared. I cursed myself for not keeping closer tabs on you; I was afraid my task had become more difficult. My options were limited: I could try to continue hitchhiking, the method you had chosen (more for economic reasons than any other, I suspected) and hope to catch up with you by mingling with others you might have met. In my opinion, that approach had only a small chance of success for someone of my age, stature, and lack of experience as a detective. Or I could switch to the relative luxury of train travel, its higher speeds giving me more time to make and correct poor guesses as to where we might end up at the end of each twenty-four-hour period. Keeping track of you wasn't as difficult as I'd anticipated; you continued to play the ugly American, creating a scene at every opportunity, declaring loudly, for example, your distaste for anything Greek despite the fact that we were already in Italy.

That wasn't much to go on, but over the next three days I managed to stay one step ahead of you as you fled up Italy's eastern coast, through Brindisi, Foggia, Pescara, Rimini, and Bologna. These were nothing more than names to you; in most cases you passed through each city seeing only the ugliest aspects of it. You took no photographs, consulted no guidebooks. You traveled night and day, sleeping only when you got a ride—preferably in a truck, among whatever cargo was in the back, and out of reach of the driver. In my pursuit I relied on guesswork and intuition; I had no idea what your final intended destination was, or even if you had one. I was always surprised when my guesses as to your whereabouts turned out to be correct, though often it wasn't clear which of us was leading and which following. By day five, I had to acknowledge that the chase was becoming somewhat tedious, despite the freezing purity and drama of the Swiss scenery.

On day six I guessed that we were both in Basel, preparing to cross into Germany. Your trail had gone cold—let's say disappeared, in fact—when coincidence intervened again: to my shock, I recognized you among a group at the border crossing who were waiting to enter Germany on foot. I realized this might be my last chance to connect with you.

I'd rented a small gray Citroen just to get me over the Alps and had an empty passenger seat I used that as an enticement, asking if anyone in the group was headed (here I took my final guess) to Hamburg and in need of a ride. Once we were both seated comfortably in the car with your backpack in the trunk, you began to unspool your story more or less as I've captured it here. Of course, there are parts of it I know even better than you do…Davey.

I didn't recognize you immediately. The six years since I last saw you have turned you from a child into a young man, still not terribly attractive, to be honest, but you'll be okay once your skin clears up. Also, you're travelling as David, no-last-name, so the coin didn't drop when I was initially assigned to be your Eagle coach. Apparently, you never knew anything about my formal role in your project, either. I should have withdrawn, or at least announced myself, when I realized the true dynamics of the situation. But I had to know how much damage I'd caused—unintentionally, of course, but real just the same. I needed to know how far you'd run from your self-loathing. I don't feel guilt for leaving you alone on the shoulder of the Autostrada, shivering in a jacket too thin for the cold, your feet freezing in canvas sneakers wet from the puddles that formed at the edges of the plowed snow. I could insist that it's just another game, like the many that we invented and played beside the pool back at Beaver Lake. I think you finally realized that there was nowhere to go that would serve as an escape from what you had discovered about yourself.

As I pulled away, I saw the startled look on your face and I couldn't help lowering the passenger-seat window and calling out, you're going to make it, Davey! You have a Wilderness Survival merit badge to prove it. And, after all, haven't you just spent a week tracking me (or were you leading?) 2,200 miles across Europe? That achievement alone should be worth a Tracking badge.

As for Androu, it's true his actions were criminal. Yet, I can't stop re-playing the incident over and over again in the theatre of my mind, until memory mixes with invention in an infinite loop that becomes… I don't know; something different than either, I guess. Something true and untrue at the same time. For me it always ends the same way it did that humid night on Philipapou, while I was trapped by the weight of Androu's grunting carcass. I know I could flee the meaning of that moment for the rest of my life and never be free of it. It had always been and now always will be part of my nature—the "something in common" that Androu had seen immediately.

The Ice (Cream) Man Cometh

All of my announcements started like this:

"Ladies and gentlemen, may I have your attention, please!"

Farrell's Ice Cream Parlor offered a free sundae if you came in on your birthday. The catch was that you had to suffer through a raucous birthday announcement full of embarrassing schtick, delivered at your table along with the sundae and a verse of "Happy Birthday" shouted above the din of the dining room. All the waiters were expected to join in. On busy nights, I must have sung the song thirty or forty times. After three days on the job, that duty had already become perfunctory.

I worked as a waiter for six months at the Farrell's in the Fashion Valley mall in San Diego before starting graduate school. At twenty-six, I was the oldest and best-educated member of the staff, older even than the manager—a balding, stringy-haired potato who had some kind of condition that made him sweat constantly. Excepting the cashier, Farrell's employees were all male, which meant that the work atmosphere was roughly akin to that of a high school locker room. Farrell's corporate theme (no snickering, please) was "The Gay Nineties;" all the restaurants in the chain were decorated in dark wood, red vinyl upholstery, and a player piano on which patrons could play paper scrolls of 1890s hits like "A Bicycle Built for Two" for a nickel a pop, with the occasional Scott Joplin rag thrown in for good measure. In keeping with the theme, the waiters augmented their standard black pants and white shirt with suit vests they purchased second-hand at Goodwill and a company-issued weird little clip-on tie thing, the whole ensemble topped off with the Styrofoam version of a common turn-of-the-century straw hat called a boater.

Farrell's signature dish, acknowledging the restaurant's origins, was the San Diego Zoo. It had something like thirty scoops of ice cream, four bananas, and five different syrups and toppings. It was built in a large silver-colored bowl and decorated with a menagerie of small plastic animals, just the right size to choke on, that began to sink into the whipped cream as soon as they were added. Franchise standards for the Zoo specified that it was to be run around the restaurant on a two-man stretcher to the accompaniment of a hand-cranked firehouse siren before it was delivered to the customer's table; it became a race against time to do so before the last hard-plastic animal sank from sight beneath the warming perma-frost of toppings. I lobbied for an animals-in must-equal-animals-out policy, but it never caught on—for obvious reasons.

Thanks to the promotional free sundae that probably cost the restaurant less than a dollar to make, Farrell's was mobbed by birthday revelers most days of the week. If there were no birthdays to celebrate, they would come for the entertainment. And by entertainment, I mean the comically insulting birthday and other announcements that the waiters were encouraged to create, often linked to the franchise's specialty dishes like the Tin Roof or the Gibson Girl or—another of my favorites—the Pig Trough. At its heart it was simply an up-market double banana split, but it was, as the menu promised "Fit for a pig!"

I see or speak of the people I knew then less and less often, but when I do we often end up reminiscing about subjects like the jobs we had in college. I only have to remind them of my stint waiting tables at Farrell's to win the "coolest part-time job" category. Of course, it wasn't cool for me; all restaurant work is dirty, poorly paid, back-breaking labor. In spite of that, when someone asks me to do an announcement from my repertoire, I'll oblige with my Pig Trough for "John" a customer. It goes something like this:

"Ladies and gentlemen, may I have your attention, please! John came into Farrell's tonight, not to celebrate his birthday, but to make a gross and disgusting pig of himself by devouring one of Farrell's famous Pig Troughs. If you look closely you can still see his snout tracks at the bottom of the bowl."

At this point, the showman in me would take over and I'd warm to my subject and audience. I'd make sure everyone saw me scrape a few streaks in the ice cream residue with the customer's spoon before I raised the evidence over my head and waited for the cheers and whistles.

"In recognition of his uh-may-zing feat, John is hereby awarded the Farrell's red badge of courage, [hands customer a small campaign-style button] which reads, 'I made a pig of myself at Farrell's,' redeemable for a five-minute romp through our dumpster at three o'clock tomorrow morning."

[To customer:] "I'll see you there, bro!"

[To the other diners:] "I'd appreciate it if all of you would help me congratulate John with Farrell's official pig call. Please repeat after me: Oink, Oink, Soo-EE, Soo-EE, Piggy-Wiggy-Wiggy. That's two Oinks, Two Soo-EE's, One Piggy and two Wiggy's. Everybody ready? Let's go!" …and the crowd joined me for the final pig call.

My shift at Farrell's was five to closing, five evenings a week. I worked there for about nine months prior to leaving San Diego for graduate school in Boston. I think I must have served a dozen or so Pig Troughs each night. That would mean I called the hogs more than two thousand times while I worked there. After the first thousand, I got over my own embarrassment. For my customers, it was always fresh.

Twenty Questions

What if you hadn't died.
What if it hadn't been two weeks before I found out.
What if it hadn't been years since I'd spoken to you.
What if you didn't live two thousand miles away.
What if I'd made the effort to visit you anyway.
What if the plaque that began to grow on your brain had never started, hadn't given you a geriatric disease when you were still young, still lovely, just forty years old. Only a year older than I. They called us "Irish twins," but no real twins were closer.

What if you hadn't ended up—despite your master's degree—working as a bartender in a gay bar in Key West, where your regulars bought you too many drinks at the end of the night and you always went home drunk. Once you'd dreamed of becoming a photographer, of capturing the wild waterscapes of the Keys on postcards that tourists could send home, writing "Wish you were here." But that went out the window, thanks to your husband.

What if you'd never met him.

What if he hadn't decided to drink himself to death.

What if, later, he hadn't told you he only married you so that you would take care of him while he did it.

What if you hadn't felt so alone, so adrift, so cut loose by us, your family, the ones you should have been able to depend upon, that you couldn't think of a way to leave him.

What if you'd fallen in love with someone who actually loved you back, someone who saw in you (in addition to your beauty) the smart, accomplished, independent woman you were, and wanted to nurture those aspects of you.

What if you could remember your strength, your daring, your curiosity, and how you drew me into your romance with the world, persuading me (for example) to hitchhike through Europe with you the summer before I turned twenty-one, each of us with less than three hundred dollars in our pockets to last us three months. You insisted that we go to see *Aïda* at the Baths of Caracalla, even though we couldn't afford it. Later, under a full moon, to save the bus fare, we walked for miles through Rome's famous squares—deserted at that hour—all the way back to our campsite on the edge of the sleeping city, while we reviewed every scene and aria.

Back when we were both in high school, we would sit on stools at the kitchen counter until one or two or three o'clock in the morning, talking about anything and everything, silly things, falling again and again into helpless laughter while the rest of the family slumbered at the other end of the house.

What if you remembered how, on one of those giddy nights, you tested the colors of your nail polish on my ragged, bitten nails.

What if you remembered challenging me, when I was seven, to a contest that consisted of climbing to the top of a six-foot stepladder and jumping off onto the barren, hard-packed soil of our front yard in Lemon Grove (the rental house where crabgrass grew in under your bedroom wall), a contest that ended when I broke my arm on a bad landing.

What if you hadn't been so adventurous.

What if you hadn't had to try everything once.

What if we could un-argue our disagreements, un-feel the petty slights, un-decide to allow the drifting apart that was due mostly to laziness.

What if I could forgive you for allowing yourself, the sister I loved, to fade away behind a haze of drugs and liquor, long before your mind began to fail as well.

What if I could forgive myself for doing nothing.

What if I could forget how I saw you last, at a family gathering, trying to join in a word game and only managing to arrange the tiles to spell your own name, over and over, like a precocious four-year-old: Rebecca Rebecca Rebecca.

Some months ago, you sent me a box of your photos, without a letter. I put them under my bed and dreamed that night of gentle Gulf swells washing against a rocky shore. I didn't realize until today that they were your postcards to me, saying goodbye.

The Wright Stuff: Excerpts from My Journal of a Trip Across America

9/21/2008

Dodging panhandlers and navigating closed streets, we eventually found our downtown Cleveland hotel yesterday afternoon. It seems to be in a nearly deserted section of Cleveland, its avenues lined with empty storefronts and pristine office towers, early skyscraper period, 100% of which are being reconstructed using a preservationist's approach. Beautiful architectural details abound, many carved into the limestone facades. In front of every office building there's a group of four or five smokers taking their cigarette break; their body language suggests that they're the only inhabitants of the buildings and of the city. There are no pedestrians, no shoppers, no motor vehicles. No one else comes or goes while we watch. The overall impression is that we have arrived at Armageddon and smokers were the only ones spared.

The main event today was a visit to the Rock & Roll Hall of Fame, designed by I.M. Pei. A pyramid (like his 1984 addition to the Louvre in Paris), large spaces below ground level, upper floors cramped and virtually unusable.

The museum has an impressive collection of costumes displayed on mannequins; their scale suggests that almost every famous Rock performer is four-and-a-half feet tall. The level of detail on the costumes for bands that routinely play in stadium shows is surprising. Especially impressive are the hand-camouflaged silver-brown shoes for Aerosmith. Nice stuff for Madonna by Jean-Paul Gaultier. Surprisingly feminine outfits for Jimi Hendrix: bias ruffles down the front of a sheer "jacket" over printed shirt, velvet pants. It's apparent that a lot of what looks thrown together onstage is professionally designed and carefully constructed by costume houses.

Overall impression of the R&RHOF is of chaos—not the creative kind—and cold. Had to wear fleece pullover even though it was 70 degrees outside. Main themes:

- R&R grew out of an appropriation of black, country, and western roots by the white market
- R&R is a product of youthful rebellion that became an iconoclastic art form that flies in the face of conventional society and revels in insult and outrage. Yay!

Good Mexican food for dinner at—once again—a nearly deserted sports bar near our hotel.

9/23/2008

Leaving the unimpressive Cleveland Botanical Garden, we found ourselves on the grounds of the Weatherhead School of Management at Case Western Reserve University and the Frank Gehry-designed Peter B. Lewis Building. Its stainless-steel roofline suggests a Brobdingnagian-scaled pile of used giftwrap. Tilted brick façade fails to integrate Gehry's building with those adjoining. Security graciously allowed us to step into the lobby; that was enough to make me claustrophobic in spite of what a gratis pamphlet refers to as "a soaring space." In my opinion, it does not soar. The building's design is all ego, reflected in the drama of the exterior. How it is to be used by humans is secondary.

9/24/2008

Left South Bend headed toward Chicago. We approached on the south side, once again impressed unfavorably with challenges shared by most large American cities we've visited: smog, congestion, poverty.

Found our way to Oak Park to visit Frank Lloyd Wright's home and studio. Wait time: 2 hours, so took the self-guided audio walking tour of the neighborhood surrounding the home he lived in from 1889 to 1913, and where he executed 24 commissions. Lots of variety documenting the transition from the Victorian era to Art Deco. Many stunning examples of design. Especially liked the exterior of the Unity Temple—a Unitarian Universalist church included on the tour. Lots of echoes of Hollyhock House/Olive Hill in LA.

FLW's home and studio again demonstrate what I've observed as typical of his interiors: impressive attention to detail in what ends up feeling like a doll house as a result of cramped spaces and low ceilings. (FLW designed spaces to suit himself more than his clients. He was only 5'8½" tall.) The children's playroom on the second floor was the only room with a reasonable sense of space, and even that room with its barrel ceiling and elaborate sconces (it doubled as a private theatre) had to be adapted to accommodate Wright's grand piano: the sounding board protrudes through the wall into an adjacent stairwell. The amiable humor of his design for the studio—a crow's nest in a library—is lost because of the cramped space.

Decorations (capitals, friezes, figural statues) all interesting and emphasizing human virtues such as truth, knowledge, strength, etc. The octagonal library's exterior decoration is bands of repeated small octagons, each one rotated x degrees so that the angle of one bisects the straight edge of the next. Ingenious! The floral light screens over the dining room table and in the playroom still anchor the design style firmly in the Victorian period.

9/25/2008

Today given over to exploring Chicago on foot, beginning in Millennium Park with Frank Gehry's "serpentine bridge" leading to an outdoor pavilion. A web of metal struts forms a roof suspended above the lawn, the seating area for informal performances. Nearby, two tall stone slabs face each other in a shallow pool of water. A filmed series of human faces is projected on them. Each image eventually forms an "O" with their lips and spits real water into the fountain.

One fascinating object in the park is Anish Kapoor's sculpture "Cloud Gate," which the public has renamed "The Bean." Meticulously fabricated, there are no seams, rivets, or other construction clues in its perfect, mirrored stainless steel form.

[Note from 2018: I understand that in May 2016 Kapoor decided the world had seen enough of the shiny version of Cloud Gate and took it upon himself to improve the sculpture by painting it black. And not just black, but a very black-black. Strange as this may seem, he is not alone among artists who can't disengage from their work, even after it has become someone else's property. I've heard anecdotally that a family for whom FLW designed a home invited the architect back for an overnight visit several years later. As he often did, Wright had designed the furniture for the home as well. When the family arose the next morning, FLS had moved all of his original furniture back to where he'd staged it before he'd handed the keys over to his patron. Any furniture the family had added was not to be found.]

Crossing Lake Shore Drive into the bustling business district, found Picasso and Calder sculptures in public plazas mixed in with modern office towers; large open spaces planted with lawn, trees, and flowers; incongruous but appreciated Adirondack chairs scattered about for resting in—lovely, and everything Cleveland would like to be. Left the city by a much nicer route than that by which we'd arrived, driving along Lake Shore Drive until it dissipated in the residential delta of the northern suburbs. I imagined we were following in the tire tracks of FLW. The married architect fled Oak Park when his affair with the wife of one of his clients was revealed. This was a pattern that was repeated more than once.

9/26/2008
On the 11am tour of Johnson Wax headquarters in Racine, Wisconsin. Tours of the Wright-designed administration building, still in daily use as Johnson's world headquarters, and the associated parking garage are very tightly regulated; it's difficult to roam or examine things too closely... which didn't keep a group of 3 French tourists from blithely ignoring the guide's instructions to stop taking pictures and stop wandering off—a safety issue, as a number of the buildings on site are still used by JW for research and light manufacturing. After the tour, the male in the group had to be removed from the industrial area by security guards. He was carrying a small drawing tablet on which I was able to glimpse some nice charcoal sketches of the complex before he was hauled away.

[A note on French tourists: during our travels, we noticed more than a few incidents in which French tourists ignored warning signs, insisted on following their own path even when it was made clear to them that they were trespassing or otherwise going where they shouldn't. Later in our trip, we stopped at Palo Verde for a few days. Walks among the ruins left by cliff-dwellers who had lived on the site for thousands of years were led by park rangers who would linger at the hike's announced starting point to allow late-comers to join the walk. Engaging in small talk at the beginning of one such walk, the ranger was asking visitors where they were visiting from, while keeping an eye on one of the male tourists who repeatedly had to be called back from trying to begin a solo tour of private areas. The third time it happened, the ranger asked him, as he had the other walkers, where he was from. The over-eager tourist stared at him with a blank expression. "French?" the ranger asked. The tourist nodded.]

The Johnson Wax administration building interior: Smaller than expected, but still impressive. Famed "lily pads" enchant in person as they do in photos. Impact lessened by major repair being carried out everywhere, especially in lobby/reception. No access to the research tower; closed for retrofitting to meet modern fire regulations. In general, Wright's structures still look startlingly modern but somehow lost or out-of-place in juxtaposition with the adjacent manufacturing complex.

[One nostalgic note: Taliesin Associated Architects is the firm FLW established before his death in 1958. They were hired to create a structure on the JW grounds to house a small museum and a theatre in which to show the short film "To Be Alive." Both film and theatre had originally been created for the Johnson Wax pavilion at the 1964 World's Fair, and I remember seeing it there when my family drove cross-country from San Diego to attend. Hard to believe that was almost 45 years ago! Unfortunately, the building created in Racine by Taliesin Associates was pedestrian: a box for the museum with the original World's Fair saucer—the theatre— plopped on top of it. The film was still moving. Taliesin Associated Architects ceased operations in 2003.] On to Taliesin!

9/27/2008

There's a category of restaurant that Wisconsinites refer to as a "supper club;" this is revealed to us by the desk clerk at the Motel 8 in Kenosha, near Racine, in answer to the question, "Where's a good place to eat around here?" After declining her first two suggestions—Pizza Hut, McDonalds—we were offered the elegant-sounding third alternative. It conjured memories of Astaire-Rogers movies, or one of the episodes of "I Love Lucy" in which she manages to talk herself into the show at Ricky's club. Was it possible that some version of club culture, circa 1930, survived among the Wisconsin dairy farms? We had to go.

It turns out that a supper club, Wisconsin-style, is a restaurant that serves steaks and fish and has a bar. And, if you ignore the brown lettuce in the salad, the brown skin on the lime in the watered-down gin and tonics, the saltine cracker appetizers served with "spread" (cream cheese mixed with chives), and the cigarette-smoke-saturated interior still sporting last year's Christmas decorations, it *is* pretty elegant, despite lacking a floor show. We had some language problems negotiating our order. Me to waitress: "How is the fish cooked?" Waitress to me, "I don't know." Several seconds of blank stares pass between us. Waitress: "Would you like me to find out?" The mahi-mahi, grilled, turned out to be quite satisfying despite the carbon footprint it left, having been air-lifted from the west coast that morning.

9/28/2008
We had a reservation for the 10:15 Taliesin tour this morning. The bus
driver had to be at least 80. Our guide was Melinda, great
granddaughter of the owner of the lumber mill that provided FLW with
much of the wood used in building Taliesin.

The tour began at what had been a boarding school run by FLW's
two aunts, now part of the still-operating school for architecture. I can't
add much to the many photos and words already produced in re: these
buildings, except to say that there was wood rot and deterioration
everywhere.

To experience Taliesin, the house itself, was thrilling, overlooking
the usual discomfort of low ceilings. Rooms were more expansive than
usual; the views of the Wisconsin countryside were outstanding.
There's little colored glass incorporated into the leaded windows;
Wright felt it wasn't needed to enhance the experience of gazing out
the window. Overall, successfully evokes the spirit of an Italian villa,
influenced by FLW's visit to Italy.

Here is one place where FLW's interest in integration with Nature
is apparent. Taliesin (Welsh for "shining brow") is situated just below
the top of the hill on which it's built, so that from the back garden the
house is invisible. It's a wonderful effect. Also wonderful: the
integration of Asian art—screens, rugs, ceramics, etc. Not so
wonderful: the overly close supervision during the tour that prevented
us from pausing to admire or absorb much of the exterior.

One anecdote from our tour guide: FLW designed furniture for all
of his interiors—including Taliesin—that was famously uncomfortable.
Late in life, fed up, he reportedly complained, "I am tortured by my
own furniture!" He eventually replaced the chairs in the sitting-rooms
at Taliesin with over-stuffed armchairs from a Chicago department
store.

All of what we see today at Taliesin, with the exception of
Wright's studio, was re-built following a murderous 1914 arson attack
by a deranged employee. His studio, with all his letters and plans, was
saved from the flames by his injured foreman. His mistress, for whom
he had built the place, her two children, and a dozen employees were
all brutally murdered. Wright himself, working on a project in Chicago,
was not present during the attack.

9/29/2008

Stopped for lunch in Mitchell, SD, yielding to the enticement of the signs we had seen every quarter mile or so for the last 300 miles. Mitchell is home to the Corn Palace, a real tribute to kitsch. The exterior of the building is completely covered in decoration made from various varieties and colors of corn. Reminded me of the style often referred to as tramp art. After all the effort some entrepreneur had invested in the roadside signs—not to mention the Palace itself—we arrived to find it closed. Looking around, I realize almost all the businesses in Mitchell are closed on this Fall afternoon in the middle of the week. OK by us. I expect we saw what we needed to see. Finally found Chinese restaurant had a reasonably tasty buffet.

This afternoon, arrived in Rapid City, SD in preparation for tomorrow's visit to Mt. Rushmore.

Notes from the road (so far):

- Best gas station name: *Kum & Go*
- Best business sign (painted 3 ft. high): *24-hour Toe Service*

We spent all of Monday at Mt. Rushmore National Park. The Black Hills scenery is spectacular, especially the numerous stone fingers that stick up—not sure whether due to earthquake or volcanic activity followed by erosion. The Rushmore sculpture itself is much more impressive than I thought it would be and can be approached via a trail/boardwalk that goes to the base of the debris pile. Twists and turns provide different views of specific heads. Biggest surprise was seeing lines suggesting spectacles on TR, only because I'd never noticed them before.

In a small clearing about halfway along the trail, a Native American park service employee had a hide from a recently butchered buffalo staked out. She was explaining how every part of the animal was used by NA hunters:

- Un-tanned hide dried hard and could be used to make storage boxes
- Un-tanned tail used as fly swatter
- Hollow horn became drinking cup, powder horn, or container to carry fire from one camp to the next
- Ligaments were dried, pulled apart into sinews, and used for laces or ties
- Hollow hooves were hung on strips outside of teepee for use as a "doorbell"
- Ribs were used as sled runners, other bones as tool handles, scrapers, etc.

• Tanned hides were used for clothing, teepee covers, rugs, etc. That evening I felt bad after dinner because I'd left the bones from my pork chop on my plate. Maybe I could have fashioned a spare car key or ball-point pen out of them.

9/30/2008

Today was an example of exactly what I'd hoped to encounter when we set off on this trip: in the middle of nowhere we saw an exit sign for Devil's Tower National Monument and took an unplanned turn. Thirty minutes later we were at the tower, which is 1250 feet in elevation and soars 820 feet above the visitor's center. According to geologists, the tower was formed by streams of molten igneous rock flowing through granite tubes and forming 5-, 6-, or 7-sided crystals. 50 million years of erosion have left the tower free of the softer surrounding layers of soil and stone.

- Best business sign in Jackson Hole, WY: *Hole Juice*
- Best business sign in Utah: *Pop Food Worms*

10/11/2008

We arrive at Taliesin West near Scottsdale, AZ in time for our noon tour. The attitude among the guides is much more relaxed than it had been at Taliesin East; we're invited to take pictures both inside and out during the tour.

The buildings were again built just below the top of a hill, with a beautiful view for many miles across the desert…interrupted by electrical towers and power lines that run across the property. These were installed during FLW's lifetime, and so frustrated him that he raised the height of the windows in the rooms facing the lines so that they aren't visible when sitting in a chair.

FLW conceived of TW as a camp. Although the buildings cover an estimated 45,000 square feet and are built of stone and concrete (it's said he wanted to use materials that wouldn't burn), many ceilings are canvas. At TW, the concrete that was one of his favored building materials is readily visible as mortar between large local boulders. FLW treated the local rocks, some with prehistoric petroglyphs, as centerpieces or totems, and placed them near the entrances to the buildings, much as he used sophisticated cast concrete planters in his commercial and residential projects.

Overall sense is of rusticity, whether by intent and developing temperament or because of lack of money for more sophisticated buildings.

While FLW was alive, he initiated the tradition of spending the spring and summer at Taliesin East and the fall and winter at Taliesin West. The entire household, including the students in the architecture school, would move as well, and would provide most of the labor that went into building Taliesin West.

10/13/2008
We had an appropriate welcome to California this morning: an earthquake. It made me think about our visit a few days ago to Chaco Canyon, an extensive prehistoric building complex in the middle of the New Mexico desert. One of the large structures we saw there had been designated as unstable by the National Park Service. They'd made the decision not to shore it up, but to let nature take its course. Though today's quake was nowhere near the canyon, the NPS policy makes me think about how we value things. Would we let Taliesin West fall if it were threatened? The prehistoric architects of Chaco Canyon were just as skilled, in their own way, as FLW's students, yet we might value their work less because they weren't white, and we don't know who they were or why they built. On the other hand, maybe the NPS is right: we shouldn't interfere with natural processes. Everything man creates is someday likely to fall or be replaced.

We'd set off from Farmington, NM on 10/9, having spent the night in the Days Inn on the edge of town. Like all the motels in Farmington, its parking lot is surrounded by a 10-foot chain link fence with coiled razor wire on top. Signs warn against leaving valuables in the car, so we'd moved all the computer equipment, cameras, etc. from the back of the Escape to our room.

We easily found the obscure turn-off to Chaco Canyon, soon passed on to the 13 miles of dirt road leading to the Chaco Culture National Historical Park. As the driver, I struggled initially with the eroded, washboard road. I thought we might have to ride the whole way at 20mph, with the car heaving violently from side to side as each wheel summitted the 4-inch ruts, then front to back with every slide to the bottom. As a small sedan passed us doing about 45, I noticed that his wheels were bouncing up and down like time-lapse yo-yos, but the body of the car looked relatively stable. I discovered that the secret to navigating a washboard road is to drive fast and focus 100 feet or so in front of the car. That way, there's not enough time between rotations for the wheels to sink into the ruts; instead, they bounce from the top of one to the top of the next. This is a really exciting way to travel; with so little tire contact with the ground, steering and braking are nearly useless. It took only a few minutes for my hands to cramp from the tension of my grip on the steering wheel. Sweat flowed from every pore. John and I took turns seeing who could scream the loudest as we flew around blind curves, hoping against hope we wouldn't meet anyone coming the other way.

At least we were now travelling at about 40mph and making good time.

According to the NPS, Chaco Canyon hosts the densest and most exceptional concentration of pueblos in the southwest. Nobody knows who the builders were or why they chose to build there, though the structures' alignment with astronomical phenomena suggests, as it does at Stonehenge, that it may have some religious significance. Analysis of trash piles suggests that no one actually lived in the main complex. There are 50 or so small settlements scattered across the valley nearby—possibly caretakers. The Chetro Ketl site, combined with Pueblo Bonito next to it, formed the "downtown" section of the city. The structures were built using sandstone quarried from the top of the surrounding canyon walls, presumably because it's harder and more durable than the sandstone at lower elevations. The builders were highly sophisticated and skilled and obviously observed a rigid aesthetic, even though they had only stone tools to work with. Right-angled shapes (exterior corners, windows, doors, etc.) were extremely precise, though circles (kivas) were more approximate. Logs for roof supports (some 2 feet in diameter) were brought to the site from 20 to 60 miles away.

The complexes were built in a "D" shape, with the curved wall enclosing a plaza. There are few petroglyphs, distinguishing the culture from that of the Pueblos. The whole place seems to have been constantly expanded and remodeled. There are no explanations for why the site was abandoned in about 1250 AD; one speculation is that the highly structured society that would have been required to construct it over 300 years was torn apart by some sort of political strife. Seeing the craftsmanship, sophistication, and ingenuity of the builders, it's difficult to understand why they never felt the need to develop a written language (unlike Aztec and Inca civilizations shortly after) that could have helped us understand them. Similar "Great Houses" are scattered across an estimated 60K square miles of Arizona, New Mexico, Utah, and Colorado. My feeling is that this was a civilization that rivaled the size and power of Mexican pre-Columbian civilizations, but because of the lack of a written language we know almost nothing about it.

One example of foresight employed at Taliesin West that the Chacoans never thought of: the deep eaves and covered walkways of TW prevent the drifting sand from penetrating the interiors of the rooms. Most of what is visible today at Chaco Canyon has been excavated by archeologists and others, but every day the desert winds and Mother Nature collude in a constant, on-going effort to cover it up again. I think I know who will win this eons-old tug-of-war.

Jeromy in Athens
A Tragedy in Two Acts

Persons Represented:

JEROMY	VOICE 1
ANDROU	VOICE 2
CHORUS	VOICE 3
2 DANCERS	A GROUP OF ACTORS

trag·e·dy (trăj'ĭ-dē): A drama or literary work in which the main character is brought to ruin or suffers extreme sorrow, especially as a consequence of a tragic flaw, moral weakness, or inability to cope with unfavorable circumstances.—*The Free Dictionary*

ACT 1

THE SCENE: *like the theatre, is in the open air on a sloping, boulder-littered hillside where the theatre of Dionysus stood two thousand years ago. At the base of the hill is a stunted forest of thick shrubs and low trees.*

THE TIME: *late summer, mid- to late-afternoon.*

> [*A lone figure,* JEROMY, *is discovered laying on his back on one of the larger limestone fragments of the ancient theatre, sleepily soaking up the last of the day's warmth from the quarried rock. He has removed his T-shirt, spreading it on the limestone as a buffer between the rock and his skin. In the theatre below, A* GROUP OF *ACTORS is rehearsing a play.* JEROMY *listens for a few minutes, decides it's Agamemnon, and returns to his nap.*]

The CHORUS, *VOICES, and* ANDROU *enter and form a rough semi-circle around the sleeping figure with the open end toward the audience. The* VOICES *begin to chant and sing, very softly, the words to the chorus of Donovan's "Atlantis." The chanting should be so soft that no one can decipher it.*]

CHORUS.   We show you JEROMY, an American college student who is spending his summer touring Europe. He has just arrived in Athens and has stumbled upon a rehearsal of Sophocles' tragedy* *Oedipus Rex* taking place in the theatre of Dionysius.

[JEROMY raises his head briefly to look at the CHORUS.]

JEROMY.   It's *Agamemnon.*

VOICE 1.   [*from within the chorus.*] Actually, it's *Orestes.*

JEROMY.   [*Firmly*] No, it's *Agamemnon.*]

> [*On the stage below, A GROUP OF ACTORS gesture and chant at each other in Greek. Jeromy does not speak Greek; to him it sounds like the men are chanting "soda-water-bottle, soda-water-bottle" and the women are crying, "RHU-barb, "RHU-barb." ANDROU who's sitting nearby, notices JEROMY and leans toward him. The CHORUS suddenly stops chanting*]

ANDROU.   You are very sure of yourself for a young man. American?

JEROMY.   [*in a challenging tone*] Am I? Sure of myself?

ANDROU.   [*With an exaggerated "Greek" accent*] Ah, I zink so. I zink vee have zometink ink common.

JEROMY.   Really? And what would that be?

VOICE 1.   [*Aside*] JEROMY didn't really ask ANDROU what the "zometink" they had in common was; that's why this is a tragedy.

ANDROU.   My name, ANDROU. I teach… [*pause, then starting over.*] I am professor at university. University of Athens.

> [*JEROMY sits up and begins to put on his shirt, preparing to leave. It's a difficult task; the shirt is damp where he was laying on it, and it takes a minute for him to pull it over his head. ANDROU takes advantage of the extra time to appreciate JEROMY's physique, which is more like that of a swimmer than those captured in the marble statues of naked gods and heroes that once decorated the acropolis. Now that JEROMY is standing, ANDROU notices that the warm sun and cool caresses of the afternoon's breeze have worked their way with the younger man's dick, which is straining against the front of his jeans. JEROMY awkwardly tries to cover both his chest and his erection at the same time. He is only partly successful.*]

ANDROU.   Sorry to stare. I thought... For moment, I think you are my student.

VOICE 1.   What, so that's a good reason to stare?

ANDROU.   You *are* a student, though—yes? You study philosophies? [*Speaking faster.*] I give you private Greek history tour, yes? Then we go and drink wine. You like wine, of course. You are old enough, yes? Come! Come!

CHORUS.   JEROMY decides he will have one drink with this strange character before heading over to his hostel. The terrain is rough and the light is fading, and there is little that could be considered a marked trail. He uses the teacher's babble on the subject of Greek philosophers to guide him as he scrambles to keep up.

VOICE 1.   JEROMY will soon discover that reading a book is a much safer method of learning than wandering around at night in unfamiliar territory in a foreign country.

CHORUS.   [*Keening, as if at a funeral, starting softly and gradually becoming louder*] Yi! Yi! Yi! Yi! Yi!

VOICES 1, 2. Oh JEROMY! Do not trust Greeks offering free lessons in the woods!

ANDROU.   [*Puts his arm around JEROMY's waist as they enter the thickest part of the forest.*] Keep me this way!

CHORUS.   It takes JEROMY a moment to figure out that ANDROU means "hold me." In Davenport, which is JEROMY's home, only queers walk around holding on to each other. JEROMY is embarrassed but decides it's okay to drape his arm across his guide's shoulder, the way he's seen young men do in the public square.

CHORUS.   [*Men only.*] Tourists should be careful not to misinterpret local customs.

CHORUS.   [*Women only, still keening*] O Jeromy! In Athens, only queers walk around holding hands with each other.

ANDROU.   [*Holding JEROMY tighter*] This is the way we do it—friends, yes?

CHORUS.   [*Men only.*] No, we don't "do it" this way.

ANDROU.   [*During his next lines, gradually maneuvering* JEROMY *from down right to down left, where there is a small clearing in the woods.* ANDROU's *arm is no longer across* JEROMY's *shoulders; it's slipped up until it's more or less a chokehold across his windpipe. As he speaks,* ANDROU *occasionally jerks his arm for emphasis, cutting off* JEROMY's *air.* CHORUS *is suddenly silent.*]

ANDROU.   You come to learn, yes? [*Jerk.*] You know who was Socrates? He was great teacher [*Jerk.*]

CHORUS.   He was a pederast. He liked to have sex with young boys.

ANDROU.   Perhaps *I* can teach *you* something…

JEROMY.   [*Struggling to pry* ANDROU's *arm from around his neck*] I. CAN'T. BREATHE!

ANDROU.   [*Abruptly breaks off his narrative, quickly re-positions the two of them so that he has* JEROMY *in a modified standing half Nelson.* ANDROU *begins to cover* JEROMY's *face with slobbery kisses.*]

ANDROU.   Mmuff, slurp, mmmmm…

JEROMY is unable to speak.

VOICE 1.   JEROMY is gagging on the older man's fat tongue, which tastes of acrid herbs, stale cigarettes, and retsina, a local wine even we Greeks consider undrinkable. He struggles with ANDROU, who's working one hand down inside the front of JEROMY's jeans; JEROMY tries to push him away.

CHORUS.   [Women only.] O, JEROMY! Why do you twist and flail so? Take it from us, it's not that bad once you surrender. Besides, you don't want to vomit on your nice clothes! [This is a mistranslation; s/b "You don't want to ejaculate"-*ed.*] Soon it will all be over, and you'll want something clean to wear for your trip home to Davenport!

> *ANDROU and* JEROMY *are still in an embrace, chest to chest, crotch to crotch, at times even cheek to cheek.* TWO DANCERS *dressed in black emerge from the chorus, displaying brightly painted forty-inch phalluses. They dance around* ANDROU *and* JEROMY, *forcing the phalli between them, rubbing them up and down and pantomiming various sex acts. This goes on for an uncomfortable length of time; the audience becomes restless.*

JEROMY.   [*Finally!*] Let go of me, asshole! [*He breaks free and runs downstage center; he's joined by ANDROU and the dancers with the phalli. JEROMY and his dancer face the audience; a long stream of confetti erupts from the dancer's phallus.*] O! O! O! [*JEROMY collapses onstage. His phallus begins to slowly deflate, like a balloon with a slow leak. Everyone freezes except JEROMY, whose squirming gradually tapers off. After a minute, the dancer carrying ANDROU's phallus begins to make small, surreptitious movements, rubbing it against CHORUS members who happen to pass by. The movements gradually get larger, until the dancer/ANDROU is chasing JEROMY and CHORUS members around the stage, holding the phallus in front of him. ANDROU struggles to keep up; eventually collapses down center. One by one, the other characters follow his example.*]

ANDROU.   [*Reaching for JEROMY*] Give me your eyes!

CHORUS.   It takes JEROMY a minute to figure out that ANDROU means "Look at me." [*When he does so, there is a repeat eruption from the phallus carried by DANCER/ANDROU. Confetti covers the audience in the first three rows. ANDROU's phallus begins to deflate. He rolls onto his side to look at Jeromy.*]

ANDROU.   You have done it this way before?

CHORUS.   [*Men only.*] What could he mean? In the woods? Standing up? With another man?

JEROMY.   [*In a calm, small voice; all the frenzy has drained from the scene.*] I'm not a faggot, if that's what you mean.

ACT 2
Immediately following ACT 1

[*JEROMY is looking around for an escape route, careful to avoid being too obvious about it.*

ALL VOICES. We show you JEROMY, an American tourist who is disgusted by his own desires and actions.

VOICE 1.   He's embarrassed. Regretful.

VOICE 2.   Infuriated!

VOICE 1.   He wants to run, but—in the darkness—which way should he go?

VOICE 2. [*Sarcastic:*] You poor, poor thing!

VOICE 3. [*Baby talk:*] Did the mean man scare you?

VOICE 1. [*Mocking:*]Did he touch your whittle teeny-weeny pee-pee?

[*ALL THREE VOICES together.*] Now comes the bad time.

VOICE 1. The shame.

VOICE 2. The regret.

VOICE 3. The guilt.

VOICE 1. [*Milking the moment for everything he's got*] The FURY!

[*ALL THREE VOICES together.*] You know you could have stopped him if you really wanted to!

JEROMY. [*Protesting*] But…I… he… *surprised* me!

CHORUS. [*Turn to each other and lisp*] Oh, well, if he *thurprithed* you…

VOICE 1. No one can find out. You'll have to kill him!

VOICE 2. Smash his face, his smacking lips! Make him sorry…

VOICE 3. Hit him with a cudgel! We're in the woods; there must be a cudgel around here somewhere…

VOICE 1. What's a cudgel?

VOICE 2. You're taller and heavier. You have the advantage…

VOICE 3. [*Holds up a small stick too insubstantial to be used as a weapon.*] Found one!

ALL VOICES. Yes! You big, fat American! You must kill him before he kills you! If he breaks your legs, No one will find you for weeks; you'll die out here in the woods.

> [*Throughout this conversation among the other characters, ANDROU is preening himself like a cat, his tongue flicking between his fingers, licking at whatever remains in his palm.*]

JEROMY. [*Watching ANDROU with obvious disgust.*] Hey! Do you know the way out of here?

ANDROU. [*Looks up, after a moment nods slowly.*]

JEROMY. [*Jumps up and gives him a kick.*] Well, what are you waiting for? Get going!

[*Everyone shuffles off-stage.*]

VOICE 1. [*Is heard, dreamily*] Isn't Athens beautiful this time of year?

> *From a distance, as if through the half-open door of a small bar or restaurant,* JEROMY *can hear a singer winding up for the last chorus of Europe's number one song that summer:*

"I beg your pardon—I never promised you a rose garden. Along with the sunshine, there's gotta be a little rain some time. When you take you gotta give so live and let live…" etc.

JEROMY. [*After he exits with the rest of the cast, notices several actors and dancers lingering in the vomitorium. He follows them around the half-circle of the theatre until they're once again on stage.*] Oh, God! [*To the world at large*] Do they have to keep playing that song?

DANCERS. [*Emerging from hiding places, apparently having had similar ideas about meeting up with the American student once the other cast members were gone. Two of them are still carrying the giant phalli*] Do you address the two of us?

JEROMY. [*Startled, then recovering.*] Show me.

> *The* DANCERS *look away.*

DANCER 1. We're *dancers*.

DANCER 2. We're not supposed to talk to, or even look directly at, you actors.

JEROMY. Show me, please.

> [*He watches intently as the two dancers—impersonating* JEROMY *and* ANDROU—*run through a pantomime of the scene they have just completed. Each time they reach the end of the action, they start over from the beginning. After three or four repetitions,* JEROMY *realizes that the* DANCERS *will continue "looping" until someone or something changes the narrative. The next time the pantomime reaches its end,* JEROMY *interrupts.*]

JEROMY. Okay, I get it. What was it ANDROU said? "I think we have something in common?"

DANCER 1. Congratulations! You have converted your tragedy into...

JEROMY.   Wait a minute! Is that it? Is that all there is?

DANCER 2. [*Quickly changing direction*] ...something other than a tragedy.

DANCER 1. How about this: There's a message carved into the threshold of the Temple of Apollo at Delphi. It says, "Know Thyself."

JEROMY.   I always thought I did. Now I realize that, in one respect at least, the only thing I know about myself that's of any importance is what I learned during two hours spent in the woods at the base of the acropolis in Athens.

END

Things Could Be Worse

How'm I doin'? Oh, you know—can't complain. What is it people say…workin' hard or hardly workin'? I guess I'd have to say I'm hardly workin'. Yeah, those days are over. It's not too bad here, though. It's nice to be outside. I find myself a comfortable spot somewhere—one that gives me a good view of the street—and spend the day just sittin' and people-watchin'. The concrete's a little cold but, you know, things could be worse.

I used to get around a lot more, when I was younger. Before I moved here. I was very long and lean back then, if you can believe it. I was quite a gymnast, really. I see you're smiling; you probably don't believe me. You probably look at me and think, there's that fat old slob that's always hangin' around. But I used to be pretty good. That's the truth. We didn't have regular equipment to practice on. I lived up in the mountains, and we did what we could with what we had. We had trees, so I'd climb those. Tree limbs were my parallel bars, see? We had boulders to jump over. We'd have contests to see who could do the most somersaults in a row. That's what we used to do.

Eventually, I ended up here and—I don't know; I just lost interest. It got repetitive. You know how that goes. You start out doing something—let's say it's climbing trees— you're having a good time, it's fun! Then one morning you wake up and think, screw it, I don't feel like doing that today. I'll do it twice tomorrow. And that's it: the beginning of the end. Tomorrow maybe you do it or maybe you don't; the next day you'd have to do it three times and you hate the idea a little bit more, and before you know it three months have passed and you can't remember the last time you did it. Well, that's life, isn't it?

I had a friend named Raff who used to live here with me. He was fun—quite a comedian, you know? He was good company, always ready with a joke or a trick, though he could have his dark moods, too. He was kind of small and would get pissed off when he overheard anyone call him "short stuff" or—this was the worst— "pygmy." Well, who wouldn't? But that's the way it goes. All his screaming and threats didn't scare anyone, because most of the time he was as sweet as could be; quite a "hedonist," if I have that word right; that's what people sometimes called him anyway. He could nap for hours, stretched out in the sun, barely moving a muscle, perfectly happy.

Raff was already sick when he moved in here, but I'm the only one he ever told about it. The day he arrived, he introduced himself and I—trying to think of something to say, you know—asked him if he knew his name means "healed by god." He had a good laugh at that one. I thought he was laughing at me at first, but when he calmed down he said Well, god better hurry the hell up. So I said I'd heard St. Peter's chariot had failed the immigration checkpoint at San Clemente, and was swinging low over Jordan at present. And he said, who the hell is Jordan? We both cracked up at that one.

As time went by, Raff got worse and people started to notice, started to make comments, ya know? On his worst days he would stay inside, huddled in a corner, and he'd mumble to himself, over and over, Any time, god. You just reach on down here and heal me. Any time. Then he would chuckle. But it wasn't like it used to be. Those chuckles would send a shiver down my back. When we became friends, he used to worry about what it would be like for me when he was gone. It was hard for me to listen 'cause I didn't want to think about what I would do if he wasn't here. Who would I talk to? Who would tell me jokes?

In the end, god didn't come into it at all; if he had, Raff would still be here. Because Raff is basically a good guy—sorry, *was* basically a good guy. So, now, I don't believe in gods. It's been twenty years since he disappeared in the middle of the night. We never said good-bye; I didn't even know he was gone until morning. I still think about him almost every day. I don't know if you ever lost someone you loved. I loved Raff, and now he's gone. And it sucks, man. It really sucks.

But I'm still here, even if I get around a little less and move a little slower than I used to. I have my favorite spot where I sit and watch the world go by. Like I said, things could be worse.

You do start to notice stuff, though. For example, kids don't seem as polite or as well-behaved as they used to be. They'll call me names and throw things at me when their parents aren't looking, just because they can. They see that I'm old and can't chase them away. And they're right: I don't have the energy to react anymore. I just look away and think to myself, screw you, you little vandal, you with your soft-drink cup and your, your...TRASH that you toss over here like my yard is your wastebasket! Screw you—yeah, you, the blonde one. You think I don't see you hiding a piece of gravel in that wadded-up napkin? You throw that and you'll be sorry. Someday you're going to be old and slow, and when that day comes, I hope some snot-nosed little sub-primate dumps a whole garbage can on you, you little twirp!

But I don't say anything. I really don't want people to think I'm a complainer, you know? The older ones who complain too much—they're the ones who disappear in the middle of the night.

Besides, nobody wants anything to do with a fat old geezer like me. Yeah, they walk up and stare at me sometimes, like they're waiting for me to do something. I sit here and stare back until they get bored and turn away. Sometimes I get the feeling, though, that they know something about me that I don't, and that's really annoying. Maybe I'm getting paranoid, imagining things, going crazy just sitting here all day by myself. Being alone here, it's not good. Not good at all.

Anyway, there's something I wanted to ask you before you leave. Oh! And thanks, by the way. You've been very considerate while I ramble on. This thing has bothered me all these years, but I can't get anyone to explain it to me. There's something attached to my front fence and I don't know what it says. There are letters, maybe whole words, written on it, but—promise you won't laugh? —I never learned to read. That's right—I can't read. I know, you're surprised. But anyway, people come by, and they stare at the words for a while, and when they turn to walk away everyone always says the same thing, again and again, all day long: "Lowland Gorilla, Central West Africa." What the hell does that mean?

Little Red Bird

Gloria has been in a twenty-four-hour nursing facility for six years. She will die there without returning home, doesn't know that her children have put her empty house up for sale to pay for her care. She suffers from a cruel disease, crippled by rheumatoid arthritis that has turned her lovely pianist's hands into twisted claws permanently clasped to her chest, as if resting from playing the final chords of a concerto. With her neck, legs, and feet similarly affected, her active mind has become a prisoner within a body that has failed her almost completely.

She can still move her tongue and jaw and therefore can chew and eat food—if someone is available to put it in her mouth—and speak, though the length and volume of her sentences, often just a single word, are limited by her uncertain ability to force air through her vocal cords. She will never again rest on her side or stomach; she sleeps, day and night, with her torso partially raised in the hospital bed, or on her back, unable even to shift position without help. She keeps a box of Kleenex on her lap from which she can manage to pull a tissue—grasping it between the thumb and immobile fingers of her left hand—to dab at the phantom drool that obsesses her. She is bathed, changed, dressed, made-up (on special occasions), fed, and wheeled about by someone else; someone she knows and is used to if she's lucky, on many days by strangers.

Gloria's nursing home is a terrible, depressing place. Not because it's worse than any other; it's better than some, and there's a waiting list to get in. Just because it is what it is. I guess one can get used to the smell of shit-filled adult diapers that drifts into the hallways and stays in your nose even when you escape outside. But it's hard to witness and, for me, even harder to participate in the desperate false cheerfulness that everyone who enters the facility tacitly adopts upon crossing its threshold. Staff, residents, an occasional visitor, all collude to act out an elaborate lie. Over the several days my spouse, John, and I visited his mother there, the plea I hear most frequently from those who can speak is, "I want to go home." Those who have been silenced by their illness just stare with what I interpret as desperation.

I wonder how many of the residents here were told, as a way of easing the transition from their own homes to this one, "It's only until you feel better." Or, "We'll bring you home when the doctor says it's okay." In reality, few patients, if any, will recover sufficiently from whatever put them here to leave this place alive. But the "return myth" helps sustain the resident patients, who cling to it in the face of dully repeated routine and ample contradictory evidence. The staff, as well, push hope as though it's a drug that can cure sadness. To do otherwise would be to acknowledge the specter that hangs over the wards. We've all seen Bette Davis in *Dark Victory*, a movie in which she shuffles off this mortal coil after excusing herself to go upstairs for a nap. For most of the residents, their final breaths will not be like that. Forgotten by friends, ignored by family, they will die only after years of suffering under our incomplete ability to cure disease or minimize pain.

To physicians, who must take an oath to "First, do no harm," modern medicine has delivered tools that take the possible interpretations of that oath into heretofore unexplored territory. In the nursing home, the doctor who holds preservation of life as her highest value is forced to confront the consequences of having the ability to extend life indefinitely. Her patients often die only after years of the soul-numbing tedium and pain that comes with chronic illness, years of repeating the same activities on the same schedule every day, years of pissing and shitting themselves and waiting hours for someone to clean them up, years spent struggling with the buttons on the TV remote in an attempt to find *something* to distract them from an endless string of commercials peopled by ridiculously exuberant pitchmen selling products the patients no longer have any use for. That's why I feel, though I don't say this to John, that his mother died six years ago. The woman we're having lunch with? She's Gloria's ghost.

At lunchtime, a staff member manages to get Gloria into her wheelchair; John and I must get her to the dining room while they're still serving. We run down long hallways, pushing her ahead of us, taking corners on two wheels, and burst through the room's double doors like Ben Hur crossing the finish line in the chariot race. We are in time; she will get her lunch, with some substitutions for what they've run out of. John and I didn't arrive early enough this morning to request a meal; we'll have to be satisfied with what's left on Gloria's plate when she decides she's finished.

In contrast to most of the other spaces in the home, the dining room—which doubles as a movie theatre, activity room, and chance-to-get-out-of-a-hospital-environment room—is large and high-ceilinged, with tall, broad windows on two sides. Gloria's reserved table is on the edge of the dining area, near a window that looks out past the trash dumpsters to the woods beyond. She doesn't like to face the room, where she'd be forced to acknowledge her fellow patients. She doesn't approve of those who are carelessly dressed in loosely secured hospital gowns, or those who sit with their heads drooping toward the gooey leftovers on their plates. I can't figure out whether this is an aesthetic issue for her or she's irritated that the hospital atmosphere has invaded even this pleasant hall. Gloria always manages to be neatly dressed and groomed when she has visitors or chooses to mingle with her fellow residents, selecting outfits from her tiny closet through a tedious "no-no-no-yes" system and paying extra to have her hair styled and make-up applied.

Outside the windows, the dense New Jersey woods form an impenetrable screen around the home, twenty feet from the building. During lunch John sits on his mother's right, facing the side of her chair, the better to guide a fork to her mouth. I sit across from her, my back to the windows. Gloria rejects the soup: too salty. We've finished the salad—a few pieces of iceberg lettuce, French dressing—and moved on to the main course, a slice of turkey in glossy gravy, cubed carrots from a can, and a spoonful of mashed potatoes that Gloria refuses for the same reason as the soup. When John next raises the fork to her mouth, she ignores it. She's staring at something outside.

"Little red bird." Gloria announces this in the emotionless voice she's adopted as her most effective means of forming speech sounds. John and I snap to attention.

"Where?" we both say at once. Subjects of conversation are hard to come by here, and Gloria rarely introduces one.

"Small bush."

We search the greenery on the other side of the glass. There are no small bushes. I go to the window, greedy for the sight of a little red bird, something to distract us. "Was it a cardinal?" I ask. "I don't see it."

John returns to the task of placing the tiny forkfuls of carrots in her mouth. Gloria chews carefully, looking thoughtful, and swallows with some effort.

"Little red bird." I'm still inspecting the masses of foliage visible from the window, much of it Sumac that, however diligent you are with pruning, lurches up like weeds every spring and grows to seven feet within a season. But there are also cedars, oaks, tulip poplars, and lanky wild azaleas. And dogwoods. Cardinals are often seen near dogwood trees; their red fall berries, when eaten, contribute to the birds' bright color.

"Your eyes are better than mine," I tell Gloria, returning, frustrated, to my seat across from her. I catch myself in the last millisecond before I say, "Can you point to it?"

"Do you see it." Gloria's speech difficulties turn questions into statements.

"Yes, I see it," John says.

I quickly turn to him. In his position beside her, his right hand and arm poised for feeding, Gloria can't turn her head far enough to see his face, and he can't really see out the window.

There's no bird, he mouths to me.

Today's is the last of three exhausting visits we'd scheduled at the nursing home. We've only about an hour after lunch before it will be time to head off toward the airport for a late afternoon flight back to California. We wheel Gloria out to a small lounge with a giant flat screen TV and find a channel she likes to watch. It's still an hour until her favorite show, Dr. Phil, comes on. She dozes under the influence of a full belly and New Jersey's late-summer heat and humidity.

Guiltily, we allow her to sleep. We're wasting expensive minutes together, but it's easier this way, without the constant struggle to find things to talk about. I wonder how John's sisters bear it, trading off every other day, year in, year out.

"What are you two whispering about." Gloria has roused from her nap. John moves around to sit in front of her, where she can see him.

"We were just talking about Laura and Connie," John says. He pauses, gathering courage for his next sentence. "Mom, we're going to have to take you up to your room a little early today. We have to catch a flight."

"Where are you going."

"We have to go home. To California."

Gloria is silent. I have a sinking feeling in my stomach; I realize that no one told her, or she'd forgotten, that we're leaving today.

I remember the tortured good-byes at the bedside of my own mother twenty-five years ago under similar circumstances, her gradual paralysis caused by the creep of ALS—Lou Gehrig's disease—from her hands and feet toward her chest and throat. Her begging me at the end of every rare visit, while she could still speak, to move back to California so that she could see me more often. (We did move, finally, after she died.)

"I can't," I would say. "I have a job, friends. New Jersey's my home now." Those things were true. The idea of giving up the life I had built for myself on the east coast and moving three thousand miles to sit at her bedside was ridiculous. What I couldn't tell her is that I didn't want to see her more often; that my visits were arranged at my father's insistence and made by me out of a sense of obligation; that three thousand miles was already closer to her than I wanted to be. Our past together was too complicated, too painful for the adult in me to really feel connected to her. Still, when she died a month to the day after my last visit, I was sorry I'd left without saying "I love you."

Back in Gloria's room, John maneuvers her wheelchair next to the bed, pointing it toward the TV, her only dependable companion. I give her a quick kiss on the cheek and croak some inanity— "take care of yourself"—through a thickening throat. I want to leave the room and make space for a private goodbye between the two of them. They're both weepers.

I wait for John in the dining room where we had lunch an hour ago, now cleared of food, trays, and silverware, and return to my daydream, gazing once again out the tall windows. There's a sudden flash of red in a dogwood tree.

Little red bird!

I spin around quickly, hoping to find another observer to confirm the sighting. There's no one. The cardinal hops to a branch closer to the window and stares at me with one black beady eye. I flatten my palm against the cold glass; he crouches, ready to launch himself into the sodden sky.

Goodbye, little red bird! Goodbye!

It has all come down to this moment, this infinitesimal fraction of a second.

I love you!

Six Yuletide Carols

1. We Three Kings and Orien Tar

"Hold it right there, Bud! What's that you're dragging into the house? What are you up to?"

My mother had an unerring nose for "shenanigans," as she called them. I must admit she was usually right to be suspicious of the experiments I claimed to be conducting in the bedroom I shared with my older brother. Beginning early in December, the answer to her question always involved the approaching Christmas holiday. As soon as my siblings and I were able to provide the extra finger that was needed to tie a perfect ribbon bow, the elders would begin to drill the younger on the shared Christmas experiences that would eventually become part of our family lore.

I ignored my mother's protestations, yelling "Christmas present—don't look!" as I charged across the kitchen toward the bedroom end of the house, clutching parts and implements to my chest like a wide receiver driving toward a touchdown. I never gave her the chance to question why I needed lengths of hanger wire, vise grips, small cans of left-over exterior house paint, Elmer's glue, black electrical tape, or any other of the many items I stockpiled in a hiding place under my bed. They would reappear eventually, usually in the evening when the dining room table had been cleared and the dishes washed and dried, as part of or attached to a gift. My father would be reading his newspaper in the living room, my mother would be nodding in front of the TV, and we kids would spend hours laboring over our presents with gift wrap and ribbons, counting on the cleverness of our presentations to distract from the simplicity of our gifts.

Some of our most memorable Christmases presents came with no wrapping paper, no ribbons, no warning, and scant, if any, instructions. One Christmas morning, we were awakened at sunrise by a series of loud gobbles that seemed to be coming from our back yard. A whispered debate ensued in the bedroom hallway between those who insisted that the unfamiliar noise justified a breach of the Christmas morning "no peeking" rule, and those who were loath to break *any* rules so near the time when presents were to be distributed.

"You kids go back to bed." That was my father's scolding, clearly audible through my parents' hollow bedroom door. It would have settled the matter under normal circumstances. But this was an extraordinary case. We moved our whispered plotting into the bedroom I shared with Daniel, finally agreeing to send him—the eldest and the only one of us who could navigate the drop to the ground outside our bedroom window—to investigate. It took him only a few moments to report back: the gobbles were indeed coming from a tall crate standing in the middle of our sunburned back yard lawn. Inside the crate was a live turkey.

The answer to the question as to *why* there was a live turkey in our back yard quickly became priority number two when someone suggested we give the bird a name. It turned out that Turkey Lurkey (the unanimous choice) had been the door prize at the Christmas Eve dance my parents had attended. During breakfast the conversation turned to the question of what turkeys eat. "Don't worry about that," my father said in as firm and final a tone as I'd ever heard him use. "He's not going to be here long enough to eat anything. He's going right back to the turkey farm. This morning." We protested, to no avail. We had to be satisfied with accompanying him when he maneuvered Turkey Lurkey, still in his crate, into the roomy trunk of our '46 De Soto sedan (the car my father had spray-painted forest green on the front lawn, to the horror of our neighbors) and drove to a nearby poultry farm, where my father exchanged the live bird for a butchered one.

Contending to be the most knowledgeable family member on this or any other aspect of family lore took up a lot of our time as kids; anyone who made an error was teased mercilessly and without end. My sister, Rebecca, screwed up "For He's a Jolly-Good Fellow" by singing the bridge—"Which nobody can deny,"—as "With strawberry candy nights." My *faux pas* was to imagine a travel companion for "We three kings" named Orien Tar. I'd created a whole backstory for a character with that name, a fourth king who, eschewing useless baby gifts like gold and myrrh, had thoughtfully packed essentials like asphalt and crazy glue. I don't think anyone in the family ever again sang the verse correctly while I was in earshot.

Although we never had much money to spend on gifts, we learned early on that an impressive wrap could bring as much pleasure to giving and receiving as the gift itself. We all accepted the modesty of our budget as just another challenge. I struggled, though, to come up with packaging that complimented the two LPs I bought for Rebecca one year when we were both still in high school. One was *Wednesday Morning, 3 AM* by Simon and Garfunkel; I think *Buffalo Springfield* was the other. Trying to disguise the records using standard wrapping techniques was pointless, of course. I decided to make it an art project. I found some eighth-inch plywood in the garage and cut two pieces the same size and shape as the album covers. Once I had wrapped the two pieces of ply and the two albums in the same patterned paper, I used Scotch Tape hinges and ribbon braces to form them into a cube with two open sides. I suspended a ball of curled ribbon in the center of the cube, *et voila!* Modern art.

Each of us kids had a signature variation on the art of wrapping that we favored. Rebecca's was the Nested Boxes technique, which required four or five boxes that would easily nest inside each other. The gift was in the smallest box, but the recipient had to unwrap multiple decoy boxes to get to it. For this technique, it's important that each box be sealed with an unreasonable amount of tape or glue, as most of the fun results from making the gifts as difficult to open as possible.

Our favorite game by far, though, was the Hidden Present Hunt. This game demands that the hunter be as familiar with the nooks and crannies of the house as they are with classical and modern literature (especially *The Lord of the Rings* and T.H. White's *The Once and Future King*), power tools, popular songs, animal husbandry, products of the Industrial Revolution, internal combustion engines and quantum mechanics. The person giving the hidden present must find good hiding places for a wrapped package and compose a string of clues. There can be as few as two or three riddles to solve, but there is no maximum.

On Christmas morning, the hunter/receiver is given an envelope containing a hint as to where the first clue is hidden. They must solve a series of riddles that lead them from clue to clue until the hidden gift is found. The clues might be straight forward—

"three from the left," for example—or hidden in a riddle or poem: "This makes a breeze / in carriages. / Its name says what / Its purpose is." To make sense of this clue, the hunter would have to know that automobiles were once called "horseless carriages" and that cars have a part called an air filter, which is where the searcher would find the next clue.

The entire family would tag along for the hunt, ready to suggest possible solutions, especially misleading ones. With six people living in a small house, it became more and more difficult to find new spots to hide packages or clues that others wouldn't discover by chance. We learned to keep quiet during the holiday season if we accidentally came across a clue masquerading as a bookmark, and never reported the messages found taped to the back of our bed's headboard or stuffed in the toe of a snow boot. We simply left them where they were. Inevitably, some clues were never found, and the house's nooks and crannies gradually filled with long-expired directives, all ghosts of Christmases past.

2. I Heard the Bells on Christmas Day

Christmas mornings we kids were up early, of course, but we were forbidden to open the door that separated the bedrooms from the rest of the house until my parents had joined us. Together, we all marched into the living room while Bing Crosby's 45 RPM single of "Adeste Fidelis" or, later, Mitch Miller and the Gang's Christmas Album spun on the record player. The position of Santa's elf—the one who handed out everyone's gifts, which were opened one at a time—rotated among family members. When it was finally my turn to open something, I tore into the glittered wrap to reveal a Boy Scout pocketknife, or a tetherball set, or the board game Mr. Doodle's Dog. It always turned out, once the last piece of glitter paper was pulled away, that the gifts I received were just what I wanted, though I hadn't realized it until that moment. Even the obligatory package of JCPenney underwear—from Santa, of course— I accepted with a show of appreciation, glad I would no longer be expected to wear my cousin's hand-me-downs. And if all the fabulous possibilities suggested by the few well-shaken and elaborately wrapped gifts under the tree became a little ordinary when stripped of their paper, ribbons and bows, no matter. There were still the after-dinner turkey sandwiches to look forward to—on

Wonder Bread, with cranberry sauce, mayo, and lettuce— if we could stay awake long enough.

3. Is That You, Santa Claus?

I don't remember ever believing in Santa Claus, so I can't claim to have been traumatized by the news that he wasn't real. He was credited as the giver of the rare expensive or milestone-marking gift, its tag boldly labelled "From Santa" in a script identical to my father's, wrapped in gift paper I'd seen my mother buy at year-end sales the previous season. He gave me my first wristwatch at age nine, a silvered-metal Timex which I promptly dropped on the tile floor of my bedroom while dressing for church on Christmas morning, cracking the crystal. I'd owned a new, perfect watch for about ninety minutes, and in the way of my family that was the beginning and the end of the story. I was heart-broken, of course, but there was a "no crying" policy in our house that banned emotional displays as well as discussions of effective remedies, like the possibility of repair or replacement. After all, wasn't Timex's slogan "It takes a lickin' and keeps on tickin'"?

Perhaps my parents couldn't think of a way to replace a watch that had a gift tag implying it had come from Santa's workshop. That was the downside of Santa's gifts: they almost always came with a lesson. "That'll teach you to be more careful" were my mother's consoling words when I showed her the broken watch crystal. If it hadn't been Christmas morning, if we hadn't been late for church, I'm sure I would have been sent to my room to contemplate the many ways I could have been more careful with the watch. Perhaps you'll understand, then, why Santa's gifts were often received by us kids with a mixture of astonishment and fear.

One year there was a brand-new Schwinn three-speed bicycle leaning against the dining room wall on Christmas morning—a gift so shocking in its beauty and extravagance that we three youngest were afraid to approach close enough to read the name on the gift tag. We all felt lust, certainly, but lust tempered by dread of the responsibility that would come with owning such a magnificent and expensive object.

Still, I hoped that mine was the worthiest case. An early growth spurt that lasted several years had left me a gangly, awkward, six-foot-tall pre-teen, condemned to ride my mother's ladies' bike when

two-wheeled transportation was called for. The bike must have
dated back to the nineteenth century and easily weighed about a
hundred pounds. You can imagine the mocking epithets and jeers
the sight of me, all knees and elbows, riding an antique ladies' bike
to school or to Boy Scout meetings, evoked from my peers. The
shiny new Schwinn was indeed mine, but not for long. I had no
choice but to resume riding my mother's old behemoth when the
three-speed was stolen from our open garage four months later.

As for the watch with the cracked crystal, I wore it on my wrist
every day for many years. When the original watchband broke, I
braided a makeshift fob out of string and continued to use it as a
pocket watch. I should have worn it as a lavalier—as my albatross,
in the manner of the Ancient Mariner. I was almost relieved when,
during a 1971 backpacking trip through Europe, the watch and most
of my other belongings were stolen from my tent in the middle of
the night in a campground outside Hamburg, Germany.

4. Keep the Yuletide Gay

One of the more puzzling presents from Santa, firmly in the
"educational" gift category, was a sixteen-inch-tall assemble-it-
yourself plastic model of *The Thinker*—Rodin's monolithic nude
male bronze—that I received when I was twelve or thirteen.
Rebecca had received a model of *The Visible Woman* at about the
same time. Her model had clear plastic skin through which one
could view its internal organs; mine had a suggestive bulge in the
bronze-plastic form where its genitals should have been. Rebecca
was meticulous, as usual, in assembling her model, but painted the
organs without referring to the color chart included in the
instructions. When it was time to paint the heart, the only color of
which she had enough was yellow. I never asked her whether her
eeny-meeny-miney-moe approach to the project was purposeful or
simply an expression of boredom.

I guess my parents thought these models were a good substitute
for "the talk." I can imagine my mother saying something like, "Put
that together and if you have questions about it, ask your teacher."
Like, my art teacher?

Looking back now, I wonder if Santa's gift that year was a
signal that my parents noticed the "differentness" in me and were
struggling in their own way to reconcile it with their understanding

of the nature of things, or if *The Thinker* was simply the last model left at the hobby store. I'll never know.

5. I'll Be Home for Christmas

In 1976, during my first year of graduate school at Boston University, I might have described my residential status as "homeless," if that wasn't such a freighted term. Perhaps "at large" is a better way of expressing how I felt. My parents had sold the house in San Diego where I'd spent my adolescence and moved to Santa Ana, not far from Disneyland. The rest of us abandoned San Diego as well. Rebecca followed her suicidal fiancé to Key West. One brother moved to Berkeley and was studying Renaissance history at the University; the other taught high-school Algebra and coached volleyball. Said plainly, I had no place where, as Robert Frost put it, "When you have to go there, they have to take you in."

I'd never lived in my parents' Santa Ana house and had no sentimental attachment to it. I'd purposely chosen a graduate program that would put a continent between me and them, hoping the sheer mass of the mountains and infinite emptiness of the midwest would somehow filter out the rumble of their daily bulletins reiterating their doubt that I could find success in a career in scenic and costume design. My plans for living arrangements during semester breaks had an "anywhere I hang my hat" casualness about them that resulted in more than a few nights spent in a sleeping bag on a fellow student's floor. I didn't really have other options. The two half-time jobs I held at BU paid so poorly that I was often penniless or forced to choose between buying food and buying art supplies for my school projects. Travel was out of the question. Despite all this, *I* was the one who suggested that our scattered family continue to exchange presents at Christmas. Isn't that what "normal" families do?

Soon enough, but too late to stop it all, I realized that I'd made a mistake.

I'm sure I'd been in line for over an hour at the tiny Allston-Brighton post office that served my Boston neighborhood, awkwardly shifting the brown-paper-wrapped parcels that were my presents to family among various arrangements of limbs as each grouping tired my trembling fingers, biceps, back, shoulders, etc. At the rate the line was moving, it looked like it would be another hour until I would pass through heaven's gates, which was how I was beginning to see the swinging glass doors that conveyed customers one at a time into the warm interior. I wasn't sure when I'd last had feeling in my hands and feet, except for my toes. They were stinging from the cold my cheap, uninsulated athletic shoes could not keep at bay. Everyone else was wearing boots and fleece-lined coats. I was making do with an old pea coat I'd acquired in a San Diego Army-Navy store, worn over a California-weight sweater. One of my roommates, Sumner, had assigned himself to be my mentor on all things Boston-ish.

"That's not going to be warm enough when the real winter comes," he'd warned me through his permanently congested nasal passages when he saw me dressed to go outside after the first snowfall of the season. "You'll get frostbite if you go out dressed like that when it's below zero. Should I assume, based on the fact that you're not wearing any, that you don't have warm gloves, either? Eastern Mountain Sports is open 'til six; get over there *right now* and buy yourself a warm coat and some gloves, or I'm gonna toss that old thing you're wearing in the trash, so you'll be forced to replace it." Sumner was a born and raised Bostonian, lazily making his way through dental school while living off an inheritance from his deceased father. He did throw my coat away, but I was able to retrieve it before the garbage trucks came. Sumner simply had no experience in the light of which he could understand that, for me, it was going to be that pea coat or nothing.

Outside the post office, the streets and sidewalks smelled like snow, though it had been several days since any had fallen. A number of dog-owners had brought their pets to wait with them, perhaps planning to combine a walk with their postal errand. Some of the smaller, well-behaved dogs waited in line with their masters, their curly heads sticking out the tops of tote bags advertising the Harvard COOP. There were several bigger dogs on leashes tied-up to the empty bicycle rack like horses at a hitching post. They paced continuously, as far as their leashes allowed, then strained against their bonds to sniff in the direction of anyone exiting the post office doors, lost in paroxysms of joy if they caught a whiff of their master. I envied their hand-knit sweaters and booties, couldn't help thinking that these dogs were better-dressed than I was.

By the time I reached the counter, it was nearly closing time; a disembodied voice assured us over a loudspeaker that those who had managed to make it through the doors would be served before the office closed. With the end of my ordeal in sight, I was emboldened to try a little "we're-all-in-this-together" humor.

"Wow," I said to the clerk. "Time really *does* fly when you're having fun."

She gave no sign that she'd heard me. What did I expect? Encouraging the Christmas spirit by emphasizing how easy it was to ship packages anywhere was part of her job (more revenue for the PO), but she had just gone on overtime. She began a methodical double-check of city against zip code before weighing each of my packages and affixing the postage label.

"92807. Anaheim." She examined the scale. "Five thawty-five," she murmured, noting the numbers on a small pad of paper next to her postal scale. I felt an anxious clench in the pit of my stomach. What did she mean by "five thirty-five"? Time of day? Number of packages she'd processed since nine o'clock$_+$? Or—and this is the possibility I dreaded—the amount of postage needed to get the present to its recipient via the US postal system?

"91775. San Gabriel." She squinted at the numbers on her calculator. "Nine fotty-eight," she announced.

I glanced at her name tag, which hung askew just below her left collarbone and had a sprig of plastic mistletoe as decoration. "Excuse me, ah…Noelle?" I interrupted. "What's nine forty-eight? What's five thirty-five? What is that you're listing?"

She held up an index finger to signal silence as she put package number three on the scale, then raised her eyes to look directly into mine. "That's what it's gonna cost yuh to get this stuff to Califawnyuh by Christmas."

I looked at the packages still piled on the counter awaiting her attention. Most were going to California, to my parents and siblings. Inside one brown paper wrapper was the five-dollar set of Russian Matryoshka dolls I'd bought for my mother. They couldn't possibly weigh more than a couple of ounces. Another held a Harvard t-shirt for one of my brothers—a splurge at twelve bucks, but one I thought he would prefer over the BU shirt I'd considered first. Again, not heavy. But as the list on the clerk's pad grew longer and the total postage costs climbed higher—up to and then surpassing the cost of the gifts themselves, then past the additional amount I'd allocated for a special Christmas meal—my spirits hit bottom. I'd accepted the fact that my celebration would not include visits with family or close friends. I knew there'd be no presents for me arriving in the mail—why kid myself? Now it was becoming obvious that, after paying the postage for my packages, my best hope for a Christmas feast would be limited to some Ramen Noodles and a couple of hard-boiled eggs.

I watched Noelle organize my mailings, stacking the brown packages on her counter by zip code. What, I wondered, was I trying to prove by refusing to give up this family tradition? Did I see myself as a hero, a lone ranger standing atop the suburban Boston hills, arms akimbo, silhouetted against the setting sun? Was I trying to deny my very real poverty, prove to myself that I could survive the trials and uncertainty inherent in the field in which I was determined to be successful in spite of my parents' doubt? Did *I* believe it myself—believe I had the talent, stubbornness, imagination to "make it?" Or would what had seemed quirky and creative and clever when I first made my plans turn out to be simply a refusal to confront reality, my loneliness a nostalgia for experiences I'd never actually had?

"Doing anything special fuh the holidays?"

It took me a moment to realize Noelle was talking to me.

"What? Oh, no. No. I may try to see some friends…"

"Well, Merry Christmas," she said as she moved a "closed" sign to the edge of her counter. She plucked one of the white berries from her plastic mistletoe and placed it in my palm, next to the change from the postage. "He-ah…this'll bring you luck."

6. It's Beginning to Look a Lot Like Christmas

It's beginning to look a lot like Christmas, even though Halloween was only last week. Silver and red mylar decorations featuring bells and candy canes hang from streetlight stanchions, awaiting the civic lighting ceremony scheduled for the day after Thanksgiving. The big box stores are selling artificial pre-lit trees in multiple colors and sizes and ready-made lawn displays that strive to convince us that Frosty the snowman did indeed visit the nativity.

There's good reason for merchants, in particular, to want to rush the season. Many businesses realize as much as one third of their annual sales income during those few short weeks, a number that's expected to soar to nearly $800 billion during the 2019 season.

But what motivation do the rest of us have for participating in what some critics call "the insanity of Christmas?"

I have a theory that *Homo sapiens* has a genetic, chromosomal pre-disposition to give and receive gifts. Why? To express interest, appreciation, or gratitude. As an expression of love or affection. To strengthen bonds or create a reciprocal obligation on the part of the recipient. To experience the emotional lift that we feel while searching for a fitting gift. So that the giver can show that they themselves are deserving of a gift. To feel altruistic: "It is better to give than to receive." To demonstrate superiority in wealth or influence over another. To distribute scarce resources among a group or tribe in such a way as to ensure the persistence of the optimal number of group members. In short, as a survival mechanism.

When observers lament the erosion of "traditional values" in modern celebrations of Christmas, I assume they're mourning the loss of religious meaning in the various forms of celebration ("Keep 'Christ' in Christmas") and ruing the excessive emphasis on the purchase and exchange of gifts. What they may not realize is that, as a tradition, the exchange of mid-winter gifts is itself a centuries-old practice that pre-dates Christianity and can be traced back to at least the Roman Saturnalia, which took place at about the same time on the calendar. These mid-winter holy days (holidays) were marked by the lighting of ceremonial candles while celebrants drank, sang, danced, and indulged in general merry- making.

Or perhaps critics are pining for the Germanic traditions associated with Yuletide—the Yule log, decorated evergreens (introduced to Britain by Queen Victoria's German consort, Albert), and animal sacrifices (ritualized in the roasting and carving of the Christmas ham). None of the critics want to hear that, prior to the nineteenth century, their beloved Christian holiday was a relatively unimportant celebration, looked-upon chiefly as an excuse for public drunkenness and street brawls.

Americans are nostalgic for the "good old days," but I doubt they mean good old Puritan days. The Puritans, who swelled the number of New World colonists, are honored in American legend for risking life and fortune by sailing to the New World in search of religious tolerance. It did indeed require bravery to risk the sea voyage and life in the colonies; it's estimated that as many as a third of the Jamestown colonists died either during the voyage itself or during their first year in the colony. But those who managed to survive had no tolerance for other sects or religions. Colonists who disagreed with their Governors were driven out, forced to rely on their own resources in a difficult and dangerous land. Catholics and Native Americans were frequent victims of discrimination.

The Puritans outlawed the celebration of Christmas and most other Catholic-appointed holidays (like Easter) altogether, recognizing (based on rather obvious evidence) that any festival that invited merriment was rooted in paganism. Christmas was particularly odious to the Puritans because there was no scriptural warrant for its celebration.

The eventual victory by the Puritans in a series of European wars and political maneuvers during the late seventeeth century made their Protestant creed, at least for a time, the law of the land in Britain and its colonies. To ensure there was no misunderstanding among the populace as to what this meant for Christmas celebrations, the victorious Protestants forced shops to remain open and churches to close. Ministers were arrested and fined for preaching on Christmas day. When it seemed these measures weren't enough, the Puritans went on to criminalize any and all acts that could be considered elements of the festival. The Massachusetts colonists, to set a good example, spent their first Christmas in the New World working in their fields.

This animosity toward Christmas traditions could not hold when conservative Protestants began to lose political influence, but there were, eventually, others who campaigned against the worst excesses of the season. One such group was The Society for the Prevention of Useless Giving (or "Spugs"), founded in 1911 by the actress Eleanor Belmont and Anne Morgan, J.P. Morgan's daughter. Within a year, the group grew to about six thousand members, propelled mostly by working-class women who resented the expectation that they would spend their hard-earned income on gifts just to satisfy a social norm. Unfortunately, their anti-materialist, feminist campaign was interrupted by the start of World War I. By that time, the group's focus had already shifted from the "prevention of useless giving" to the "promotion of useful giving." That change of focus didn't eliminate criticism—note parodies like Stan Freberg's satirical 1958 release "Green Christmas" and the popular song "Grandma Got Run Over by a Reindeer" and even the ultra-louche "Santa Baby" as twentieth-century examples. But with the financial success of so many people and businesses dependent on just the type of gift-giving that Spugs and other critics abhorred, we no longer have any real choice as to whether or not or how Christmas is celebrated; any other approach would be economically disastrous.

It's mid-December as I write this, and among the ads in today's paper is a photograph of a young girl clutching a spangle-covered fabric star as she gazes upward, transfixed by a decorated tree glittering against the studio backdrop of frosty windowpanes. If only it were an ad for trees. "Making Christmas Memories," the ad copy reads, "with *New Windows!*"

It's been almost fifty years since I stood in line at the Allston-Brighton post office juggling a stack of presents for my family while slowly succumbing to hypothermia. I've been successful in sticking to the resolution I made that day, even though I miss the challenge of coming up with novel ways to present awkwardly-shaped or -sized gifts. But when socially acceptable Christmas presents include windows, water heaters, and automatic weapons, I understand why my father eventually gave up on gift-giving altogether and began to send checks. At least they fit in a Christmas stocking.

Call It Fiction

I don't know if I can tell you why, at the age of twelve, I came to be standing in our garage on an early fall Sunday evening staring into an open drawer in my father's workbench, trying to pick the right tool to use to injure myself. By which I mean, of course, that I'm not sure I *want* to tell. Or maybe, from a distance of almost fifty years, I have no confidence that I *remember* why—or, rather, that I remember it accurately—even though I've started to tell the story a dozen times.

> *Every day I watched with dread as the hands of the clock on the classroom wall swept toward my hour in hell, when I would be in gym class with the other boys. Most days the organized game we were supposed to be playing would quickly break down as my team gathered around me, poking me with their index fingers and screaming "you fuckin' faggot!" in concert with threats of violence and general demands that someone "kick his ass." The captain who had been unlucky enough to have me forced onto his team as his last pick would bring his face an inch from mine, to where I could smell lunchtime's tuna sandwiches and milk fermenting in his belly, and hiss, "If you miss another ball, you're dead!"*

Yeah, I wrote that. My memory tells me it happened just as I described it. Does that make it "true," i.e., factual? Or am I describing my own typical adolescent self-loathing through eyes of classmates? And, even if true, should it matter now? By choosing to expose it, am I trying to suggest that the incident had an important impact on my developing personality, something more insightful than the realization that adolescent boys can be cruel? Is my writing about it, in and of itself, evidence of a faith in its deterministic power? Or is it a simple self-indulgence, a puling, self-centered plea for attention from a whiny crybaby looking for sympathy because life has not lived up to his expectations? Poor me. Boo-hoo-hoo.

I don't remember ever meeting anyone who loves to talk about how great their childhood and adolescence were. That, of course, includes me. In the *theatre intime* we called "home," my sister, Rebecca, and I, born thirteen months apart, performed a stumbling duet as collaborators, casualties, and POWs in the dramatic, ongoing battles fought by the crazy people who cast themselves as our parents. Our two brothers were, respectively, too old and too young to be anything but an audience. I have my parents' wedding portrait, as deceptive as any cast photo, and sometimes still search for understanding in the face of my mother—insecure, cruel, jealous, depressed, with her tentative half smile concealing a will of iron—and the blank eyes of my father, as deep, kohl-ed, and silent as Valentino's.

The weapons deployed in their decades-long internecine battle—she consistently advancing, he perpetually retreating—were as often emotional as physical. My mother made sure we knew she had never wanted children; to her we were unfairly advantaged competitors for the attentions of a husband who reminded her of her own stern, laconic father. She once confided to me that the only reason she had decided to produce offspring was so we could take care of her when she grew old. She had no other aspirations for us.

Another time, during a conspiratorial moment, she drew me close to whisper that I was her favorite child. I struggled to reconcile this professed love with her confused history of indifference, jealousy, and violent, arbitrary punishments. Years later I read Pat Conroy's novel *The Prince of Tides*, in which the narrator's abusive mother makes the same confession. Later he finds out she told each of his siblings the same thing.

During her bouts of real fury, the causes of which were usually a mystery to me, my mother's abuse turned physical. These thrashings—I won't describe them in detail—involved vigorous application of "the strap," an old belt that had lost its buckle that was kept snake-coiled in a kitchen drawer. These episodes, which I'm sure in the present day would attract the attention of the Department of Youth and Family Services (DYFUS), usually ended with her beating time with the strap on my cowering body as Rebecca calmly waited her turn: God! Damn! You! To! Hell!

The bad memories—sometimes I feel I have a million of them—come easily, even across half a century; but their age alone makes them suspect. I remember the beatings as being frequent—or did it only happen once, or only a few times? The detail in my mind's recollection of the belt's cracked, well-worn leather argues for repetition. But other, fainter images of my mother also emerge: baking cheesecake in aluminum pie tins, soaping a stenciled image of Santa and his reindeer on the front windows at Christmastime, a rainy day when she made a train out of empty cardboard boxes linked with pieces of rope and pulled Rebecca and me from room to room across the polished hardwood floor. And me, on my way home from school, stopping to pick an illicit bouquet of Sweet Peas for her through spaces in our neighbor's fence. Why are the good memories less distinct? Why do they feel less important?

When I began to write, it was not with the intention of dredging up the bad old days. Gradually, though, I was drawn in by this zeitgeist: the urge to write a complaining memoir. Stop into any creative writing class in the country and I'm willing to bet you'll find students aged twenty to eighty busily dredging up painful memories and trying to massage them into works of creative non-fiction. What's behind this enthusiasm for wallowing in the traumas of our individual pasts? The exploration may offer a possibility of catharsis for the writer; but I wonder about the value for author and audience of airing these depressing stories in public, a process I think of as "the Jerry Springer effect." It usually goes something like this:

Author (being interviewed by Jerry): "My self-confidence, trust, and ability to have meaningful relationships were destroyed because of the way my parents/ siblings/ friends/ spouse dissed me."

Audience (both singly and as a group): "Wow! I may be screwed up but at least I'm not as screwed up as that poor asshole!"

Or could it be one of these contemporary positions:

- Everyone has a story to tell and all stories are equally legitimate, important, and meaningful to others
- Society, under the influence of gangsta rap, soft-porn music videos, and tearful confessions by transgressing Christian fundamentalists, has succumbed to the idea that we should all "let it all hang out"
- The absence of self- or societal control or criticism; no one is going to step forward and say, "Don't go there."
- Diminishing acceptance of drunkenness and cigarette smoking as ways of dealing with strong feelings; now our choice of dysfunction is between becoming addicted to painkillers and writing a memoir

- Growing public admiration and financial rewards accruing to memoirists with tragic stories: you can become rich and famous off your pain
- The impulse to "get even" with childhood torturers by permanently recording their crimes in "literature"

The list could go on. For myself, I found that exploring the past helped me to understand and forgive those I believe wronged me and to achieve some level of detente with my demons. But seeking public sympathy for my trauma—ending every chapter or story with an implied self-pitying "poor me"—doesn't make it any more legitimate. And it won't make me any happier.

Then there's that nagging issue of "truth." Occasionally I'll bring up our common past with my two brothers, and rediscover that our past is not common at all: they each have different memories and feelings—all less dramatic than my own—about what happened in our household and our parents' role in it. I would turn to Rebecca for validation if I could—if she had not left us behind on her journey through drug addiction, failed marriages, alcoholism, and early dementia. These facts alone might seem to support my version of our shared childhood, but like her they are incoherent. Which "truth" is the "real" one? In one sense none are; in another sense all are: they are each child's own unique personal history.

I'm sitting at my laptop as I write this, feeling the lure of my own stories of hurt and betrayal waiting impatiently in the fan-cooled circuits a half inch below my fingertips. Gathered in drafts, fragments, folders, chapters, their electronic hum is a siren song tempting me to self-indulgence, to make myself the subject of their weepy sentences. "We're tales that should be told!" they cry. "We can help other people feel less alone, start them on their own paths to understanding! I'm determined to tell stories—even painful ones—but without indulging the need to feel "special" by making myself the real-life victim at the center of them. I want to write stories of redemption rather than persecution; about what's right with us all rather than what's wrong. I'll give my parents, my siblings, my friends, my classmates, and the guy behind the counter at Starbucks a break by acknowledging that they were doing the best they could at the time. And when I write about the bad old days, I'll seek respect and admiration for my inventiveness and imagination rather than sympathy for my suffering. I'll call it fiction.

Life As Opera:
An Abecedarium

A *ida's* plot does not include a stock car race, a bullfight, or swordplay; hence one may be excused for failing to consider the odds of being killed while watching it. In 1971, my sister Rebecca and I were spending the summer touring Europe on a budget even more meager than that detailed in one of the best-selling books at the time, *Europe on $5 a Day*. We saw the posters advertising a production of *Aida* at the ruins of the Baths of Caracalla, near the Roman Coliseum. We couldn't afford the tickets. We didn't have appropriate clothes. We had no idea how we'd get back to our campground on the edge of the city after the show, when the Roman buses would no longer be running. Rebecca was insistent. That evening, we didn't have to wait longer than the middle of the overture for the experience to become even more dramatic than we could have imagined.

The venue for this *Aida* was outdoors, which meant there was plenty of room to load up the stage with supernumeraries, exotic animals, and dancing girls, all celebrating the victorious return of Radames from a war with Ethiopia. As the orchestra reached a crescendo, four matched black horses galloped over the rise at the back of the raked wooden stage, pulling a chariot containing the tenor singing the part of Radames and a driver.

For whatever reason, the right-most horse stumbled and started to go down as he came over the rise, dragging the entire team to the right. This interference tripped up the second and third horses which, with their cadence broken, veered left. The fourth horse managed to keep his footing, but it was a moment-to-moment victory. From our vantage point, we could clearly see terror on the faces of the chariot's passengers, both now part of a four-ton mass of thrashing horseflesh and slashing, metal-shod hooves that was sliding downhill toward the orchestra pit at alarming speed. The conductor, with his back to the stage, was alerted to the impending disaster only when four of the violinists dropped their instruments and tried to flee by scaling the wall that separated them from the audience. Rebecca and I were seated just behind the timpani; if the pile of horse and human had actually made it as far as the pit, I doubt any of us would be alive today. As it was, once everyone managed to come to a stop and sort themselves out, they rejoined the orchestra (which had never stopped playing), proving once again the universality of the adage, "the show must go on."

B *The Bartered Bride* was my introduction to what would turn out to be a love affair with performing in opera choruses at San Diego State College. The college presented two operas each year. Students didn't have to audition to be in the chorus; we simply signed up for a one-unit credit. This "come one, come all" attitude resulted in choruses peopled by a cross-section of the student community, ranging from those who barely knew what opera was to seasoned performers who aspired to become professional singers.

In act three of *The Bartered Bride* opera, a circus comes to the small Czech village that's the setting for the piece. When it was time to cast the circus performers, the director faced the choristers milling about on the stage and shouted over the din, "Do any of you perform old-fashioned circus tricks?" One of the men in the chorus stepped forward and answered, "I can eat fire." It's a phrase one just doesn't expect to hear during a random casting call. Joined by a juggler, an acrobat, and a dog act, the entire circus scene was cast from the chorus in about five minutes.

C *The Crucible* was my first major lighting design credit, for a set designed by Don Powell. Don taught scenic design at the college for many years, and the college's main stage was renamed in his honor when he passed away in 1987. *The Crucible* was both the first and last show I worked on that my parents came to see. Afterward, I was chatting with my mother when my dad interrupted and asked, "Can you tell me again what you did for this play?" Behind him, my mother put her palms together in a prayer gesture and tipped her head to one side. Translation: he'd slept through it.

D *on Giovanni* presented yet another opportunity to perform in the opera chorus, but also marks the turning point at which I changed from being a scholar to pursuing an eventual career as a theatre artist/craftsman. I began to volunteer in the college's costume shop during preparations for Don Giovanni and soon was working in the shop as much as sixteen hours a day, neglecting the courses required for my triple major in history, economics, and political science. When I arrived at the theatre on opening night, the shabby, much-used doublet I'd worn through all the dress rehearsals was not on the chorus wardrobe rack. Next to my name tag was a jacket I'd never seen before, one (it turned out) that the paid staff had made for me as a "thank you" for my volunteer work on the show.

A note on the title "Don:" There are at least a dozen operas named *Don* Somebody, which may confuse those who don't know that "Don" is a modest honorific, similar to "Mister" in English. The comic opera *Don Pasquale* is another example of a "Don" opera and was the first show for which I designed costumes as an MFA candidate at the University of Illinois.

E *The Importance of Being Earnest* is an example of the way in which plots, characters, themes, and titles are often re-used in telling a contemporary story. This type of borrowing has taken place thousands of times in the history of the arts, and doubtless will continue to take place in the foreseeable future. This entry is for *The Importance of Being Earnest,* the twenty-first century opera based on the nineteenth century play by Oscar Wilde, which I've never seen or heard. But I did design the costumes for a production of the *play* while a graduate student at Boston University.

F *ourth Composer.* That was the first actual character role I [performed, in a production of the operetta *The Great Waltz* that was mounted by San Diego's Junior Theatre group. My part was to la-la-la my way through several bars of "Tales from the Vienna Woods" in the first act, then retire to the back of the chorus for the remainder of the show. When I exited the theatre after one of the performances, a young girl— I'd guess age nine or ten—rushed up to me with her autograph book and pen in hand and breathlessly asked for my signature. She was so thrilled when I added my own child-like scrawl to those more confident examples in her book; I was really taken aback. An older woman— grandmother? Aunt? Hovered protectively in the background. I found myself wishing my parents had been half as supportive of my childhood enthusiasms.

For me, working in the theatre was never about seeking fans or other forms of popularity as a performer, though when others found out I worked in the theatre they almost always assumed I was an actor.

I just liked to create cool things, and I liked to make them with minimal interference from anyone else. My graduate design teacher, James Berton Harris, warned me more than once against the risks of over-designing a show. "You don't want an audience to leave the theatre humming the costumes," he'd say. Oh, but I did.

There was one incident that nearly awakened in me a desire to seek the roar of the crowd. It was a planned fancy-dress spectacle that occurred during performances of *A Night in Venice* (see below under N). At the beginning of the second act, the eight-member women's chorus came on-stage one at a time wearing elaborate off-white Baroque-style ball gowns arranged over pannier undergarments that made their hips appear to be about four feet wide. The front of each gown was festooned with silk brocade drapes in various shades of pink, drawn back by jeweled birds to reveal the white gown underneath. Each chorister entered at the top of an up-center staircase, pausing just long enough to allow the audience to take in the splendor of their jewels, feathers, and draperies before coming down the stairs on the arm of her escort. It was very reminiscent of (if a great deal less elaborate than) Edith Head's costume designs for the ball scene in the movie *To Catch A Thief.* On opening night, I was standing in the back of the theatre, disheartened by my count of extra-large chrome safety pins that had accidentally been left in the lining of The Prince's coat. They flashed in the ellipsoidal light every time the singer shifted position. Standing next to me was Bill Schroder, my friend of some twenty years at the time, and the designer who had convinced LOOM to hire me in his stead. As the audience reacted with round after round of applause, Bill leaned over and said into my ear, "That's for *you.* If he noticed the sophomoric mistake, he didn't mention it.

G *The Good Soldier Schweich at SDSC* was the second collaboration between me as lighting designer and Don Powell as set designer.

H D Simulcast, as "Presented in…." I remember from childhood the live Saturday afternoon broadcasts from the Metropolitan Opera House in New York City. These are the longest-running continuous classical radio series in American broadcast history. To me, the singers seemed superhuman; I tried to imagine what it would be like to be able to produce the noises they did with no tools other than their own voices. Today, that effect is magnified by high-definition technology. I recently attended an HD simulcast of the Philip Glass opera *Akhenaten,* produced as part of the Met's 2019 season—something I would otherwise never have had the chance to experience.

I *phigenia in Brooklyn*, aria from, attributed to P.D.Q. Bach by Professor Peter Schickele. I've included this aria in the abecedarium as a representative contradiction to the idea that there is no real humor among classical music and musicians. In addition to many works by Schickele's alter ego, P.D.Q. Bach, we have as evidence the late careers of Anna Russell (perhaps best known for her thirty-minute version of Wagner's complete *Ring* cycle), Victor Borge, (who did stand-up while seated at his piano), and many others.

J *Leoš Janáček* composed the opera *The Cunning Little Vixen*, produced by New York City Opera, with costumes designed by children's book author Maurice Sendak (*Where the Wild Things Are*). The cast list included various domesticated and wild animals and insects. Many of the costumes were created at the Studio, the costume house where I worked at the time. For *Vixen*, I was responsible for making chicken feet for the women's chorus. Critics have praised this production as "an example of New York City Opera at its prime." During the same era, City Opera mounted imaginative productions of *Candide* and *The Mikado*. I created all the headgear for *The Mikado*, which was the focus of a feature article in the magazine *Opera News*.

K *"Kill the wabbit, kill the wabbit,…."* For the millions of us who were Bugs Bunny fans in the fifties and sixties, the 1957 cartoon *What's Opera, Doc?* was often our introduction to operatic and classical music. The lines above were sung by Elmer Fudd to music clipped from Richard Wagner's *Die Walküre*.

The *Merrie Melodies* series of animated musical shorts were produced at Warner Bros. *What's Opera, Doc?* has been preserved in the National Film Registry by the US Library of Congress, which deemed it as "culturally, historically, or aesthetically significant"; it also holds the number one spot in the 1994 book, *the 50 Greatest Cartoons: As Selected by 1,000 Animation Professionals*.

L *ucia di Lammermoor* is the opera being performed with an alien cast in the concert scene in the film, *The Fifth Element*. Albanian soprano Inva Mula is the voice-over performer of the aria "Il dolce suono."

M *anon* was the first and only SDSC production in which I had a speaking role. I had two lines as the Captain who accepts a bribe to release Manon to her brother in the final scene. Two of my siblings—younger brother John and sister Rebecca—were also in the chorus, which made the production the only time the three of us were all on stage at the same time.

N *A Night in Venice* at the LOOM was my first and last off-Broadway show as the principal costume designer. It called for about sixty costumes; the women's chorus dressed up in high-style Baroque dresses with paniers for a second-act masquerade ball. I had eight weeks between signing my contract and opening night. My relationship with the producers began to unravel almost immediately, partially due to the fact that William Mount-Burke, the renowned founder of the company and the director of *A Night...*, was blind as a result of advanced diabetes. There was a tense series of good news/bad news discoveries. For example, I was fortunate to have a construction crew provided by the company.

Unfortunately, the "crew" was one person.

Unfortunately, she was also the wardrobe mistress.

Unfortunately, she was a part-time employee.

I only saw the woman who was supposed to be my assistant three times during the build period, which is part of the reason I found myself, late one night, standing at a cutting table in the company's costume shop, dabbing at my face with a scrap of muslin, trying to find the source of the bright splashes of blood that were dropping on the piles of fabric on the table in front of me—fabric that had to be cut into ready-to-assemble pattern pieces before morning. The fountainhead turned out to be my nose. My blood pressure was so high that I had experienced a spontaneous epistaxis—a nosebleed.

I couldn't really be mad at my assistant for her lack of attention to my show; by the time she finished doing the laundry and repairs for the show that was running while mine was being built, she had pretty much used up her four hours per day. I probably will never know who arranged it, but about a week into my construction phase my friends and co-workers from the Studio started showing up in the evenings to work on my show for a couple of hours. They were true volunteers, stepping in to come to the rescue of a colleague who had bitten off more than he could chew. I couldn't pay them; I didn't have money for extra help in my budget. But the mood in the shop was far from grim.

Under the influence of the evening volunteers, the whole gambit took on a bit of an Andy Hardy flavor—a situation in which all the world's problems could be resolved by putting on a show. Of course, Andy and Judy didn't have to work in a building that was built to be the city morgue, and their director wasn't blind, as mine was. As you might guess, *A Night in Venice* was the show that convinced me I was in the wrong business. I started brainstorming ideas for a new career as soon as *A Night...* fell.

O*pera* in performance is a form of human expression intended to entertain, teach, provoke, politicize—in short, to hold up to its audience a mirror that reflects and illuminates a dramatized point of view on contemporary and historical issues. Terms like "Operetta" and "Light Opera" describe variations that serve the same purpose but in a less forbidding, even humorous manner. The dictionary definition of "opera" has expanded almost continuously throughout the twentieth century, evolving to include what their creators refer to as "rock" operas like *Jesus Christ Superstar* and *Tommy*, which otherwise might be considered song cycles (*Spoon River Anthology, Chess.*)

The word "opera" is Latin in origin, the plural of "opus," and is translated to Italian simply as "work." As with other theatre and performance arts classified under this taxonomy, opera audiences look for pieces that focus on three elements: a pot-boiler plot that's often gleaned from current events or based on a popular novel or national folk tale; some dramatic music which, again, is better appreciated if it includes variations from contemporary tunes; and drama, or better yet, melodrama.

The art form blossomed in Europe during the second half of the nineteenth century (somewhat earlier by hundreds of years in the far east) more or less in lockstep with the rise of Romanticism and with a keen sensitivity to feelings. Many opera plots are formulaic and rely on tried-and-true standard plot devices: lovers whose passions are thwarted by political or religious differences; misunderstood beliefs or thoughts that trigger tragic consequences; and so forth. In most Romantic period operas, the plot is resolved with the triumph of good over evil and one or more of the main characters dead, down center.

Because of these characteristics, calling something "operatic" usually means it's filled with moments of high drama and emotionally affecting music. This makes an operatic musical quote perfect for use in product advertising. I remember going to drive-in movies in the 1960s and hearing the musical ad for the snack bar, which was sung to the tune of the toreador song from Bizet's opera *Carmen*:

> *Have a hot tamale full of roasted meat.*
> *Have a hot tamale—they're mighty good to eat!*

P*acific Conservatory of the Performing Arts* (PCPA) at Alan Hancock College, Santa Maria, California was the west coast version of summer stock. I was hired as the assistant milliner for the season because I was one of two people in the company who had ever made a hat. Because of this distinction, I was paid the enormous sum of $300 for eight weeks of work. (That's total, not $300 a week.) The sting was leavened by the knowledge that everyone else was getting the same. Lodging, food, and transportation were all at our own expense; I trace my intimate knowledge of ways to dress up a cup of Ramen noodles to that summer. We had to create the costumes (and headgear) for six shows in four weeks; the summer I worked there the rep did *Gypsy*, *As You Like It*, *Romeo and Juliet*, *The Utter Glory of Morrissey Hall*, *The Ballad of the Sad Café*, and *Candide*. I'm going to argue that the last one qualifies PCPA to be included on this list because *Candide* was also produced by New York City Opera in 1982. It was also the piece selected to open City Opera's comeback season when it emerged from bankruptcy in 2016. Bottom line: I could never leave PCPA off a list of my best theatrical experiences. I loved the whole summer stock environment; It was one of the most exciting, difficult, and rewarding experiences of my theatre career.

Q*Don Quichotte* is a 1909 opera by Jules Massenet based on the novel by Cervantes.

R*The Ring* Cycle made up of the four operas *Die Valkyrie*, *Siegfried*, *Der Ring Des Nibelungen*, and *Götterdämmerung*, is considered to be Richard Wagner's masterwork. Any opera company that wants to be taken seriously must present the cycle at least once every ten or fifteen years or so. New York's Metropolitan Opera phased-in its latest realization between the 2010 and 2018 seasons, with an entirely new set and stage direction by the Quebecois director Robert Lepage.

The controversial stage set for the series, which is referred to by both fans and critics as "the machine," was made up of dozens of mechanized platforms controlled by computer—sort of like a giant game of Tetris. It reportedly cost the Met sixteen million dollars to build a set that could achieve Lepage's vision.

S *The Seven Streams of the River Ota* is not an opera, though its scope and lyricism invite the description "operatic." It's mentioned here because of its six-degrees-of-separation relationship to the Met's *Ring*, director Robert Lepage, his French-Canadian theatre troupe, Ex Machina, my friend Rebecca Blankenship, and me. *Seven Streams* is a seven-hour summing-up of world history beginning with the dropping of a nuclear bomb on Hiroshima and ending with a dramatic commentary on the AIDS crisis. A Robert Lepage production, it was created in 1995 with his French-Canadian theatre troupe, Ex Machina. Among the cast was my long-time friend Rebecca Blankenship—the same Rebecca Blankenship with whom I'd shared the crafts table and cups of café con leche at the Studio twenty years or so earlier; the same Rebecca who had abandoned New York for Vienna and Basel out of frustration with the scarcity of opportunity in the US for up-and-coming classical singers. She had blossomed and was thriving in the richer cultural environment of the European capitals and had become a much-admired and popular performer as a dramatic soprano, singing primarily Wagnerian roles. In spite of numerous successes, she spoke of feeling hemmed-in by the rigidity of a typical operatic career and began to question her motivation for continuing it. She eventually made the decision to cancel all of her upcoming operatic appearances, an action that virtually ended her singing career. She came to stay at my home in Plainfield, New Jersey—a visit that continued for about two years, during which she explored her poetry and her interest in psychodrama.

Rebecca remained in touch with Lepage, who invited her to work with Ex Machina on a new theatre piece that would eventually become *Seven Streams*. Her role in the ensemble cast was that of Ada, an American opera singer. When Lepage was engaged to direct the Met's *Ring* cycle, it was natural for him to turn to Rebecca as a subject-area expert and his advisor. She's listed in the program for the Met as an artistic consultant.

T *osca* was my last work for a theatre company—in this case, New York's Metropolitan Opera—before I started my new job and career as a computer programmer for a large Wall Street firm. It was the follow-through on my middle-of-the-night decision, back in LOOM's costume shop *nee* city morgue, to find a less stressful career.

The Met's 1985 production of *Tosca* was double cast: Placido Domingo and Hildegard Behrens first, followed by Luciano Pavarotti and Jessye Norman. There was quite a lot of literal weight on stage in the persons of both these couples, though perhaps a bit more in the case of Pavarotti and Norman. Putting aside the tired aphorism about the fat lady singing, I will just note, for those who are unfamiliar with opera, that the art form values voice over acting ability and requires from its audience a willing suspension of disbelief regarding much of the physical stage business the director hopes to draw from the performers. In the *Tosca* cast, the differences were most striking when comparing the performances of Behrens and Norman, the two lead sopranos. In the final scene of the opera, for example, the action called for Tosca to commit suicide by leaping from the parapet of the Castel Sant'Angelo in Rome. When the moment arrived, Hildegard Behrens dove into her final action with gusto, dashing from down center to the upstage wall and flinging herself into the void with nary a pause nor stumble, landing on an inflated stunt cushion hidden upstage. In contrast, Jessye—*very* overweight—sang her final words from a position near center stage, then paused to neatly gather her taffeta stole around her shoulders, turn, and stalk off into the wings stage left.

My contribution to the production was to make twenty-five quick-change wimples for the women's chorus in the finale of Act One, where they were all dressed as nuns. It was a very straightforward cash-and-carry arrangement, all my work done off-premises to be delivered by a certain date. But I discovered through the experience a bonus benefit in the Met's approach to crediting artists who contribute to a production. I was listed in the program for *Tosca*'s opening night at the Met as an assistant milliner—ironically, the same job title under which I'd been hired for my first paying job in the theatre, at PCPA. But the quirk I mentioned is that the Met repeats the list of artists/contributors from the production's premier every time a set is re-used over its lifetime, which could be many years. In the case of the 1985 production of *Tosca*, an audience favorite, it was hundreds of performances over twenty-five years.

U*nderstudy*: this isn't an anecdote about opera, but I wanted to slip in an observation that everyone should have a chance—at least once in their life—to perform in a theatre in front of a sold-out audience. SDSC had planned a production of the musical *1776* in recognition of the American bicentennial, and I decided, on a lark, to audition for it. I figured that, with what was essentially an all-male cast, I should be able to easily capture the role of some minor signer. It turned out that wasn't true; instead, I was asked to understudy the entire cast, and I agreed. Then I found out that the actor playing Benjamin Franklin—one of the principal roles—absolutely could not be there for the final dress rehearsal. I was going to be Franklin for one performance, and that performance, free to all students, would be SRO.

Everything went well in the first act, where Franklin opens the show with a solo scene. But in the first scene of the second act, I "went up," a term that means an actor has forgotten their lines. I stood on stage, silent, staring at the actor playing Thomas Jefferson while I ran lines in my head, desperately hoping I would stumble onto the right one. Officially, the performance was a dress rehearsal; it would have been entirely proper for me to turn to the stage manager, who was following along in the script, and ask for my next line. That simple solution never suggested itself. After a pause of an uncomfortable number of seconds, Jefferson launched into a lengthy monologue, during which the *real* actor/Franklin arrived at the theatre in his street clothes and bumped me off stage. But living through those few moments of panic and embarrassment gave me a standard against which I could measure every other appalling life experience and still know that things would be okay.

V *Giuseppe Verdi* may be the most beloved opera composer of all time. He wrote twenty-five of them, including favorites like *Aida, Falstaff, La Traviata, Nabucco,* and *Il Trovatore.* His fans, it's said, were so enraptured by *Otello*'s premiere in Milan that, at its conclusion, the streets near the opera house filled with the excited crowd to the point where the startled horses hitched to Verdi's coach driver were unable to maneuver through the throng. His fans reportedly unhitched the team and pulled the carriage through the streets from the opera house to his hotel themselves, singing choruses from *Otello* as they went.

In today's celebrity-engorged entertainment environment, I suspect that the composer, whose name in English translates to "Joe Green," would not have made it to his first publicity event without a name change.

W *Kurt Weil* wrote *The Threepenny Opera,* for which I designed the set when it was produced on the Music Hall stage at San Diego State University. The budget for this show approached zero, but in rummaging through scenery storage I was able to cobble together a respectable set out of thrice-used framed and painted canvas flats. It helped that the pieces I used were supposed to resemble trash. That's what I told everyone, anyway.

X *erxes* is one of two operas commissioned from Georg Fredrich Handel for the King's Theatre in London in 1737. Its plot is a typical eighteenth-century muddle of unrequited love, mistaken identity, and plotted revenge. Its cast of characters also provides an example of a practice that's difficult for modern audiences to accept: in early European operas, men's roles were often sung by castrati—boys who had been castrated just before entering puberty. The reasons are many, but all are based on the opinion that the adolescent male soprano voice is the purest and most agile, and thus the most beautiful. The practice began in the 1600s and was outlawed in the 1870s, after which date the roles that had been sung by castrati were given to countertenors or mezzo-sopranos, who (in the latter case) would perform them as trouser roles—women playing men. The stage could quickly become confusing in terms of gender roles.

The best-known aria from *Xerxes*, "Ombra mai fu," is a love song addressed to a tree and can be sung by either by a castrato or a countertenor.

Y *eomen of the Guard*. Gilbert and Sullivan. San Diego State University. I was in the chorus. Always fun.

Z *Franco Zeffirelli* died last year on June fifteenth, age ninety-six. I purposely avoided including anything related to the Maestro, as everyone called him, in the entry for *Tosca*. Of course, he was the director/designer for the 1985 Met production; it bore his signature hyper-realistic style that made even his stage prisons seem picturesque. I never actually met the Maestro, though we were in the same room at the same time on a few occasions. But I can say this about him: he was the only designer I know of who was able to walk into a cathedral, stand in the middle of the nave, and say, "Build this" without anyone laughing. But then the scenery would be built (mostly out of painted canvas-covered wooden one-by-three frames—an age-old technique), the three-dimensional elements added (columns, statuary carved from styrofoam), and the lighting cues set, and behold! The interior of the Church of Sant 'Andrea Della Valle stood before us, exactly as the Maestro wanted it. Of course, this type of verisimilitude does not come cheap; Opera is one of the most expensive type of theatre to produce.

Twenty-five years later, his iconic costumes (including my quick-release wimples) and beloved sets were officially retired in favor of a new production designed by David McVicar, a thirty-five-year-old west coast designer, thus restarting the wheel of artistry and creativity on a new, inexorably evolving path. One final coincidence: in my senior year of high school, the number one hit on popular radio was "A Time for Us," with lyrics set to Henry Mancini's instrumental "Theme from Romeo and Juliet"—a movie directed by Franco Zeffirelli.

Twenty-One

I figured the party was being planned as a surprise, if only because, as the date approached, there was absolutely no sign of preparation. If it were an ordinary birthday, plans would already have been made for a special dinner. There would have been a discussion of what kind of cake should be prepared, and questions about what I wanted as a gift. My answer to this last one was important; one lapse when I turned thirteen had resulted in my receiving an awkwardly gift-wrapped safety razor and a stick of deodorant with a bow around it. Now I worried that there'd been no birthday-related questions—not even about the dinner, much less a party. No slip, no peep, no hurriedly shushed conversation, no clumsy attempt to secretly compile a guest list through "innocent" inquiries, no clue at all as to what was being planned. It had to be big. After all, this was not an ordinary birthday. It would be my twenty-first.

I was living at home, in my old room, just for the summer. My job at the University had petered out between sessions, leaving me penniless and dependent on my parents' particularly Puritan brand of generosity. The summer days sweltered, with no relief at night; our discomfort served as testimony to the fact that my parents didn't believe in air conditioning. That is to say, they believed that it existed, and weren't shy about spending brief heat vacations in the air-conditioned shops in the village, but they never signed on to the idea that we deserved to have it at home. Soon, as she did every year, my mother would greet the first break in the heat that seemed it might be permanent with a triumphant cry of victory: "We made it! We made it through another summer!" As though simply surviving was an achievement, something to be proud of. But until then, the household would wake every morning exhausted by another night of sweaty, fitful sleep, and my mother and I would run through some variation of what I called "the job questionnaire."

"Are you going to look for work today?" she'd ask.

Me: "Yeah, I thought I'd try the hardware store."

Mother (disappointed): "Oh, Bud—you don't know anything about hardware, do you? Don't you think you'd do better if you tried for a job you know something about?"

She was right. I knew almost nothing about hardware, certainly no more than I knew about bicycle messengering, operating a cash register at one of the local antique stores, or any of the other jobs I'd applied for in recent weeks. I was majoring in telecommunications and film at school, but our village didn't have a movie theatre or even a camera store. I think we both knew I wasn't going to get a summer job at this late date, and to be perfectly honest, I was pretty much satisfied with the status quo. I only had a month until the next semester started, anyway. Yeah, a birthday party would be a welcome distraction. It should be a big one. With lots of presents.

Early on, I fantasized that my twenty-first birthday might be an event important enough to draw my older siblings back to the homestead for a couple of nights. But neither of them had a desire to risk their painfully reconstructed self-respect against the flame-thrower that was my father's regard, even if birthdays were truce days in our on-going internecine battles. Besides, my older brother lived too far away, was already married, had two kids and a teaching job in a Los Angeles slum that kept him out

of the Vietnam draft. My sister, one year ahead of me at State, was hitchhiking through Mexico for the summer. My younger brother still lived at home, biding his time while he finished high school, planning his own eventual escape.

None of us who thought about it at all understood what made our family the way it was—what made us react to each other the way we did. Sometimes I think the soil of the failed citrus orchard our house was built on was poisoned, and that over the years that poison leached out of the dirt and into our flesh and bones. My parents had purchased the land to build a shore house, but it was too far east of the ridges of low, brown coastal hills to catch the freshening fog that rose off San Diego Bay. Whatever curse had been cast on us had long ago soured the very fiber

of my parents' relationship. They should have seen at a glance that the arid climate and the ruined soil would never nurture anything, animal or vegetable. Yet it was here, among the bitter oranges and mealy lemons on the orchard's remaining trees, that my parents had chosen to raise four children.

As soon as we were old enough to have a friend outside our family, we discovered how different most parents were from ours. My first friend, Halyard, who was also the first gay person I knew, was disbelieving when I told him how my mother had force-fed me cheddar cheese because I'd made a casual remark that I didn't like the smell of it. As for my father, he always accused us of lying when we gave him unwelcome news. If we complained of pain or injury, he assumed we were trying to avoid assigned chores. One summer morning before he left for work, he told me to mow our half-acre of weedy lawn with our old push mower, despite a pain in my abdomen so sharp I couldn't stand up straight. It turned out to be appendicitis; the organ burst as the surgeon was removing it. I would have died if my mother hadn't decided to ignore my father's instructions for once and take me to see a doctor. Even so, I ended up with peritonitis and nearly died. My father was somewhat chastened by the incident, but once I was out of danger he returned to his old habits.

One good thing I can say about my father is that he rarely hit us. I can't say the same for my mother. She used an old, cracked leather belt that had lost its buckle. We referred to as "the strap." It existed for the sole purpose of whipping us. Our most banal misbehaviors aroused an unchecked rage in my mother; her favored punishment was to order us to bring the strap from its storage place in a kitchen drawer and hand it to her, whereupon she would beat the crap out of us with it. My sister coped by becoming more withdrawn with each incident until, at eighteen, she simply moved out of the house and disappeared for nearly a year.

I lost count of the number of times I ran away, usually heading first for the safety of the dry canyon whose western edge ran along Glen Cove Drive, the street we lived on. I knew the canyon well enough to find my way in the dark when I needed to; neither of my parents would follow me there. My siblings and I all used the canyon for sanctuary at one time or another. All we knew of family relationships was abuse, and so we beat each other up on a regular basis. One time my older brother, eight years my senior, got hold of a BB gun and emptied a load of shot at me from the back door of the house while I huddled, trapped, in the fenced corner of the orchard. I would have had to run past him to make it to the canyon, and therefore had violated the cardinal rule of our family relations: always have an escape route.

My younger brother was the one who finally broke the cycle of punishments. He had reached his adult height early, as I had, and by age thirteen was about nine inches taller than my mother's five-foot-four. One afternoon when she came at him with the strap, he caught the business end of it mid-air on her first stroke. A firm, unexpected tug was all that was needed to yank it out of her hand. My brother leaped forward to press his advantage and pinned our mother against the closet door, shaking the fist that held the leather lash. "Don't. Ever. Hit. Me. Again," he said through gritted teeth. She got the message without him appending the "Or else."

Before I met Halyard, as I've said, I had no idea that our home life was unusual. I thought all children lived as indentured servants until they managed to escape. When we were both thirteen, Halyard invited me over to his house to have dinner with his family. I was too embarrassed by my poor table manners to relax and enjoy the experience. I kept waiting for a fight to break out; I even had an insult ready for Halyard, who chewed with his mouth open, like a dog. Somehow there never seemed to be an appropriate moment to trot out that observation. "What holiday is it?" I asked Halyard later, as he was walking me home. I explained that civil conversation at dinner at my house meant that a twenty-four-hour truce had been formally declared in honor of a national holiday or another important event, with the expectation that we'd pick up the fight where we'd left off at the next opportunity. Christmas and birthdays, in particular, were sacrosanct, days on which weapons would be sheathed and we would enact the roles of "family." Halyard simply stared at me with an expression that suggested I was insane. When we had walked a couple more blocks and there was no danger we would be seen from either house, he put his arm across my shoulders as if to comfort me. It just made me more nervous; I knew what would happen if anyone from school saw us. I shrugged his arm off, and we walked the rest of the way to my house in silence.

Fried chicken was my favorite meal. I'd asked for it on my birthday every year since the age of eight, when it had unseated my devotion to waffles with Velveeta cheese sauce. I loved the sensation of biting through the crusty greasiness of a drumstick to savor the hot chicken juice as it rushed into my mouth, salty and rich with fat. No one else in the family liked fried chicken, so my mother never fixed it other than on my birthday. Now I worried that I hadn't been given the chance to confirm my choice, but decided that, after thirteen years, my mother had figured it out. Still, I hunted out of the corners of my eyes for hidden presents, secreted cakes (chocolate with green mint icing, she knew, was my favorite), anything that would give me a hint as to what was coming.

When the day at last arrived, I'd still seen and heard nothing. There hadn't been a single breach in what I'd come to think of as my parents' conspiracy; I was proud of them for managing to work together on the project without fighting. As the morning passed without comment and the afternoon stretched toward dinnertime, I began to worry that it was past a reasonable hour for a party to begin. Well, it was Wednesday. Perhaps the party was planned for the weekend; that would be easier on everyone's schedule. There was still my special meal to be enjoyed. No need to worry about that; I'd heard my mother giving my brother the job of mashing the potatoes. But when the four of us took our places at the cardinal points of our round kitchen table, I was not staring at generous piles of browned, breaded drumsticks, nor at plump, crispy chicken breasts, but at four plates of glazed Spam with mashed potatoes and boiled carrots.

Something was terribly, terribly wrong. No one, not even my mother, with her atrophied sense of humor, would dare suggest that the pink slab of vacuum-formed pork resting on the scratched sea-green melamine plate in front of me was an acceptable substitute for my birthday-entitled chicken. As everyone else began to eat, my last hope faded. I had been foolishly optimistic, fantasizing that at any moment my aunts and cousins would arrive, their arms full of presents and buckets of Kentucky Fried (original recipe), Styrofoam cups packed with sides of runny coleslaw and watery cut corn, and waxed-paper envelopes filled with the Colonel's doughy biscuits. But that, it turned out, wasn't the way we were going to celebrate my official transition to adulthood. No, we were going to celebrate with a plate of Spam and some over-cooked carrots. No party. No presents. No cake.

I watched and waited. My brother informed my mother that the Spam was poisoning all of us, to which she replied, "If only!" They began to argue the question of whether there was any actual pork in Spam if you didn't count the gristle, and whether cloves cause cancer. My father was yelling at them to stop arguing at the dinner table. No one noticed I hadn't touched my plate. When I couldn't take it any longer, I interrupted.

"Excuse me." My calm was supernatural. "I'd like to propose a toast. Oh, wait—I can't, can I? I don't seem to have anything to toast with." Caught without a script for this scene, my dinner companions sat and waited.

"Okay. No problem." I picked up a water glass painted with cartoon characters that had been a premium for buying a half-ton of frosted flakes or something.

"I'd like to start by thanking all of you, *la mia famiglia*, for honoring me with your presence tonight. That's without a 't,' by the way, in case you didn't notice. After all, I'm only going to turn TWENTY-ONE once in my life, right?" Awareness began to dawn in my mother's eyes, but to say she looked embarrassed or regretful would be a stretch. Did I see a slight shoulder shrug?

"I know a lot of families make a big deal out of this MAJOR MILESTONE by giving gifts, maybe having a party.... But I'm glad to see that this family is no longer wasteful in that way. No, for us a modest meal of processed pig pudding and the hope of a small swig of wine will have to suffice on this momentous occasion."

I was still gripping my water glass, which had a quarter-inch of liquid at the bottom. I dumped it on my un-touched meal and held it out as if to pass it to my mother. When she spoke, her tone was conciliatory.

"Oh, I'm sorry, Bud. Happy birthday. Would you like a glass of wine?"

I fixed on the square, half-empty cast-facet bottle of Manischewitz concord grape on the table. I'd gagged on the small sips of it I'd been stealing since I was twelve. Why my parents were so fond of the sweet, sticky wine I'll never know. They weren't even Jewish. But one thing I realized: I definitely did not want a whole glass of it now. I set down the water glass, turning it so that I didn't have to suffer Tony the Tiger's exaggerated grin. Was *I* the one who was behaving badly here? Was *I* making a big deal out of nothing? After all, I was just squatting at my parents' house for the summer; it had been three years since I'd lived there, officially. Maybe they liked it that way. Maybe I was acting like an entitled a-hole, returning home when it suited me, or I was broke, or both. I really needed to go, for everyone's sake. Not in a month, not in a week, but tomorrow.

There was more pleading than righteous indignation in my final words. "I can't believe it," I said. "You all actually forgot my twenty-first birthday. Thanks. Thanks a lot." I stood up. "Well, there must be someplace in this burg that serves fried chicken."

Valley Grove is a small town with only a few restaurants, even if you count the pizza parlor. The first two I stopped at didn't serve fried chicken. I pulled into the third, under a sign that spelled out "Lucky Chinese Food" in blinking script. The lights were out on the "L," which could be one reason there were only five cars in the parking lot.

"Do you have fried chicken?" I asked the hostess.

"Yes, yes; fried chicken," she replied, nodding. After finishing an order of chicken wings—all bones and skin—and two beers, I confided to my waitress that it was my birthday.

"Ah, your birthday, yes?" she agreed, tapping the Chinese zodiac printed on my placemat. I noticed that her finger pointed directly at the pig.

My bill came, accompanied by a saucer holding a sectioned orange and a fortune cookie.

"In life," the fortune read, "you must taste the sour to enjoy the sweet." I considered this bit of wisdom just long enough to pay my bill and eat the cookie. The orange I left on the table.

Unnatural Selection:
A Sociological Study

Salamanders, skinks, snakes. Gophers, mice, rats. Spiders and crickets. Bees by the dozen. These are some of the local fauna that have drowned in the bright-aqua collecting jar of my backyard pool. One day last August I arrived home to find a large lizard standing stock still in three and a half feet of water. It was on all fours, legs straight, gazing upward, and seemed unperturbed, as if waiting for something or someone to come to its rescue. Something like a nearby branch bending to touch the water's surface; someone like a sunburned human with a leaf net in hand.

The *Sceloporus orcutti*—granite spiny lizard, a Web search informed me—was about fourteen inches long. Smaller examples, hatchlings in particular, manage to float for quite a while if they're fortunate enough to end up near a bobbing leaf or twig; long enough to be rescued if I see them right away. The one I found last summer probably sank like a stone, too heavy to float even for a second. His ingenious defenses—the ability to change color or shed his tail when threatened by a predator—had been useless against deep water.

The half-tropical-rainforest, half-dry-chaparral environment I've created by irrigating part of the hot, arid San Diego hills and canyons that surround my house must seem as alien as a new continent to the abundant local wildlife. Roses grow next to cacti. Pine, ash, sycamore, birch, eucalyptus, and native oaks thrive among palm trees of every variety and tree ferns from Australia, Tasmania and New Zealand. The abundant (though rationed) water in the pool, which has been transported hundreds of miles south in open-air aqueducts from the snowmelt in California's Sierra Nevada mountain range, is a powerful draw for animals accustomed to living in a desert. They realize too late that a pool edge is not like the gradually deepening shore of a small pond or seasonal puddle and end up going in headfirst. Few emerge again.

I think it was *Sceloporus orcutti* that inspired me to start a journal to document the insects, lizards, and rodents, recently deceased, that I retrieve from the pool. The large lizard was my first example. I admired his calm demeanor, his almost military bearing. Web searches to establish species inevitably draw me in with descriptions of lifestyle, eating habits, natural defenses against predators, reproduction, all of which I note. On some level, I think of my list as a tribute, something that makes each death into more than a clumsy accident. But if not that, what? The misjudgment that leads to drowning in my pool is the only thing that connects them all. Once they realize—almost instantly, I would guess—that their decision at the waterside was a dead end, they assume an attitude of calm acceptance. There are never signs of struggle: no bloody lizard claw marks on the cement of the pool wall, no desperate stretch toward the surface. I am disappointed, I admit, for strictly aesthetic reasons when I come upon a corpse floating belly-up. For me, that position implies a last-minute panic that dishonors the victim and embarrasses the observer with its utter lack of dignity.

Sentimentality has no place in my post-mortem research. One must steel oneself against the cruel and the bizarre: the mantis that bites her mate's head off, the house finches that eat their own young. One day there was a cicada hawk (*Sphecius speciosus*) standing well underwater on the pool's second step in a pose similar to the one the granite lizard had struck. My research on the bug killed any sense of ennobling character, however. The female cicada hawk—actually a large wasp that can grow up to two inches long—provides for her young by laying her eggs in a cicada she has paralyzed with her sting. She seals the cicada in a prepared tunnel in the dirt and dies. A few days later, her young hatch as grubs and devour their still-living host as their first meal.

Last spring my yard guy, Carlos, informed me that my lawn had suffered an invasion by gophers. I wasn't surprised; I'd found one, *Thomomys bottae*, on the bottom of the pool a few days earlier, where its waterlogged fur, buck teeth, and dead, staring eyes made it one of the least attractive corpses I've encountered. Carlos was more concerned about the lawn, where he pointed to several small mounds of soft dirt that served as periods at the bottom of three-foot-long exclamation points of dead grass. He offered to catch and dispose of the gophers at twenty dollars a head, but when he showed me the trap, I hesitated. It was an oblong, eight-inch, metal clam shell, the hinged edge designed to rest on the floor of a gopher's burrow. When the animal tried to exit, it would step into the trap, the two sides would snap together, and several sharp spines would pierce the neck or forequarters of the unlucky rodent. The idea was that it would be killed almost instantly, but I had my doubts. Besides, accidental death—even in an environment as artificial as a swimming pool—is one thing. It's quite another to plot to kill an animal. Carlos convinced me it was a choice between my lawn and the gopher; in the end I gave him the go-ahead to set two traps. Javier, Carlos's nine-year-old son, discovered the first victim on their next visit.

"A gopher! A gopher!" he shouted as he ran toward me across the lawn, dancing with glee and swinging a trap in which, a small dead animal was caught by its tail.

"Okay," I yelled. "I believe you. You don't need to bring it over here!" I waved my arms wildly, as though I had just stumbled into a swarm of bees. "I don't need to see it up close!" I silently ran through my Spanish vocabulary, which consisted of about five phrases, searching for a translation. I came up with "*No veo.*" I think it means something like "I no see." Javier stopped his advance, taking a cue from my frantic gestures, but helpfully extended the hand holding the trap toward me so I could get a better view.

"I kill it with the shovel," he exulted. "I swing it over my head like this...." He struggled to mime the fatal blow one-handed, not willing to release the trap and its prize long enough to accurately re-enact the drama.

"Okay, Javier. *No description necessario!*" I was pretty sure *description* is description, just pronounced differently.

Even from eight feet away, the wear and tear on the gopher's rat-like tail was obvious. I tried to avoid imagining the desperate rodent, who must have envied the lizard its ability to shed its tail at will, chewing at its own hind end the way a fox or wolf has been known to chew off its leg when caught in a trap. Yet I was glad the thing had been caught only by the tail, even though it meant an executioner's blow to the head from Javier's shovel. At least it was spared a more painful and prolonged death from the trap's multiple piercings. That's what I told myself, anyway.

As the weeks passed, Carlos laid more traps. He brought Javier with him whenever he came to work on my yard in the afternoon, and Javier was happy to take responsibility for checking the traps and announcing the body count during each visit. If I was outside when Carlos pulled up in his battered Ford Econoline with its jumble of tools, ladders, and tarps stacked to the ceiling in the space behind the front seats, Javier would bounce out of the van carrying some version of a ball (one that almost always appeared to be an under-inflated found object) and try to engage me in a game of catch or soccer. It never lasted very long; he was overweight and un-athletic and soon tired of lurching around the yard. I was always anxious to get back to my writing, and often refused to be drawn into a game. On those days, after checking the gopher traps, Javier would flop down in a spot of shade and turn his attention to whatever he'd brought with him to ease his boredom while his father worked. Lying on his belly on the lawn in his worn jeans and Spiderman T-shirt, he would sketch birds or his favorite superheroes on pieces of paper torn from his school notebook. The sketches were good for a nine-year-old, even if marred by the irregular thickness and sudden accidental changes of direction in the pencil line due to the grit that had worked its way under the paper.

Just after the first gopher was trapped, Javier found a dead ruby-throated hummingbird below the dining room window that he proudly showed to his father and me, prodding it with a gentle forefinger as it lay in the palm of his hand, as if to prove that the bird wasn't merely stunned. He carried it in his jeans pocket all afternoon, despite my efforts to convince him that the best place for a bird found dead on the ground was in the trash, delivered with a minimum of touching and stroking. On his next visit I asked him what had happened to the hummingbird, and he told me he still had it in his room at home.

"I want to collect all kinds of animals—*todas las clases!*" he said. I was afraid to ask what he'd done with the dead gopher.

As the season progressed, the gopher dead grew in number until, in my imagination, they approached the scale of casualties of the Trojan Wars. I handed over one twenty-dollar bill after another and wondered where it would end. In fact, only six gophers died in my yard that year— five in traps and the one that drowned in the pool. The last one trapped must have been caught a short time after the trap was set. Two weeks later, on Carlos's next visit, there was little left of the gopher but some bits of fur and the stink of dead rodent. From my inspection of the scene, I theorized that, caught in the trap and unable to flee, the animal had been torn apart by one or more of the crows, owls, hawks, or kites that wheel through the canyon. Even Javier's enthusiasm for the hunt seemed dimmed by the imagined violent postscript to this last trapping. Or perhaps he was just disappointed by the lack of a corpse to examine.

I grew up in a lower-middle-class neighborhood barely five miles away from where I live now, though I spent thirty-five years in the interim in Boston, New York City, and various New Jersey towns. I'm uncomfortable making this comparison—our circumstances are very different and most likely always will be—but here it is: when I see Javier resting in the grass, concentrating on his sketches of birds, I see myself at his age, fifty years ago, sprawled on the brown and beige oval braided rug in front of the TV in my family's living-room while my brothers and father, on the battered couch, struggle to stifle their shouts of triumph or moans of disappointment in reaction to the ebb and flow of the Sunday afternoon football game. The volume is turned down; my mother is in her bedroom, as she often was, napping under the influence of Elavil or Valium or both. My sister is beside me on the floor, attempting, amid the *sotto voce* chaos, to read a novel. I'm ignoring the game, engaged in copying a map of Brazil out of the family's thick world atlas. I couldn't have cared less which country it was. My subjects were chosen by color and my favorite color was pink. On the current page, the pink country happened to be Brazil.

Like Javier, I'd collect every animal and unusual insect I could find, from horny toad to tomato worms to stray kittens, though I preferred my temporary pets alive. I say "temporary" because—to their good fortune—I never managed to keep these objects of curiosity under my inept care longer than a few days. When I had the idea to start a salt-water aquarium, I convinced my sister, one year older and the possessor of a new driver's license, to drive me down to the La Jolla cove at dawn to search for catchable sea life in the coastal tide pools. I managed to take a sea anemone and two small fish home in plastic bags, but they didn't last a day in the tank I had prepared for them by dumping some table salt into tap water.

Javier had one obvious advantage when compared to me at his age: a doting father. Over the years, each time a holiday or special occasion neared, Carlos would confide in me that he was saving up to buy the fifty dollar "zombie doctor" Halloween costume Javi had begged for, or the forty-gallon fish tank to keep piranhas in that Javi hoped to get on Three Kings Day. The cost of these gifts might represent the totality of Carlos's earnings for a day of labor.

My father kept food in our mouths and clothes on our backs, though my clothes included hand-me-downs from people we didn't know, and food was rationed to last for an arbitrary number of meals. We were taught to not be "uppity," not think we were better or more deserving than others. When it turned out I was a good-enough student to be accepted at a prestigious private college, my father refused to provide the financial information that would qualify me for a scholarship, torpedoing my chance to attend. "The state college is good enough for your sister," he told me, "and it's good enough for you."

It's not that we didn't have enjoyable family moments, but a dominant teenage memory is of the Sunday my sister, Rebecca, and I, having dutifully suffered through a morning church service and Sunday school, refused to return to church in the evening to attend yet another meeting. My father ended up storming up and down the hallway between our two bedrooms with a leather belt, beating one of us, then the other. He had every intention of continuing until we both agreed to go and was only dissuaded by my mother's hysterical weeping. My father walked with a very measured step; once I learned to recognize it I would be overcome by panic whenever I heard him coming down the hall. The Young Churchmen rebellion was one of the few instances in which we were able to stand up to my father, but the legacy of those beatings and others is that I still flinch when someone touches me unexpectedly.

I haven't said much about Javi's mother, and for good reason: I've never met her, and neither Carlos nor Javi volunteer much. I've been told that Carlos has a wife and several children back in Mexico; that certainly wouldn't be unusual in the highly porous border region that stretches almost two thousand miles across Baja California. Or perhaps she stays away for her own protection; I've seen demonstrations of Carlos's temper, and I wouldn't want to be on the receiving end of it.

One afternoon, Carlos arrived at my house an hour late and in a huff. Javi climbed down from the van with less than his usual enthusiasm. There was a constant buzz from Carlos's cell phone as we struggled through a Spanglish discussion of the work to be done that day. Finally, he pulled his phone from his pocket and gave it a brief glance.

"She calls me now," he said, obviously seething.

"Who?"

"My girlfriend—Javi's mother."

I waited, not sure what to say.

"On the way here, I see her in the Jack-In-the-Box with someone else," he said. "I call her and tell her, 'I see you, you fucking bitch!'" Spittle flew from his lips; he pronounced the last three words perfectly, without a trace of an accent. When I glanced at Javier, who was listening from a few feet away, it was obvious that he was deeply embarrassed. After all, he was eleven or twelve by then and profoundly mystified by adult behavior. At that moment he looked as though he wished he were somewhere—anywhere—else.

I spoke to Javier about his mother only once. It was near Three Kings Day, the one that would feature the forty-gallon piranha tank, but I hadn't heard about that yet. I asked Javi what he wanted from his parents as a gift, and he told me that the only Christmas gift he can remember ever getting from his mother was a pair of women's prescription sunglasses with one lens missing.

I wasn't sure how to respond to this revelation. On the one hand, Javi was old enough and savvy enough to have made the story up; enough to have intentionally left out the mitigating circumstances, but also young enough to recite something simple and true without pretense. Regardless, it was pitiable on both their parts. I thought it was one of the most pitiable stories I'd ever heard.

My father told me that, when I was born only eleven months after Rebecca, he'd felt he had to make a choice between focusing his attention on us—"saving us," I think is the way he put it—or on my physically and emotionally overwhelmed mother. He chose to save my mother. Growing up, I'd felt the effects of that secret decision as a mysterious, unidentifiable force, like gravity, whose existence could be proved only by showing that it explained everything Rebecca and I didn't understand. It shadowed our entire childhood and adolescence. Between my mother's drug-induced mastery of the ability to be physically present but emotionally unreachable, and my father's chosen path of detachment, my sister and I were left alone, like feral cats, to raise each other.

When I was in my thirties, my father visited me in New York City. I was attempting, with moderate success, to pursue a career in the arts—something of which he thoroughly disapproved and, in fact, had done his best to sabotage. We were walking home, toward my fifth-floor walkup on West 49th Street, when he asked me—with an eye, I guess, on his legacy—if I didn't want to get married and have children. I was caught by surprise; it was a subject I'd thought about a great deal, but one we'd never discussed. I stopped and turned to face him.

"Dad," I said, "I'm never going to have children."

"Why not?" he asked.

I could have told him the truth, could have said that I was afraid I'd learned too much from him, that I would end up (despite my best intentions) being the kind of father *he* had been—cold, distant, aloof from his family, picking and choosing from among his children which ones to love, which to abandon. I could have said I was afraid his style of parenting had wormed its way into my genes, and that if I had children and ended up treating them the way he'd treated his I wouldn't be able to live with myself. I could have tried to hurt him.

What I said was, "I don't think I would be a good father. I'm too self-centered."

"Oh, I do. I think you would be a good father."

That's the only occasion in my life I can remember my father encouraging me in anything.

My list of drownings in the pool has almost filled the slight journal I record them in. I can't yet discern what lesson is to be learned from these biographies, but I'm sure I'm nowhere near the end of the catalogue of cruel, violent, murderous things that nature has taught her children in the interest of survival. One piece of news—I'm not sure whether it's entirely good or not—is that I haven't seen any sign of gophers for two years now. Of course, that makes me wonder about the well-being of the coyotes, snakes, and hawks that should be preying on them. (Perhaps they've been supplanted through competition. I've seen an Internet video of a blue heron, likely an escapee from one of the man-made lakes nearby, swallowing a gopher whole.)

Javi would be thirteen now. The last time I saw him, which was a while ago, he was almost as tall and wide as his father. We were talking about his upcoming graduation from middle school at the end of the year, and I asked if he'd thought about what he wanted to be when he grows up.

"I dunno," he'd replied.

"Well, how about a veterinarian?"

"What's a veterinarian?"

"A vet—*veterinario*," I guessed. "A doctor who takes care of animals."

He shrugged his shoulders. I wanted to remind him of the gophers that so fascinated him at age nine, the dead ruby-throated hummingbird he'd carried in his pocket until it was just a feathery wad of bony bird-mess. I wanted to remind him of the afternoons he'd lie in the dirt, drawing pictures of imagined heroes in his school tablet. With effort, I wanted to tell him, he could learn to be a lab technician, an illustrator, maybe even a graphic novelist.

I suspect, instead, that his history will turn out to be his destiny; that someday I'll catch a glimpse of him in someone's yard, rake in hand, the skin on the back of his neck browned like his father's, hand to hat brim against the sun, staring into a future only he can decipher.

Gorillas in Our Midst

There are eight forty-five-pound iron weights on the barbell of the Smith leg machine. They wobble and ring against each other as one of the weightlifters slowly lowers himself to a squat. Even more slowly, now in the power stroke of the lift, he returns to an upright stance. Maybe he grunts a bit on the way up, pauses a moment at the top to enjoy a moment of triumph even though his legs and arms are shaking from the stress of supporting the extra 360 pounds.

The eight stations of the Universal Gym are all busy—all have lifters waiting to work in between your sets. At one station, someone is doing shoulder pull-downs. At another, a moaning beginner is overdoing cable arm curls, hoping to achieve a miraculous overnight transformation from ninety-eight-pound weakling to muscle god. A driving drumbeat blasts from the overhead speakers, daring your heartbeat to try to match its rhythm. There are lyrics to the music, but you can't make them out above the yelling and clamor: shouts of encouragement, grunts forced out by almost unbearable effort, a scream of despair when one lifter fails, a shout of victory when another reaches a new milestone and drops a barbell with a hundred and eighty pounds on it on the rubber floor. It bounces once, clangs like a bucket of horseshoes. If you close your eyes and just listen to the screams and wails, you'd be forgiven for concluding that, two stations down, someone's being tortured to death.

Between each set of ten repetitions, the serious lifters turn toward the eight-foot-tall mirrors that typically cover at least one wall of the gym in the free-weight area. Those new to the experience assume that the mirrored walls are a setting for self-admiration by the mix of aspiring amateurs (who tend to favor the controlled movement of weight machines) and the more confident regulars (who line up to wait impatiently for their turn at racks of free weights.) Well-muscled members of either group might earn the "gorilla" sobriquet—never within their hearing, of course—but even those who mock are sufficiently self-aware to know that their disparaging words spring from envy. They would be surprised if they could hear the stream of savagely critical invective the gorillas mutter to themselves, swearing at a six-pack that refuses to pop, agonizing over the lack of definition in the veins of a forearm, despite the compliment from a passing fellow lifter: "Nice vascularity, man." As is true of those with eating disorders, what the gorillas see in the mirror is not the reality others see. When they look at their reflection, they feel only that something's *wrong* with their bodies, that something essential is missing, something that, were it present, would allow them to finally fix the wrong-ness; something they cannot even name. All they can do is work—morning, noon and night, no time off for good behavior, weekends and holidays included. They work and work and work in the hope that one day they will discover whatever it is that will finally make them whole.

I think of female ballet dancers—ballerinas—as the athletes most like weightlifters in this sense: both disciplines seek constant visual feedback on their form to assure they're doing a movement or pose correctly; both studying and adjusting posture, position, angle, and attitude. Attention to these details is a way of avoiding injury, among other benefits; but there is nothing natural in the dancer's steps or the body-builder's freakish shape and form. If the legitimate purpose of muscles is to support the effective functioning of the skeleton and internal organs, then these have another, non-essential *raison d'etre.* The muscles that allow a ballerina to stand in a foot-crushing *en pointe* position, or that actually impede the weightlifter's ability to cross his arms over his ballooning *pectoralis major* muscles, are developed purely for the pleasure of touch or the thrill of exhibition; they are otherwise useless.

As the gorillas flex and pose, they're critically comparing their achievement to the airbrushed, photo-shopped images of hyper-masculinity they've studied by the hour in *Men's Health* or *Muscle and Fitness* magazine:

SIX PACK ABS! the teaser on the cover trumpets for what seems like the thousandth time.

BIG LEAGUE BICEPS!

Lose Your Belly Fast: Going, Going, GONE!

30 Red Hot Sex Secrets!

The ads inside are for cars, watches, colognes, shoes, vodka, muscle-building protein powders, Botox—everything one might expect in a mens' version of *Cosmopolitan*—pushing product to dandified metro-sexuals and post-adolescent minimum wage workers alike.

I'm looking through the thirtieth anniversary issue of *Men's Health* magazine, which features an un-smiling thirty-year-old Arnold Schwarzenegger on its cover. It's obvious that he has not been airbrushed. He stares directly at the camera, as if surprised by the click of the shutter; the portrait ends up looking like a mug shot or a Wal-Mart employee's ID badge. He holds out a smaller photo of himself in full flex as though offering it to the photographer as a souvenir. His limp, greasy hair, parted down the middle, is long enough to cover his ears.

But his body… well, his body is simply magnificent, even if the photos serve only as cautionary examples of the other-worldly shapes we can coax it to adopt. I wonder if the sweating strivers I see in every gym would work as hard as they do if they knew that recent medical research suggests that genes, not exercise, bear eighty percent of the responsibility for how fit we are as adults? The implication is that most would-be gorillas could pump iron from here to Sunday, run hundreds of miles on treadmills that will never actually take them anywhere, and still not reach their physical ideal. It's just not in their genetic cards.

In the mid-1940s, American psychologist William Herbert Sheldon developed what he believed was a scientific way of describing human body types. Looking mostly at men, he identified three: the thin, lean ectomorph; the well-built mesomorph; and the soft, flabby endomorph. Soon he went on to associate characteristics such as intelligence and emotional maturity with body type as well; then drilled down even further to connect individual personality traits. When I studied myself in a mirror, I saw the classic ectomorph: tall, thin, lightly muscled, flat chested; cerebrotonic (an intellectual), secretive, inclined to enjoy isolation and solitude; self-aware, anxious, and restrained in posture and movement. He described Endomorphs as slow, sloppy, and lazy. Mesomorphs are popular and hardworking, and ectomorphs were seen as intelligent but shy loners. The name he chose for this "science" of association was Constitutional Psychology. Sheldon's theories reached their height in popularity in the mid-1950s, about the time I started kindergarten, but they lingered in practice for several more decades. By the time I enrolled in middle school at Palm Junior High in the small town of Citrus Grove, California, I knew enough about these classifications to resent them, even though I saw how they might be applied. When I studied myself in a mirror, I saw the classic ectomorph, a ninety-eight-pound weakling: taller than average, thin, lightly muscled, flat chested; cerebrotonic (an intellectual), secretive, inclined to enjoy isolation and solitude; self-aware, anxious and restrained in posture and movement. Although Sheldon's theories were eventually dismissed as racist, sexist, and a bunch of hooey, his conclusions based more on personal stereotypes, observational bias, preferences and prejudices than science, they are still an example of how appealing such theories can seem.

There was one artifact of the period that was enthusiastically adopted on a national scale, especially among high school and college teachers, doctors, anthropologists and other program professionals—all the way up to President Eisenhower himself. I refer to the report from the President's Council on Physical Fitness, which took the form of a fitness test developed by Swiss researchers and administered to four thousand American children and three thousand youngsters from Switzerland, Italy, and Austria just after WWII. The results for the American group were devastating: fifty-eight percent failed the test, while only 8 percent of the Europeans did so.

Eisenhower knew this had to be remedied if America was going to remain dominant in international affairs, but the council he organized argued to a stand-still on the subject of whether military preparedness or fitness-for-fitness's-sake should be the council's main goal. The researchers made it clear that their intent had been to encourage general fitness; Eisenhower, a war hero, was more interested in military preparedness. The schism was made obvious in he first edition of "the "Blue Book," so named for the color of its cover, which was the report-out from the first President's Council on Physical Fitness. Eisenhower had won; the exercises and tests it suggested made it clear that the program's goal was military dominance. Kennedy's "improvement" to the program, reflected in the Blue Book's second edition, was to make the test competitive by attaching rewards to successful student athletes and their mentors.

For every winner, of course, there has to be a loser; in groups of adolescent boys they are fair game for harassment, insult and often, physical abuse. Frequently, the adults that are supposed to be policing this behavior are complicit in it.

(One Phys Ed teacher at Palm kept a wooden paddle in his desk drawer that he used to mete out punishment on the spot when one of the students committed a minor rule infraction, acting as judge, jury, and executioner. He had drilled holes in the paddle to lessen its wind resistance and make each swat sting a bit more. Even at age thirteen I could sense that he knew he was doing something wrong; on the one occasion I was ordered to the coach's office, he drew the blinds across the window between it and the shower room so that he couldn't be observed when he ordered me to pull down my gym shorts to receive the paddles on my naked buttocks. He had just administered swat one of a planned five when the door to the office opened and the department head strode in. The remaining swats were given quickly, with half the energy the first one had delivered.)

I remember well how hellish the semi-annual weeks of testing for the President's program felt, as my lack of athleticism caused me to fail test after test, suffering the ridicule of the other boys. The punishment/reward model added to the test while it was under Kennedy's administration was, in retrospect, simply public shaming on an enormous scale for the less-athletic students. To make matters worse, someone in the hierarchy decided that the Palm coaches would do President Kennedy one better during his tour of responsibility for the test: they established a requirement that each student sew onto his gym shorts a felt square that took the guesswork out of determining what level of accomplishment each student had reached on the President's test. The colors indicated the ranking: Gold, of course, was the highest, followed by silver, brown, green, red, and pink.

On a Friday at the end of one of the testing cycles, I brought home my gym shorts and my pink square and told my mother that one had to be attached to the other before I left for school on Monday. She seemed unable to grasp the purpose. "What does it *mean?*" she kept asking, as I struggled to find a way to explain its meaning that didn't include the words "piece of crap." Years later, when I learned about the pink felt triangle that homosexual internees in German concentration camps were forced to sew onto their clothes, I felt a deep and sudden sense of kinship with the tens of thousands of gay men who were among the six million murdered by the Nazis. Imagine my surprise when I set out to research this topic and found a photograph of a German WWII-era chart that could have been ripped from the locker room wall at good old Palm Junior High. The chart was the key that decoded the significance of the variously colored patches worn by prisoners in the camps: red triangles for political prisoners, green for common criminals, black for Gypsies, pink for homosexuals.

Americans have become inured to the discovery that many of our national heroes had feet of clay. It seems nary a day passes that we don't discover some racist, sexist, or fascist detail in the lives of our national heroes. Witness the disclosure that Charles Lindbergh, whose thirty-foot-high portrait, until recently, graced the side of a building at the San Diego International Airport, was an admirer and enthusiastic supporter of many Nazi ideals. He even travelled from the US to Germany several times to participate in a eugenics program that encouraged him, in the interest of breeding supermen, to impregnate as many German women as he could during his visits. It's interesting that the Nazi program approached the challenge by treating their supermen like so many cattle and assumed that the same breeding rules applied.

I would guess that mandatory fitness classes have all but disappeared from the curriculum of US schools, with the exception, perhaps, of military academies. In spite of the misery, I associate with my hours in gym classes in middle school and high school, I *do* believe that everyone should strive to be and remain physically well. What saddens me is that the reason for the disappearance of these programs is *not* that the administrators realized the great injury to self-esteem they can inflict if the program isn't positioned correctly, but because we, as a nation, don't value wellness enough to make it a budget priority.

If I sound like a pitchman for fitness programs, there's good reason: it's been twenty-five years, but I've at last broken my oath, taken when I graduated from high school, to never step foot in a gym again. This time it's just for me, a private and solitary pleasure, no color-coded patches or wall charts to be found, done as part of an effort to discover just how much I can ask of a forty-five-year-old body, joining the would-be Gorillas at the racks of free weights, waiting my turn to test my strength and endurance against that of my peers. In fact, I've become so involved in fitness that I ended up pursuing a course that led to certification as a Personal Trainer. I've just added a boxing coach to the list of my trainers; sometimes I think I'm still preparing for those middle and high school confrontations I ran away from as a teenager.

Finally, to all you ectomorphs out there: don't listen when someone like me tells you that you'll never be a mesomorph. If I can do it, anyone can. Just remember to slow down and enjoy the journey.

October 31, 1958

Robert's palm was already sweating, trapped within Susannah's much-larger hand, as the two crossed the quiet street and paused at the bottom of their neighbor's driveway. It had already been an unusual and upsetting day, nothing happening in the order he considered routine. Dinner had been rushed, his mother urging the two children to finish quickly "before it gets too dark to see where you're going." They were dressed in the odd clothing their mother had spent the afternoon assembling at her sewing machine. The two children carried empty brown paper bags on which she had drawn somewhat impressionistic pumpkins with the various shades of red and purple crayons from Robert's coloring set (the oranges and greens, for some reason, were missing).

He had never been out after dark alone with Susannah, who was full of the confidence of a six-year-old who was about to be given charge of her four-year-old brother for the first time. She was showing off a bit for Robert, who had only vague memories of similar past outings. They hurried through the gloom at the end of their neighbor's driveway, Robert's hand still in Susannah's, who had taken it as they crossed the deserted street. He edged closer to his sister to put her between him and a grinning jack o'lantern, whose flickering candle made a small, irregular beacon on the grass near the Fitches' mailbox. A nervous shiver started in the pit of Robert's stomach, then shook him from head to toe.

"Just do what I do," Susannah said. She shifted her grip on her brother from his hand to his upper arm. "Come *on!*" she urged, nearly dragging him along in her haste. As the two reached the porch, Susannah stretched forward to ring the doorbell.

"Trick or treat!" she shrieked, timed to coincide with the exact moment the door escaped its latch. Inside the house, the air currents found a new pathway past the opening door, carrying a warm draft of caramel-scented air from the kitchen, where Mrs. Fitch was busy dipping candy apples, to the two children waiting on the porch. A huge figure seemed to fill the home's entry hall, at first just an unidentifiable silhouette in the glare of the bright interior light. But as Robert stared, the image resolved into the outline of a man with a hump on his shoulder, just like the one he had seen that afternoon on TV. He was surprised, never having seen a hunchback in his life before, that today he had, so far, seen two. During "The Early Show"—San Diego's afternoon movie program—Robert had been distracted by Susannah's repeated attempts to explain the title of the day's movie. She would say, "It's notter dam, stupid," which Robert didn't believe because he knew "damn" was a bad word. Susannah finally ended the argument with the summary announcement, "It's French," an assertion he lacked the knowledge to dispute.

And now, having seen a hunchback for the first time only that afternoon, in the movie, here was a real live monster, so close that Robert could have touched him if he wanted to, which he most definitely did not. The monster's features were distorted by what looked like a woman's stocking pulled over his head and face. It flattened the black hair on his forehead and twisted his nose and lips into a hooked snarl. The door had swung fully open, and Robert could see thin puffs of condensation coming from the monster's nose and mouth as he breathed into the cold night. The effect was terrifying. It hardly mattered that this monster wore the uniform of a mailman and was holding a large bowl of Tootsie Rolls. Had it not been for his sister's firm grip on his arm, Robert would have turned tail and run home, even if he'd have to do it alone.

"Aaaarg! Who be knockin' at me door?" raged the monster in his best pirate-ogre voice. "I'll take thee down to Davey Jones' locker...." His voice trailed off when Robert, following Susannah's lead, stepped forward into the light and held out his empty treats bag. Now Robert could see that the hump on the shoulder of the man in the doorway was just a trick of the lighting and realized a moment later that the monster had to be their neighbor and mailman. Still, it took all his courage to confront this version of Mr. Fitch, so unlike the cheerful, if officious, character Robert saw almost every day.

"I'm a flying purple people eater!" Susannah chattered as Tootsie Rolls tumbled from Mr. Fitch's bowl into her proffered bag. Susannah's starched gauze mask, splashed with spots of purple paint, slid up and down her face in time to her words; the wrinkled magenta lips only occasionally matching her own. "See?" She dropped her bag, already heavy with Tootsie Rolls, and let go of Robert to flap her freed arms and the chiffon wings, tacked at shoulder and wrist, that her mother had fashioned from an old set of kitchen curtains. Mr. Fitch hardly took notice of her pirouette, his attention still focused on her brother.

"Very nice—uh, Susannah, isn't it? And who is your little friend here?"

He continued to stare at Robert while he dropped five or six Tootsie Rolls into his otherwise empty treats bag.

"Where do *you* live, honey?"

The evening's first fruits! With the transfer of Mr. Fitch's candy as an example, Robert had grasped the mechanics of the transaction immediately: you ring a neighbor's doorbell, they open the door and give you candy. Why they should do so was not yet clear, but as he turned away and looked out over the neighborhood of modest bungalows Robert no longer classified the beckoning lighted porches by reference to how many kids lived there or which one had a new car in the driveway. For tonight, each was simply a potential source for candy or other treats. In the morning, and for as long as his personal collection lasted, Robert would refer to "the house that had popcorn balls" or "the one with candy cigarettes."

The Tootsie Rolls in Mr. Fitch's bowl were not a favorite. Robert didn't like the way they stuck to his teeth, and so wasn't much disappointed in his small portion. Susannah wasn't a big fan of Tootsie Rolls either, but she had been anticipating this moment for weeks and was short on patience. She hurriedly unwrapped one and bit off a piece. Robert followed her example, unable resist sugar's siren song any longer. In his mouth, the candy softened to a viscous glue that cemented his upper and lower jaws together as one.

Mr. Fitch tried his question once more.

"Who's your little black girlfriend, Suzie?"

Both children stared at him, made dumb by the sticky toffee in their mouths. Susannah had raised her mask to rest on the top of her head while she consumed the Tootsie Roll, and now pointed to her bare cheek and exaggerated her chewing efforts as an explanation for her silence.

Little *black* girl, Mr. Fitch had said. Little black *girl*.

Robert thought back to earlier in the evening, his mother rubbing burnt cork on his face, his neck, the backs of his hands. It had been fun at first, watching his hands turn from pale to soot-colored. But when she moved on to his face and he could no longer watch his own transformation, he'd grown tired of the frequent demands to keep still and bored with the warnings to not rub soot into his eyes. He'd begun to argue over nearly every detail of his costume. He'd readily agreed to wear one of his father's old white work shirts with the collar cut off but refused the red and white checkered skirt she'd made from an old tablecloth. He'd insisted on wearing regular pants, afraid that someone he knew would see him in the skirt and make fun of him. And besides, the rubber toes of his sneakers kept getting tangled up in excess fabric.

They'd reached a compromise when his mother agreed to shorten the skirt and let him wear his blue jeans underneath. Somehow, as part of the deal, she'd talked him into letting her smear his lips with bright red paste from one of the gold-colored lipstick cases that cluttered her dressing table. The final touch was a white head-wrap that covered his light brown hair. His mother had found two curtain rings she could use as earrings, and sewed them to the headpiece at the two points where it covered his ears.

Now Robert stood in the glow of the Fitches porch light while he recalled the evening's preparations, absent-mindedly rubbing one of several new mosquito bites on the back of his left hand. As he rubbed, a spot of his own pale skin color emerged from the black soot.

Black soot. Robert looked past Mr. Fitch to the tall, mirrored umbrella stand that stood in the house's entry hall, facing the front door. One panel framed Susannah, dressed in her ballet tights and leotard, filmy wings hanging loosely from her long sleeves. A second panel, set in the wood at a slightly different angle, reflected the figure standing next to Susannah: a little black girl in a long skirt and white blouse, gold earrings swinging from her ears.

If Robert had been able to speak, he would have shouted, "It's Robert, Mr. Fitch! It's me, Robert!" But the sticky toffee in his mouth made it impossible. Susannah was paying no attention, absorbed in her own bag of candy; her instruction to "do what I do" forgotten.

The fact was that Robert had never seen a black child other than on TV, in the Tarzan movies he and Susannah would sometimes watch on Sundays after church. He was certain, likewise, that Susannah had never seen a purple people eater, and guessed that Mr. Fitch had never met an actual ogre. The full understanding of what Halloween was all about began to dawn on him: it was a day, he realized, that he could pretend to be anything he wanted to be. If Susannah could pretend she ate purple people and Mr. Fitch could pretend to be an ogre, why couldn't *he* pretend to be a little black girl, just as Mr. Fitch saw him?

He tried to recall what he'd seen the younger black girls do in the Tarzan movies, and began to sway to a half-remembered, half-improvised drumbeat, moving his hips from side to side, both arms extended and one hand still clutching the trick-or-treat bag. Then HOP—he jumped forward toward the Fitches' open entryway. HOP—he jumped backwards, lifting the front of his skirt in the air, shaking it to chase spirits away, dancing the way the children in the Tarzan movies danced.

Susannah emerged from her reverie, grabbed Robert's arm and hissed in his ear: "What are you doing? It's time to go!" The two turned and began a stumbling, disorganized retreat down the driveway. "Oh! Thanks for the candy, Mr. Fitch," Susannah yelled over her shoulder.

"Hey, Susie, I asked you who's the black girl?" Mr. Fitch shouted after them, stepping through his front door and out onto the porch.

Robert danced down the driveway, following Susannah, saying nothing. As they reached the sidewalk, his sister turned around once more to look back at Mr. Fitch's silhouette in the glowing doorway.

"Don't you know, Mr. Fitch?" Susannah called out. "He's Aunt Jemimee!"

Robert turned left, heading for the next house on their street, swinging his treat bag through the air, hopping and swaying: a little black girl dancing to the music of drums only she could hear.

Truth is a Stranger

Fiction is obliged to stick to possibilities; Truth isn't. —Mark Twain

1.

I hadn't seen or spoken to Susan since I was in graduate school, some thirty or more years ago, so to say I was surprised when an email message from her popped up on my computer screen would be an understatement. It took me a good minute or two to attach a face to her name. I didn't recognize the woman in her Facebook thumbnail even when I squinted until my eyes nearly closed. Based on what I could remember, I was pretty sure she'd had some work done.

We'd been in some shows together back in our college years, me always in the chorus, she usually in one of the lesser supporting roles. She had always struggled with weight, and that kept her out of the principal line-up. Her character would have one or two lines in the show, just enough to merit her own credit in the program. She was a nag to the tech crew, demanding changes in the set and lighting. She would take her costume home the night before the show opened and return with it the next evening, the gown recut to a shape she considered more flattering and the trim enhanced with sequins or rhinestones. I guess she figured she would glitter from the wings if she couldn't make it to center stage. I remember her as being quick with a quip or a pun; we'd amuse ourselves during long hours of rehearsal by adjourning to the Green Room between scenes. There we'd sit and tell each other jokes or share rumors about goings-on in the San Diego classical music scene while we waited for our next call to the stage. Sue was, in the parlance of the time, what we uncharitably referred to as a fag hag.

After she contacted me, we exchanged several emails; hers were pleasant, newsy. She was married, she said; had two children, grown; had recently decided to start singing again with a small local opera company in the mid-west. I waited for a clue as to why she had decided to contact me after so much time. Then she let drop this bit of news:

she told me she had been working for the Central Intelligence Agency during the early seventies—the years we were hanging out together. Her job was to report on student groups and political protest activity at San Diego State University, particularly those protests aimed at stopping the war in Vietnam.

I laughed. She had to be kidding. It was ludicrous to think there might have been anything involving me, my friends, or any of our activities that could possibly have been of interest to the CIA. Besides, I thought I remembered that the CIA was prohibited from acting against American citizens on their home turf.

"Good thing you never found out about the Weapon of Peace I was building in my basement," I joked.

"Oh, we knew about the weapon," she said. "And everything else."

I wracked my brain trying to think of something—anything—I'd done during those paranoid years that could possibly be construed as suspicious or un-American. The worst I could come up with was that I'd wandered past the top of the Greek Bowl on my way to where my motorcycle was parked one evening while Angela Davis was delivering a lecture on Feminism, Communism, and Black Power. I guess, now that I think about it, that someone who didn't know me well might have conflated my attendance at the lecture and my appearance in photos of the sit-in at the college's Administration Building to conclude that I was a dangerous radical. The truth is, I was just curious to find out what it felt like to be inside the razor wire, behind a phalanx of riot police. I became suspicious of "Susan" when she didn't react to my reminiscences about the "weapon of peace." The real Sue would know that I could never live in a house with a basement. I've never seen a CIA file, but if that's the kind of stuff that's in them, mine must be the most boring one ever.

Sue's messages stopped coming as suddenly as they'd started, and I decided she was either unhinged or she was gaslighting me. She had once been famous for her practical jokes, but thirty years is a long time to wait to pull one off. Either way, I wasn't interested in continuing our conversation. I just wanted to do a couple of internet searches before I closed the subject permanently. I started with the keywords "CIA" and "domestic spying." When my screen lit up with page after page of search results and forty or more branches ("see also…") all the fear, uncertainty, violence, and desperation of the era came flooding back. How could I have possibly forgotten?

The CIA's codename for surveillance of the student groups was Operation CHAOS (or KAOS, if Sue had anything to do with it.) It was exactly the kind of inside joke that Sue would have loved to perpetuate. I chuckled again when it occurred to me to wonder whether any of the agents assigned to the project had claimed "Maxwell Smart" for their nom de guerre froide. According to Wikipedia, the CIA's information-gathering effort began in 1959—when I was eight years old—and finally ended in 1974, my senior year at San Diego State, in the wake of the Watergate scandal. At its busiest, the operation had sixty agents assigned to it, secretly gathering information on more than seven thousand American citizens "Officially," says Wikipedia, "reports were to be compiled on 'illegal and subversive' contacts between United States civilian protesters and 'foreign elements' which 'might range from casual contacts based merely on mutual interest to closely controlled channels for party directives.'" What was I to do with this revelation, other than to wonder how deep and wide it had gone, how many of my friends and colleagues had been spies or victims of spying, how many knew about it and said nothing? I didn't want to reestablish contact with Sue; the thought of confronting her made me sick to my stomach. In the end, I was paralyzed by indecision. I never heard from Sue again.

In truth, I wasn't much of a political activist during my college years, especially after the Selective Service lottery reduced to virtually nil the possibility that Uncle Sam would invite me to visit Vietnam as a member of the US Army. Once I was freed from the fear of being drafted, I changed my major from history, economics, and political science to design for theatre. My parents were dismayed by my decision; my father because he couldn't imagine I'd be successful in an occupation that required artistic talent, my mother because she didn't want me to move three thousand miles away, to the east coast. I began to enjoy the reduction in the sense of menace that had seemed to dog all my life-affecting decisions—especially those that might have had an impact on my draft status. I became a subscriber to that generally liberal school of undergraduate thought that regarded with suspicion any policy or project proposed or enacted by politicians. I guess you could say I had an apolitical general distrust of authority, which sometimes led me into activities that were foolish and dangerous, but rarely illegal. What I was doing was learning. Isn't that what we were supposed to do in college?

2.

During the winter of 1975 my younger brother, John, and I were living in San Diego, though I was scheduled to start graduate school in Boston in September. I had no idea when, if ever, I would return to the western states and the great National Parks in which I'd loved to hike and camp. John and I decided to go to Yosemite for a week over the winter break. It had been snowing in the park for several days, and sodden clouds continued to drop additional inches every twenty-four hours. We were cold and miserable but, with our campsite one of only two in the whole valley that was occupied, we had plenty of room to spread out. Other than the cold, the only inconvenience we faced were the bands of starving raccoons, who sported tree-climber claws and jaws that could snap a broom handle, that marauded on the other side of the thin tent canvas every night. They had overpopulated the valley during the summer, relying on food from park visitors who left them too fat to climb trees.

The racoons followed us everywhere, even into the heated restrooms, begging for something to eat. When we asked one of the rangers what would happen to them, he shrugged his shoulders. "At some point," he said, "we're going to have to let nature take its course. They're in trouble now because of human intervention. Over the long term we may have to let some starve to reestablish balance." At the time, that seemed an overwhelming cruelty, but the only thing we could think of to do was to make sure we didn't store the food inside our tent.

There are many great views in the park, but my favorite is from the top of Yosemite falls. From an observation point at the lip of the falls, you can see the whole valley spread out before you. A few inches beyond your toes (depending on the time of year), thousands of gallons of the Merced river are flung into space every second as they rush over the edge of the fourteen-hundred-foot upper falls escarpment. With most man-made structures in the valley hidden by trees, it's easy to imagine James Savage and John Boling coming upon the scene for the first time in 1851 and being astonished by the lost world it suggested. I had been to that observation point many times, as a child and as an adolescent, during family summer vacations, plagued by the tourists that swarmed over the mountain like horseflies on a dead fish. I was determined to make the trek once more, in winter, when the park would be empty, before I left for the east coast.

John and I inquired at the ranger station every morning as to the status of the trail to the falls: open or closed? Every day the answer was the same: closed. On the fourth day, a different ranger, after giving us the same answer, added, "That trail is seasonal, always closed in winter."

Outside the station, John and I huddled with Carl, a friend of his who had driven up from San Diego to join us.

"Listen," I said. "They probably close that trail because they can't be bothered to maintain it when the park is so empty. I'll bet we can still make it to the falls."

John and Carl were loath to give up a day of saucering down a slope near our campsite, where we had created a near-perfect run, but finally agreed to start up the trail and "see how it goes." I accepted the compromise; it would have been foolhardy to attempt the trail on my own. It was nearing noon. The park service's trail guide listed the hike as a "very strenuous six- to eight-hour round trip." If we wanted to complete the hike before the sun went down, we'd have to get a move on. I took the lead, and we set off.

What the Park Service's elapsed time estimate hadn't taken into account was the thirty inches of snow on the sections of the trail not protected by trees. I began to understand why they opted simply to close it. Blazing a trail through the heavy snow was slow work, but I made up some ground on the forested stretches and, fueled by determination, I soon left my companions behind. I stopped at one point to wait for them to come into sight; after five impatient minutes I resumed the climb alone.

Shadows from the setting sun were creeping across the canyon walls by the time I reached the short trail extension to the viewpoint. I had been able to hear the steady, low-pitched roar of the water growing in volume as I approached, though the falls remained hidden from view by an outcropping. Rounding this last obstacle, a dizzying view of the snow-pocked valley opened in front of me. I made my way toward the rocks and boulders that formed an approximate stairway down to the observation point, and saw they were slick with ice from the splashing water. Ice likewise coated the metal railing that was intended to keep viewers from falling off the cliff, and the boulders I would have to traverse to get back up. It would be stupid, under the circumstances, to try to make it down to the platform. What if I got stuck down there? I hadn't seen John and Carl for at least an hour; I was certain they were no longer coming up behind me.

224

Now I was frozen not by the cold but by my inability to make a decision. I knew I would regret it if I chose not to go down, perhaps for the rest of my life. On the other hand, the time it would take to go down to the observation point might constitute the rest of my life if I wasn't careful.

But I had to climb down; otherwise, all my effort up to that moment would have been pointless. As I eased myself across the sleeted boulders, gripping the frozen railing as tightly as I could, I knew that a sort of insanity had seized me, brought on by the pummeling thunder of the water, the vertigo-inducing awareness of the drop to the valley below, the utter solitariness of the specific spot of Earth under my feet. Driven by a fear that both seduced and repelled, it was impossible for me, in my excited state, to understand the real risks of my situation. Surrounded by the breath-stealing rush of water, I nearly swooned from the sense that the entire mountain was rushing toward its annihilation; the whole landscape was on the move. A thought crossed my mind: I wonder if this is how people die in these mountains? I was keenly aware of being nearly alone in a vast, indifferent wilderness, in a spot so dangerous I dared not let go of the railing, even though the cold of the ice-sheathed metal began to numb my fingers through my gloves. That awareness made me recoil against the granite walls as though I'd been pushed by a physical force. As my heart did its best to keep pace with the rushing water, I balanced on a knife-edge between existence and oblivion. I wanted to stay there forever.

But the sun was setting; time was running out. I moved back up the crude steps on all fours and started toward our campsite as the sun dipped below the valley's rim. A stroke of luck: the rising moon was full, and with the snow as a reflector the open spaces along the trail were quite bright. After some time, I was able to spot reassuring footprints, headed downhill, in the snow. I kept expecting to find John and Carl waiting for me around the next bend, but there was no trace of them other than footprints. At one point the prints and the trail disappeared at the edge of an open slope, and I realized that a small avalanche had recently covered the path. It was a relief when the downward-pointing prints reappeared on the far side of the meadow.

Two hours later, I stumbled into our pitch-black campsite. It was deserted; no sign of John or Carl, and I had the horrible thought that I'd misinterpreted their tracks on the mountain in the dark. The prints could have belonged to anyone, I realized; after all, it had really been too dark to be sure. I began to compose in my head the rational-seeming appeal I would use to convince the rangers that John and Carl's situation was an emergency, that they must launch a difficult nighttime search and rescue on the treacherous mountain. The searchers, I knew, would need long poles to probe for bodies under the snow in the slide area. An image of two curled, frozen figures filled my imagination.

How could I justify ignoring the ranger's warning and the "closed" sign posted at the trailhead? How would I deal with the consequences of my insistence that we climb anyway?

Then I heard voices coming from the brightly lit restroom. That's where I found John and Carl, whose first words to me were, "What's for dinner?"

I was torn between relief and fury; I could have murdered both of them on the spot. The fury came from the fact that they had abandoned me on the trail with (I imagined) no thought for my safety. The relief came from finding out they were all right, and that I wouldn't be called upon to explain the series of bad decisions I'd made. The fact was, I was somewhat pleased that they hadn't made it to the top with me. That experience would remain my secret, personal, transcendental adventure.

3.

I had another secret, one that I'd lived with going all the way back to recess on the Monterey Heights Elementary School playground. When my classmates called me "faggot"—based, I guess, on my preference for playing hopscotch with the girls rather than kick-ball with the boys—there were two things I never could have foreseen: first, the discovery some years later that I actually am a faggot (though, back then, I didn't even know what the word meant) and, second, that a county clerk would someday marry me and my partner of fifteen years in a public ceremony at the San Diego County administration building. I was fifty when I met the man who would become my husband; he's nine years younger. That means there are a lot of pivotal life experiences I have to fill in for him. And that's why, earlier this summer, John and I (yes, I married a guy with the same name as my brother) found ourselves in Yosemite National Park.

We weren't camping this time, and it was spring, not winter. I wasn't sure before we arrived that I wanted to try to return to the upper falls; the trail hadn't become any shorter in the last forty years and was still classified as "very strenuous." There's plenty of other stuff to see, even (at that time of year) several other more easily accessible waterfalls. But the memory of my winter experience nagged at me. Every time we stepped outside our room at the Lodge, a short walk from the trailhead, the falls beckoned with their power and challenge. Thanks to a week of rain just before our arrival, the river was swollen with runoff; the water raced over the cliff's edge into thin air and crashed onto the rocks below with a sound like the beating wings of fallen angels. Easily audible through the open windows of our room, the constant white noise dared us to come closer, then warned us away. There was a now-or-never urgency to our decision: I was pretty sure I would never return to Yosemite.

When I was sixty-three, I was diagnosed with an incurable progressive degenerative brain disorder. If this were a Batman comic like those I remember from my teen years, the news would have been delivered like this: Incurable. (WHAM!) Progressive. (POW!) Degenerative. (OOF!) I couldn't believe this was happening to me. I was looking forward to long, post-career years during which I would accomplish all the dreams and adventures I'd been saving for a lifetime. There would be plenty of time to travel, to hike and camp, to write (a new interest), to learn to play the guitar that I'd owned for twenty years but had never taken out of its case. All those plans were suddenly laughable; it turned out I was to be the butt of a personal cosmic joke. The friend who had come out to me as a CIA spy once told me, "Your problem is that you could do anything." Consequently, I now thought, I've done nothing—certainly nothing of importance. And when I tried to think about the future, all I could picture (like a lazy screenwriter looking for a cheap plot device to end a scene) was a series of slamming doors. I'd taken for granted my body's readiness to meet the challenges I'd set for myself; nature, genetics, and fortune seemed determined to deny me all of them. In the end, it's not my heart, lungs, liver, eyes, blood, bones, muscles, or connective tissue that are failing me. The culprit is the three pounds of gray jelly that fills my skull and controls all those things.

There were plenty of reasons John and I should not have attempted the climb. For one, my illness makes my sense of balance uncertain, and the trail to the upper falls has numerous sheer drop-offs. Even with a walking stick, which I use primarily to remind my brain where the edge
of the trail is so that I don't walk off it into thin air, there was a real risk

of falling. Too, there was that "very strenuous" designation in the hiking guide. In my college days, my young lungs had been able to quickly adapt to the thin atmosphere. That couldn't be assumed now, at an altitude five thousand feet above what we were used to. On the positive side, the trail length was listed as just over seven miles round trip, and half that—which, admittedly, would include the difficult, up-hill part—is about the distance John and I walk through the hills surrounding our home for our weekend exercise. "We can start out and see how it goes," John said. "We can always turn back if we need to." The argument seemed familiar; it's the one I'd used forty years before to get my brother John and Carl to start up the same trail. We set the hike for our third day in the park, in the hope that our bodies would be somewhat acclimated to the trail's 10,000-foot elevation by that time.

On the chosen morning, it was seventy degrees, cloudless, and calm. We laced up our hiking boots, packed water and sandwiches, and set out.

The trail, as I've said, started across the road from the lodge. It ran first along level ground cushioned by needles fallen from the indigenous Ponderosa pines. It was easy going for about a quarter of a mile, until the trail took a sharp right and began to climb along a narrow rift in what, from a distance, had appeared to be a sheer rockface. As soon as the trail shifted from dirt to stone, I knew I was in trouble. My stability depended on a level, regular surface, but this trail was covered with what were essentially very large cobblestones, interrupted at intervals by uneven stone steps—some two inches high, some twelve inches high. My speed of ascent in the thin atmosphere slowed to a creep.

If you've ever explored the most challenging trails in any of the nation's parks, I probably don't need to mention the relatively recent growth in distraction caused by the impatience of the (much) younger folks of both sexes, in T-shirts and running shorts, flip-flops on their feet, who line up behind slower climbers—some politely, some impatiently—waiting for a wider point in the trail where it would (in their estimation) be safe to pass. At that point, if you're smart, you'll press yourself against the mountain like it's your long-lost mother if you don't want to be (literally) bumped off by the younger climbers who leap past and lope ahead as though they're late for a class being held at the summit. I guessed that one reason for the heavy traffic on this particular route is that it continues north past the top of the falls to meet up with the Pacific Crest Trail, the one made famous by the movie Wild. But then, I've encountered the same attitude on other trails, so maybe it has nothing to do with that. The sprinters' annoyance is discouraging because, in their goal-oriented rush to the top, they miss the beauty of the trek. In May, nearly every crack and crevice along the trail sports a tiny garden of orange or yellow flowers; the larger patches of wild grasses, still brown from the winter, cover sprouting greens. It's an aspect of Yosemite that the sprinters will never see. They're in too much of a hurry to look.

During most of the upward climb, the three segments of the falls—the 1,430-foot upper, the 675-foot middle cascades, the 320-foot lower—were neither audible nor visible, hidden in a recess formed by the crumbling edge of the upper falls. After about three hours of painful and painfully slow climbing, we were rewarded with the growing roar of the water. Our hearts rejoiced: we were almost there!

I might have crawled the last forty feet if there hadn't been a small audience of other recent arrivals whom I imagined I could impress with my vigor. I drew myself up and, assisted by John, marched around the last obstacle. Before us, in all its glory, was...the base of the upper falls.

We were nowhere near where we thought we were. We had gained about a thousand feet in elevation, but we had another fourteen hundred vertical feet to go if we wanted to reach the top. At the rate we were climbing, that would take about another three hours, assuming we could summon the physical strength it would require. I wasn't sure I could do that, and I had to save something for the downward trek. I knew the unevenness of the trail would challenge me almost as much going down as it had coming up. And I had to be wary of downward momentum. If I built up any speed, I might misstep and fall or run right off the trail. It was a good time to sit down, eat our sandwiches, and ponder.

My next announcement went against pretty much everything I'd lived by up to that point. "Look," I said to John as I chewed my sandwich of smoked turkey and Swiss on Pumpernickel. "Everyone has their limit, and I think I've reached mine. I'm willing to wait here while you go on to the top, but I think this is the end for me. This is as far as I go." I was glad I had the sandwich to stuff in my face; it made it easier to hide my watering eyes—the result, I figured, of a high-altitude allergy of some type.

"I don't need to go to the top," he said. And just like that, our adventure was over. We had gone as far as I could go, and for John, who made no pretense of being an outdoorsman, that was far enough.

Whatever his motivation, he was willing to skip the experience of making it to the top, of facing off against the extreme, of looking Death in the face and not blinking. As with my brother and Carl forty years ago, he professed no driving need to complete the adventure. As for me, I felt each difficult step down the mountain as a betrayal of the winter vision I had kept in my heart and mind for decades.

On our final day in the park, we set out to hike to Vernal Falls. With the additional burden of exhaustion from our experience of the previous day, we weren't able to complete that hike either. But I was not willing to leave Yosemite for the last time without declaring victory on at least one front. Since no one would be able to contradict our claim, I proposed to John that, should anyone be rude enough to ask, we can tell them that yes, of course I'd hiked to the top of the upper falls many times. I didn't have to be too specific about when those hikes had taken place. John just had to say nothing.

When I try to list (for the benefit of my own memory) the major events of my life, I don't think first of travelling from San Diego to Boulder, Colorado on my motorcycle—a trip during which I had three accidents, the last nearly fatal; of spending a week in a houseboat on Lake Powell, floating along shores topped with cliff dwellings that could now be reached only from the water; of running in front of the bulls in Pamplona, Spain, during the European summer I spent with my sister, Rebecca, following in the footsteps of Earnest Hemmingway; of walking down Fifth Avenue beside Senator-to-be Hillary Clinton during New York's Gay Pride Parade in the year 2000; of travelling to the Dominican Republic, Grand Cayman, and St. John's with my first partner, Ralph; of seeing my name in the Metropolitan Opera's program (as a minor craftsperson) for Franco Zeffirelli's production of Tosca; of meeting Ralph in Central Park on a day a hurricane was expected, or of the love and support that came my way when he died of AIDS five years later; of marrying my current husband on the steps of San Diego County administration building in 2013. All these events are important. But first, I will always go back to that moment of winter solitude on the icy granite at the top of Yosemite Falls, where the mica-flecked stone returned the fire of the setting sun in a thousand tiny mirrors—a moment suspended between past and present, joy and sadness, hope and regret; a moment when I could be certain, finally, that Truth is not a stranger. If I'm lucky, I may yet have new adventures like these; if so it will be my goal to live them slowly, carefully, more mindfully now, and with more gratitude.

Uneasy Listening

A few million years from now, if scientists' conjecture is correct, an alien civilization inhabiting a planet in a different solar system—perhaps Proxima Centauri's—will detect the first signs of our existence. Their evidence will be the sound waves that have for centuries been hop-scotching their way through space on the gas clouds that drift across the lightyears that separate us. Ignoring every rule of physics, I like to imagine that wave carrying a snippet of some exquisite example of humanity's artistic accomplishments. Yo-Yo Ma playing one of Bach's suites for cello, for example. Walt Whitman reading from *Leaves of Grass*. Maria Callas singing the aria "Vissi d'arte" from Puccini's *Tosca*.

Other times, I fear instead that the first thing our celestial neighbors will hear from us will be the blood-curdling shrieks and foul-mouthed braying of Johnny and Angela. They were the constantly bickering couple I lived next to for ten years after leaving New York City for what I imagined would be a tranquil existence in Plainfield, New Jersey. During the worst moments of our forced, arms-length association, I pictured the sound waves carrying their screams and threats racing past all competitors (no doubt flipping them the finger as they went by), advantaged by sheer volume and vileness of content, being the first Earth-originated sounds to be detected by unsuspecting non-terrestrial listeners. Those poor star-children, even if ignorant of the details of human anatomy, will be so shocked by Angela's promise to cut Johnny's heart out if she catches him cheating, and so alarmed by his retaliatory announcement that he's going outside to shoot the dogs (all six of them), will realize that living only 4.22 light years away from Earth is too close for comfort. They'll quickly pack their things and move to a quieter sector of the universe.

Johnny worked the three-to-eleven shift at the Ford assembly plant in Metuchen, New Jersey, for twenty-five years, until it closed in 2004. He would get home around midnight, eat a meal, and then go to work on the junkers that littered his back yard. There were always two or three back there: one in the garage, a couple others parked helter-skelter on what used to be lawn but now—thanks to the frequent comings and goings of the heavy vehicles that had compressed the clay-like soil into hardpan—supported plant life only in the fringe of tall weeds that extended two feet or so from the chain-link fence separating our back yards. On my side, ivy and ajuga grew as groundcover in the shade of old pines and copper beeches. Rhododendron, azaleas, and seasonal peonies filled in the mid-level landscape. Occasionally Johnny would lean over the fence to offer neighborly advice on how I could improve my yard. It usually included the suggestion that I cut down the 100-year-old deciduous trees to save myself the bother of raking leaves in the fall. Once he gave a demo showing how he thought I could improve my landscape by cutting down three feet of the hedge that separated our property in front because Angela thought maybe she had seen a leaf of poison ivy among the foliage.

The most annoying thing about living next to Johnny—worse than his six mutinous border collies who squirmed under the fence to take their dumps on my grass; worse than the ruined engine block he elevated to the role of front-yard lawn ornament; worse than his unasked-for advice—was the amount and volume of the noise he made. From the moment his F150 roared into his driveway at midnight or one in the morning, radio blasting, until the moment he roared away again at two the next afternoon, he generated a nearly constant stream of offensive, obscenity-laden speech, shouted at top volume over the heavy metal music blasting from his radio, the mid-tone rev of his air compressor, and the deep-throated chug-chug of whatever motor he was working on. I don't know when he slept, but I never noticed a pause in the demonic symphony that was the soundtrack for his life, which carried clearly across the driveways that separated us and through the walls of our separate homes. When he was inside the house his rage was focused on Angela, who gave as good as she got and whose soprano range carried even better than his baritone. I wondered for a time how his neighbors on the other side, who occupied the home that served as the rectory for the Baptist church in downtown Plainfield, dealt with Johnny's antics, until it occurred to me that cautionary "Johnny Stories" had probably served as inspiration for many a Sunday sermon. If you're a preacher, there's an advantage in being able to hear everything that goes on in the devil's house.

The irony is that I'd broken off my ten-year affair with New York City and moved to suburban Plainfield partly to escape the unhealthy noise and nerve-shattering hustle and bustle of the city that never sleeps. Make that "The city that never shuts up," complains a July 2017 article in the *New York Times,* decrying the whine of refrigerated grocery trucks, the incessant banging and high-pitched wail of construction equipment, the deafening rat-a-tat of jack hammers, screeching subways, honking taxis, wailing police sirens, and loud cellphone chatter.

A 2012 *Times* investigation found dangerous noise levels in restaurants, bars, stores and gyms, and since then things have gotten worse rather than better. Noise levels in these establishments can reach 96 decibels (dB) or more—as loud as a power mower—and cause permanent damage to hearing if exposure lasts three hours or more. In one nightclub, the noise level averaged 99 dB over twenty minutes and reached 102 dB during the loudest five minutes. Note that dB is a logarithmic measure; an increase of 6-10 dB translates to a doubling of perceived noise volume.

My retreat from the city to bucolic Plainfield was only marginally successful in lessening my exposure to noise. The first night I slept in my "new" five-bedroom Victorian (which I'd purchased for $50,000 *less* than I had my 600-square-foot New York co-op) started out well. I snuggled into my bed and prepared for a quiet night of restorative sleep. A cheery twittering outside my second-story bedroom window made me think of fields of wheat swaying in the breeze and stands of spreading oaks and beeches. Soon the complexity of the uninterrupted birdsong led me to wonder if the nightingale—for such I assumed it was—ever had to stop for a breath. I waited for a hesitation, a triumphal crescendo; anything, even if only a fraction of a second, that I could label "The End" so that I could stop listening and go to sleep. Instead, the on-going twittering devolved into a trill without a pause. This new form, full of vocal swoops and loud punctuative bursts, reminded me of a traditional Chinese opera I once suffered through. *Okay,* I thought. *That's enough. I'll just roll over...* But my night visitor had other ideas. Without reprising a single musical phrase, he began an improvised fugue that commented on a string of notes he'd chirped—if I wasn't mistaken—well over ten minutes ago. I remembered the old nursery rhyme about four and twenty blackbirds. That reminded me of the sappy (and lengthy) Christmas song, "The Gift." Then I thought, *If that f-ing bird doesn't shut the hell up I'm going outside to strangle it with my bare hands.*

I waited ten miserable years for Johnny to die of apoplexy or a heart attack, but no such luck. He did, finally, suffer a heart attack, but it didn't kill him; ten weeks later he was back, his tirades very slightly dulled by the tranquilizers he'd been prescribed. That's when I realized that I would have to be the one to leave.

When I did finally move, I chose a house in the middle of a 4.5-acre wooded lot where I couldn't see my neighbors for the trees and, I assumed, wouldn't hear them either. Come fall, the leaves were on the ground, the sightlines to my distant neighbors much clearer. The first snow of winter weighed heavily on the brittle branches of the tulip poplars and black walnut trees, causing them to splinter and drag down the power lines. The next morning, I awoke in my new home—where, without juice to power the electric furnace, the inside temperature had fallen to a cool forty-five degrees—to the sound of gasoline-powered electrical generators running full tilt at every neighboring home, and *that* noise, accompanied by the roar of snowmobiles racing across a treeless nearby hill, continued off and on for the next three months.

We are living in an age of noise. Or, rather, we are living in the age of a specific noise: that of the internal combustion engine. Noise is everywhere; we encounter it at every turn, and the people making it— far from feeling self-conscious about their contribution to that particular kind of pollution—revel in it. I can remember when automakers emphasized how quiet their cars were, inside and out. Now ad agencies give us an endless string of video commercials showing their clients' cars spinning on a salt flat in choreographed slo-mo, a pounding rock score in the background and the roar of a something-point-something-liter engine up front. Who would do that with an auto they just paid $35,000 for? It doesn't make sense, but we've been trained by years of exposure to advertising to follow its simple logic: if you buy this car you are allowed to drive that way. Their "trained driver on closed road" disclaimer is a buzz kill and is treated as such—so much so that in some recent car commercials the warning is literally transparent.

I live now on a street that used to be a quiet country lane. Over the years, and particularly during the last couple, it has become a primary source of air and noise pollution thanks to the introduction of GPS applications like Apple Maps and Waze (from Google) that direct freeway traffic onto surface streets if there's a slow-down or obstruction reported on the main route. I'm able to monitor the sound emitted by a thousand vehicles a day, of all types. The loudest, as you can probably guess, are motorcycles. A device called a muffler is a standard part of every gasoline-powered motor a factory builds, from earthmovers to go-carts to chain saws. As its name suggests, its role is to muffle the sound of the engine. But for some motorcycle owners—perhaps those hoping to increase their perceived manliness—a quiet engine is too girly. (Women account for only 17% of bike owners.) They want to announce their comings and goings with tooth-rattling pops and booms and head-splitting rat-a-tats. No problem: the art of altering mufflers to make an engine sound louder is a time-honored tradition. An after-market device can do the trick for about thirty dollars, but do-it-yourselfers can reference an E-bay "how to" that shows you how to alter a standard muffler to achieve similar results. "For those riders that like to attract attention as they travel the roadways," it begins, "there are options for increasing the sound output from the exhaust."

And that's the heart of the matter. Bikers want more than transportation from their hogs. They want transportation that *says* something about its owner, the way the choice of a pickup truck over a fancy sedan does. Bikers want to say it LOUD, and what they're saying is, "I'M HERE. LOOK AT ME!" Unnecessary engine noise is aural graffiti, a way of drawing attention to the noise-maker. They don't care if the attention they get is born out of annoyance.

No single inventor—and certainly not Henry Ford—can be celebrated as the inventor of the gasoline-powered internal combustion engine (ICE) most of us are familiar with today. Early on, competing engine designs and technologies made it impossible to identify one individual in the crowd to whom that honor is due; later the rapid, iterative development and enhancement of different levels of competitive explosion-fueled motive-power-emitting techniques made the situation even more confusing. What's clear is that by 1791 there were several experimenters working on the technology.

The first American ICE was built by John Stevens in Hoboken, New Jersey, in 1798. He also built the first American steam locomotive and the first American steam-powered ferry. By 1900, a number of American car manufacturers were producing about 4,200 automobiles a year, of which 1,700 were powered by steam, 1,575 ran on electricity, and 925 used gas-powered internal combustion engines. The main advantage of steam cars over ICE-powered vehicles? They were QUIET.

It's an interesting thought experiment to theorize about the ways our culture and collective lifestyle would be different today if manufacturers had been willing to stick with steam technology long enough to overcome its perceived disadvantages. The complaints about having to make frequent stops to take on water and the comparatively long wait to build up a head of steam would, even at the time, have been trifling challenges easily resolved had we spent a similar amount of time and treasure on perfecting and miniaturizing steam that we have on improving internal combustion. Meanwhile drivers could have been enjoying a century of nearly noiseless, low-emission autos capable of travelling over 1,500 miles between stops. The current Steampunk sub-lifestyle celebrates the mystique of steam through re-imagined Victorian-era aesthetics, clothing styles, and concept-vehicle prototypes that owe as much to the novels of Jules Verne as they do to actual steam technology. But the possibility of silent, steam-driven cars, boats, trucks, and motorcycles—all operating without the need for fossil fuels—and lawnmowers, chain saws, leaf blowers, and weed whackers that could play your favorite tunes while you used them, is real.

What killed the steam car? It was mainly the demand for motors to be used in World War I that could start quickly with an electric ignition. But we shouldn't discount the influence of Henry Ford as an advocate for internal combustion. With his assembly lines, he was able to flood the private automobile market with cheap product that became the de facto standard for mass consumption.

There's a medical condition called hyperacusis that affects the way the brain perceives noise. I thought I might have it, partly because I'm the only one among my friends who's downloaded a decibel meter to their phone. People with hyperacusis can't tolerate sounds that may not seem loud to others, such as the noise made by a running faucet, by walking on leaves, or by shuffling papers. Please! Try living in my neighborhood, with a screaming parrot, a shrieking five-year-old, and a revving circular saw to which you're forced to listen for hours on end. Yet the parrot and child live, the circular saw has not mysteriously disappeared from my neighbor's garage. Consider that to be evidence of my powers of restraint.

A publication written by the Purdue University Department of Chemistry suggests that 70 dB, the level of noise emitted by a vacuum cleaner, is about the maximum a human can comfortably tolerate for several hours. The article lists other common devices and how they compare to the vacuum in decibels emitted. Each 6-10 dB increase means the perceived volume has doubled. For example, a garbage disposal, dishwasher, or food blender emits nearly 80 decibels; each is twice as loud as our 70 dB vacuum cleaner. A power mower, edge

trimmer or leaf blower is around 90 dB, four times as loud. As for
traffic noise, a diesel truck sounds off at 80 dB, a motorcycle (with a
standard muffler) at 90. At 110 dB, from one yard away, an automobile
horn breaks the average pain threshold at 16 times our vacuum's
volume. If you're less than 28 yards away when a passenger jet takes
off, its 150 dB will rupture your eardrums.

There are loud sounds in nature, of course. On a recent walk in a
local park, decibel meter at the ready, I caught what I think was a
California towhee sounding off at 72 dB. More typical, though, is the
sound of rustling leaves: at 20 dB, one thirty-second the volume of the
towhee and our constant, the vacuum cleaner.

I would love to live in a 20 dB world, if it were possible. And I
imagine it must be somewhere. Instead, I'm stuck with barking dogs
and screaming birds, a different cast of puling children each week at the
Airbnb next door, and garbage trucks and yard services that invade our
quiet side streets nearly every day. Some months ago the local natural
gas utility put up several orange signs, the kind that warn drivers of
planned roadwork. There seemed to be a lot of information on the one
near my home, but no place to pull over to read it. The best I could do
was slow down and snap a picture with my phone. When I un-pinched
the photo at home, my heart sank. "Closed to thru traffic," it read,
"from 10/19 to 3/4 for gas main construction." True to their word,
they were working 25 feet away from my home—with jackhammers,
backhoes, skip loaders, cement trucks, paving vehicles—every piece of
roaring, beeping heavy equipment you can think of—for each of those
120 workdays, from 7:30 in the morning until 3:30 in the afternoon.
While they were working, the street alternated one-way, with a flagman
at each end, creating an exhaust-puffing, horn-blowing line of
passenger vehicle traffic outside my studio window. When they were
done for the day, they covered their excavations with metal plates that
rang like steel drums every time a car ran over them. I thanked the gods
every night for the invention of foam earplugs.

I heard recently that, back in Plainfield, Johnny'd had his second
heart attack. I wish I could feel sorry for him, or at least for Angela,
who no longer has someone to fight with. But they were such miserable
creatures and made so many people around them miserable as well, I
think they got what they deserved. I hope their nastiness never made it
to Proxima Centauri.

I still dream that one day I'll find my 20 dB spot, far from traffic.
I'll let the grass grow without mowing or blowing; I'll get rid of my

blender and forbid the use of the garbage disposal. I'll insist that visitors park their cars 100 yards away and ban motorcycles entirely. I'll hold a funeral and bury the vacuum cleaner that's been my reference point for twenty years. And when I've done all that, perhaps I'll finally be able to sit down and enjoy the rustle of the leaves.

Me, Myself, and I

Don't you just love those long rainy afternoons in New Orleans, when an hour isn't just an hour, but a little piece of eternity dropped into your hands, and who knows what to do with it?
—*Tennessee Williams, A Streetcar Named Desire*

It was about two years after I was diagnosed with Parkinson's disease that I began to experience hallucinations. Such phenomena are common to those with PD; it's an open question as to whether they are a symptom of the disease itself or a side-effect of one or more commonly prescribed PD medications in combination.

I'd heard others who have Parkinson's describe the experience of climbing into a bed that was covered with black spiders, or of overhearing conversations being carried on in an empty room. I was grateful that my hallucinations were simple and benign, at least in the beginning. They occurred most often when I was outdoors, usually working in the garden, and took the form of a small dog that would dart around a corner of the house and be gone in the split second it took me to try to see it clearly. My brain readily accepted the reality of these visions even though the figures of the dogs were two-dimensional black silhouettes, devoid of mass or weight.

That slowly changed, until I was playing the same game of hide-and-seek with full-sized human male cutouts who seemed to favor specific locations throughout the house. One preferred the living-room, where I would encounter his long black form stretched full length on the sofa. He would linger long enough for me to separate his shape into its components. The sofa itself formed his torso; three throw-pillows were confabulated by my brain into a crooked arm supporting a heavy head. I don't know why he was wearing a cowboy hat and boots.

When I first told my neurologist about the hallucinations, she asked the obvious questions: do you feel frightened or threatened by the figures? How difficult is it to convince yourself they're not real? She was loath to suggest that I give up the advantages of pramipexole, a dopamine agonist and prime suspect as the cause of the visions. It is itself a well-known trickster, brewed specifically to seek out dopamine receptors in the brain and convince them it's exactly the thing the receptors are searching for.

Over time, the hallucinations have become more bothersome. They were never hostile, but I've grown tired of the one that stands behind me, looking over my shoulder, waiting to critique my effectiveness at whatever task I'm trying to accomplish. In the kitchen, I've arranged to work in a corner where I know there isn't enough room for the two of us to stand side-by-side. I squeeze through narrow doorways like a whale scraping off its barnacles against the pilings of a pier. My neurologist suggested I reduce my dose of pramipexole by cutting the tiny oval tablets in half. The tiresome hoverer immediately went missing. A few months later, my spouse and I moved into a house in which one living room wall had been covered entirely with floor-to-ceiling mirrors. Suddenly, my hoverer is back, and now, especially when the two of us are alone in the mirrored room, I can see him quite clearly. He looks exactly like me.

I've become used to the sensation that he's always there, even when I move to non-mirrored rooms or otherwise lose sight of him for a while. I worry about the mischief he might be up to when I don't feel him looking over my shoulder: running up credit card charges on home shopping TV channels, switching labels on the condiments in the refrigerator, or deciding to take a walk on the freeway. But then, I worry in the same way about the batterer who rains down blows on my spouse when he's in bed next to me, trying to sleep—epic one-sided battles of which I remember absolutely nothing when I wake in the morning. The only evidence of the attack is the defensive stockade of pillows that's sprouted between us.

My inability to remember these events is so complete as to suggest that the forgotten hours have been ripped from the timeline of my experiences, like the hour lost when we turn our clocks forward in spring. What was supposed to happen during those sixty minutes that now goes undone? What was created in that short-lived second between one and two in the morning, and what destroyed? Who is responsible? Is it Me, or could it be my hoverer, whose motivations, actions, and appearance were so like mine that he's earned the name "Myself?"

At my next ophthalmologist's appointment, I struggled to describe the visual frustrations of my experience as "Me." I saw different versions of movies than my friends did; in my version the stars were always identical twins. During the interview portion of the appointment, I described the problem as "double vision;" I had only to speak those words out loud to throw the doctor's office into scramble mode. An immediate appointment time was found with a specialist I typically waited six months to see. Later he explained that true double vision is a sign of brain injury, which had to be treated within an hour or two if permanent damage was to be avoided. I didn't have a tumor or trauma, but further investigation confirmed a third theory: because of my Parkinson's, the muscles that control my eye movement were no longer acting in concert, and my brain was struggling, often unsuccessfully, to reconcile the two slightly different images it was receiving from my eyes. Nothing could be done about it, the doctor said. Thus, we became a trio, like Siamese triplets sharing a single brain: "Me," the one whom everyone could see, fighting to maintain the status quo; "Myself," the master of mirrors, monitor of multiples, my "spitting image," the silent hoverer who came and went as he wished; and "I," the cowboy hallucination to whom I eventually became so accustomed that I would set a place for him at the dinner table.

Yesterday I found a letter that I'd written to my mother when I was ten years old—nearly sixty years ago—on the occasion of her trip from San Diego to New York to attend my grandmother's funeral. I was going through a box of family photographs I'd found during our move, wondering what the hell I should do with them, when the letter fell out of the stack I had in my hand. It had more to say about some dinnerware my father had gotten as a premium on our grocery purchase than anything else. I think the breaking news I was anxious to announce was that our car had a flat tire.

The picture the letter paints of the ten-year-old Me is unfamiliar. For one thing, the name I'd used on my stationery was "Jimmy," a diminutive I'd come to loathe for a reason I don't remember. Perhaps I felt that Jimmy went too far in infantilizing (and feminizing) "James;" "Jim" was a respectful half-way point. I regret now that I didn't know "Jay" was an option. I do remember announcing the name change to my family over dinner one evening; I seem to recall it was taken up immediately.

I think of myself as having been a rough-and-tumble adventurer as a child, one that would free-climb up to a treehouse someone had built high in a California pepper tree on the edge of a nearby vacant lot; one who, despite my claustrophobia, would shimmy down through the curb-high opening into a storm drain that exited in the canyon across the street from our house.

I definitely do not remember having personalized stationery, though there it is—my name and address pre-printed in blue on small sheets of off-white notepaper sized to slip easily into a three-by-five envelope, similarly imprinted. We had recently moved from the rental house my father had taken when he was first transferred to San Diego into a home he'd had built on a hill that had been the fruit orchard for the house behind it. On my stationery, the address of the rental was neatly crossed out (too neatly to have been done without a ruler) and the new address written-in with careful block print.

The best that could be said of the text of the letter is that it was dull, as though the author had been ordered to write it as homework (as I may have been). It was clear that I'd found no pleasure or amusement in its composition. I'd probably convinced myself that my narration of the activities that filled our evenings was sophisticated and clever, but it came off more as prissy and conceited.

I realize now that I've constantly been re-inventing the Me that I present to the world, at least as far back as the ten-year-old who typed his letters on personalized stationery. Who did I think would like him? Who would want to be his friend? Was he the same ten-year-old that liked to play hopscotch with the girls rather than kickball with the boys at recess? Was he the same teenager who found himself in his father's garage one hot August evening, staring down at a drawer full of tools, trying to select one he could use to injure himself just badly enough to be kept out of gym class? Was he the man who would need twenty more years to understand where the foundation of his own happiness lay, who never had a real home until he made his own in the arms of a dying lover?

I am all of these; or perhaps I should say they are all Me, the pragmatist struggling, as long as possible, to walk the straight and narrow. I am also Myself, the hoverer, the critic, ever watchful. And I am I, still the adventurer, the journeyer, the seeker, the one who is and is not here.

What's Good for the Goose
A Tribute to Edward Albee (1928 – 2020)

The lights come up on a somewhat shabby living room decorated in standard suburban just-getting-by style. On one wall is a number of framed photos of two girls at various ages—maybe school pictures. The furniture looks inexpensive; all of it is positioned to achieve the best possible sightline to the TV. MARSHA, late middle-aged with professionally styled hair that doesn't suit her, is sitting on one end of the couch, her legs tucked under her, a closed book in her lap. There is a floor lamp behind her. She is watching DICK, her husband—about the same age, but a frump—who is sitting in a broken-down armchair on the other side of the room, his face hidden by the spread-open newspaper he's reading. A second, mismatched floor lamp is behind him. There is no extra lighting in the room; the corners are dark. There's a sense that the two of them are trying to maintain as much distance between them as possible while bound by the confines of the room. Marsha speaks.

MARSHA
You know, Dick, you don't have to make *everything* into a confrontation.

DICK
You're right, Marsha, m'dear, as usual. I don't *have to* turn everything into an argument. On the other hand, if I didn't do so, I honestly don't know what we would have to talk about. Current affairs is out, since you don't read newspapers. Family news is out; *(puts down the newspaper, peers at her over the top of his reading glasses)* your drunken performance when we were at Christy's during our Thanksgiving family get-together

took care of that. No, I don't think we'll ever be asked back to *their* house. We'll have to have them here, if they come at all, and based on what went down on turkey day I don't think they will. So, I think I have the right to be a little apprehensive when you open with "Can I ask you a question?" Some year you'll realize how much that irritates me. What if I said no? Don't ask if you can ask a question. Just ask it, for Christ's sake!

MARSHA

Dick, are you happy?

DICK

Am I *happy*? Are you kidding me? That's what you wanted to ask me? Am I *happy*?

MARSHA

Yeah. I want to know. Are you happy? That doesn't seem such a hard question to answer, does it? Because—let me tell you—I am not. I'm not happy in the least. There is nothing that makes me feel happy. Happiness is not in my vocabulary. I don't recall a single solitary day during the last forty years during which a felt happy, even for a moment. My life is a demonstration of what the absolute antithesis...

DICK *(Breaking in)*

OK, OK, got it, no need to continue. Of course, your misery is all *my* fault. I see this is going to be one of those nights. Do we really have to do this now? It's one in the morning. I don't have the energy.

MARSHA

That's just it—you always want to put things off 'til morning. Then you make up some errand you have to do, and I don't see you again 'til dinnertime. I can't take it anymore, Dick. We never talk. We don't spend time together. I don't think we even enjoy each other's company. You're almost a stranger. I don't know where you go during the day or what you do when you get there. We've become two strangers who eat and sleep in the same house. If I thought you had the balls for it, I'd guess you're having an affair. I *wish* you were having an affair. That would at least be a sign of life.

DICK

Strangers. Oh, that's funny. I don't know how we could be strangers—we've been married for 40 years. We have two kids. We raised them right here in this house. Did you notice? Do you remember?

MARSHA

The kids are gone, Dick They've got their own lives. It's time for us to reclaim what's left of ours.

DICK

What's left...! Why are you talking this way? What's wrong? Are you sick? Is that what this is all about? That's what you're trying to tell me, isn't it? You've got breast cancer. That's it, isn't it. Oh, my God, Marsha. When did you find out? Well, I'll tell you one thing *(emphatically):* we are not going to do anything until you get a second opinion. These local doctors don't know what they're talking about.

MARSHA

No, I don't have breast cancer, you dolt! You are so fucking dramatic! I'm not sick, Dick, unless you count sick and tired. I'm sick and tired of *you.*

DICK

Really? *You're* tired of *me.* That's rich. *Very* rich. *Supremely* rich! Okay, you want to get into it, I'll let you in on a little secret, Ms. I-am-woman-hear-me-roar: it ain't no picnic on my side, either. You want to know where I go during the day? You want to know? I'll tell you. Today I went to the library. The *library*, Marsha. I sat there in the middle of a bunch of homeless people for six hours! That's how desperate I was to get away from your nagging, your whining, your constant questions, your mind-numbing need to talk, talk, talk! Sometimes, during these little chats you're so fond of, do you know what I'm thinking? Can you guess? I'm thinking, "God, would you please just shut her up? I don't care how. Please, God!" The fact that you're still here, living and breathing, is final proof that there *is* no Supreme Being; if there were, you'd be a carpet spot made up of smoke, piss, and ooze at this point.

MARSHA

And you, on the other hand, can't say three little words: "I'm not happy." Go ahead and say it, Dick. Try. "I'm not happy." You can't do it, can you? Do you know how infuriating that is? I'd gladly throttle you with my bare hands. I'll bet I could do it, too.

DICK

What do you want me to say? I've done my part for the species, Marsha. I worked hard for 42 years, paid taxes, got married, raised two children. It wasn't easy, but I did it. I earned my retirement. I don't owe anybody anything. I'm done. I like things the way they are. I don't *want* to change.

MARSHA

What about love, Dick? What about you and me? Do you remember that we used to be in love? Have you given up on *that*? Is your plan to just sit in that chair and decompose in place?

DICK

I'm not dead yet, Marsha. You'd be surprised.

MARSHA

Well, surprise me then, because from where I'm sitting you have no vital signs. You *are* dead, as far as I'm concerned, and you're killing me too.

DICK

What do you want from me?

MARSHA

Dick, can I ask you… *(stops just in time)* Will you answer this: do you still have any affection for me at all?

DICK

Oh, come *on*, Linda! We're not teenagers. We're two old farts doing the best we can under the circumstances. Can't you accept that?

MARSHA

No, I can't accept it. *(Pause. It seems neither of them is sure what to do next.)*

And since you asked, what I want is a divorce. I want half our savings. I want to get as far away from you as I can while I'm still alive, while I can still have a life.

DICK

Take half our savings? I'd like to see you try. You're not leaving me. You've never been on your own, never written a check, fixed a car, mowed the lawn. A couple days without me and you'll come crawling back on your hands and knees.

MARSHA

It's the 21st century, Dick. People don't write checks any more. And what about you—who's never fixed a meal, washed a load of laundry, used the vacuum cleaner. Do you imagine you'll be able to get along without *me*?

DICK

You think I'd have to worry about fixing a meal? Have you seen the fast food places along Conway? They open a new one every other day. You can get whatever you want, no dishes to wash, and the worst of it tastes better than the crap you've been feeding me for 40 years. I'll tell you what, Linda; if this is the way you want it, your wish is my command. Bring it on. Nothing could be worse than having to listen to you piss and moan about it. I guarantee you'll be crawling back to me

before the week is over. Go ahead Ms. "I am woman, hear me roar."
Pack your bags. Get out.

MARSHA

My bags are packed, Dick.

DICK

What?

MARSHA

My bags are packed. I'm ready to go.

DICK

What do you mean, you're ready to go? When did this happen?

MARSHA

This afternoon, while you were communing with the homeless, I guess.

DICK

(Almost to himself, with wonder.) You're really going.

MARSHA

Yes, I'm really going.

(Her trembling voice betrays the show of strength she's determined to display)

DICK

Where?

MARSHA

None of your business. *Then, genuinely curious,* Why do you want to
know?

DICK

Why? Do you think you can just walk out of here without telling me
where you're going, how to get in touch with you? What am I supposed
to say to Beth and Christy when they ask where you are?

MARSHA

Obviously embarrassed; she speaks so quietly that Dick has to strain to hear her answer Okay, Okay! I'm going to stay at Anthony's for awhile.

DICK

Anthony's? Who the hell is Anthony?

MARSHA

I met him at the salon, if you must know. What difference does it make? He loves me.

DICK

(Incredulous) Oh, my God! I can't believe this! You're throwing over 40 years of marriage to…what? Hang out with some mincing little hairburner? Just tell me one thing, Marsha. Did you let him fuck you? Did you let him stick his wormy little hairdresser's dick up your ass?

MARSHA

I don't know why I thought we could get through this amicably…

DICK

What about it, Marsha? Did he or didn't he? I'm asking you. Did you let some little shit of a *hairdresser*—what did you say his name is?

MARSHA

His name's Anthony. I'm not going to say any more. You're obviously not able to deal with this calmly.

DICK

You expect me to be *calm*? My wife of forty years just told me she's become the village bicycle, and now she wants me to be calm. Wait a minute. *(snapping fingers.)* Wait a minute. What is this "Anthony's" *last* name?

MARSHA

What difference does it make? He loves me; you don't. It couldn't be simpler.

DICK

What's his last name, Marsha? WHAT IS HIS NAME?

MARSHA

Why do you keep shouting the same question at me? I told you, his name is Anthony. But it doesn't make any difference to me what his name is. It only matters that he's taking me away from this crappy house full of cheap furniture. Away from you.

DICK

It wouldn't be Bruno, would it? Tony *Bruno*? Please don't tell me you're running away with Tony Bruno. Please!

MARSHA

What... How...How do you know his name?

DICK

Oh, my God, Marsha! What have you done?

MARSHA

I don't... What do you mean? Do you know...?

A cell phone begins to ring.

DICK

After looking at the number of the incoming call

Your phone's ringing, you'd better answer it. it's "Anthony."

MARSHA

Wait, though... What...? How...?

DICK

Not going to answer? Allow me.

MARSHA

Please, stop!

DICK

(into the phone)

Tony, you fucking son of a bitch! Yeah, it's Dick. Who the fuck else would it be? I'm just having a little chat with Marsha. It's funny, we were talking about *you*. Yeah! Very, very funny. So, listen up, asshole, 'cause what I'm going to tell you I'm only saying once. What we had is over. I never want to see you again. I want you to stay away from me. Stay away from Marsha, too. Stop calling her. And stay out of the library. If I see you in the men's room again, I'll beat the shit out of you, and then I'll call the police. I don't want... I don't want.... It's.... Oh, Tony, you cock-sucking bastard! Why did you have to screw everything up?

(Dick starts to cry.)

I thought you loved me! You *told me* that you loved me!

Blackout.

What I say Instead of Nothing

1

I first met Rafe in 1985. I'd made a quick lunch date with him after being sent home from my job on Wall Street because of an approaching hurricane. At the last moment, the storm turned toward the ocean, leaving me with a weekday afternoon off under dry skies with only New York's normal, nearly unbearable August humidity to contend with. I dialed the number he had given in his letter on the off chance that he was home as well. The day might be salvaged if I could talk him into joining me for a couple of early-afternoon drinks at one of Ninth Avenue's deserted Puerto Rican bars, or inviting me over to his (hopefully air-conditioned) apartment. Or why not both? Then, if he made a good impression (or even if he didn't), there was the possibility of sex with a relative stranger, an outcome that could redeem the dullest conversation and render temporarily invisible the network of fine wrinkles around the eyes of a fifty-year-old who claimed he was thirty-five.

His phone rang four times; I waited for the familiar click-buzz of an answering machine picking up. At the last possible second, the fifth ring was cut short as the receiver was lifted at the other end. *Ah-hah!* I thought. *The gods of pleasure have blessed me today!* No such luck. Rafe suggested an impromptu picnic in Central Park, and I agreed. I slipped the picture he'd sent with his letter into my pocket for reference and went out to wait for him on the corner of 59th Street.

I spotted him walking toward me from a half block away. He had a lazy athlete's stride (something I couldn't have anticipated from his letter), deep-set brown eyes whose depths no mere photo could plumb, a mop of dark hair, and too-red lips under the moustache I would never see him without. A tangle of sweat-dampened black hair sprang from the V-neck of a blue and white football jersey; his navy shorts only half-covered his muscled thighs. Watching him approach, I knew immediately that I would gladly hand over my soul to see him naked. Who among us has never contemplated such a bargain?

Looking back now, I realize that both our destinies changed that day, and that the events that would eventually devastate and nearly destroy both of us had already been set in motion. I often wonder whether—had I been able to foresee what would grow out of our less-than-chance encounter, the suffering and sorrow that would come with the joy—I would have had the courage to begin.

2

To say I fell in love with Rafe that day would be an exaggeration. In truth, I spent most of the afternoon in a daze, confused by the novel mix of feelings I'd never experienced before: intimidation, lust, fascination, rapture—but not love, not yet. I had him repeat questions I was too distracted to hear the first time he asked them; stared at his lips to avoid the intensity of his eyes; barely restrained myself from seizing his hand each time he reached up to tug with his left thumb and forefinger at a spot in his mustache he had made bald with that nervous gesture (which, I later learned, is called trichotillomania).

Through all these distractions and observations I wove an unspoken monologue, explaining to myself why someone so beautiful would never be interested in me. When that subject was exhausted, I allowed my mind to wander, to silently bemoan the tortuous path and typically wasted effort that had brought us to that moment. It began with the struggle to write the perfect classified ad to place in the personals section of the *New York Native,* the city's gay newspaper—one that would strike just the right note of rut or romance within the paper's thirty- word limit for free ads. Then the exchange of letters and photos through anonymous post office boxes, the trading of phone numbers and the screening of calls on answering machines. Next would come first meetings, like this one, where one or both parties would decide, usually within the first few seconds of the encounter, that the real person they're confronted with bears no resemblance to the correspondent they had idealized in their imagination, and the whole delicate structure of possibility would fall apart. The well-mannered way to handle the situation was for the disappointed advertiser to spend a polite five minutes faking interest, and then announce, "You seem like a nice guy, but I don't feel a connection here," and depart quickly, leaving both parties' self-respect intact. Often it was messier than that.

My hopes had soared during our first phone conversation when we discovered that we lived six blocks apart in a city of six million, as though proximity implied affinity or compatibility. But one glance at the living man had shown me he was out of my league. *At least I didn't have to take the train out to Queens or Brooklyn for this one*, I thought. I can only imagine how diffident I must have seemed in response to Rafe's attempts at conversation; I figured we were just killing time as a preface to his polite rejection. I was rude enough that, at one point, Rafe, exasperated, asked, "Do you have any questions for *me*?"

It took me a minute to come up with one: "How was your sandwich?"

On the walk home, when we reached the point where our paths diverged, I offered my hand for a formal, final goodbye. He took my hand in his, pulled me close enough that I could feel his warm breath on my ear, and whispered, "Can I see you again?"

The last time I saw Rafe was five years and four months later, when I left him in the emergency room at NYU medical center. I'd brought him in early in the evening; he was hallucinating, which was something new for him. I'd been standing beside his bed for hours, holding his hand, and he finally seemed to be sleeping comfortably. I didn't want to leave, but it was 2:30 in the morning; there were no visitors' chairs in the crowded ER, and I needed some sleep myself if I wanted to be ready to once more negotiate the process of getting him officially admitted to the hospital the next morning. I kissed him good night and told him I loved him.

An hour later I was in our bed, dreaming that Rafe and I were riding bicycles through Central Park toward Belvedere Castle. There was snow on the ground, and my wheels slipped as I rode, while Rafe raced ahead. My bicycle had a bell on it like one I'd had as a kid, the kind that attaches to the handlebars. I called out to Rafe, telling him to wait for me, and pressed the bell's lever over and over. It sounded exactly like a telephone.

I leapt up in a panic. How long had the phone been ringing? I fumbled with the receiver as I tried to decipher the hands on the bedside clock. Did it say 3:30 or 6:15?

I sat on the edge of the mattress; the booming of my startled heart nearly deafened me, but the voice at the other end of the line was calm, dispassionate. I tried to absorb what he was saying: Rafael was gone. He had stopped breathing and had died peacefully.

Thus it came to pass: Rafael Reyes, age forty, AIDS patient, died alone in the busy NYU emergency room in the middle of a Thursday night less than three weeks before Christmas, becoming U.S. victim number 122,464.

3

How long after the line went dead did I sit staring through the open bedroom door and across our tiny, dark apartment, the dimness broken only by the needle-shaped glints of moonlight flashing from the tinsel on our stunted Christmas tree? They reminded me of the infusion needles stored in the drawers of our demi-kitchen, beside the syringes, alcohol wipes, sterile packages of coiled plastic tubing, and glass ampules of heparin and saline that were supplied by tze home nursing service. It was a small pharmacy of medical supplies, souvenirs of a battle decisively lost. They were suddenly useless to me other than as impersonal reminders of a futile struggle waged against impossible odds.

I don't remember the exact order of what happened next.

A call came from Palm Coast. Hurricane Madeleine— Rafe's sobriquet for his mother—alternated between screaming and wailing in non-musical counterpoint. "Is it true? Is it true?" And then: "Why didn't you call me? Why didn't you tell me he was in the hospital? Why didn't you tell me he was dying?"

The hospital must have called her, Rafe's official next of kin, after talking to me. I wanted to say, "Maddy, he's been dying for five years. Where have you been?" But all I could manage was, "I'm sorry," even though it had been Rafe who made the decisions about what to tell her and when to tell it. It was much too early in the morning, but I called Rafe's good friend in New Jersey anyway. "Joyce, he's gone," was as much as I could get out before I dissolved into a blubbering mess and began to weep the desperate tears of the abandoned, tears more for me than for Rafe. "Shhhh, shhhh, it's okay, it's okay" she kept saying. "Shhhh—it's all right."

At some point I got hold of my friend Will on the upper West Side, who promised to meet me later in the morning to help make arrangements. We went to the hospital first. I headed for the emergency room, expecting to find Rafe where I'd left him, smiling his smirking little smile as if to say, "What's wrong with you? Did you really think I would leave you?" But we didn't go to emergency, and I realized for the hundredth time that morning that, to the rest of the world, there was no longer anything urgent about Rafe's case. His was just another death in the middle of the night in a busy big-city hospital. Will and I went to the property desk, where the clerk handed me a baggie containing Rafe's gold chain bracelet and the ring I had given him on the fourth anniversary of our Central Park lunch.

How had it all come to this? I stood in a glossy maze of fluorescent-lit hospital corridors; an environment that had become all too familiar. I held a bag of inexpensive gold jewelry in one hand; over the other arm was the small pile of Rafe's folded clothes and jacket. My dead lover lay under a sheet somewhere in the basement, awaiting the attentions of Reddens funeral home on 14th Street. I was thirty-nine years old and had spent the last five years fighting for someone else's life. Suddenly I had nowhere to go and nothing to do but to try to make sense of the senseless, to face the fact of my failure and the prospect of a future alone.

You have to think about what you dread in order to dread it, and I had thought about this possibility a great deal. I had even—secretly, shamefully, hating myself for it—allowed myself to accept its inevitability. Maybe it had been in October, when Rafe had contracted a new infection. Maybe it was November, when his eyesight began to weaken for a reason his doctors weren't able to discover. That was when his doctor had called me at work from his office, with Rafe sitting beside him. "There's nothing more we can do," he'd said. When I didn't respond, he continued. "Do you understand what I'm telling you?" I'd struggled to keep my resignation from showing, but one day Rafe said (in an echo of our first meeting), "You never ask me how I feel in the morning anymore," and I told him he had given the same answer so many times that I couldn't ask again, that I couldn't face the day with his litany of complaints I could do nothing about lingering in the air between us, that I had to be able to hope he would get better in order to do what I needed to do each day. I wanted to say, "You can tell me about it the day you wake up and feel better." But the truth sat like a dead weight on my chest and left me breathless, as though I were watching an accident happen in slow motion and was powerless to do anything about it.

4

At one point, when it was clear his health was failing, I made Rafe an album of photos of our life together, hoping it would encourage him to remember better times. It still serves that function for me. There are snapshots of the two of us in Grand Cayman, the Dominican Republic, and Key West—one in which Rafe posed so close to a resting brown pelican that most people who see the picture assume the bird is stuffed. There are photos from Disneyland, Big Sur, and The Pines on Fire Island. There are pictures of Christmas trees, birthday parties, and graduations. And of apartments. So many apartments! Five in the three years we lived together.

When I look at that album now, it's not the empty pages at the end that evoke sadness, but the gaps at the beginning. How could we have been so careless with those first months and years? How could we have wasted our time on petty jealousies while we followed the whims of our faulty characters? In the beginning, lovers always feel that time stretches infinitely before them. They luxuriate in it as if in a warm bath, taking perverse pleasure in the needless injuries they're able to inflict on their beloved because of his longing, and unaware (the embracing infinitude so warm, so comforting) of the scarlet drops leaking from their own wounds, measuring out their time together as deliberately as the ticks of a clock.

For Rafe and me, the heat of our August meeting faded through the autumn months. By the time Christmas arrived, Rafe was in Puerto Rico on a winter vacation he had planned with other friends. I was alone in the bitter cold of New York's late December, with its slushy, deserted streets bound by piles of dirty snow and frozen dog droppings, and store windows already advertising post-holiday sales. When he came home, Rafe presented me with a souvenir—a T-shirt: "Sun of a Beach"—and broke up with me. But in the warming days of spring our need for each other sprouted again, as determined as the crocuses blooming in Central Park.

Approach, avoid. That went on for a while. I don't remember his revelation that he was HIV-positive having anything to do with it. Back then we had only a vague idea what that meant, and the AIDS acronym hadn't even been adopted yet. As the meaning became clearer, the injustice of it fed Rafe's rages, whose destructive force scared me and which I credited to an unfortunate gene inheritance from his mother. Once, while we were still living separately, I tried to reassemble the splintered cabinets in Rafe's kitchen using a bottle of white glue and some C-clamps after he kicked them in during a particularly violent incident. Another time, I visited his parents' house in New Jersey, before his father died of cancer and his mother moved to Florida, to help Rafe re-paint their living room. It was the first time the walls had been touched in twenty years. Madeleine took me on a tour of the modest bungalow, and I stopped to examine a fist-sized hole in the wall of what had been Rafe's teenage bedroom. "Yes," she said in her Spanish-accented English, "he did that. You must understand. He does everything with the whole heart."

Everything except love, I thought.

But then, gradually, it was love; love that we eased into like a favorite shirt, that grew in our hearts like an acceptance of something inevitable.

Among the photos in the album I made for Rafe are some from our first shared apartment, the upper half of a roomy, high ceilinged, two-family in the Kingsbridge section of the Bronx. We were far enough away from Manhattan that we could afford the rent that gave us shade trees outside and a second bedroom within—the safety valve that allowed us the option of solitude while we adapted to the idea of living together. One photo from our time in Kingsbridge shows the large sun porch that faced the street, a perfect spot for our Christmas tree. We returned from a local lot with an enormous balsam fir that we barely managed to wrestle into the room, leaving a trail of needles all the way from the front door. We scoured the district's stores for strings of tiny lights that were available locally only in the gaudy magentas and pineapple yellows of our Dominican neighborhood. From the surrounding streets, the tree, with its hundreds of lights and glittering icicles, was a beacon that blazed through the porch's many-paned windows and guided twenty or so guests—parents, brothers, cousins, friends—to our house for a traditional Christmas dinner. We were a family at last.

We did our best, through that long winter and the spring that followed, to believe we had escaped, had somehow left the ever-pursuing specter of disease and death behind, to believe our idyll could last despite the almost daily stream of bad news in the papers and the regular appearance in Rafe of new symptoms. I was tempted to think of our story as a grand drama, the two of us the heroes who, by dint of love and virtue, would prevail against all odds. Certainly, war was being waged—a perfect environment for heroes—but the enemy had all the advantages. We had no weapons with which to fight this silent, invisible, apparently unstoppable foe. It was winning, and we, all humankind (or so it seemed), were being slowly, inexorably tortured and then destroyed.

Could the battle have been turned in Rafe's favor if governments had stepped in quickly, rather than sitting back with grim satisfaction while society's undesirables died off in a plague that many thought was only what they deserved? Being poor, gay, black, or addicted was suddenly a possible death sentence. What a relief that normal, god-fearing Americans couldn't catch it! Then it turned out, as scientists had warned from the beginning, that anyone could catch it—men, women, children, gay, straight, bisexual, atheist, Christian, Muslim, Jewish, rich, poor, black, white, brown—and, as the number of victims doubled and doubled and doubled again year after year, the research money finally began to dribble in.

All of it too late for Rafe. In 1984, the year he was diagnosed, only about 7,200 AIDS cases had been reported in the US. By 1990 there were 160,000, and more than 120,000 of them had died.

I have a terrible confession to make. I didn't care. I didn't care about the thousands or hundreds of thousands; I didn't care about friends, even, who sickened and died. I was focused only on the survival of one person, and that was Rafe. If you want to talk about callousness, about self-interest, here's an example: I forced myself to invent a brutal game of give-and-take, a game of bargains (very different from the first bargain I had offered that day on Ninth Avenue, the day we met) in which each death that was not Rafe's meant that he would live a little longer. I was spellbound by rumor as I searched through the details of obituaries. This one had toxo; Rafe didn't have toxo, he would be okay. That one had been a smoker; Rafe had quit smoking, he would recover. The third one spent his spare hours at the baths; Rafe had never visited them.

I wasn't a hero. In truth, when it came to this disease, there was nothing special about either of us; nothing in our profiles distinguished us from thousands of others threatened by the same or similar circumstances other than Rafe's determination to face it down, to survive somehow. The closest thing we had to heroes were the doctors who stuck with us, even though they had little to offer but palliatives and flimsy hope, even when their spirits were nearly broken by the flood of new, desperately sick patients they faced each day. Among the sick and their partners and helpers, timelines for plans and goals were shortened; no one knew whether they would be alive in six months or a year. People learned to not ask questions when someone was absent from a meeting or event, but there would be whispered consultations afterward: "Where's Roger? Has anyone seen him since Tuesday?" I attended a weekly support group for caregivers and watched the entire membership of the group change over the course of a year as their partners died and the caregiver left, only to be replaced in the circle by another. The fact that I was still there, that Rafe was still alive, served, in my mind, to validate my heartless game of bargains.

But there was no way of hiding from the dangers that stalked us, no bargaining when all we had to offer was what fate could seize whenever it wanted. Rafe was taking AZT, a cancer drug adapted to combat HIV, on an experimental basis even before its FDA approval. No one knew what the effective dose was. Rafe took twelve capsules a day, and suffered the anemia, headache, and nausea that were the drug's side effects. Yet his T-cells continued to dwindle, as did his weight: he was starving to death on a full stomach due to a cytomegalovirus infection. He did his best to swallow the huge, calorie-laden meals I prepared for him in a desperate attempt to stop his weight loss: fatty fried pork chops, mashed potatoes with butter and sour cream and grated cheese, sugary desserts washed down with milk shakes. The rich foods nauseated Rafe, and I gained twenty pounds.

5

We tried our best to live normal lives. I built a wire cage to house a pair of budgies, who we then had to banish when bird down and empty seed shells combined on the carpet to form dust balls that rolled from one end of the apartment to the other, sending Rafe into coughing fits. We bought a cheap car—one without a radio, to discourage break-ins—and began to enjoy brief escapes from the city: to Jones Beach to see Diana Ross and a Chicago concert, to Port Washington to visit Rafe's cousins.

Life in the Bronx was difficult for me. Our landlords downstairs spoke a little English and were the only people in the neighborhood I knew by sight. As far as everyone else was concerned, I was an unwanted foreigner, isolated by my downtown business drag and my nearly complete ignorance of Spanish—handicaps Rafe didn't share. It was only forty-five minutes by subway to my job in lower Manhattan, but in the evening the smell of stewed pork, the knock-knock-knock of wooden pestles fusing green plantains and garlic into fragrant mofongo, and the throbbing beat of meringues that spilled from the second-floor apartments onto the crowded sidewalks all made the atmosphere thoroughly Caribbean. The older neighborhood residents watched warily from their doorways and windows and gave me a wide berth on the sidewalk, suspicious of my business suit and obvious Anglo identity. I relied completely on Rafe for any local business transactions after spending a frustrating quarter hour one October day trying to get a sullen grocery clerk to admit he knew what "pumpkin" was.

The group of Dominican and Puerto Rican punks who sprawled in the middle of the otherwise empty subway car most evenings as I neared my stop was a bigger concern. I was careful to keep my eyes on my book or newspaper as they mumbled to each other in low voices. Then, one night, a distinct phrase: "Hey, that guy is queer." I had to walk past them to get to the station exit as they lingered on the dark Kingsbridge platform. One called out, "Yo, faggot, you wanna look at my dick?" as he pissed onto the elevated tracks. I pretended to be deaf and dumb.

I waited a day to tell Rafe the story and tried to make light of it, in a guess-what-happened-the-other-night kind of way. He listened, silent and expressionless, and remained so for a few seconds after I had finished. Then, two words, final and irrevocable: "We're moving."

I tried to convince him he was over-reacting, that it was an isolated incident, but I didn't try very hard. Rafe's decision was made in a moment; he was determined to leave the neighborhood where he no longer felt I was safe. I never found out how he convinced our landlady to allow us to break our lease—he may even have told her the truth—but in another month we were back in midtown Manhattan, in a one-bedroom not even a third the size of our Bronx floor-thru.

6

For some reason, that became our pattern. We never stayed in an apartment for a full lease term of one year—at least, not until the current one—and we never spent two Christmases at the same address. Everyone we knew understood that they should have pencil and eraser ready to update their address books when they received our holiday cards. I used to joke that I was renovating New York City one apartment at a time as we went from one rental to another, building sleeping lofts, installing air conditioners, replacing kitchen floors. Then, finding each polished space lacking in some essential quality, we quickly moved on.

I think Rafe sensed the shortening of days. Everything he did seemed urgent now, driven by an awareness of a shrinking timeline. I was putting the final touches to the re-painting of our fourth apartment, another midtown address, when Rafe came in and sat on the bed. He watched silently for a few moments before speaking.

"Jamie, I have to talk to you about something."

I was kneeling on the floor, carefully brushing the baseboard with off-white semi-gloss and trying not to get it on the carpet. My crisis radar had fired up automatically when he called me Jamie. He knew I hated that nickname and only used it when he wanted me to pay close attention. I sat back on my heels. "Okay. What's up?"

"I'm not feeling so good. I don't know if I'm going to make it."

That caught me by surprise. Rafe never wanted to talk about "not making it," but I didn't need to ask what he meant. I felt a little sick to my stomach and wondered if I was ready for this conversation.

"There's one thing I've always wanted to do," he continued, "but you're not going to like it."

My stomach did another flip. I put down the brush and waited.

"I've always wanted to live in the Village."

I nearly laughed with relief. Is that all? Was it really just another move, something we'd already been through four times? Still, I said nothing, but looked around the apartment, lingering on the "dusty rose" walls—a color Rafe had insisted on—and the eight-month-old couch we'd purchased for this place when it turned out that the heavy furniture, we had been dragging around with us wouldn't fit. There was no point in arguing about the move, since Rafe knew I could deny him nothing. But I was tired. And the Village! What was he thinking? I doubted we could afford an apartment there, unless it was a little room where we'd be tripping over each other all the time. If I could delay things—even for a few months—so that, this one time at least, we could stay put for a full year, I could later relent and we would look for another place together.

"Rafe, I'll make a deal with you. You know we can't afford a higher rent right now. But if you can find an apartment in Greenwich Village at least as large as this one, for the same rent, I'll move."

The next day Rafe found our Village apartment.

"And the rent is *less!*" he crowed triumphantly.

I still live in the apartment Rafe found, on Barrow Street just off Hudson. It's on the ground floor, usually undesirable because of the risk of burglaries. But we couldn't afford an elevator building, and Rafe was too weak to climb stairs. We made our compromises gratefully. After all, we were, finally, in the kind of upscale, gay-friendly neighborhood to which Rafe had always aspired. The apartment's six hundred square feet is divided into three compact rooms and an entrance hall which, with the typical oddity of older New York City buildings, is as big as the kitchen. Raymond, an enormous orange tabby who adopted us when he walked in through an open door on move-in day, found his spot on a sunny windowsill where he could watch the resident old ladies feed pigeons on the sidewalk, and I allowed myself to hope that we were finally home.

If, as they say, timing is everything, ours was more than a little off. I think Rafe spent as much time in the hospital as out once we moved to Barrow Street. He was always trying to get home, and once devised a scheme that involved me sneaking him out of the hospital for an Italian dinner and a quiet evening watching TV with Raymond in his lap. He tried not to mope when I dropped him off back at NYU Medical Center just before bed check, but he really didn't see the point. He wasn't getting better.

Rafe had been HIV positive for at least five years by this time and had survived longer than most of his doctors' other patients. But he was not winning the war against the virus and its opportunistic allies; he had merely achieved a temporary standoff. He hadn't been able to rid himself of CMV; he had lost fifty pounds, nearly a third of his healthy weight, as a result. His doctor prescribed something called TPN as part of a new plan to end Rafe's slow starvation. It was a nutritional bag of milky fluid that had to be forced into his vein through an infusion pump—bypassing his unreliable stomach—for eight hours a night. I barely slept during that period, waking again and again to listen in the dark for the soft weep and sigh of the machine at the head of the bed and the sound of Rafe's breathing. I rifled his body like a pickpocket to reassure myself that the needle was still in his catheter, that the tube wasn't kinked under his arm. Inexplicably, perhaps from exhaustion, Rafe slept long if not well, mumbling through his nightmares without waking.

I used to wonder whether he would have been willing to suffer through the years of his illness if he had known how bad it would be. The Rafe who had flirted with me on that muggy August day five years earlier was gone. His beautiful olive-toned complexion had turned pallid and wan; most of his hair had vanished—the victim of an assault by his own immune system and the drugs he was taking—and his skin draped loosely over bones looted of muscle by a body desperate for protein to keep its essential organs running. All the pain, disappointment, and failure that had accompanied his desperate search for treatment were written on his once-handsome face; his robust physique had been replaced by that of someone twice his age. He could no longer affect the confident stride that was the first thing I had noticed about him; now he walked slowly and took several minutes to climb the subway steps. Even I looked careworn and older than my years. Had I been able to foresee all this, would I have been brave enough, generous enough, to love him?

Perhaps you think the answer should be no. But I see I've left out part of the story. Sure, there were challenges, disappointments, pain, and sorrow. But they came with a flip side. If it hadn't been for Rafe, I might never have learned to enjoy life the way he did, to schedule vacations first and relegate work to the months left over, to act on a whim (like stopping in at the half-price ticket booth in Times Square on a weekday just to see what's available and then spending the evening at a Patti LaBelle concert). Had I not met Rafe, would I ever have learned to thoroughly enjoy *tostones con ajo* or a simple plate of baked ziti? Would I ever have found myself in a hut in the Dominican Republic, on an otherwise deserted beach near Punta Cana, ordering fish for lunch and then watching the waitress's brother push off in his boat to pull my struggling entrée from the still, clear water of the Caribbean? Suddenly, I see that I've cheated you. The flip side is the real story. The pain, the struggle, the disappointments—that's all just bad luck.

And in spite of all that happened, all the suffering we endured together, all the physical changes Rafe's mirror documented in pitiless exactness each morning, he was essentially an optimist. He had plenty of chances to give up, but deep down he always expected to survive, to overcome whatever came his way. When he seemed on the verge of losing hope I would remind him: "Rafe, in the entire history of disease there has never been one that killed everyone who got it. You can survive this. You may be the only one who can, but if you can, you must!" And when we had a good day—and there were many—Rafe would say to me, "These last five years have been the happiest of my life," and that would make me happy, too.

7

I finally got to celebrate two Christmases in the same apartment. A full year. Rafe almost made it, too. He died just three weeks short. It's ironic because he had actually been feeling better for a while. How could we have known that a quite ordinary tumor had been secretly growing in his brain, ignored by his overburdened immune system? The mystery of his dimming eyesight was finally solved.

One afternoon—about a month before he died—we had one of those good days I mentioned. Rafe was home from the hospital. It was once again December in New York, clear and cold. The mounds of snow that the plows had pushed from the street onto the sidewalks had not yet been blackened by soot and exhaust. We bundled up and went out to wander through the neighborhood we had come to love, window-shopping at the small stores that crowded the narrow, tree-lined streets winding among elegant nineteenth century townhouses. I doubt there's anything more beautiful, more hopeful, than the Village at Christmastime. Rafe and I decided to go into a store on Bleeker Street that had given over its display window to an arrangement of fifty-dollar tree ornaments. While Rafe perused their collection of Santa Clauses, I carefully lifted two delicate crystal snowflakes and held one up to each ear lobe.

"Look!" I called out to Rafe. "Who am I?"

He studied my pose. "Hmmm. My guess would be you're going for Liza, but you look more like what's-her-name...the puppet...Madame!"

Me: "You mean they're not the same person?"

Rafe, appearing to give it serious thought: "Not the same; similar. They both have a gay boy's hand up their skirts..."

"Wow," I said, replacing the snowflakes. "You know, we could have just left off with Liza."

Another customer, wearing a black cocktail dress, stiletto heels, and coyote coat, frowned at us as she stalked out of the store. I tagged her as an East-sider, an example of the type of New York woman that Tom Wolfe once described as "an exquisitely starved X-ray."

"What's her problem?" I wondered out loud.

"I don't know," Rafe whispered as we followed her out, "but don't get too close. I'll bet she killed that coyote herself, with her bare hands!"

Back outside, we turned the corner onto Grove Street and stopped in front of a leather store. There are lots of chaps-and-bondage shops in the Village—so many that they're like dog turds on the snowy sidewalk: you only notice them to avoid them. But this one is different. It sells expensive coats and jackets in the extreme styles that are the latest fashion, with extra zippers and tabs everywhere. Sort of punk meets "The Wild One." It was exactly the kind of excess that Rafe loved. We knew we couldn't afford leather coats—not from this shop—but we charged into the store anyway, moving briskly and trying to look as though we might actually buy something. We tried on one coat after another, admiring or, when appropriate, mocking the transformed beings revealed in the store's mirrors.

Unexpectedly, I discovered among the fashion-victim-ready designs a simple saddle-tan leather jacket with a Russian closing—a zipper that ran from the left side of the waist diagonally across the chest to the right side of the collar. I slipped it on, half zipped it, and admired my newly elegant figure in a mirror. Unlike the store's more aggressive-looking merchandise, the leather of this jacket was soft and supple. It followed my body's contours but was tailored in such a way that it broadened my shoulders and narrowed my waist. I thought I looked twice as butch as I had a moment before, and the soft silk satin lining, padded for warmth, conjured up delicious feelings of luxury and sex.

I saw in the mirror that Rafe was beside me. "Now I know how a woman feels the first time she tries on a fur coat!" I whispered, turning to face him.

Rafe smiled, tugged the overlapping lapels tighter around my neck, and kissed me gently on the lips.

Just before we left the leather shop, I noticed Rafe in conversation with the salesman. I didn't think anything of it; Rafe can strike up a conversation with anyone. But a few days later, a clumsily wrapped jacket-sized package with my name on it appeared under our Christmas tree.

That was more than twenty years ago. I don't remember opening that present on Christmas; in fact, I don't remember opening any gifts that year. I had to have taken down the tree at some point before it became a fire hazard, and I had to have done something with the presents from Rafe's friends and family. But the large ribbon-less box wrapped in snowman paper came to represent for me the dividing line between living with Rafe and living without him, and it took a while for me to be ready to cross that line.

I had a dream about Rafe a month or two after he died. I was at a party with dozens of other people, all strangers to me. Suddenly there was a commotion at the door, and Rafe appeared with a group of friends, chatting and laughing, their arms draped easily around each other's shoulders. All signs of his illness were gone; he looked as he had the day we met. He left his friends and came over to me, his impish smirk playing across his lips. "Well," he said, "I guess you didn't love me that much." I don't know what he meant, but he was wrong, of course.

It didn't happen for a long, long time, but I was fortunate in eventually finding other relationships. Now I have a husband to whom I've been legally married for two decades—an outcome no one could have imagined in 1990. Had Rafe managed to survive just five more years, his life might have been saved by the new anti-retrovirus drugs that restored a normal lifespan to so many HIV+ men and women. Unfortunately, some at-risk groups misinterpret this development and fail to understand the difference between the words "controlled" and "cured." The official count of people who have been cured of AIDS— through complete bone marrow transplants—is two, while thirty-two million have died. Out of the confusion, a new absurdity has emerged: a "game" played by men too young to have experienced the horror and human suffering of the plague years who purposely have anonymous, unprotected sex with HIV+ partners just for the dangerous thrill of it all. It's the next generation's version of Russian roulette.

George Santayana made the much-quoted observation that "those who cannot remember the past are condemned to repeat it." Often it seems in the case of HIV that the experience and learning of nearly four decades of persecution, protest, tragedy, and loss—a history many Americans would prefer not to learn or, being forced to learn by personal familiarity, try to soon forget—is relegated to textbooks and the observation of anniversaries. Some of us still grieve and want to remember, even if we shudder at the re-telling of the history of those years when a diagnosis of HIV was a death sentence that killed by the thousands, when a friend you saw last week was dead three days after your visit, when men who "acted gay" could be thrown out of their apartments or off of buses or planes because they "looked sick," when a new medication that was rumored to save lives could only be had for hundreds of dollars a dose and you gladly paid it, only to find it did nothing or made things worse. I feel the responsibility of having custody of these histories, of keeping the pain of all these trials and betrayals alive, and at the same time to proudly celebrate the activists among the gay community who dedicated their own lives and fortunes to finding solutions.

This is what I say instead of nothing

Made in the USA
Columbia, SC
14 September 2021